RISE

OF THE

LESSER

PRINCE

By

Christopher Joyce

The Lord of night and shadows,
In Aclevion, he rests.
With ancient Soul, his will bestowed
on lands from east to west.
Of elves in fair Eonis,
No wars nor battles waged.
Their watch will keep, while Soul does sleep
A balance, they dictate.
Of mages, dwarves, and barrens,
No songs are sung in tale.
Until one eve as fate decrees,
A chance, its head will raise.
The mighty hand of darkness,
Oppressive, cold, unjust.
Should weigh down cruel upon the fool
Who bravery does trust.

And so foretells the journey,

A chosen hero, brave.

Should join the hands, unite the lands

And Gibrion, will save…

PART I:

THE PRICE OF HOPE

The year 307, in the ninety-ninth cycle of Aether

Prince Vinadan set out from the citadel longing for the rustling of leaves; for the sound of birdsong; for the feel of the cold grass beneath his bare feet, and for the solitude of the woods. He did not have a mind for murder, but oh, how quickly one's plans can change.

*

"Who are you?" asked the young girl, looking up at the man who had strode so softly toward her in the Fairweather woods, east of Acelvion.

"You do not know me?" he asked.

"No," she replied simply, "are you a ghost?" Her hand, and the apple it contained, paused above her waiting wicker basket. The man smiled, and chuckled a little under his breath at the question.

"Well, I can see why you would think that," he said, glancing down at his long, silken robes which were as white as his hair, "but no; I am quite real.

My name is Prince Vinadan. I am your ruler; I am the lord of all of Gibrion."

The girl could not hide her confusion as she tilted her head and narrowed her eyes.

"Lord? Ruler? I've never heard of you," she replied, turning her attention once more to her apples. This time Prince Vinadan laughed openly.

"Oh, the honesty of children," he said with a shake of his head. "Still, I am troubled by your words. How old are you, child?"

"I'm eight years old," she replied with pride in her voice.

"Really? And your parents have not spoken of me? Surely you will have seen my likeness upon your altar, or hanging in the halls of your academy?"

"No, we don't have an altar. *We're as free as the wind*, my parents say."

"Is that so?" Prince Vinadan asked, lacking some of his earlier warmth and charm. "How *quaint*. It is a shame, without doubt. Your parents, girl, are wrong – *dead wrong*. Perhaps it is time they learned that; perhaps it is time they *all* learned that."

Without warning, Prince Vinadan's skin burned with a hundred small runes of an ancient kind, the runes for *Domination* and *Obedience* repeated over and over in strange patterns. Suddenly, as if propelled under the influence of some unknown power made manifest by the burning runes, the girl was lifted high into the air. Branches tore at her skin as she went up, high into the trees, and Vinadan grinned. There she remained, suspended, and Prince Vinadan stared up at her triumphantly, savouring her screams. After a long moment, he waved, a mere gesture of his hand, and the girl's screams were choked short as her neck snapped. She fell unceremoniously back to the woodland ground with a sickening *thump*, and all was silent.

Vinadan collected one of the apples from the girl's overturned basket, and resumed his journey. He did not look back as he strode away through the woodland, savouring the pleasant feeling of cold grass and breaking twigs underfoot, and the sharp, sweet taste of the apple upon his tongue.

The basket of apples would remain upon the ground, rotting and forgotten; as would the girl, for the dominion of Prince Vinadan was absolute, and would suffer no insult.

Chapter One

Sometime later…

The rain had started to fall in the early morning, and had not let up all day. Now, the lanes and thoroughfares in the centre of town were little more than a mess of mud and puddles. The night had turned cold, and barely a soul could be seen outside at this hour. Inside The Broken Staves, however, an open fire burned while a young female barren picked her way nervously through a melancholy tune on her old lute. Her skill with the instrument was not in question, but the presence of the three or four orrecs who wandered here and there, keeping an eye on the patrons and generally acting as a visible deterrent to even the flicker of discontent, troubled her deeply and set her nerves on edge.

At a table in roughly the centre of the crowded inn, Horith waited until the orrec captain had passed behind him before continuing to speak. His voice was guarded and hushed with caution, and his eyes darted to and fro around the crowded inn.

"You see? This is exactly what I'm talking about," he hissed. "Orrec patrols at an inn? Come on; there's no reason for it! What would you call it if not intimidation?" His friends had heard this speech before and did not necessarily disagree, but they knew better than to openly question or criticise Prince Vinadan in public, even here in their homeland.

"We know, Horith," replied Ruli, matching Horith's urgent whisper "but you must hold your tongue before you get us all killed." He turned his attention back to his ale.

"We cannot go on like this," continued Horith, shaking his head in the gloomy golden light of the inn. "More go missing with every new day, and half of our wages go straight to the capital, straight into Vinadan's war chest. And you know why."

"Don't, Horith; please. I beg you. Say no more," pleaded Gerdan, placing his hand to his forehead in growing frustration at Horith's diatribe. Horith paid no mind to his friend's warnings and continued, growing louder with each new exclamation.

"The Soul," he said with finality. "Without that thing - that relic - he'd be little more than a…" The orrec captain turned his substantial neck in their direction at the sound of Horith's remonstrations. Ruli,

Gerdan, and Miseldi sighed deeply and busied themselves with their drinks. The captain lumbered over to them, his hand resting suggestively on the hilt of the large, serrated dagger which hung from his enormous leather belt.

"Do we have a problem 'ere, you barren scum?" he snarled at the four. Horith's companions each fixed him with a look which required no translation.

Look what you've done, it said without words.

It was Miseldi who spoke first, making sure to answer before Horith could open his mouth and make matters worse for the group.

"No Sir, no problem here. *Our friend was just leaving*," she said, staring pointedly at Horith.

The orrec looked each of the barrens in the eye in turn before deciding they weren't worth his trouble. "Move along then, you pointy-eared vermin," he said to Horith, who drained the last of his ale and slammed the tankard down hard upon the wooden table, eliciting anguished looks from his friends.

"As you wish. *For the might of Aclevion,"* he said through gritted teeth, raising a clenched fist to his forehead.

"For the might of Aclevion," the others repeated as one, fists similarly raised, as Horith strode away in anger. The door slammed shut behind him, and Ruli, Gerdan, and Miseldi returned to their drinks exchanging knowing looks, rolled eyes, and micro shakes of their respective heads. Once outside, Horith stood alone in the dark, cold night. The stars were beginning to break through the canopy of clouds which hung heavy over Ehronia, and the muddy streets were all-but deserted. He could feel his frustration and anger growing, boiling up from the pit of his stomach and threatening to explode out of his chest. He kicked out at a wooden signpost from which hung the crest of The Broken Staves Inn, sending a sod of mud flying from his pitted work boots, and causing the sign to swing and sway on its chains.

The fools; the spineless fools, he thought as he set off toward home with his head down and his hands in his pockets. The rain was still falling heavily, and to Horith, it somehow felt heavier in the darkness.

Obedience and servitude; raking around in the mud for a few measly kreons while Prince Vinadan sits on a dragon's fortune in his fortress, laughing at us from behind his walls, surrounded by his orrecs and the Asarlai.

He continued to make his way home, a little unsteady on his feet as the rain fell. His long hair was now as wet as his clothes, and he flicked it out of his face, sending water flying over his shoulder.

No, he thought, *we cannot continue to live like this.*

Horith was almost home, and through the rain he could see the small, wooden domicile in which he and his few worldly possessions resided. Ehronia was not a wealthy land, but it was his home, just as it had been home to most of the barren race for centuries. Its wooden structures, muddy lanes, and boggy farmlands were all Horith knew of the world. He had never seen the lush forests and towering woods of his elven cousins who, though virtually identical in appearance to Horith and his kin, were possessed of a magic with which his kind had not been blessed. *Barren,* they were named in mockery, centuries ago, as more and more elves were born without innate magical abilities, and a schism opened among the elves of the south. The barrens had been declared an abomination; a perversion of the will of the goddesses, and they were summarily banished from the elven realm of Eonis, exiled in shame. To the west they fled, and the land of Ehronia was chosen as the place they would call their new home. They would settle here, raise families, forge new destinies and live their lives free of the scorn of their haughty elven cousins. And they thrived; in time what was once considered an insult was reclaimed, and the barren elves were now recognised as a people in their own right, quite separate from their forebears.

The night grew darker, wetter, and colder. Lost in his ruminations and wishing for nothing more than a tall goblet of blood red wine and his warm bed, Horith nearly overlooked the shape in the darkness of the trees away to his left. Nearly.

He raised his head and glanced toward the figure, hoping the gesture appeared as casual as he had intended it to be. He could tell the figure was male but could not identify its race in these conditions. He made a mental note of his observations and continued forward, acting as if he had not seen the stooped and bearded figure, nor the tall wooden staff upon which it leaned.

At length, he arrived home, and as he stepped inside his house and closed the door behind him, he inhaled a long, deep breath, hoping to calm his mind before he retired for the night. He tucked a stray strand of dirty, wet hair behind his pointed ear and made for the pantry to pour that goblet of wine he had so looked forward to. Before he settled himself down into his favourite chair, Horith lit a small fire to warm his bones against the evening chill which still shuddered through him, despite his arrival indoors. The fire roared and crackled, and Horith began to feel the cold leaving him, and by degrees he ceased to shiver. A feeling of warmth, soothing, and relaxation seemed to caress him; to wrap him up snugly in intangible hands. He took a large and very satisfying gulp of wine and began to feel much better about the evening's events almost immediately. He sat for a while, unmoving but for the rhythmic rise and fall of his chest as he savoured the pleasure of his own company. Try as he might, however, he could not seem to shake the vague and disjointed feelings of dread and foreboding which crept up his spine and crawled into his throat each time he unwittingly called to mind the hunched silhouette he had glimpsed in the rain.

*

Despite the nebulous concerns he had harboured the night before, Horith was able to sleep soundly and awoke alert and refreshed, the effects of the previous night's wine notwithstanding (in fact, he later thought, his deep sleep may have been thanks in no small part to the very wine the excessive consumption of which he now lamented), and had all-but forgotten the figure he had glimpsed in the trees. He brewed himself a strong, hot, herbal tea, and enjoyed the feel of the warm ceramic cup in his hands. He stared out of the window as he drank, and watched as the moody, muggy grey veil was slowly pulled aside, lifting the gloom from the world as the sun rose.

He finished his tea and ate a small breakfast of nuts and fruit. As he sat at the small table, his gaze fell upon the floor, and he watched, mesmerised, as a thin shaft of light from the window made its inexorable crawl across the stones and rugs as the sun made its ascent. Once he had bathed and was dressed in his stained but reliable work clothes, he pulled on the muddy boots which he always kept by the door. He locked the door behind him and sighed deeply, steeling himself for the day ahead. He turned and set off on foot toward the farm in whose fields he and his friends worked. It was an all-too familiar routine, borne of many years spent in the service of the landowners who, in turn, were in the thrall of Vinadan and subject to the unwelcome yet ever-watchful gaze of his orrecs.

Thankfully, the rain had cleared overnight and the air felt uncharacteristically warm for this time of year. Horith was soothed by the feeling of heat on the back of his neck as he made his way along the muddy tracks toward his place of work. His route would lead him to an inevitable meeting with his friends along the way - usually at the intersection where Horith's street ended and the road wound sharply toward the main town square - and they would complete the journey to work together, as they had done a thousand times before, taking the opposite fork and heading away from town, outside of the main population centres of Ehronia.

"Feeling better today?" asked Ruli as the four came together. The youngest of the four, Ruli was a quiet but determined soul, and he was worried by the turn which the previous night's drinks had taken. Horith thought fondly of Ruli, and was sorry to have placed the young barren in such a volatile situation.

"Yes, thank you Ruli. I'm sorry about last night; I just get so angry sometimes…"

"Don't worry, Horith; the day you turn into a loyalist is the day we'll *really* be worried," chided Miseldi, nudging her friend in the ribs in jest. They walked the rest of the way in near silence, and soon enough the four friends were hard at work, along with countless others of their kin. With scythe in hand, they each worked the fields for what crops they could reap; it was hard work, but they were heartened at least by the warmth the new day had brought with it. It was their penultimate shift of the week, and they were planning to spend the weekend together at Horith's house. To them, it was a time they coveted dearly; an opportunity - rare enough in these dark days - to merely chat, to drink - usually too much, in Horith and Gerdan's case - and to laugh. More than anything, though, the four of them would simply savour the time spent in each other's company, away from the prying eyes of the ever-watchful orrecs, free to live and to lark; to wish and to weep.

Horith was lost in his thoughts, working his scythe on muscle-memory alone, when the orrec foreman Shan-Gatt decided that that was quite enough daydreaming for one day, thank you very much.

"Oy, you! Get back to work, unless you want to go a couple of rounds with *Motivator*," he shouted, indicating the rather appropriately-named whip upon his belt. Horith bit his lip and swallowed down hard on the defiant and unsurprisingly sarcastic response which had threatened, just for a moment, to spill free of his lips.

"Yes Sir; sorry Sir," he replied instead, lowering his head in a placatory gesture. Horith hated the orrecs; he really, truly hated them with every fibre of his being, and as he still bore the scars from his last encounter with Shan-Gatt and his *Motivator*, he was understandably keen to avoid a repeat performance. Still, it pained him to show such a display of obedience, such a show of deference - however feigned - to show such *weakness* in front of his friends. While his countenance was one of civility and respect for his masters, his resolve was further strengthened; fuelled by the burning fires of his hatred for the spawn of Elgiroth. He was more determined than ever to do something - *anything* - to free his kin from the shadow which lay over both their lands and their lives.

Horith had hatred within him, to be sure, but he did not seek to temper it; he sought not to dampen his rage, and his fury fed his resolve, as fuel provokes a burning flame. Though he would never admit it - not even to Miseldi, Ruli, or Gerdan - some days, his hatred was all that kept him going.

The light had started to fade by late afternoon, and each of the workers felt as if they had personally drained the sun of its daily quota of heat, as the air once again turned cold and sent shivers down their spines. The shift was nearly over, and Horith ached from the day's exertions. He stopped for a moment to stretch out his aching back, which gave a satisfying *click* as he flexed his spine. He rotated his hips from left to right to further loosen his tight muscles and, as he glanced back over his shoulder, he caught sight of the man from the previous night, standing in the trees and watching Horith keenly.

Afforded a much better view in the afternoon light, Horith was able to discern the man more clearly.

A mage; a human mage, he realised, noting the man's long, greasy black beard and matted hair, which were the perfect companions to his dirty robes and twisted wooden staff. Though a fairly common sight in Gibrion's wider lands and quite prevalent in the capital, humans were rare in Ehronia and the country of Iollen in general, and human mages almost unheard of in these parts.

That's it, he thought, feeling his anger swell. He turned and picked up his scythe, determined to confront his unlikely observer, but when he spun on his heel with blade in hand, the mage was gone and the treeline stood empty once more. His previously-high spirits had been well and truly extinguished by the second appearance of the old man - the second that he *knew of*, that is - and he declined his companions' invitation to The Broken Staves in favour of a swift return home following their day of toil and labour.

His head was on a constant swivel as he made his way home; his keen ears and sharper eyes alert for any sign of the old human who appeared to have taken a keen interest in him. He arrived home in record time and, once inside, he immediately locked his door - a task usually reserved for bedtime. He helped himself to a small plate of food, but barely registered what it was that he was eating, so distracted was he. His mind was buzzing with confusion, conjecture, and questions, and he did not have to wait long for answers.

Knock, knock knock.

A momentary dread seized his stomach, and he ignored what little food remained on his plate. He stood, walked cautiously over to the door, and moved to peer through the small pinhole, despite already knowing in his very bones the identity of the evening caller. He looked through the hole in any case, and felt an overwhelming shudder run the length of his body as he gazed out into the face of the old mage.

"I know that you are looking at me, Horith," the mage said from the other side of the door.

He knows my name? Horith thought, more confused than ever.

"Who are you? Why have you been following me? What do you want?" he demanded. The door remained locked.

"Well," said the human at the door, "that was three questions in a single breath, and I should like some wine if I am to answer them. Them, and more besides, I do not doubt." There was something of a twinkle in his eye, and the knot in Horith's gut began to untangle somewhat, his breathing returning to its normal pace. There was something about this old fool which reassured Horith, and some of his earlier misgivings were starting to evaporate in spite of his caution.

"May I come in?" the stranger continued. "It's turning frightfully cold out here and I think you'll be most interested in what I have to say. Quickly now, before the next orrec patrol passes this way." The mention of the orrecs and the old man's seemingly earnest desire to avoid the foul creatures sealed the deal. With a deep breath, Horith unlocked and opened the door to allow the old mage safe passage inside.

"Thank you, my boy. Now, about that wine…"

"First things first," said Horith, pointing a finger at the old mage and not taking his eyes off him for a moment, "who are you?"

"Ah yes, question number one. Well, I did say I would answer. I am Montagor of Aclevion."

"Aclevion?" Horith demanded.

"The very same," said Montagor, "but do not look so worried, young Horith, I am no longer associated with the citadel, and I do not serve Prince Vinadan." He fixed Horith with a pointed stare.

He has sad eyes, Horith thought, *weary eyes. There is memory there; memory, regret, and pain.*

"I am old," the mage continued, seeming to read Horith's thoughts, "but I have not stepped foot in that accursed city since before our *good Prince Vinadan* was even born." This he said with conviction, but Horith was not yet convinced.

"Is that right?" replied the barren, keeping his emotions tightly guarded, "so why have you been following me?"

"Question two, I see," said the old man with a wry smile. "I have been following you, Horith Nindrius, to… how best to put it… *size you up*. I wanted to confirm my suspicions and see you for myself."

"Size me up? What suspicions? *What do you want*?"

"And there's question three," said the old man. He was clearly enjoying himself a great deal more than Horith was, and he helped himself to a seat by the fire and turned his gaze toward his host. His jaw tightened, just for a moment, and his brow furrowed.

"Word has reached my ear of your, shall we say, *disenchantment* at your current situation. I have heard that you are garnering a reputation as something of a troublemaker; a malcontent among an otherwise obedient race."

"How-"

"No, do not interrupt me; how I came by this information is immaterial. In answer, therefore, to your third question, the question of what I want, Horith, the answer is quite simple: *you.* More specifically, I want your help as I embark on a perilous mission."

Horith had also taken a seat by this point, and was looking at the old mage with interest - not to mention a good deal of confusion - from the opposite side of the open fire. The flicker and spark of the flames reflected in his eyes as he weighed up the old man's words.

"What mission?" he said at length, "what are you talking about, old man?" he asked.

"See? Did I not tell you there would be further questions? It is clear to me that you are all too aware of the source of Prince Vinadan's power: the relic, the Soul. You know also that the immense power of this artefact is ultimately the source of your suffering, the one thing keeping your kin and countless others across all the lands of Gibrion under the thrall of Aclevion and at the constant mercy of Vinadan's orrecs."

Montagor had Horith's attention.

"What do you know of the Souls, Horith?" he asked, leaning in closer.

"Not much, not really," replied the barren with a shrug of his shoulders and a shake of his head. "I know that Vinadan has one in Aclevion, and that the Asarlai guard it day and night. I know there is a second, too, which the elves of Eonis hold. Hold, but do not use."

"Exactly, my boy; *exactly,*" replied the old man, grinning and waving his finger in Horith's direction. "Your woodland cousins hold within their grasp an immense power, an ancient, wondrous power; the very power, in fact, to challenge the so-called *might of Aclevion* if they could only be persuaded to do so."

Montagor had grown louder and more animated as he spoke, and Horith was beginning to get the impression that there was something about the Souls which sparked a fire inside of the old mage; he had a passion for the relics which Horith did not yet understand, but was beginning to recognise.

"But Eirendollen is a neutral country, Montagor, you must know this! They have not concerned themselves with the affairs of humans, dwarves, barrens - anyone - for centuries; anyone but themselves, that is. My 'cousins', you say… ha! They are no kin of mine. The only reason they still guard the Soul of Hemera is to maintain the peace and deter incursion. Everything they do - or don't do, for that matter - is in their own self-interest."

"Believe me," said Montagor, his palms held outwards, "I am all too aware of the stubbornness of the elves. But if they could be convinced to use the Soul, to harness its power, they could turn back the tide of darkness which blights our lands despite the illusion of peace and prosperity the capital continues to promote." Montagor was pointing at Horith, his plea beginning to sound more like a lecture to the young barren. "And this is where you come in, Horith," the mage continued, "I need your help if I am to convince Keya and her kind to break with their ancestral tradition of inaction and actually do some good for a change."

"Why me?" asked Horith with a small shrug and a weary shake of his head. A long moment passed between the two, and in the intervening silence, Montagor chewed his bottom lip and frowned. He absentmindedly reached up and touched the back of his neck as he framed his answer.

"I am old, for one thing, Hortith," he said with a humourless grin, "and for the most part I am but a healer, though I am not without certain other talents. As for you, it is your passion, your rebellious nature and - perhaps most important of all - your yearning to be free which we will need if we are to succeed in our quest."

"*Our* quest?" said Horith, enunciating the first word and raising his eyebrows.

"Oh yes, my boy," replied Montagor, grinning. "Please do not insult my intelligence by continuing to act as if you are not already completely sold on my offer. Besides," he added; a shadow of concern crawled across his face, making the old wizard look older still, "if I have heard your name, Horith Nindrius, others may also know of you and your…. opinions. They will come looking for you, Horith, at the behest of the lord of Aclevion. Your friends are not safe as long as you remain in Ehronia." Horith offered no reply, but slowly nodded. The crackling fire was reflected in the barren's eyes, and Montagor fancied that he could see a burgeoning tear begin to coalesce there. The mage stood, and clapped his hands together. He made his way over to the long couch and kicked off his boots, sending flecks of mud against Horith's walls, before stretching out his legs along the full length of the comfortable sofa.

"Right," he said after he had wriggled himself comfortable, "we leave at first light. Our first port of call will be the dwarven capital of Torimar, in the land of Toraleth, to the east."

"The dwarves?" asked Horith.

"Oh yes; Torimar is as good a place as any to begin. Plus, if we are to come eventually to Eirendollen and into Eonis, Torimar is on the way."

Horith nodded along slowly and placed his hands upon his hips. He took a moment to gather his thoughts, then nodded faster, more definitively, his mind having been made up.

"Now," said Montagor, throwing Horith a wry wink, "how about that wine?"

Chapter Two

Horith and Montagor were indeed up and alert at first light, though Horith was still a little unsure as to whether he had invited Montagor to stay the night or if the old man had simply decided this for himself. Either way, the end result was the same. They wasted little time as they made their preparations; at the mage's instruction, Horith had packed a bag of essentials which was now securely strapped to his back. Clothing, food and water, and camping gear were deemed the most crucial items, although Montagor was certain that the dwarves of Torimar would allow them to restock and rest awhile in their realm, were the travelling duo to simply request it. A gruff and short-tempered race were the dwarves, but they were not without their manners and traditions, and hospitality, Montagor explained, was chief among them. However, though the country of Toraleth and its capital Torimar were - as Montagor had put it - *on the way*, a long journey still lay ahead, and it would not be without its dangers. So Horith packed the essentials and considered the space he had left; of more pressing import than spare socks, however, was Horith's fine ash bow. It had only recently been restrung, and was presently accompanied by a full complement of intricate, silver-tipped arrows. Though they were not a battle-hardened race, the barrens knew their weapons, and some of the finest smiths and fabricators in all of Gibrion were to be found in Ehronia. Of Horith's exquisite arrows, though he counted fletching among his hobbies, these were far beyond his burgeoning skills. No, these had been a gift - an expensive gift - given to him upon his twenty-fifth birthday by Ruli, Gerdan, and Miseldi. Ruli had later told Horith that the arrows had been custom-made for him by Feanil, arguably the most skilled among all barren weapon makers. Feanil also happened to be Ruli's cousin, which was the only reason they had been able to afford such a gift. They were as unique as they were intricate, and Horith's heart was heavy as he picked them up. He had intended to keep them as display pieces, but - according to Montagor - they would be needed, and soon.

The barrens may not be possessed of their cousins' magic, but preternatural skill with a bow was in the blood of every elf, whether they called Eonis their home or not. While he was, admittedly, not as skilled a shot as Ruli, Horith was no exception, and he was confident in his abilities. With his bag now secured and his bow stowed, Horith stopped for a moment to consider whether or not to take his sword along, too, and ultimately decided against it. He trusted his bow, and should any orrec, hoblin, or raider dare to get too close, well, he had a dagger or two secreted about his person just in case.

"Ready?" asked Montagor, as Horith fastened and tightened the last of his straps and strings.

"Yes. I suppose I am," replied the barren, sounding anything but.

"Then we must leave," said Montagor, motioning toward the door, "and quietly."

They stepped out into the cold darkness of the early hours, putting one foot in front of the other as they began their quest. They knew that their first priority was to get out of Ehronia unseen, and therein lay the first challenge. From there, they would head northeast toward the open plains - *the wild lands* as they had come to be known among some of the older, less adventurous barrens - which surrounded Ehronia and bridged the gaps between it and the other, smaller inhabited areas of Iollen. Ehronia itself was a land of boggy fields and damp, soggy lanes; the sweet and sickly reek of sodden wood and damp vegetation were a constant companion, as ubiquitous as the morning rains. It was through these dark, cold lanes that Horith and Montagor now trudged. They moved on, crouched, constantly alert for any sight or sound of Vinadan's orrecs. With each corner they peeked around, and every wall they dared to peer over, Horith became more and more convinced that they would be spotted and caught. In this manner they continued on until the air - subtly at first - began to smell colder and sharper; the rank, damp smell which had followed them like their own shadows eventually dissipated, and fresh morning air filled their lungs at last. Horith had not breathed such clean air in a long while, and he paused for a moment to savour it.

"Come Horith," said Montagor, snapping the barren back to his wits, "we cannot linger. The morning is upon us, and soon the orrecs will come. It will be light at any moment. We must reach the borders; quickly now." Redoubling their efforts, the barren and the mage moved in near silence, constantly alert for any sign of the incumbent orrecs. They continued this way for a while, and as the light increased, so did Horith's anxiety, until at last they could see the edge of a stream which was lined with small but densely packed trees. Their crossing would mark their departure from the main population centre of Ehronia, and would signal their arrival into the outskirts which would eventually give way to the open, wilder regions of Iollen. It both thrilled and terrified Horith to be this close to the borders of his homeland, and a hope began to rise within his chest.

"Come on, you pointy-eared scum! Get a move on."

Horith and Montagor turned as one, their eyes wide and hearts beating unusually fast. The voice of the orrec captain was unmistakable,and it rang out from somewhere not very far behind them. They looked back and saw with immeasurable relief that the orrec was facing in the opposite direction to them, a hundred yards or so back toward the main streets of Ehronia. It was surrounded by a large group of barrens who had just left their homes ready for another day at work.

"Don't turn around, don't turn around…" Horith mumbled under his breath, willing the orrec to remain ignorant of their presence. Montagor grabbed him by the shoulder with a strength which belied his age, and dragged him onwards toward the stream and the safety of the open plains beyond the treeline, where they would be hidden from prying eyes.

"Come on, Horith; move, at once!" the old mage hissed. They crouched low as they pushed forward, eating up the last of the ground which lay between them and the shallow waters which marked their way-point. Upon reaching the stream, the pair wasted no time in stepping straight in and wading through the knee-high water, yearning for the safety of the trees beyond, and sparing only fleeting, nervous glances back over their shoulders.. As they sloshed and splashed their way out of the water, the orrec captain's ears twitched and his eyes narrowed. "Hmmm," grunted the orrec as it started to turn its head toward the direction of the stream.

"Oy, orrec!" shouted Ruli, attracting the captain's attention once more. "Which way are we going today then?"

"*Oy orrec*? Who do you think you're talking to, you barren scum?" the orrec demanded as he marched over to young Ruli and gave him an almighty shove down onto the muddy ground.

"You're going this way," said the orrec, pointing west, "to the fields; same as always."

As the orrec captain pushed and cajoled the gathered barrens down the lane and towards the farmlands, Ruli stood and dusted himself down. He smiled to himself, recalling the sight he had glimpsed moments ago off in the distance behind the orrec.

Horith, thought the young barren.

I don't know what you're playing at, nor what company you keep, but good luck, my friend.

Chapter Three

"Well, I must say," said Montagor, catching his breath, "that was much closer than I would have liked, my boy." Horith couldn't agree more. The orrec had almost turned round, almost caught them.

"I was certain he was going to see us," said Horith, wiping sweat from his brow and trying to ignore how wet his feet and legs were. "Something must have caught his attention," The look on Horith's face amused the old mage who smiled knowingly at the barren.

"Let's just say that our departure didn't go *entirely* unnoticed," he said, cryptically, "but enough of that, we must press on. Torimar is days from here and the journey may prove even more perilous before we reach the dwarven lands."

Horith nodded his agreement and busied himself checking his equipment and shaking some of the excess water out of his boots, and the duo set off once more. Onwards they walked, each step taking them further and further away from the more populous areas of Ehronia, until at last they passed beyond the border of the city entirely. There was no marker or signpost to punctuate their passage; no fence nor wall separated Ehronia from wider Iollen, it was as if the land simply spat the pair out of one realm and into another. The day grew bright and warm as they pressed ahead. Insects of all shapes and colours buzzed and flitted about them, and birds flew high in the sky, standing out vividly against the clouds. The difference between the boggy, sticky streets of Horith's homeland, and the soft grasses and open meadows, littered here and there with rocks and boulders, was stark. A dark, gloomy place they had left, and a bright, verdant land they had found. Still, there were many miles ahead of them and hunger soon began to claw and scratch at their bellies. Neither humans nor elves - barren or otherwise - were particularly renowned for their appetites and could survive on even the most scant allocation of food and water, at least for a while. The dwarves on the other hand, and the orrecs - now *they* could eat.

Ehronia was by no means the only inhabited part of Iollen, and as Montagor and Horith forged ahead, they began to see small structures - spires, chimneys, bonfires - which signified other, smaller settlements scattered against the horizon. Horith could not remember the names of every such encampment and township, though he had spent some time in Parghest as a child, and he found himself lost in a memory of running, laughing, and of playing games in the sunshine. He smiled at this unbidden recollection, but his countenance was tinged with sadness.

Montagor seemed fairly certain that the orrecs maintained no presence in the smaller outposts, but, as sure as he was that they were unlikely to be accosted or in any way assailed, he and Horith decided it would be beneficial to give them a wide berth in any case and stick to the wilderness as they went. Two hours later, having trudged through seemingly miles of green and brown nothingness, Montagor and Horith came upon the crumbled remains of a settlement, long since abandoned. The moss-covered corpses of stone structures were as foreboding as they were eerie, to Horith's mind, and he was immediately on high alert.

"Where are we?" he asked Montagor, whispering for reasons he did not entirely understand.

"This, my boy, is Al-Dreccen, or what's left of it," said the mage, looking around at the silent ruin.

"What happened here?" said Horith, finding his voice.

"No one knows for certain," admitted Montagor, "though various legends and old tales persist about this place." The feel of soft grass and moss underfoot stood in stark contrast to the white-grey stone of the empty structures all around them.

"Some," continued Montagor, "hold that there was a great battle here, a long time ago - even before your kind made a home of Iollen. The story holds that a great and powerful elven king betrayed his oath, and sacked the city he had sworn to defend. *Unworthy*, the history books call him, and a betrayer of his own kin."

Horith was only half-listening to Montagor's story, as most of his attention was upon his surroundings, and the deep unease he felt in his stomach, and the tingle of cold like a dead hand upon the back of his neck.

"These days, Al-Dreccen is given a wide berth by most - elves especially. They say it is haunted, you see; that whilst it looks to all appearances to be a dark, deserted place, many hold that the poor souls who fell at the stroke of Ealdris' betrayal never actually left this place."

"Are you saying this city is haunted? Cursed?"

"Don't ask me," said Montagor, cryptically, "ask that feeling on the back of your neck."

They moved through the dead city in silence, senses on high alert; Horith's fear screamed silently in his ears, and more than once he fancied that he caught a flicker of movement in his periphery, though he dared not turn to look.

As they crossed beyond the boundaries of Al-Dreccen, Horith felt an enormous, practically tangible sense of relief. It was as if a dark cloud had passed, leaving nothing but clear blue skies. His heart felt lighter, yet he dared not turn to look over his shoulder. That a thousand ice-cold gazes, staring out from the grinning faces of long-dead elves, were now fixed upon his back Horith knew instinctively, but had no wish to confirm it by sight.

The light had begun to fade rapidly, and Horith ached from head to foot. Montagor leaned heavily upon his staff and looked just as weary as Horith.

"We will need to find shelter," said the mage, as if reading Horith's mind.

"Actually," he added, thoughtfully, as he looked around at their location, "I wonder if…No, surely not… Ha! I knew it; I *knew* that I knew it, and know it, I did!"

"Montagor?" Horith prompted.

"Horith, I must ask you two things. First, I ask you to trust me. Second, I ask you not to pay any mind to anything he says or does."

"He?" asked a puzzled Horith. "He *who*?"

"Ignus," replied the mage with a smile.

"*Ignus*? Who in Hemera's name is Ignus?"

"An old friend," said Montagor with a wide grin, "he lives just beyond that hill, over there. But Horith," Montagor added, growing serious.

"Yes?"

"The thing you must know about Ignus," said the old mage, circling his finger at his temple, "he's really *quite mad*."

*

Within half an hour, Montagor had led Horith over the crest of a steep hill, and into a small clearing on the other side. The available space between the hills and the surrounding trees was small, and Horith wondered at the decision to build a hut in such an odd spot. Consisting of rudimentary stonework and topped with a rickety-looking wooden roof, Ignus' home was certainly quaint. Montagor knocked on the chipped and flaking wooden door without preamble, and the sound of thumping feet upon creaking floorboards could be heard from inside. The door was thrown open, and a short but powerful looking human man stood in the doorway, wearing an angry expression.

"Who the f-" he began, but his face instantly lit up as he identified one of his unexpected visitors.

"Montagor?" he practically whispered, "well I'll be a lizard's gizzards; come in! Come in!" He made way for Montagor - and Horith - to enter, though his one good eye never left the young barren.

"Thank you, old friend," said Montagor in reply, "I'm sorry to drop in on you like this."

"No problem," said Ignus, "no problem at all; *anyfing* for you, my - erm - anyfing for you, Montagor."

"Again, we thank you. Ignus, this is my friend, Horith; one of the barren folk of Ehronia."

"Nice to make your acquaintance, 'orith," said Ignus in a thick human accent Horith did not recognise. "So," he continued, clapping his hands together, "'ow may I be of assistance?"

"We need a place to rest tonight, Ignus, and thought you may be able to put us up, as it were," Montagor said.

45

"Of course, of course! Allow me to fetch some ale and some bread - might be a bit stale, mind you - back in a bit." Montagor held up a hand to protest, but Ignus had already scurried away into what Horith assumed was a kitchen or pantry. He returned shortly after with a tray of bread and a gourd of wine, the stems of three goblets carried precariously between his fingers.

"'elp yourselves, gents, and don't be shy if you want some more." Ignus looked very pleased with himself, and sat down heavily into a well-worn armchair. "So, what are you two doin' all the way out 'ere in the middle of nowhere?"

"We are on our way to Torimar, truth be told, but it's still a long way off, and the night has sadly overtaken us," Montagor replied.

"Torimar, 'ey?" replied Ignus, growing stern. "Thyrus?"

"Thyrus indeed," said Montagor, offering no more.

"Well," said Ignus, brightening, "I hope that fat 'ol bastard has sorted his bleedin' attitude out these last, how many years has it been?"

"You know Lord Thyrus?" asked Horith before Montagor could respond.

"Do I know Thyrus?" Ignus echoed incredulously. "Well a-course I know Thyrus; hasn't our good Montagor here told you about…"

"Oh, I don't think we have time for that," interjected Montagor, forcing a laugh into his voice. "We're not here for tall-tales, Ignus," he added with some finality.

"Fair enough, old pal, fair enough," said Ignus, holding his hands up. He turned to Horith.

"Shame, mind you, as I have some absolute doozies I could tell you about my time in Aclevion."

"Aclevion?" said Horith, stunned.

"Oh yes, my lad! Blimey; Montagor really hasn't told you who I am, has he?"

"Ignus," said Montagor, but their host paid the old mage no mind.

"I was Vinadan's bodyguard, I was. For a time, at least. Grew up wiv him, you see. I was in the same academy as him, back in the day."

"Come now, Ignus… We've talked about this," Montagor said, with a little more ice in his tone than he perhaps intended.

"Yeah, you're right, sorry," the man said, "pay no mind to me, young 'orith. Mad as a box of tits, I am." His eyes never left montagor as he spoke, and his voice was clear and controlled.

"I did once see me a witch though," he continued, his voice once again jovial and his face animated. "Just south 'a the capital. Pretty fit, she was, too. Red 'air and nice, well - you know... Funniest 'fing though," he added conspiratorially, leaning in close to Horith, "she was chattin' away with a dragon - I kid you not - chattin' away like they were old mates or something. Strangest 'fing I ever seen. More wine, gents?" He stood and took the gourd from the small table upon which it sat, and disappeared back into the other room.

"You see?" hissed Montagor, "he's completely and utterly mad. Though he means well, poor soul, and will do us no harm. We will rest safely here tonight."

And so they did; at Ignus' behest they played cards and drank wine, and all the while the man regaled Horith with tales of adventure, intrigue, betrayal, and dark sacrifice. He had murdered a farm owner at Vinadan's command; had personally trained a battalion of orrecs inside Elgiroth itself; he was quite sure that the late Queen Arianrhod- Vinadan's mother - had a bit of a 'thing' for him; and had single-handedly repelled a band of mercenaries who had dared to attack Aclevion under the cover of night, and had ultimately been banished from the capital by a mage who sat upon the former king's council.

"Mid-something, I 'fink his name was."

And Horith did not believe a single word of it. The man was clearly delusional, but the young barren knew in his heart that Ignus was not a threat to him, despite the misgivings he harboured. Here and there, now and then, Horith would catch Ignus staring at him, and did not like the look in the man's one remaining good eye. There appeared to be a hint of menace upon the man's countenance, but his bearing and nature contradicted this underlying malice. Montagor, too, appeared at pains, as if spending time in Ignus' presence, whilst necessary, was also dangerous, somehow.

That there was a secret - or secrets - between the two humans, Horith had no doubt, but at length considered it none of his business and did not press the mage for information.

Old friends, old battles, he thought, taking a long gulp of the astoundingly mediocre wine.

It was growing late, and Montagor was keen to set out early upon the following morning. Ignus offered Montagor use of his bed, Horith the use of the bedroom floor, and he himself took the couch. Horith's sleep came easily, but his dreams were troubled, and he awoke feeling almost as tired as he was the night before.

*

They thanked Ignus for his hospitality and bid him farewell. Hortih was aware that the man was standing at the threshold waving at their receding backs, and was also aware of the stern set of Montagor's jaw and the deep furrow of his brow. They pressed forward in earnest, and did not speak for a while as they picked their way through dense, claustrophobic woodlands. The trees were thick and virtually impassable in places, and more than once Horith and Montagor were forced to turn around and find another way through the mire. The trees eventually began to thin, and the pair soon found themselves out upon open lands once more. The sun was high in the sky now, and before too long the duo found themselves hungry and in need of a break. They stopped beside a large boulder, and Horith dropped his backpack, and sat down upon the grass with a grunt. He extracted the components of a small cooking tripod from his pack, from which he hung a small pot. Expertly piling a bundle of sticks beneath, Horith took out a match with which to light the small pyre, but Montagor held up a hand to stop him and threw a wry wink at the barren. The old mage clicked his fingers theatrically, and the pile of sticks burst into flames, their meal beginning to cook in earnest.

So, noted Horith, *the old man has some skill with pyromancy.* What Horith had failed to notice, however, was the strange, glowing rune which had appeared on the back of Montagor's hand as he brought forth his magic. It was gone as quickly as it had appeared. Shortly thereafter, barren and mage alike were tucking into a hearty broth, each with a bread roll to dip. They relished the opportunity to rest their legs and fill their stomachs, and no sounds but the singing of birds, the chirping and clicking of insects, and the low murmur of the wind was to be heard as they ate. A cloud passed in front of the sun as they ate, and the wind gained a little in intensity, though it remained warm and pleasant. Once the much-needed meal had been consumed and Horith's bag was restocked, the pair took to their feet once more and resumed their journey.

The day passed uneventfully, and their sleep was untroubled. Though the wild grasses and shrubbery they laid down upon were hidden from sight under the cover of trees, and was deep enough within the woods to keep the pair away from the icy fingers of the chill wind, it was not comfortable. It was in this vein that the pair continued for the next three days and nights. They kept to the wild lands and hugged the treeline where they could, and came across other beings only rarely. Even then, Horith and Montagr went to great lengths to remain concealed, or at very least draw no unwanted attention. Their luck did not hold indefinitely, however, and as the duo risked a more direct route, choosing to utilise a more established road in order to save daylight, Horith's keen ears heard voices to the north-east.

"Montagor," he said, pulling at the mage's sleeve, "we have company." Montagor squinted his eyes, and held up a hand to block out errant rays of sunlight which dazzled his eyes.

"Men," he said, "four of them. All armed."

"Yes," replied Horith, whose elven sight had already discerned the number and species of the oncoming group, "we have to move, quickly."

"There, Horith," said Montagor, pointing to the stump of a large tree trunk; the only cover to be found at this point upon the road, "hide. I will deal with this." Horith's eyes went wide at Montagor's suggestion, but he did as instructed and hid behind the trunk, pressing his back to the bark and trying to make himself small. He did not know for certain that the men would be a threat, nor that they would even be interested in him at all, but at very least, he rationalised, the sight of a barren and a human mage would not likely be forgotten. Horith held his breath as the men came near, noticing Montagor.

"You lost, old man?" Horith heard one of the men say in a mocking tone.

"Me? Lost?" replied Montagor, "good grief, no. I am exactly where I need to be."

"These lands are under our protection," said another of the men, though Horith did not dare look out from his position to get a look at which one, "under orders of Aclevion."

"Aclevion, you say?" replied Montagor, an edge of something unidentifiable tinting his words, "Well, gentlemen, allow me to explain my business more *definitively*." Silence ensued, and Horith could not stand it. He risked a glance from behind the tree stump, and saw Montagor huddled close to the men, deep in hushed conversation. Though the mage's back was to Horith, the barren could well imagine Montagor's face as he… what was he doing? Horith knew not, but prayed that it would end well. Montagor nodded, and the men shook their heads. He held up a finger, they waved it away. He placed his hands on his hips, and raised his head to the sky in exasperation. Lowering his head, he straightened his back and folded his arms. Horith did not dare risk being spotted, so he ducked back into cover. A moment later, he heard a gasp of surprise, and a chorus of "For the might of Aclevion!" issued from the mouths of all four men. Horith closed his eyes tight, fearing he had been betrayed by the old mage, but breathed a long sigh of relief at the sound of the men continuing on their way, not so much as sparing a glance in Horith's direction.

"You can come out now," said Montagor, "it's quite safe."

Horith slowly stood and walked toward the grinning mage, leaning to look further down the road to make sure the men had truly left, and were not simply waiting to spring some elaborate ambush.

"What happened?" Horith asked at last, "who were they?"

"Mercenaries," said Montagor with disdain, "worse than orrecs, if you ask me. They would slit the throats of their own kin if there was money in it. Come on, we must not linger."

"But I don't understand," said Horith, making no move to follow Montagor, "how did you get away? What did you say to them?"

"Oh, that?" said Montagor, casually, "I simply reminded them that I too was once in the service of Aclevion. I rather - how best to put it - *pulled rank*. Now, please; we must move on.

They walked in silence for a long while, with Montagor speaking only occasionally to point out the various items of interest, or particular features of the landscape, offering anecdotes along the way. Horith spoke only to offer polite responses to the old mage, and occasionally to reassure himself of their location and general bearing. At length, the brightness of the day began to fade, and the warm air took on a sharp edge as night drew in. Though the land still appeared wild and vast from their point of view, they found that they were not far from Haneth, the second largest city in Iollen. Again, the pair decided to forsake the comforts the city promised, and agreed that the long way round would be the best bet. Once they passed the predominantly human centre, there would only be a smattering of smaller, scattered settlements and townships before they would finally pass beyond the borders of Iollen and into the southernmost region of Korrigand.

"We must find a place to make camp, Horith. Preferably somewhere quiet; somewhere hidden from view," suggested Montagor.

Horith agreed. He was unfamiliar with these lands and did not like the prospect of being caught out in the open by some creature or other in the night. As a child, he had been terrified by stories of the haemori, and as he looked up into the darkening sky, watching as the moon made its first appearance, he fancied that he could almost see one or two of the soulless, deathless creatures swooping high on unnatural leathery wings; their ice blue eyes gleaming upon pallid faces, and ivory fangs prominent in rictus grins. He shuddered at the thought, and involuntarily touched a hand to the side of his neck.

On they walked, and with each step they took, their visibility reduced incrementally as the moon continued to muscle in on the sun's territory, as it had night after night for cycles beyond count, and would continue to do until the light of the Souls burned out.

At last they found the perfect spot; the grass was tall and soft, and large boulders formed a crescent of sorts around them. Horith would rather have been hidden from view completely, hemmed in tight on all sides, but he knew as well as Montagor did that this was as good as they were going to find while the light held. Horith once again dropped his bag onto the ground and set about constructing their tents. Before long, two were up and ready. Though their camp was constructed, the barren and the mage remained outside for a time while the last of the light still held sway. Horith was distant, seemingly lost in his own thoughts, but eventually looked up at Montagor who had not interrupted the young barren's silence.

"What are our chances?" asked Horirth, "I mean, *really?*"

For all his joviality and wit, the old mage met Horith's concerned gaze with one of his own. He took a deep breath, and then blew it out heavily.

"Much depends on the dwarves, truth be told," Montagor began. "Without the numbers which Torimar commands, we cannot hope to sway the elves. And without the elves, there can be no victory against Prince Vinadan and the armies of Aclevion - especially with the Asarlai at his command." The old man shook his head and rubbed at his temples.

"No, we must journey on to Torimar and seek an audience with Lord Thyrus if we are to have any hope of succeeding."

Horith's frown remained in place as he pondered the old man's words.

"What is it about the Asarlai? Why do they worry you, so?" he asked at length.

"The Asarlai are an ancient order," Montagor began, "named for the first of their kind. Daedan Asarlai, you see, was the first to interpret the runes, though countless had tried across the centuries. He was the first to harness the power of the Souls to manifest the power locked away inside those ancient shapes and symbols. In short, he gave magic to men. Before Asarlai, Horith, it was only the elves - your cousins - who could wield that sort of power. Asarlai levelled the playing field. And they killed him for it." Montagor's eyes glazed over and lost their focus as his mind whirled and drifted somewhere else, momentarily.

"Some call them warriors," he continued, turning his attention to Horith once more, "others believe them to be merely monks, locked away in their monastery high above Aclevion, ignorant of the wider world. But neither view is true, Horith, nor are they necessarily false," the mage said with a wink. "The Asarlai answer to no-one, you see - not truly - and that is what makes them dangerous. They possess magic, yes, but it is not the magic of the elves; magic derived from nature, from living things; theirs is a magic of an altogether darker kind. Whispers of witchcraft and the forbidden arts surround the order, and the fire they possess within can be used to conjure burning flame into existence out of thin air. Though no man has ever mastered the rune, rumours of necromancy surround their order. The Asarlai have dictated the tides of power in Gibrion for centuries, though they have done so subtly; unseen; pulling hidden strings in the darkness."

"And now they serve Prince Vinadan," Horith concluded.

"Correct, my boy," said Montagor with an approving nod, "as they served his traitor father Entallion before him, and his grandfather Ondellion before *him,* so on and so forth for centuries. While they have rarely marched openly into battle, they are a very real and constant threat nonetheless. But enough of that; here…" the mage said, producing two pewter goblets and a flask of a deep red liquid from somewhere within his robes. He poured a hearty amount into each goblet, and handed one to Horith.

"To victory," he said.

"For the might of Aclevion," Horith added with a grin. The laugh was just what the travellers needed, and they drained their goblets gladly. They helped themselves to a refill,then another, and they talked and laughed around their small campfire. Smiles still pulled at the corners of their mouths as they eventually bade each other good night and retired to their respective tents. They had a long day ahead of them tomorrow, and they needed to sleep soundly tonight. The red wine helped greatly, of course, but Horith's dreams were troubled. Though he would only remember fleeting images and abstract feelings come morning, Horith's sleep was beset by darkness and foreboding. Here, a red-robed Asarlai conjured a bow of pure flame. There, one of the haemori, newly come from their home in the eastern lands, stretched long, thin fingers out toward Horith as it bared its fangs. He glimpsed fire, death, and suffering. He saw his friends upon the battlefield, drowning in their own tears. He saw himself, from a distance, as he crawled upon the ground, his hands flailing for traction but slipping on slick crimson. He heard the guttural shouts of orrecs, and the high pitched screeching of hoblins in answer. And as the hours ticked by, his dreamscape grew darker and darker as a shadow loomed overhead. Dream-Horith looked up, the simple act requiring an immense feat of strength, and as he locked eyes with the dragon which hurtled toward him open-mouthed, Horith woke.

*

The night grew colder with the appearance of every new star, and a silence lay over the lands. The cover afforded by the rock formation had eased Horith's mind somewhat although he was still uneasy as he recalled snippets of his dream. He heard the low, rhythmic sound of Montagor's breathing as the old man slept, ensconced within his own tent. The sound lulled Horith back into restfulness, and as his exhausted body courted sleep once more, Horith heard a sound. He sat bolt upright, and strained his keen barren ears, attuned as they were to even the slightest of sounds, and his stomach churned with a wave of dread as he discerned the unmistakable voices which seemed perilously close to their precarious position.

hoblins, he thought as he quietly picked up his weapons.

Though human ears were not nearly as sensitive as those of elves and barrens, Montagor, too, had heard the hoblins. The mage tapped delicately on Horith's tent, and held a finger over his mouth as his barren companion emerged with bow in hand and eyes keen in the darkness. Confident that Horith had indeed taken his meaning, Montagor now held up a palm to communicate to his companion that he intended for them to *wait*, to let the rabble of short, sinewy hoblins pass by their location, and to hope that they did not see the tents in the darkness. Cautiously and silently they crouched, hidden on three sides by the rock formation, but all-too aware of their tents which still stood erect in the darkness. The companions held their breaths as if the very act of exhaling would draw unwanted attention, and both Horith and Montagor grimaced as one of the hoblins raised the alarm.

"What's this? Lads, over 'ere!" it shouted as it broke from the pack and started toward their makeshift camp. The travellers had already concluded that their chances of remaining unnoticed had long since vanished, so Horith readied his bow and Montagor assumed a defensive stance with his staff held in both hands.

"We cannot wait for them to encircle us," said the mage, charging into the open and away from the closed-in camp. Horith nocked an arrow, and followed Montagor out into the open. Once he had cleared the rock formation, he was able to discern the hoblins more clearly and counted fifteen, his sharp elven eyes darting to-and-fro in the moonlight.

"Get 'em, lads!" shouted the lead hoblin, and his companions drew their blades in unison. Horith did not stand on ceremony, and loosed three arrows in lightning-quick succession, killing a trio of hoblins within seconds. Montagor broke off from Horith and headed toward a group of the hoblin raiders. He gritted his teeth, and raised his staff high above his head as the hoblins drew nearer, slamming it back down into the dirt when they were within mere feet of the mage. A wave of angry red flames burst forth from the point of impact, searing the grass and scorching the ground, and it spread outward, engulfing four of the hoblins as they charged, instantly reducing them to ash.

That's about half of them, thought Horith as he nocked and loosed arrow after arrow, reducing the hoblin numbers even further, moment by moment. The remainder of the snarling and screeching hoblins had closed the gap, however, and were now in melee range. As one hoblin raised his sword overhead, Horith tried in vain to fumble his long dagger out of his boot holster and could only dodge wildly to the right, falling to the ground as the hoblin brought the blade to bear. Horith screamed out in pain as the hoblin blade found his shoulder, but was finally able to draw his dagger from his prone position. He thrust his arm upwards with all his strength, impaling the hoblin where it stood. Horith bit down hard on his lip as he clutched his injured shoulder, and grimaced in pain as he beheld bright orange and red flashes away to his left. Montagor was busy deploying his pyromancy against the horde, and the old mage was a whirlwind of fire. For an old man, he was more than holding his own against the hoblins. Horith clambered back to his feet and saw that the hoblins were no more, having succumbed to the precision of his own bow and the fury of Montagor's supernatural inferno. The wizard turned to regard his barren companion and, noticing he was injured, hurried toward him.

"Rest easy, my boy. I've got you," he said, lowering Horith back to the ground. He drew a purple gemstone from within his robes, and held it to his lips as he whispered an incantation that Horith did not understand. The stone blazed brightly as the mage spoke, a metallic, shimmering light emanating from the heart of the strange gem. Once Montagor had completed his recital, he moved the shining object toward Horith's injured shoulder.

"This may sting a little…" he cautioned. Horith gritted his teeth and groaned in pain as contact was made, but the feeling soon passed, and the deep cut in his shoulder began to heal itself before his very eyes. Montagor noticed the surprised look on his companion's face, and laughed a little under his breath.

"I *did* tell you I was a healer," he said with a lopsided grin. .

"I've never known a healer who could summon fire like that," Horith replied, betraying more of his awe than he had originally intended.

This time Horith did notice the numerous glowing runes which were beginning to fade from Montagor's hands, wrists, and neck. The old mage registered Horith's curiosity at the appearance of these strange symbols but did not acknowledge it openly.

"Yes, well… I served in the king's court for a time - a lifetime ago it now seems. Living and working alongside the Asarlai, as I did, well; let's just say I learned one or two of their tricks. I only hope that this was both the first and last time I'll have to use it. It takes a lot out of me," the mage said wearily. Now that he was no longer focused on his pain and the adrenaline of battle had worn off, Horith noticed that the old man did indeed look exhausted. He tested his shoulder, and was pleased to report no pain or swelling from the wound. He exhaled heavily, and turned his attention to the sky, noting that the stars had begun to recede a little. Morning couldn't be far away.

"Are you okay to travel?" he asked Montagor, "I think it's best that we press on."

"I wholeheartedly agree, my boy. And don't worry about me; one or two more of these and I'll be right as a rainstorm," said the old mage as he pulled his flask out from beneath his robes and took a long, deep swig of the blood-red liquid within.

Humans, though Horith, shaking his head.

They dismantled the tents and packed away their belongings in short order, and were soon on their way once more. Having narrowly survived the encounter with the hoblins, they resolved not to make camp again unless they absolutely had to, and even then they would sleep in shifts. Camp dismantled and bags packed, the pair stood and assessed their position in the growing daylight. The sky was now a soft white-blue, and the high peaks of the distant mountains served as a waypoint as the mage and the barren turned once more to the road. On they pressed, moving at a faster pace than they had the previous day, spurred on by the memory of the hoblin ambush. They wanted nothing more than to leave the open lands behind them, with all of its mystery and dangers, and reach the safety of Torimar and the halls of Lord Thyrus without delay.

Then the real difficulties would begin.

Chapter Four

Between Horith's home in Ehronia and Lord Thyrus' mighty halls in Torimar, stand a number of human outposts and small villages. Jo'Thuun, to the east, offered a promise of warmth and shelter, but its human residents had grown insular and suspicious over the centuries, and mostly kept to themselves. Were Horith and Montagor to seek refuge there, even for a mere night or two, the travellers would not likely be met with warmth and hospitality, but with hostility, and the cold edge of decades-old prejudice and disdain for outsiders. The humans would be neither sympathetic nor particularly useful to Horith and Montagor in any case, so they would be best avoided. No, the travellers would not head toward the human lands, but would instead simply forge ahead, trusting only in themselves and their own wits if they were to make it as far as Torimar still in one piece.

They allowed themselves only the most fleeting of breaks to take on food and water, and slept only in fits and starts in the days and nights following their encounter with the hoblins. Taking great pains to avoid a repeat and choosing speed over comfort, Horith and Montagor passed into the land of Toraleth a little ahead of their earlier projection. As wild grasses began to give way to harder ground, the very world around them seemed to shift from green to grey. In the distance stood a mountain range which seemed to spread infinitely northwards, and whose tips were greedily swallowed up by the clouds. They held their course, and Montagor led them incxorably in thc dircction of thc tallcst mountain among the Toralethian range. Horith had not been aware of an incline, at least not a steep one, but as he and Montagor found themselves standing at the precipice of an impossibly deep gorge, he was surprised at just how high up they were. As if reading his mind, the old mage offered an explanation.

"The dwarves are miners, ancestrally speaking. They excavate deep into the ground, and sculpt great caverns within the very rock underfoot. So while we may look down upon their realm, it is not us who are elevated, it is the dwarves who are beneath us, as it were. They have made their home beneath the ground for centuries beyond memory. *Torimar,* they name this place which, as I understand it, roughly translates to *Stone Hearth,* or at least something close in the dwarven tongue. We are now at the liberty of Lord Thyrus and his kin, Horith. Come,"

Montagor said, moving forward once more. Just as Horith was about to ask how in the name of Hemera they were supposed to get down there, Montagor began to descend the lip of the precipice.

Stairs, Horith realised, dumbly, placing his hand over his face. Noting now the huge walkway hewn into the very rock of the gorge, he carefully followed the mage and they zig-zagged their way down. Further and deeper they went until at last they reached the bottom. Horith looked up over his shoulder and his feet swayed beneath him as he beheld the gargantuan wall they had just descended.

It seems much, much higher from down here.

Two dwarves approached them as soon as they had made footfall on ground level, and Montagor held up a hand in friendly greeting as they approached.

"Who are you; what is your business here?" the lead dwarf asked.

"Greetings, friends. I am Montagor, formerly of Aclevion, currently of, well, *everywhere*, I suppose. This is my companion Horith of house Nindrius. We are here to speak to your Lord Thyrus, if our presence would be permitted by your graces." Montagor spoke kindly and in deference to their hosts, and bowed low at the conclusion of his words. Horith had always imagined the dwarves to be a tempestuous, short-tempered race, but their hospitality surprised him.

"We will notify Lord Thyrus of your arrival at once, master mage. Follow us and we will provide food and chambers; Aether knows you look like you could use it," the dwarf said with a wry smile. Horith and Montagor followed the dwarves as they left the open gorge, and journeyed through a hewn archway which led deeper into the mountain. It had concerned Horith that they had been able to so easily enter Torimar via the stair, and had not been challenged until they had reached the bottom. But passing through the archway and into Torimar itself, Horith was struck by the number of armed and armoured dwarves which lined the passageways and corridors. While one may indeed descend the stair into the valley, they would not be permitted inside without leave of the dwarves.

Before long, the barren and the mage were seated at a long, stone table which appeared to have been carved seamlessly from the very rock beneath their feet. Hot meat, crisp vegetables, and all manner of sweet breads and cakes lined the table, and the visiting duo were grateful to fill their bellies. The dwarves had provided tall carafes of wine, ale, and mead, all of which Montagor was keeping a very close eye on. As Horith and Montagor began to slow down their eating, their long since stomachs full, the dwarf who had greeted them earlier returned to provide an update.

"Lord Thyrus is at your service, master mage; master elf, if you would follow me." The dwarf stepped aside and gestured toward one of the many natural passageways which led away from the mess hall and deeper into Torimar. Montagor paused to finish his wine in one long gulp and motioned for Horith to follow the dwarf while he quickly refilled his flask at the dwarves' expense. They followed the winding caverns by the light of torches affixed to the rock walls, and they soon reached a huge set of heavy wooden doors guarded left and right by dwarves clad in golden armour. The dwarf leading the unlikely travellers nodded to each of his kinsmen in turn, and they dutifully threw open the heavy doors to permit the group.

A long, narrow hall lay beyond, at the end of which stood a throne, also hewn from the very rock of Torimar. Atop the throne sat an elderly dwarf whose long grey hair and beard clashed starkly with his golden, gem-studded armour, not to mention the similarly-adorned ceremonial battle axe mounted above the throne. Upon a dais to the left of the throne sat a crown of steel and bronze which bore a large purple jewel. More noteworthy to Horith, however, was not the grandeur of the crown, but the fact that it did not reside upon the dwarf's head.

"Lord Thyrus," Montagor boomed, bowing low in reverence to their esteemed host. Horith followed suit and inclined his head toward the dwarf.

"Come closer, mage," Thyrus bade in a deep, velvet voice, the heavy accent of the mid-lands unmistakable in his words. "We do not receive many guests here in Torimar," he continued, "let alone humans and elves."

"Barrens," said Horith, in spite of himself.

"Excuse me?" said Thyrus.

"Barrens; I am a barren, my lord. The green woods of the south are not my home, and the ancient magic of the world is not mine to command. I am no elf, Lord Thyrus."

"I know of the barrens, my friend," said Thyrus, kindly. "We dwarves are not possessed of magic either, whether of the old world or the new. So I suppose we are all barren in the end," Lord Thyrus said with a small grin. He continued, addressing the pair once more.

"So; why do you come before me, travellers?"

"My lord," began Montagor, "we have come before you to seek your aid in our quest to free Gibrion from the oppression of Prince Vinadan and the armies of Aclevion." Thyrus' eyebrows stood high in surprise.

"Oh, is that all? For a moment there I thought you were going to ask for something utterly ludicrous," said Thyrus, with velvet sarcasm dripping from his voice. Montagor continued undeterred, and Horith stood silently at the mage's side and listened to Montagor's impassioned plea for help. The old man rationalised that the might of the dwarves, allied with the power of the elves and the ancient Soul of Hemera they guarded, would be enough to break the grip which Vinadan had placed around the throat of each realm, each race, and each being in Gibrion. The mage's passion and speech-craft moved Horith, and stoked his determination, setting the fires of rebellion burning hot in his gut once more.

"...and only together can we be free of this evil; only together can we build a better world." The mage was finished. Lord Thyrus had sat in silence throughout Montagor's plea, and so he remained for a while after the old man had finished speaking. He sat and stared at Montagor before turning his gaze upon Horith, and his eyes narrowed as they lingered a while upon the barren. At length, he turned his attention back to the mage.

"The skies will be dark soon. You two should rest. Go now, and help yourself to whatever food and wine you should like. I will have rooms prepared for you in the meantime, and you will sleep comfortably and safely this night. You will have my decision in the morning." Montagor and Horith bowed low in agreement and were led from the hall without a word passing between them. Horith believed in the mage now more than ever, and only hoped that Lord Thyrus had been as convinced by Montagor's plea, and would decide to commit the strength of the dwarves to this unlikely quest of theirs. Without the dwarven army at their backs, the elves would not so much as even consider Montagor and his proposal, and all would be lost. With the leave of their hosts, Horith and Montagor carried food and wine - plenty of wine in Montagor's case - back to their rooms, or rather back to Montagor's room. They ate and drank as if friends of old, talking not of Lord Thyrus and the pivotal decision before him; talking not of Prince Vinadan and the prospect of war with Aclevion, and talking not of their strategy to win over the elves of Eonis. They spoke instead of matters trivial and deeply personal in turn, with Horith's discussion of his homeland tugging at his heartstrings and prompting him to picture his friends. He saw Gerdan and Miseldi, laughing with goblets raised in some toast or other. And he saw Ruli. Ruli who, of all his friends, was perhaps closest to his heart. Montagor talked at length of his travels and the adventures he had undertaken in his long years, and told tall tales of the lands he had seen and the folks he had met, long ago.

"Where do you call home, Montagor?" asked Horith, "Where will you go once all this is over?"

"My dear boy; were I to answer you truthfully, you would name me false in any case," the mage said with a wink, and Horith decided not to press the matter any further.

There is little sense speaking in riddles at this hour, he thought. More they talked, more they ate, and more they drank, until they could talk, eat, and drink no more. Well, that was true of Horith at least; Montagor, it seemed, had no upper-limit where wine was concerned, especially dwarven wine. At length, they decided to call it a night. Horith bade the mage goodnight and made for his own room, laying down upon the soft, warm sheets and allowing sleep to take him in its grasp within moments. He slept more soundly than he had in a long time, and his dreams were filled with glimpses of hills, lakes, mountains, and clouds. Horith's sleeping mind presented images of wide, sweeping landscapes, of adventure, and of exploration among trees and across streams. No darkness encroached upon his rest.

Before he knew it, he was awoken by a heavy knocking at his door, and he was alert instantly. He strode across the room and opened the door, and found himself looking upon a dwarf he did not recognise.

"Lord Thyrus will see you in one hour, master barren; I have already notified the mage," the dwarf said, before nodding sharply and turning on his heel. Horith closed the door and set about washing and dressing in preparation for their fateful meeting with Lord Thyrus, upon whose decision so much depended. He hurried and met with Montagor in the mess hall, and each partook of a quick breakfast before being led once more into the hall of Lord Thyrus.

"Good morning, my friends; I trust you slept well?" the dwarf began earnestly.

"Yes, my Lord. Your hospitality knows no bounds," replied Horith with equal sincerity.

"Right," began Thyrus, "I will not talk in circles, but will rather get straight to the point." He paused as if for dramatic effect, and continued.

"I agree that the oppression of Aclevion and the iron grip of Prince Vinadan is indeed a blight on all our lands. That being said - and I'm sure it will not have escaped your attention - his orrecs make no home of Torimar, nor Toraleth in general." It had not in fact escaped their notice, and Horith was all too aware of the fact he had not seen a single orrec since stepping foot inside dwarven country.

"We do not suffer like many others, and we are a strong, proud race, more than capable of defending ourselves should the situation call for it," Thyrus continued. "As it stands, the situation has not yet called for a show of force, nor have we been forced to fight. Vinadan fears us, perhaps; or more likely, he has yet to decide our fate. Either way, I am under no illusion that the foul stench of orrecish flesh will likely taint our halls sooner or later." Thyrus' face grew grim, and his tone was dark as he spoke, and Horith began to feel a flicker of hope kindling inside his chest, as a match trying to catch fire in the wind. He held his tongue, and the dwarf lord continued.

"It is for this reason," he went on, standing from his throne and descending the steps toward Montagor and Horith, "that I accept your proposal, gentlemen. I hereby commit the dwarves to your cause, and I mean to accompany you to Eonis personally to plead our case to Lady Keya."

Neither Horith nor Montagor could keep themselves from grinning openly at Thyrus' words, and Horith had not failed to notice the emphasis the dwarf placed on the word "our".

"My Lord, I cannot tell you what a pleasure it is to receive such welcome news," said Montagor.

"You make a strong case for action, master mage, and I feel I can trust you. There is a familiarity to you; if I did not know better, I would swear that you and I had met before," said Thyrus.

"Well, I was often present in King Entallion's court," said Montagor, offhandedly. "It is not unreasonable to allow that you and I may indeed have crossed paths once or twice."

"I knew him, you know," said Thryus.

"The king?" asked Horith.

"Vinadan," said Thyrus, "Entallion Daelectus was more than just our king, you see; he was my friend. He and I shared many a hangover in our time. He was a good man, and a good friend. Vinadan, though…" he trailed off, shaking his head. "Vinadan was a petulant, sickly child. When he was small, he and Entallion were all-but inseparable; he adored his father, and would often sit upon the king's lap on the very throne of Aclevion as Entallion held court. As he got older, though… As I understand it, he suffered a great ordeal, but that does not excuse his actions."

Horith listened intently; he had no idea Lord Thyrus had actually known Vinadan. Montagor's face was still and impassive as he listened.

"When I saw him last, he…" Thyrus sighed heavily and shook his head. The beginnings of tears glistened in the old dwarf's eyes. "They did not deserve what happened to them, despite what that wretched boy says. Entallion and Arianrhod were my friends, yes, but they were also wise and noble leaders. They would never betray us; they would never betray the kingdom. And as for Prince Valahir…" A tear now rolled openly down the dwarf's cheek as he spoke, recalling a horror he had not given voice to in decades. "That boy was the image of his father; a strong, proud warrior, and a kind and generous man in his own right. He would have made a great king.On my honour, and that of my house, I tell you now that Valahir was no turncoat. The lies of Vinadan, and the brutality he employs know no bounds."

Montagor's left eye twitched a little, but his face remained unreadable.

The sadness upon Lord Thyrus' face was replaced with a look of sheer, unfiltered anger.

"Make no mistake, gentlemen; for me, this is personal. I cursed Vinadan that day, and he renounced my kingship in return," he said with thunder in his voice. "Torimar is a free realm, and while I remain its leader, I am no thrall of Aclevion. I will instruct my captains to ready a host, one-hundred strong, immediately. We will travel in convoy at daybreak tomorrow, and head south-east toward Eonis. With luck, we should arrive within a week. Onward to Eonis, and our common destiny."

Tomorrow, Horith thought with excitement, *tomorrow we make for the woodland realm. We are so close.* He turned to face his companion, and found Montagor casually observing Lord Thyrus' resting crown. Horith was encouraged to see the wide grin which was now etched upon Montagor's face.

Chapter Five

The following morning brought with it as much agitation as it did excitement, as Horith's nerves began to get the better of him ahead of this vital leg of their quest. He stood beside Montagor and Lord Thyrus at the foot of the great stair, and idly fidgeted with the straps and ties of his clothing and equipment. For his part, the mage helped to put the barren's mind at ease with tales of his adventures serving as a much-needed distraction while they awaited the readiness of Lord Thyrus' forces. Though day had dawned, the skies were still a deep, inky blue, and the birds had not yet risen to sing and circle above the dwarven lands. They did not have to wait long, however, and as a great horn boomed out in the early morning half-light and reverberated wildly within the confines of the great gorge, the hairs on Horith's forearms stood on end.

Here we go, he thought.

Lord Thyrus led the way, followed by Montagor and Horith, and they made ready to ascend the stair down which the travellers had trudged mere days before. Behind them, coming three abreast, marched a host of dwarves, resplendent in their armour and helms; razor-sharp axes and colossal war hammers carried proudly and with poise. After what felt like an age to Horith, the dwarves emerged from the depths of Torimar and out onto the higher ground above the great gorge. Once all were above ground and accounted for, Lord Thyrus poured an almighty breath into his own dwarven horn which he carried upon his back, and as one, the soldiers took up the march. Onwards they proceeded, heading south toward the elven land of Eirendollen and the capital Eonis. The journey would not be a short one, and they planned to stop only to take on food and water, marching at the first light of the rising sun and not stopping until the stars shone brightly above. They pushed onwards in convoy, the great army silent but for the heavy trudging sound of armoured boots on the ground. At the head of the column, Montagor and Thyrus were deep in conversation whilst Horith listened on eagerly.

"What do you know of Lady Keya, master dwarf?" the old mage asked.

"Not much, truth be told. Not unlike myself, I know that she lost her crown when Vinadan came to power. I am aware, also, that she is a popular but ruthless leader, and that she had to fight twice as hard as her predecessors to be taken seriously due to… well, you know," the dwarf replied, shrugging his shoulders in mild embarrassment.

"Yes," Montagor nodded, "it is high time the woodlanders and the night elves put such inconsequential differences behind them. Maybe Lady Keya can be a force for change in her realm."

"I wouldn't count on that, master mage, though I must confess I hold some measure of fear to enter so freely into the hands of one with a temper such as hers."

"Well, my good dwarf," replied Montagor with a wink, "you'd better just make sure to *play nice*."

Horith was infinitely more confident now the dwarves were in tow, and had no problems setting up his tent and falling straight to sleep as they made camp on the third night. Their journey had been long but uneventful, and there were more than enough dwarves to keep watch as they slept. Horith knew that the relative ease of their march had less to do with the safety of the lands they passed through, and more to do with the fact that no hoblin pack, orrec patrol, or band of marauding scavengers would dare attack a gathering of armoured dwarves, whether the night provided cover or not. Horith awoke at first light, and took a moment to look around, assessing their position. He wandered through row upon row of dwarves asleep atop blankets but otherwise exposed to the open air.

Hardy folk, these dwarves, Horith reflected with an approving grin. He continued on a little further, and he gradually became aware that they had come to rest on an area of higher ground, though it was neither hill nor peak. From this modest vantage point Horith, with the keen eyes of his kind, could just about make out a point of glistening, shifting light, sparkling in the early morning sun some miles off to the south, and a gargantuan mass of green further to the east.

Eonis.

He stood a while, taking in the view, and considering their next move. Were they to replicate the previous day's pace, they would reach the elven lands - the home of his ancestors - in two days or less. Horith was lost in his thoughts and calculations when Montagor walked up beside him.

"Eonis," the mage said, making Horith's own thoughts tangible, "and the great lake of Ideen lies beyond. Our path will lead us away from the lake, regrettably, but it is truly a sight to behold should our paths ever lead us back to this part of the world."

Horith nodded, but did not speak. The lake *did* look impressive; pure blue waters which must stretch miles from shore to shore, yet it troubled Horith to imagine the manner of creatures which would name the depths of Ideen their home.

"Come along, my boy, we are ready to depart," said Montagor, leading Horith away by the shoulders. Shortly afterwards, they were away on foot once more. Thyrus took up his position at the head of the convoy, flanked by his newfound mage and barren allies, with the might of a hundred dwarves thumping along behind. On they pressed, on and on towards their destination, keeping conversation to a minimum. All wanted to make progress; it would not do to tarry. Horith's earlier projections regarding their pace and destination indeed proved correct and they reached the borders of Eonis while some sunlight still remained in the skies above on the day after he woke to the distant sight of Ideen.

The trees were tall and thick, and scarcely any light could be seen through the mass of green and brown. Despite his earlier optimism, a wave of unfounded dread passed through Horith, turning his stomach. He could not quite discern the cause of his unease, but being this close to his ancestral home was undoubtedly a daunting prospect to the young barren. The eyes and ears of elves are sharp indeed, and Horith and Montagor's host were met at the edge of the immense woodland by a contingent of elves, equally as armed and equally as armoured as the dwarves. The elves held their bows tight, with arrows nocked but facing the ground. One elf broke from the pack and strode confidently yet cautiously toward Horith, Montagor, and Thyrus.

"I am Thalnon Meldreth, guardian of Eonis. Explain your presence here at once," said the elf.

"It is an honour to make your acquaintance, Thalnon Meldreth; I am Montagor. This is Lord Thyrus of Torimar, and Horith of house Nindrius, barren elf of Ehronia."

Thalnon regarded the unlikely trio with one eyebrow raised, before turning his gaze over their shoulders to consider the army of dwarves on his doorstep.

"It is a rare thing to receive one of our western cousins these days, Horith of house Nindrius, and what curious company you keep."

"We seek an audience with Lady Keya," replied Horith. "We have travelled far and our business is of the most pressing importance." Thalnon did not reply immediately but continued to scrutinise the trio and their dwarven legion with unblinking blue eyes. He sensed no ill-will from Horith and reached a decision.

"You, Horith, are permitted inside. As are you, Thyrus of Torimar, and you also, Montagor. Your forces must remain here, but I will send provisions from within." Thalnon turned and bade the trio follow him as he and his company of elves weaved their way deftly through trees and branches, stepping over logs and threading around foliage with a practised grace - one which Lord Thyrus in particular lacked. Deeper and deeper they went into the dark woods, the very air around them seeming to grow brighter and brighter with each step, and at once they emerged into a huge clearing in which stood immaculate structures of smooth wood, as impressive an adaptation of the surrounding trees as Torimar was with its native stone. Thalnon held up a hand to halt the trio and turned to face them once more.

"Lady Keya is expecting you," he said.

"How could she possibly be expecting us?" replied Thyrus, his confusion written upon his face for all to see.

"Because I have just told her you are coming, master dwarf," Thalnon replied.

"Well, I didn't hear you," the dwarven lord grumbled in reply, and Horith smiled.

"He didn't say it with his *mouth*, Lord Thyrus."

Thalnon led them through the central plaza of wooden structures which were built in and amongst the trees of Eonis. Light permeated this place, though Horith could not quite discern the source. Their path led them upwards as they zig-zagged their way higher and higher into the trees on intricately carved walkways and bridges which spanned the gaps between the trees. Eventually they arrived at an immaculate, covered walkway which wound up and up, sculpted as it was from the very trunk of the mightiest tree. From this dizzying path they emerged and beheld a throne room not unlike Lord Thyrus' own, but radiant and smooth as opposed to dark and rough. Upon the throne of oak and thorns sat an elf with long, dark hair, dark eyes, and a hue to her skin which leaned closer to blue than most of her woodland kin. Though not an uncommon tone, it was rare indeed for one such as Lady Keya to take the seat of power in Eonis, as Lord Thyrus had alluded to earlier in their journey.

"My Lady Keya," said Thalnon, bowing low to his matriarch, "may I present Horith of Ehronia, the mage Montagor, and Lord Thyrus of the dwarven realm of Torimar."

"Welcome, travellers. It is a long way to Torimar, let alone Ehronia. Pray, tell me why you have come here, and please do tell me why you have brought an army," Lady Keya said with a tone of menace in her voice. Her bodyguards tightened their grips on their long, curved swords.

"Please, my lady, you have us all wrong," said Montagor with both palms raised in a placatory gesture. "My companion, Horith, and I set out from Ehronia some two weeks ago to seek an alliance with the dwarves of Torimar. I am happy to report that - rather obviously - Lord Thyrus was sympathetic to our cause and has pledged his armies to us. I, in turn, pledge them to *you*. The force beyond your border is Thyrus' personal guard, nothing more."

"You pledge a force of dwarves to me, mage? Why? What is this cause of which you speak?" Keya asked.

"Peace, my lady; our cause is the pursuit of *peace*."

"And how do we - nay - how do *I* figure into your schemes?" she asked. A darkness fell over Lady Keya's face, and Horith started to get the impression she knew *exactly* where she figured into the plan, and was merely playing along with this charade, toying with the trio for her own amusement.

"The Soul of Hemera." Montagor answered, "we need you to use it. With the combined strength of Torimar and Eonis, and with the power of the Soul brought to bear in your hands, only then can we possibly hope to defeat Prince Vinadan and his foul legions."

Lady Keya regarded the mage with curiosity rather than interest.

"No," she said after a lengthy pause.

"No?" replied Montagor, who did not even attempt to hide his disdain, "but, my lady…" the mage continued, taking a step toward the throne. Horith, sensing that this was why he'd been brought along in the first place, also stepped forward.

"Lady Keya, please," he began, holding his arm out to stop Montagor in his tracks, "I am just one being, and a barren, at that. I know that you look down on me, and I know that my kind were long ago disregarded by the elves of the woods. But even *I* know there is hope. I know that we can defeat Prince Vinadan; I know that we can defeat his orrecs, and I know that we can defeat the Asarlai, should they interfere. I know all of this because I have *hope.* I have done more and seen more in these past days than ever before in my life. My kin, my friends, those I love… We are a proud race but we suffer. We suffer under the whips and chains of Aclevion. We suffer under the oppression of one for whom magic, power, strength, and control come easily, and are amplified by the Soul of Aether in Aclevion into something truly terrible." Horith swallowed hard, and continued, taking a step toward Keya.

"I feel as if I have broken free of my chains of late. I have stared darkness in the face and yet I have pushed forward. Now I implore you to do the same. The elves of Eonis take no part in the wars of Gibrion; this I know. But I ask you - I beg you - shake free the shackles of tradition, be brave, and join us. Use the power of the Soul to overthrow the darkness which lays over all the lands of Gibrion. I beg you to do the right thing. I beg you to see that there is *hope*."

Lady Keya had listened intently to Horith's plea without interruption, and regarded him with a new-found respect in the silence which followed.

"Perhaps I have misjudged my barren cousins; perhaps there is a power within them after all. Not magical, of course, but power of a different sort. Belief, determination, the will to act, the power of hope." The smile which had threatened to show itself on her stoic face as she addressed Horith disappeared as quickly as it had arrived.

"But my mind is unchanged. I will not help you. Leave, and withdraw your forces at once." Horith, Montagor, and Thyrus each opened their mouths to argue their respective cases, but Lady Keya stood up from her throne and held up a stalling hand. Her dark eyes were hard and unflinching, and were fixed on the trio whose words caught in their throats as if gripped by some sort of…

Magic, Horith realised.

"Leave this place. I will not say it again." Lady Keya's guards each took a step forward, closing the distance between themselves and the travellers. Noting that the elves' hands had gone to the hilts of their weapons, the despondent trio turned and began to walk back toward the throne room door. Montagor stopped in his tracks, and turned to face Lady Keya.

"Would you at least allow him to see it, my lady?" he said.

"What?" she replied, not taking his meaning.

"My friend, Horith, your western cousin. Would you at least permit him to look upon the Soul of Hemera, just once, before we depart in peace? He has come such a long, long way only to leave with nothing," the old mage said. Lady Keya considered his proposal for a long moment, silently weighing up the human's audacious request. At length, she sighed and shook her head.

"Very well, it shall be so. You three, follow me," she said, motioning to human, barren, and dwarf in a single gesture. She stepped down from the dais upon which her throne stood and motioned for two of her guards to flank her. She walked around behind the throne, and toward the wall at the back of the room. She closed her eyes and raised a hand toward a seemingly innocuous stretch of plain wall. It promptly shimmered and resolved itself into a great door, and opened at a gesture of her fingers. Lady Keya walked inside, flanked left and right by her guards, and her three guests followed behind into the huge, round auditorium. There was no roof to speak of, and they were granted a view of the stars in the deep blue night sky which hung like a veil above the large room. In the centre of this hitherto hidden chamber stood two gargantuan pillars of wood, each decorated with carved runes of a hundred different shapes which were somehow familiar to Horith, even if he could not read them. Suspended within the pillars, held in place by flashes of blinding green and blue lightning, was the Soul or Hemera.

What struck Horith most about the awe-inspiring scene in which he found himself was that the Soul of Hemera was not a solid, physical object as he had imagined, but a pulsating, undulating mass of liquid, gas, and energy. It was held together, moulded into a rough approximation of a sphere, by forces and energies entirely unknown to Horith, and the barren's mouth hung open wide at the sight of it.

The next thing which struck Horith was the colour his blood appeared under the maelstrom of the Soul. His eyes went wide, and he clutched his newly-cut throat. He turned, and laid his eyes on Montagor who stood with a dagger in his right hand, eyeing Horith menacingly. Lord Thyrus lay dead at the feet of the old mage, blood flowing freely from the dwarf's own throat. Horith's eyes were wild with confusion, and he fell to the floor. Such had been the deftness and speed of the Montaor's actions that neither Lady Keya nor her guards had heard anything over the din of the undulating Soul, and they continued to gaze up at the relic, unaware of the carnage behind them.

Montagor stretched out an arm toward the Soul, and a lick of angry green lightning tore loose of the colossal relic to leech into the mage's palm. At this, Lady Keya and her guards finally turned, and were unable to reconcile the horrific scene which met them. Before either of the elven guards had a chance to react, Montagor incinerated both with a click of his fingers, and summoned Lady Keya toward him, propelling her across the room under the force of some hidden power. The lightning and energy of the Soul of Hemera continued to pour into him, encircling his body as he drew on its power. He caught Keya by the throat with one hand and plunged his blade deep into her chest with the other before dropping her at his feet where her own guards, Lord Thyrus, and Horith also lay. Montagor released the dagger and spread his arms wide victoriously. He laughed aloud as the Soul's energy continued to encircle and engulf him. Horith stirred, and managed to drag himself up onto his knees to face the old mage.

"M... Mon... Montagor?" Horith spluttered.

"Not exactly, my boy. Not exactly..." said the mage. He winked at Horith, and his long, dirty beard began to recede, until his clean-shaven jawline was visible once more. His tangled mat of black hair straightened and began to change colour, haloing his head in long, white locks. His wrinkled skin and dark eyes were also gone, and Horith beheld the smooth, handsome features of a much younger man. A man with long, white hair, a smooth, clean shaven face, and emerald green eyes. The face of Prince Vinadan, Lord of Aclevion. With one final, mocking grin, Vinadan turned on his heel and ran from the chamber, leaving Horith, the dead, and the now-empty pillars in his wake.

Chapter Six

Horith tried in vain to claw his way forward toward the fleeing Vinadan, who had exited the eerily quiet Soul Chamber. The door to the throne room was still open, and Horith could discern the flashes of green and blue, punctuated by the dying screams of elves which confirmed Horith's suspicions that Vinadan, who had played him for a fool all along, was intent on a massacre here in fair Eonis. He almost felt like laughing at the irony of it all; should any of Lady Keya's elves survive, they could no longer sit by as impartial spectators, and if they were all killed…. Well, what difference would it make? War had finally come to their lands in the most direct, most intimate way possible. Horith's eyes began to darken, and he felt an overwhelming tiredness like no other he had ever known, yet he felt no pain and marvelled at this. His breathing slowed and his entire body, his very *spirit* felt heavy. He knew he could not catch Prince Vinadan; he knew that he would be powerless to stop him even if he did.

He knew this was the end. Before his strength finally failed, and before he breathed his last, Horith of house Nindrius, barren elf of Ehronia, spoke his final word.

"Ruli…"

*

If the power of one Soul was too much for mere mortals to contend with, then the power of two was something else entirely. It was heresy, a perversion of the natural order. The Souls were not meant to be united, and their power was unstable in Vinadan's hands. Wave after wave of elves threw themselves at the prince as he strode his way mercurially through the woods of Eonis, every inch of his exposed skin now ablaze with glowing runes. He slaughtered warrior and citizen alike, with no regard for gender, age, nor station. Some he incinerated with a wink, others he would rend limb from limb with his own hands, fuelled by the intoxicating power of the Souls. More still, he *unmade*, for the power of the Souls was an ancient, dangerous thing. From within the cover of the trees he finally emerged, leaving Eonis behind him and sauntering toward the dwarven forces amassed beyond the border of the forest. Seeing this stranger emerge from the elven realm caused disquiet among the forces of Torimar, especially given the absence of their lord Thyrus and his companions. Unsure of what to do, the dwarves tightened their grips on their weapons and set their feet in the dirt.

"It's him!" one of the dwarves in the forward section shouted suddenly.

"It's Vinadan!" Shouts of panic and rallying cries went up among the dwarven contingent, and they charged forward toward the human prince. Unfazed and unconcerned, Vinadan tilted his head to one side and smiled.

All the better, he thought, *one fewer force to challenge me*.

He spread his arms wide and raised them slowly, and the power of the Souls crackled and sparked upon his skin and clothing. He grinned, and moved against the dwarves. Not so much walking as hovering above the ground, he began to cast his dark powers at the dwarves, taking down one and then another in a hail of mystic fire. Some of the dwarves survived long enough to close the gap and swing their weapons at Vinadan, but the prince of Aclevion deftly dodged and ducked, before employing his ancient arts to the destruction of the dwarves. Mere minutes later, it was over. Vinadan did not deign to so much as cast a look back over his shoulder, but simply continued to walk forward, unchallenged, smiling in the night's cold breeze. Had he wished to, he would have gazed upon nothing more than a pile of smouldering, dismembered corpses where a force of dwarves had stood mere moments before, but nothing could, at that point, have interested him less.

Vinadan paused, just for a moment, and looked down at his hands, delighting at the sight of green and blue lightning, sparking and flickering over his skin. He took a deep breath, exhaled, and began to walk once more. Before long, Eonis was nothing but a dark shape in the distance at his back. Columns of smoke rose high into the inky night sky and Vinadan grinned, but still he did not look back.

CHAPTER SEVEN

From their position in the doorway of the monastery high above the capital, two members of the Asarlai stood in the darkness, robed and hooded against the chill wind. They kept a watchful eye on the city below while their brothers slept, studied, or stood sentinel over the Soul of Aether, housed inside the Soul Chamber deep within the mountain. The Asarlai monastery had stood for centuries, and the two shapes in the doorway were among the order's most senior members. The unmistakable orange glow of torchlight below caught their attention, and they turned to see a dark shape ascending the stair which led from the citadel below to the monastery above, carved into the very rock of the mountain, not entirely unlike Torimar. The Asarlai shared a quick glance at one another, but did not speak. Before long, the dark shape had resolved itself into the prince of Aclevion.

"I trust your mission was a success, my lord?" asked Alma, the older of the two ordermen, as Vinadan came close.

"As we knew it would, brother," replied Vinadan. "Now to secure my prize," he said, motioning for the Asarlai to follow him as he walked past them and made his way into the mountain. Once they reached the outer door of the Soul Chamber, Vinadan dismissed the guards and led the two Asarlai inside, gesturing for them to give him space. He looked up at the Soul of Aether, crackling and pulsating within its own pillars of marble, as it pulsed and rolled in orange and red lightning. As it sparked and undulated within its energy field, the runes carved upon the stone pillars likewise pulsed and glowed in synchronicity with the Soul. Vinadan smiled and held out his hands. With a cry which was half pain and half pure ecstasy, green and blue energy burst forth from his outstretched limbs and poured into the chamber. When the last of the arcane energy had left his hands, Vinadan collapsed to his knees in exhaustion as his prize resolved itself into a shape. A sphere; an orb; a Soul, floating upwards to first join its sister between the pillars.

The mystical artefacts began to orbit each other. He had done it; he had taken the Soul of Hemera, the ancient power of Eonis into himself, had contained its mighty power, had borne it all the way back to its sister in Aclevion, and he had survived. He regained his feet as the beginnings of a grin tugged at the corners of his mouth. The grin became a smile, and the smile erupted in fits of laughter, as the lord of Aclevion beheld his glorious accomplishment. Once he had ceased in his laughter, he bade the two brothers follow him out of the chamber and into his private quarters where he poured three large glasses of a thick red wine.

Alma and Xebus accepted the proffered glasses, and the three men drank deep in celebration.

"It is as I told you," said the grinning prince, "*Hope*. Hope will be their undoing. Give these imbeciles, these cretins, a glimpse of hope and they will destroy themselves. They will blindly follow to whatever end you can craft, should you possess the wit to devise the crafting." He drained his glass, and poured another

"Keya is dead. Thyrus is dead. The elves and dwarves are defeated and demoralised. Without the protection of Eonis and Torimar, the other realms will quickly fall back into line, and any hope of open rebellion will be dispelled with the death of Horith Nindrius. We shall make an example of him; we shall show all of Gibrion that there is no power in these lands to challenge the might of Aclevion."

Vinadan continued to smile as he drank the expensive wine. "We will now begin the next phase, gentlemen; we will tighten our grip, double the patrols, increase the taxes… whatever we need to do to maintain control." He looked up, fixing the Asarlai with a pointed stare. "My rule is absolute."

Xebus and Alma exchanged a fleeting glance as Vinadan continued.

"With Hemera and Aether now under one roof - *my* roof - I am a *God*. There is no one left to oppose me," he smiled, draining his wine once more. The Asarlai wore expressions as black as the shadows which hid their faces beneath raised hoods.

"No, my lord," said Xebus.

"No one."

PART II:
New Allies; Old Wounds

"How do you kill a god?" asked Xeb, as he sat across the table from Alma inside the other man's cold, dusty chambers. Alma smiled back at his charge and shrugged.

"Let's just finish our wine and call that a start," he said in reply. A dusty bottle stood on the table between them, a '270 red; the finest wine in all of Aclevion.

Chapter Eight

Betrayal was not a new concept to Prince Vinadan, and the slaughter of innocents seemed to follow in his wake like a crimson-stained shadow, ever trailing unapologetically at his feet. He sat virtually unopposed upon his throne in the land of Aclevion, capital of Etain in the north. With its impenetrable walls and its legions of loyal orrecs to protect the prince, no force could hope - nor dare - to march against him, were there indeed any force left in Gibrion with the numbers and inclination to attempt such a move.

The dwarves of the mid-lands and the elves of the south had been left reeling in the aftermath of Vinadan's coup in Eonis, licking their wounds and attempting to rebuild and restore what they had lost. They turned inwards, shunning the lands beyond their own borders in the wake of Vinadan's atrocities. The cost of boldness and alliances was too high to pay, it turned out. As for the human inhabitants of Gibrion, they were a weak and superstitious lot. With the odd exception here and there, they generally lacked both the courage to act and intelligence to determine when it was necessary, and instead chose to keep to themselves. It was known among the other races that human folk were content to look to the past for comfort and validation; reflecting upon the glory days of centuries and cycles long since past, all the while offering blind devotion to their deities with neither an original thought nor questioning look ever passing between them. Whilst humans could always be counted upon for labour and servitude, they were not so readily looked upon for counsel, so followed the prevailing wisdom. Some worshipped the light, offering prayers to Hemera, whilst others bowed to the darkness, naming Aether as their goddess. To a man, though, they cowered before the power of nature, fearing the darkness of the woods, and heeding legends of witches, dragons, and giants. Over the centuries, the crimes which humans perpetrated against those - of their kin or otherwise - who hailed the goddess Gibrion and revered the power and beauty of the natural world, were as numerous as they were bloody.

Of the orrecs, the humanoid beasts who named the desolate slopes and burning fires of Elgiroth in the eastern region of Tol Peregon their home had long been held in the thrall of Aclevion. The constant heat and scorching dust which hardened the orrecs from birth and could set the very air ablaze, also enasured that the great furnaces and forges which produced weapons and armour for Prince Vinadan's armies never ran cold; the orrecs slaved to spit out steel and iron from daybreak to nightfall.

Vinadan had grown fat - not physically, of course, to which his legions of admirers would attest – but in his arrogance and his unyielding belief in his goddess-given right to rule over all of Gibrion. From Aclevion in the north, his influence spread like a virus to the south, east, and west. Not three weeks ago, he ordered a legion of orrecs to make the long journey from their base at Elgiroth into the city of Markosh, which sat upon the border of Tol Peregon and Skyoliin. Another battalion marched further southward and were now mere days from the thriving and prosperous human settlement of Adeniron. The orrecs already held sway in Ehronia - home to the late Horith Nindrius and his barren elf kin - and from there they stood sentinel whilst the barrens toiled and slaved away in fields and farms, producing food and materials for Aclevion, and receiving only scant payment and zero gratitude for their efforts.

Yes, Vinadan had grown fat indeed, and the ancient order of the Asarlai who had served the throne for centuries, deftly positioning the lords and ladies as if mere pieces upon a gameboard of their own making, had noticed.

*

"How fare the stores?" demanded Vinadan from his throne.

"The stores are healthy, my lord; more provisions arrive each day by horse and ship," replied Lant, who stood at the foot of his master's raised dais in the grand and ostentatious hall. "We want for nought, and-"

"It is not my provisions to which I refer, but to my gold," interrupted Vinadan, cutting off the Asarlai mid-sentence. *My provisions… My gold,* thought Lant, noting – and not for the first time - the selfish manner with which the Prince of Aclevion conducted himself.

"The wealth of Aclevion – *your* wealth - is unrivalled, my lord. The coffers are full, and the citadel of Ondellion thrives. All is proceeding as planned, my prince." Lant bowed low at the conclusion of his report, but Vinadan was unsatisfied.

"My wealth is unrivalled and my stores overflow with meat and mead. With the combined power of the Souls, I am the most powerful being in all of Gibrion." He paused, and every courtier and advisor in residence remained silent.

"Yet resistance remains," he continued. "Whether their fealty is to be borne of love or fear, I would have it. It is better to be feared than simply ignored. With all of your wisdom, Lant, with all of the so-called power of your brotherhood, can you not tell me why there are still those throughout Gibrion who do not bow to me? You are supposed to be advisors, so go ahead: *advise* me." Vinadan's countenance was a mask of insincerity as he sneered.

Silence permeated the throne room, and all around cheeks turned red whilst eyes darted here and there. Lant met his Lord's piercing gaze and opened his mouth to respond, but was beaten to it by a voice from the back of the hall.

"If I may, my lord."

"Xebus Anatalis; on you at least I can usually count. Proceed," said Vinadan, gesturing for Lant to make way for his brother Asarlai. Lant seized upon the opportunity without hesitation and retreated into the crowd.

"Thank you, your excellency," said Xeb, as he made his way to the foot of his master's throne. His deep red cloak billowed behind him, and though his hood was raised and his face cast in deep shadow, he nevertheless met Prince Vinadan's gaze evenly.

"It occurs to me, my lord, that it is perhaps mere ignorance, rather than open defiance, which is the root from which this so-called resistance has grown." Vinadan's eyes narrowed and his long white hair fell across his forehead as he tilted his head to the side in appraisal of Xeb's words.

"Continue," he bade.

"My lord, the people of Gibrion do not openly oppose you. Rather, many are simply... *unaware* of you. The lands are wide and vast, my lord, and the masses are an ignorant, selfish lot."

"I assume this line of thought is leading somewhere, Xebus. What do you propose?" asked the prince.

"Oh, it is quite simple, really," said Xeb, casually, "allow me to spread the word, my prince. I will travel abroad at once and, shall we say, *educate* the masses. I need not be gone long, and my brothers-in-order are as capable as I in matters of state and divinity." Xeb offered no further word but stood before his master as the prince mulled over his proposal.

"Hmm," muttered Vinadan, placing a hand upon his chin. "One must assume, of course, that the unenlightened folk are precisely that: unenlightened. It would indeed follow, therefore, that the need to educate is indeed a pressing concern. Unchecked, the people will turn to others to lead them. They will raise their own idols, unaware that a god already sits atop a throne in the north. Very well; I will allow it, but the arrangements are yours to make, and any expenses your own to bear."

"Very good, my lord," said Xeb with a bow, "I shall make haste to spread tidings of your glory across each realm and race in turn. I will preach your name in the streets, and should they wish to see your benevolent power for themselves, I will of course return these loyalists to the capital."

Vinadan simply waved him away from sight without further word and called an end to the day's audience with the merest of nods. As was his custom, he would retire either to his private chambers deep within the citadel, or make his way to the library high up in the mountains above Aclevion. The ancient and fragile arcane texts housed within were guarded by the Asarlai come sun or moon, within the very caverns and hand-hewn anterooms of the mountain where the order of Asarlai practised their arts, eyes cast ever-downwards, keeping watch on the seat of power in Gibrion. The prince would hold court until he deemed his time spent, and would from there take his leave to study the ancient texts and push the limits of his powers, and neither man nor mage was permitted to disturb him. A human he was, as were all of the Asarlai, but where the unenlightened, pious masses of his kin scattered throughout Gibrion were ignorant to all things magical, the lords of Aclevion had long studied the arcane arts, and had in doing so gathered to themselves the means to rival the natural magical abilities of the elves.

Each and every day, prince Vinadan dismisses his court and retires to pore over his texts, with the ultimate goal of enhancing his powers and strengthening his grip on Gibrion in turn. All who observed him recognised that he had grown more petulant of late, as the power of the combined Souls – a unified power unprecedented in this era – had proven somewhat unstable, unyielding, as if it were unwilling to give itself over to the prince until he had earned it. So he toiled; he practiced and he studied, often forsaking both food and sleep in exchange for knowledge. And he had grown strong. His mastery of the runes was unparalleled, though some of the more complex incantations still eluded him.

The Asarlai, and the throne's multitude of hands and servants were not unhappy with this arrangement, as it kept the tempestuous and impulsive lord out of their way, and they were, to a man, woman, and child, more than happy for Vinadan to believe his daily solitude to be entirely of his own making. That his servants, his subjects, his *pets,* the thirty-thousand-or-so citizens who called the land of Aclevion their home, would not only appreciate but actually come to covet the time during which he was absent, had not occurred to him in even his most paranoid and fretful humour. Xeb was counting on this to continue.

Chapter Nine

The fires of Elgiroth burned, as they had for cycles since The Spoiling. The orrecs who inhabited the desolate, dusty wastes were as accustomed to the heat and dirt as the deep-sea creature grows accustomed to the cold and the dark. The forges, which were long ago constructed beneath the slopes of the colossal volcano from which the city took its name, continued to churn out weapons and armour apace. The orrecs were proficient and effective, their product utilitarian and strong. From the largest of the forges came the best and strongest weapons, as it was overseen by an orrec commander the gaze of whom none of his workforce would dare to draw, let alone provoke his temper.

For Malgorth they worked. For Malgorth they worked *hard.*

He was at least two feet taller and far broader from shoulder to shoulder than most of his kin, but while his physical strength marked him as distinct from the rank and file orrec under his command, it was his intelligence which really set him apart. The orrecs, while strong and loyal, were not known for their wit nor cunning. Malgorth, on the other hand, had something of a talent for tactics, and could be counted on to lead on the battlefield as well as he could inspire the forge workers. He wandered here and there as the orrecs worked around him. Molten ore was poured into moulds, and all around the sound of hammers against steel echoed. He inspected the weapons and armour at random as they were churned out of the fires. He picked up a still-glowing blade with his bare hand and held it out in front of his face, one eye closed to gauge the heft and craftsmanship. Satisfied, he placed the blade onto a waiting cart and clapped the trembling orrec responsible for its creation upon the back.

"A fine weapon, forgemaster. For the might of Aclevion," he said to the orrec, with fist raised in salute.

"F… For the might of Aclevion, my c…c…commander."

Malgorth grinned at the orrec's obvious anxiety, and continued on his rounds, checking, inspecting, confirming, and discarding as he went. To some he offered words of encouragement, to others he offered words of advice and guidance. That was, at least, until he reached the arrows. Through smoke, steam, noise, and the hustle and bustle of carts laden with all manner of weapons he strode, terminating at a small, stone table upon which two orrecs were fletching arrows and tossing them into a waiting crate. At his approach, both orrecs stood with their backs stiffened and each turned an even deeper shade of green than their natural hue.

"My commander," said one orrec, bowing low yet quivering at the shoulders. His partner followed suit and the pair held their postures until Malgorth motioned them to stand tall once more. He reached into the crate and withdrew a handful of the completed arrows. One by one he turned them over in his hands. One by one he closed one eye and extended them to check their shaping, and one by one he picked and pulled at the fletching.

He was not impressed. His head did not move, but his eyes did as he cast his gaze upwards from the arrows in his hand to the orrecs in front of him, who both began to sweat and fidget in his wake.

"M… my commander?" offered one of the pair. Having received no response from their orrec superior, the second tried his luck.

"Is… is all to your liking, my com-" He never got to finish his sentence as one of the arrows was thrust upwards with lightning speed, entering his throat, straight up through the top of his head. Sticky black blood poured down Malgorth's forearm but he paid it no mind and simply tossed the limp body off to one side where his fellow orrecs were already scrambling to take it away for orderly disposal. To the remaining orrec he simply turned his head, and the smaller creature moved as if the very wrath of the Aether was upon him. He emptied the crate onto the floor and kicked away the offending arrows, turning immediately to begin anew. Malgorth did not have to tell the orrec to ensure the next batch was better, he already knew it would be. The orrec's life quite literally depended on it. Malgorth turned his back and renewed his rounds, silently amused at the sudden urgency which seemed to have gripped his workforce following his appraisal of the arrows. He had decided he would take a short break to clean the filth from his hands and arms when he was beckoned by an orrec from the entrance to the great forge chamber.

"My commander! Commander Malgorth!" shouted a frantic orrec from the doorway. Malgorth turned to view the orrec and discerned that the creature was a scout, and he clearly wished for the commander to come to him as opposed to him entering the forge.

Clearly, he had something to say which he did not want the worker orrecs to overhear.

Very well, thought Malgorth, as he made his way to the entrance and continued outside, motioning for the clearly distressed scout to follow him out onto the acrid plains of Elgiroth. The rock underfoot would have split and blistered the feet of lesser beings, but to Malgorth it was as the soft sands of the southern beaches. Once he was at a suitable distance from the forge chamber, he took a deep, cleansing breath, filling his lungs with the smoke and sulphur he longed for after so many hours inside the claustrophobic chamber. He turned to scrutinise the other orrec more closely, and recognised him.

"You are part of captain Ogarsh's raiding party, are you not?" he demanded of the smaller creature who, to his credit, met Malgorth's gaze evenly and did not cower in his presence.

"Yes commander. I am Agnaz, scout and raider," he replied.

"Then why are you not in Adeniron, scout Agnaz? Where is captain Ogarsh?" he demanded.

"Here, commander" said the orrec, producing a stained black hessian sack. He untied the string which sealed it, and tipped out its contents onto the hot ground below. Even had he not beheld the sight of Ogarsh's severed head which now lay at an unnatural angle at his feet, the stench which had emanated from the newly opened sack had already confirmed Malgorth's suspicions.

"What happened, scout?" said Malgorth calmly, his voice betraying not a modicum of the fury which now burned deep within his mighty chest. "How did a warrior of Ogarsh's calibre come to lie at my feet in a manner such as this?"

"We sacked Markosh with little difficulty, my commander, this you know, and from there made our way south toward Adeniron. We didn't even get as far as the outskirts before we were ambushed, sir." Agnaz bowed his head, but whether he did so in shame or deference, Malgorth could not be sure.

"*Ambushed*, you say? By whom?"

"By men, commander Malgorth. And elves."

"Do not take me for a fool, scout, as it will be the last thing you do. The men of Adeniron are fools, and Lady Keya's elves were decimated in Eonis. Speak truly, or I will have *your* head."

The orrec scout fell to one knee.

"I *do* speak truly, my lord! A great host they were not, but they were organised. A host of men on horseback and a group of elves. The pointy-ears were shooting from the cover of the trees by the river; it was all I could do to escape with the... *evidence*." He nodded toward Orgarsh's head on the ground between them. Malgorth nodded slowly and let out a series of long, deep breaths.

"Okay, scout. Okay. I judge your words as truth indeed. Now, retire at once to rest awhile. Heal your wounds and catch your breath. When your strength returns, take on such meat and mead as you can, and meet me here - on this exact spot - at daybreak tomorrow. Help yourself to the best gear and weapons from my forge and be ready to travel."

Scout Agnaz slowly returned to his feet, and furrowed his leathery brow at Commander Malgorth.

"Travel?" he asked cautiously. "Where am I going, my lord?"

"To Adeniron, scout, as planned," replied Malgorth, "and you will not be going alone."

Chapter Ten

Xeb could taste the salt in the cold air as he pulled his hood up over his head and tightened his cloak against the early morning chill. He had begun his descent from the mountain at the first sign that the new day had dawned, and found himself at the most north-westerly point of Gibrion, beyond the borders of Aclevion and into the wilder parts of Etain. He made his way southward toward the small port at the foot of the enormous mountains which enclosed the capital. Though his ultimate destination could be reached upon horseback or even by foot, he felt that travel by boat presented the better choice for this particular leg of the journey.

On he pressed, hugging his arms across his chest against the cold; the wind blew strong this close to the sea, and Xeb felt the cold in his bones. He continued on, stepping carefully upon sand and rock at intervals, until the rickety old wooden jetty he sought came into view at last and, as he had hoped, a modestly-sized boat floated lazily at the end of a frayed and blackened rope. Xeb could make out a hooded figure slumped against the post to which the vessel was bound, and the Asarlai was almost certain the man was either drunk or dead. To his surprise and relief, however, the man stirred at his approach.

"Good morning, sir!" the man offered, first standing tall then bowing in deference.

"And a good morning to you too, boatmaster," Xeb replied in kind, inclining his head.

"Are you just passing through, milord, or do you wish to charter my *Imelda*?"

Xeb looked from the man to the old boat; its paint was all-but faded to nothing and its hull was a patchwork of repairs and shoddy fixes.

"Is she seaworthy, good boatmaster?" Xeb asked, not quite succeeding in keeping the frown from his countenance.

"Seaworthy?" asked the other man, feigning great offence. "Why, she's as seaworthy as any ship in the Three Ears, m'lord! Not that I'd ever venture that far south, o'course. Those elves… you know what I mean?" he threw a knowing wink at Xeb.

"Yes, I know what you mean," Xeb responded, though in truth, he did not have the first idea what the man was referring to. Whether it was an utterance of prejudice, or a thinly-veiled innuendo, Xeb would never know. He decided it best to simply ignore the comment and move the conversation along.

"How much to convey me to Vitrius, my good man?"

"Vitruis?" asked the boatmaster. "*Vitrius*, sir? Why would a gentleman such as yourself want to go to such an accursed place?"

"How much?" Xeb repeated, feeling no imperative to explain himself to a being such as this.

"Well, let me see now… For you? Twenty gold mullions, milord."

Reasonable, Xeb decided. "Very well; twenty it is. We leave at once," Xeb declared as he strode toward the waiting *Imelda*.

*

"…and that's when I said to her, I says: "you can't go doing that to no horse, it's just not good manners…" and then *she* said-"

"How long until we make landfall, good boatmaster?" interrupted Xeb. He had been forced to endure the man's ceaseless, banal chatter ever since they had set sail, and he had just about run out of patience.

"Oh, I'd say within the hour, milord," replied the man, smiling, and quite oblivious to Xeb's frustrations.

"Then we shall make it twenty-five gold mullions if you would hold your tongue 'til then and allow me peace to think awhile, good boatmaster."

To his own credit, and much to Xeb's relief, the man happily did as requested and kept his mouth shut until the sea eventually gave way to sand, and the *Imelda* made landfall. Xeb stood and stretched out his aching back, casting a furtive glance at his surroundings as he did so.

Nobody here. Good, he thought.

"So…" said the boatmaster, rubbing his hands together nervously, "I think we said twenty-five, milord." Xeb nodded and fixed the man with a stern glare.

"We did indeed, good boatmaster. What say we make it thirty-five, and you forget both my face and my destination?" The man's face lit up in surprise and greed.

"Thirty-five, sir? Yes! Yes, I can do that, milord. *For the might of Aclevion*, milord"

"Good man, here-" said Xeb, tossing the man a velvet coin-purse.

"Thank you, milord. And should you ever require my services again, sir, my name is Imelda."

Xeb smiled. *Of course it is*, he thought, as he turned and strode away into the dark forest which stood like a silent guardian over the narrow shoreline.

*

Xeb pressed on through the trees, thankful that the sun was now higher in the sky and his way was much better lit than he was expecting at this hour. Still, the forests which now covered the way on all sides to the small, long-abandoned township of Vitrius, were foreboding by their very nature. The men of neighbouring Frostpeak to the east and Dinann to the south no longer ventured to Vitrius – anywhere near it, for that matter - steadfast as they were in their belief that the land was a cursed and haunted place. No living creature stirred here, they say; at least not in the manner they understood. There were beings which dwelt within, however, but beings of an altogether darker breed. Legends had grown up in the human lands of sorcery and witchcraft; of dark magic and necromancy; all with Vitrius at their heart. It had long been said that any who dared venture into the forests, whether borne of ignorance, thrill-seeking, or desperation, were never seen nor heard from again. Whether this was actually true or merely another layer of embellishment added around a campfire, none really knew for certain.

Xeb had the unshakeable feeling that he was about to find out. He kept his wits about him as he went; eyes and ears strained for any sign of movement. On he pressed, heading further and further into the forest, when a sudden flicker of movement away to his right caught his attention. He spun, senses alert to any potential danger, and exhaled heavily upon finding himself face to face with a large brown hare. It stood on its hind legs, sniffed at the air, then darted off into the trees once more.

Calm yourself, Xeb thought. The myths and legends were clearly pressing on his mind, despite his belief that he already knew the truth of this place; he just had to confirm it. At length, the trees began to thin, giving way to the charred and crumbling remains of structures. Wooden huts and homesteads, all-but burnt to the ground, littered the clearings, and Xeb understood that he had now reached the outskirts of the former township. Centuries' worth of charred and decomposed structures lay all around him; the very settlement a corpse, to his mind. He ventured further, neither encountering a living soul nor hearing so much as a bird in the sky. All at once, the landscape seemed to change, and the burned and charred remains of the former settlement gave way to greener and more verdant ground. He changed direction to follow this new course; the increasingly abundant plants and a plethora of aromatic flowers in his path were at direct odds with the unease in his stomach, so strong he could almost taste it. He moved on slowly, rounded a corner, and was taken back by the sight he beheld. A circular courtyard lay before him with a large, ornate fountain at its centre. At the far side of the courtyard stood an unusually large greenhouse, most of its glass panes still intact, if a little dirty. It was not the courtyard nor the greenhouse which gave him pause, however, but the beautiful young woman who sat upon the fountain's edge, filling a pristine silver gourd with some of the clearest and purest water Xeb had ever seen.

"My lady," he offered in greeting. The young woman turned her flawless blue eyes to face him, and he discerned a playful smile on her lips.

Beautiful, Xeb thought, feeling a heat beginning to swell in his chest. No sooner than he felt the sensation, he forcibly shook the thought from his head.

Damn it, he thought; he had indeed confirmed his suspicions. The young woman stood, and tilted her head to the side, allowing her long brown hair to play over her face. She turned to stride barefoot across the courtyard and toward the greenhouse, throwing a suggestive look back over her shoulder at Xeb.

So that's how they do it, he thought, and followed the woman. Upon entering the greenhouse, Xeb was nearly overwhelmed as he was assaulted by myriad aromas, tastes, sights, and sounds. The whole place seemed alive, as if the very ground beneath his feet were breathing, and the air around him seemed to radiate a heat not entirely of the world he knew. He shook his head as if to banish the intoxicating effects of this place.

This place holds great power, he thought, *but so do I.*

Having regained control of his wits, he smiled to himself as he noticed the same brown hare from earlier, now sitting inquisitively at his feet. His mind cleared he also became aware of a dishevelled brown cat which sat grooming itself over in a far corner, while a magpie circled lazily overhead. Xeb loosed a small snort of amusement.

Of course, he thought, slowly shaking his head.

"I see you have met Morrigan," came a voice from deep within the greenhouse. The hare turned and hopped further inside, and Xeb followed closely until they came upon the source of the voice. There, at the far end of the greenhouse, stood a large, strong, wooden table laden with all manner of exotic instruments and unknown ingredients. Here, a mortar and pestle; there, a pile of dried herbs and spices. Beside a large silver bowl lay a long and angry-looking dagger, and inside the bowl, the severed head of some rodent or other listed unnaturally to one side. Behind the table stood three tall-backed wooden chairs, and in each chair sat a young woman, each as beautiful and alluring as the next. On the right sat the brown-haired woman whom Xeb had first encountered, on the left, another with long red hair. In the centre sat a third who also sported fiery crimson locks, though she wore it shorter than her sisters. It appeared to be the middlemost of the women from whom the voice had rung out.

"Morrigan, my lady?" replied Xeb.

"My hare. I see you have met my hare," she clarified, indicating the animal without taking her eyes off Xeb for a moment.

"Ah, yes. We met, though we were not formally introduced," he answered, forcing calm and a tone of deference into his voice. The woman's face gave nothing away, and her intense eyes seemed to stare straight through the Asarlai.

"That a man would walk freely into our domain troubles us greatly," she said without further preamble. "What business brings you here?"

"I am not merely a man, my lady. I am Xebus Anatalis of the Asarlai. I have come from the mountains above the fortress of Ondellion to seek your aid."

"Our aid?" Her eyes narrowed as she scrutinised him openly.

"Whatever aid you believe we can provide is denied to you forthwith. You have risked much to come here, Xebus, and your efforts will come to nought. You feign strength with your words and your titles, but you are just as weak as all the others who have dared to defile our sanctuary with their salt sweat and foul breath."

"Please, my good ladies, let us not get off on the wrong foot; I mean you no harm nor offence-"

"Stop. We will hear no more. We did not invite you here, Xebus Anatalis; we have only ever wanted to be left in peace."

"Peace?" replied Xeb, his frustration beginning to show. "Peace is a myth. Look around you. You are ladies of nature - the very blood of Gibrion herself runs through your veins. Surely you have noted the signs. There is a shadow over all our lands, a darkness who calls himself *Lord*." No response came from the trio. After a long moment, the woman on the left began to rise, smiling.

"Come now, good sir. You take yourself much too seriously. Allow me to… *relax* you awhile."

Xeb involuntarily bared his teeth in anger. "I think not, *crone.*"

At the last word, the three women stirred, and Xeb could sense their own anger crackling in the very air around him, like the herald of lightning on a stormy night.

"*Crone?*" repeated the woman on the left. "You would dare to-"

"I do not *dare* anything, my lady, but please, let us not keep up this charade. I can see you for who – for *what* – you truly are, my good ladies, and I am at your service nonetheless."

"At our service?" asked the brown-haired woman on the right. "What service could you possibly render which we cannot provide for – or *to* - ourselves?"

Xeb shook his head in disappointment. "There is a war coming, and it will come to all, no matter how deeply they choose to hide themselves away in the forests of the world. It will find you, no matter how resolutely you seek to hide your true natures behind so thin and obvious a glamour. Show yourselves true, my ladies of the forest, and I will do likewise."

The short haired woman in the central chair continued to stare at Xeb for what seemed like an eternity, then she laughed. It started as a small chuckle, playing out at the corners of her mouth, but built to a piercing crescendo as her formerly soft voice became an inhuman screech. She stood, pressing her long thin fingers into the dark oak table, and her sisters followed suit. Before Xeb's very eyes, their perfect skin began to pale and thin, their bright, beautiful eyes darkened and clouded. Their radiant, sweet-smelling hair grew dank and musty, the very stench of death emanating from lank and greasy locks. As their formerly immaculate, enticing feminine figures began to bulge and contort, Xeb had to repress a shudder as the three seemingly ethereal beings who would have ensnared the very hearts and loins of lesser men, revealed to him their true selves.

Old, haggard, bent double, and rank to the very core, the Crones of Vitrius showed Xeb toothless and joyless grimaces in place of their formerly supple and enticing smiles.

"You win, Asarlai," said the central crone, who Xeb had long-since concluded to be the leader of the coven. "I am Karsha," she said, "and these are my sisters; Yilmé, and Grema." indicating the red-haired and brown-haired sisters respectively.

"Xebus of the Asarlai, at your service," he bowed.

"My sister speaks true, Xebus," said Karsha, "we neither need nor want your service. But should we ever find ourselves needing something to be knocked over, smashed, or molested, or if we ever feel the need for two pieces of driftwood to be nailed together, we will be sure to let you know." The crones shared a mirthless laugh.

"Having said that," continued Karsha, raising a crooked finger as if seizing upon a stray thought, "countless of our sisters have suffered the wooden constructs of men for centuries, and it did not end well for them. Nor will it end well for you, Xebus, if you do not leave us."

Xeb made no move to leave; Karsha, Yilmé, and Grema began to advance.

"Please; I cannot do that, lady Karsha."

Xeb drew back his arm and called to hand a flail of pure fire, conjured from the very air around him. As the fiery weapon sprang into existence in his right hand, an orange glow shone upon the back of his left, slowly resolving itself into a shape of some kind; a symbol. The ancient rune of *Nature* it was, brought forth from the dusty pages of ageless scrolls and tapestries housed within the Asarlai monastery, high in the mountain above Aclevion, now cast in burning colours upon Xeb's skin. He had called upon this specific rune to fuel his magic for a reason which he hoped was not lost on his present company. The crones paused in their advance, the flaming weapon casting unnatural shadows on their horrid, decaying faces.

"A huge, flaming weapon. How very… *male*," snarled Grema. Xeb ignored the jibe and continued to entreat the crones.

"All of our lands are in great peril. Prince Vinadan will stop at nothing to bend all life to his will. His greed and arrogance will only be satisfied once every being in Gibrion kneels before him. I cannot let that happen, and I need your help to defeat him."

"Defeat him?" spat Yilmé. "That boy doesn't even know we exist. We have lived here, in peace, for centuries. We do not concern ourselves with the petty squabbles of men."

"Yet here you live, among plants and trees. You have a love of nature, of fertility; a love of *life itself*. Prince Vinadan respects only death." He lowered his arm and extinguished his flail into nothingness, the rune upon his hand fading in turn. The crones stood their ground and regarded him, weighing up his words.

"You have great power, Xebus of the Asarlai," began Yilmé. "But you fumble at its edges as a mindless child fumbles with a broken doll."

"Then *help me,* my good ladies of the forest. You do not have to share your magic with me, but I beg you to deploy it against Aclevion." Xeb's words seemed to echo unnaturally around the overgrown greenhouse; it was Karsha who broke the ensuing silence.

"Were we to agree; were we to aid you in your goals, we would invite great danger to ourselves. We have survived this long only by secrecy; only by ensuring that word of our existence has never reached the ears of men."

"How have you accomplished this, my ladies? I have to ask. How have you remained hidden all these years?" The three smiled as one.

"Let's just say we've never been so wasteful as to pass up perfectly good fertiliser when it wanders so freely into our path." A sudden dread welled up inside of Xeb, and though he did want to look down, he did so in any case. A sudden realisation dawned on him, and he closed his eyes.

Of course, he thought, *none who enter ever return, indeed. How else could the plants grow so green and strong in such a desolate land?* He shuffled, adjusting his feet nervously now that he was aware of exactly what it was he was standing on.

"I understand your concerns, my good ladies, but the risk you would take in action is nothing compared to the risk of inaction. You do not have to answer me here, in this moment, but I beseech you to be strong and pledge to join me against the darkness. I will leave you now - in peace. When the time is right you must seek me out. Fight with me, fight with me against Vinadan. And his *men*." Xeb hoped that the emphasis he added to the final would lend some small weight to his pleas.

"Should we agree to help you, Asarlai," asked Karsha, cautiously, "where would we find you, and how would we know the time is right?"

Xeb showed them a playful smile as he gestured broadly, holding his hands out and looking around the greenhouse at the arcane tools and ancient texts which filled every space not currently occupied by greenery.

"Oh, come now lady Karsha," he said with a wink. "You are the fabled crones of Vitruis; surely you will divine it."

Chapter Eleven

The air was thick with the stench of death as the small band of men and elves worked in pairs to dispose of the orrec bodies as quickly as they could, tossing them by their hands and feet into a shallow and hastily-dug pit. They would burn them later. As the soldiers performed their grim duty, the leaders of the group were crouched around the single surviving orrec a little further back into the treeline.

"You will tell us all you know, orrec filth. You *will* die here; the only choice you have is how quickly and painlessly your end will come," snarled Tyan, spraying spittle into the orrec's face as well as his own unkempt beard. Tyan was a gruff and perpetually angry man who had managed to escape the slaughter of Markosh some two months back with a handful of men and horses. Most of the town's other inhabitants were not so lucky; the attack had come suddenly and without warning, and hundreds had perished at the hands of the orrecs. Tyan and his men had since made it their personal business to destroy each and every orrec from here to the very halls of Ondellion in the north.

Alongside Tyan knelt Gael of Eonis. Her long and intricate curved dagger was held perfectly still, never more than a few millimetres from the orrec's throat, despite Tyan shaking and shoving the injured creature by its collars.

"My friend here is quite right," said the elf. "Whether your suffering is brought to a merciful end by my blade, or whether we simply leave you here to bleed out, your days are at an end. Tell us what we want to know: where did you plan to go once you had sacked Adeniron? How many more of your raiding parties are out there?" she asked in a calm and even tone. The orrec tried to laugh, but the sound it made was gargled, and rank blood bubbled at its black lips.

"I'm… I'm not tellin' you nothin' elf scum! Why don't you ask your brothers and sisters in Eonis? Oh yeah, that's right…" it taunted.

"Speak no more, spawn of Elgiroth, or I will cut out your tongue," replied Gael, refusing to rise to the bait.

"For the might of Aclevion!" it spat back, continuing its strained laughter. Tyan had heard quite enough, and planted an elbow squarely into the orrec's chin, sending a haze of black blood onto the grass below. He grabbed the orrec by its hair and brought its face a mere hair's breadth from his own.

"I'm only going to ask you this one more time, filth. *Where were you going?*" The orrec spat blood into Tyan's eyes and resumed its laughter.

"Go *shiv* yourself, human worm!" it snarled. Tyan shoved the orrec hard, and enjoyed the thud its head made against the tree trunk. The creature came to rest, dazed, slumped up against the tree as Tyan and Gael stood. The elf held out a silken handkerchief and Tyan accepted it gratefully, wiping all traces of the orrec blood from his face in one movement.

Thank Hemera for the magic of the elves, he thought to himself as he passed the gleaming, unsoiled item back to its owner. Gael stowed the enchanted item into her pack and turned to Tyan, frowning.

"There is little we can learn from a creature such as this. It is senseless to reason with the senseless." She shook her head, her long blonde braid swaying at her back as she did so. She reached into her pack once more and produced a map. "We must look to all eventualities," she said, handing the map to Tyan. "From Elgiroth they have come," she continued, "moving south through Barkash and Markosh." Tyan swallowed hard at the mention of his homeland.

"We believe they meant to sack Adeniron, of course, but where would they go from there?" Tyan narrowed his eyes as he studied the map. Trying to second-guess the logic of orrecs was not an easy business, and he could feel the burgeoning sting of a headache beginning to form at his temples.

"Okay, so we know they would not head south-east to your homeland of Eonis," he said, pointing to the map.

And he was right, of course. The slaughter of elves and dwarves in the land of Eonis some months earlier, coupled with the murder of Lady Keya had crippled the formerly powerful and influential realm and forced it onto the back foot. Prince Vinadan's seizure of the Soul of Hemera which had resided in Eonis for centuries had hamstrung this city and rendered it all-but worthless.

The orrecs did not need to break that which was already broken. And Gael knew it. As Tyan had fled the butchery of Markosh, so too had she escaped the devastation of Eonis and the slaughter of the elves. As one of the late Lady Keya's most loyal military commanders, Gael had survived the massacre and had taken a small but trusted cadre of lieutenants and warriors into the woods to the east, toward the coast. They meant to hunt. They sought revenge. At length, they had come across Tyan's people and – upon discovering they were united in both grief and purpose – their forces became one.

Another they had met on the road. Like them, he held anger in his heart. Like them, he meant to kill. Like them, he had Vinadan and his forces squarely in his sights. It was from the trees - quite apart from the rest of Gael and Tyan's alliance - that this one stood with raised hood and keen, dark eyes, watching the leaders as they continued their deliberations above the gargled curses and insults of their stirring captive.

"I do not believe they would seek to cross the sea to Skellt or Grior, or they would have made the crossing from the port at Barkash," said Tyan.

"Agreed; we must therefore assume they meant to continue south toward…" Gael traced a finger across the map, indicating the destination.

"Earon?" asked Tyan. "You believe they would attack the Three Ears?" Gael rolled her eyes at the use of the colloquial name men had given to the closely-knit elven lands of Earon, Olon, and Eldon. Earon itself was primarily a port town, with the isles of Olon and Eldon serving as trading posts for the import and export of fish, wood, silk, and various herbs and ingredients commonly used by elven alchemists and healers. A trio of elven lands, they were, so the *Three Ears* they became.

"It would make sense, would it not?" asked Gael. "How better to keep down an already defeated people than by disrupting their access to food and medicine?" She was now more certain than ever that she was correct.

"Okay, I admit it does make sense. But orrecs are mindless beats; they have neither the foresight nor the wit to plan such a complex operation," argued Tyan. Gael was not convinced. She had heard rumours of an orrec commander who was developing a reputation as something of a strategist. She feared such a being, and with Prince Vinadan at the centre of the web, pulling the strings and driving the machine of war inexorably onward, they could ill-afford to dismiss anything at this point.

"Either way, we must continue on to Adeniron if we are to eat and sleep comfortably tonight," she said. "Have your men set the pit ablaze and let us put an end to this one." She motioned over her shoulder to the orrec captive, still gurgling out insults between bouts of vicious, taunting laughter. Gael and Tyan turned to face the stricken orrec, and both reached for their daggers. Before they could unsheathe their weapons, a fine, silver-tipped arrow cut through the very air between their heads, and struck the orrec hard in the small recess between its nose and upper-lip, severing its spinal column and practically splitting its head in two.

Tyan and Gael removed their hands from their weapons and smiled. Gael turned to face the hooded figure still crouched low in the trees behind them.

"Once more you impress me with your bow skills, master barren."

"Thank you, commander," replied Ruli.

Chapter Twelve

The orrecs had truly made themselves at home in Markosh. The few human inhabitants still alive in the sacked and burned town were now in chains, forced to carry their fallen brothers, sisters, wives, and children to the shallow pits in which they were to be unceremoniously dumped and burned. The stench of death was interwoven with the acrid taste of smoke and cinders in the air; homes were reduced to cinders, and all around smoke billowed from pyres. Commander Malgorth inhaled deeply, savouring the chaos. Agnaz and he had not long arrived in the stricken town, and were now surveying the carnage and destruction as more civilised beings would appreciate a fine work of art. Upon seeing the looming shape of the orrec commander striding purposefully through the muddy streets, the members of the orrec raiding party stiffened, and threw clenched fists to their brows in salute.

"For the might of Aclevion!" went the cry, as orrec after orrec showed their respect for their towering commander as he passed. Malgorth nodded at each in turn and congratulated the soldiers on a job well done; their mission here was a resounding success worthy of medals and promotions, to his mind.

"Please... please..." came a low, timid whimper from one of the chained and kneeling humans. A female, Malgorth noted as he stopped to appraise the mewling creature. Clearly she recognised his status and sought an audience with him to...*to what, exactly?*

"You would dare address the commander, you filthy animal?" roared the scout Agnaz, stepping in front of his commander. Malgorth put an arm across the orrec and gently pushed him aside.

"It is okay, Agnaz, I want to hear what this... *thing* has to say."

"Please, sir... Please... I just want to go home... My... my daughter is hurt, you see? And I...I just..." The young woman broke down in tears as she tried to plead with the orrec for her freedom. She hoped beyond all hope that the mention of the injured child at her feet would appeal to something inside of the commander. She thought that, if she could just make a connection with the powerful orrec, he might spare her from her servitude and allow her and her daughter safe passage. Instead he merely grinned.

"Daughter, you say? Ah yes; she carries your unique stink," said Malgorth, sniffing in their direction for dramatic effect.

"She is hurt, correct? Allow me to take a look." He knelt down before the shackled young woman, and reached for the child with a softness which belied his appearance. He touched the back of his hand gently to the child's forehead, and deftly picked at her clothing to discern the wounds she carried beneath. Satisfied with his assessment, he nodded, and turned his face to the young woman, concern writ large upon his countenance. "I fear you are correct, human. This little one will not likely last the night without immediate care and medicine." The woman's eyes grew wide with hope; a faint hope; a chance that her appeal had not fallen on deaf ears.

"Pity," said Malgorth, "I was hoping to keep my hands clean." In a flash, he had drawn back his powerful arm and brought his fist crashing down upon the stricken child's head, shattering it in an instant and sending pieces of skull and tissue in every direction. The young woman screamed an inhuman scream of pain and horror which caused even Agnaz to wince. Malgorth regained his feet and held his gore-soaked right arm out to his side. One of the orrec raiders immediately ran to the commander and placed a vicious looking mace into his waiting palm.

"We do not treat with scum," said Malgorth over the woman's insufferable wailing. He drew back the mace, then swung the weapon downwards with incredible force. The town grew silent once more.

Malgorth withdrew the weapon from the young woman's decimated corpse, and held it up in the air before him, turning it around in his hands a few times and nodding. He turned to the orrec raider who had handed him the mace and fixed him with a questioning stare.

"Of… of course my commander! It would be my honour!" he said, taking Malgorth's meaning.

"Excellent. What is your name, soldier?"

"Gumaz, sir," the orrec replied, bowing low.

"I take this weapon and rename it *Matriarch*. In return, I name you Captain, Gumaz. You are to hold this town under all circumstances, or I will turn your former weapon upon your own skull when next we meet."

"Yes Commander, of course. Thank you, Commander," said captain Gumaz, who seemed to be standing a few inches taller than he had been moments earlier. Malgorth gestured for Agnaz to follow him with a subtle movement of his head, and the two visiting orrecs resumed their stride once more through the blood-soaked streets of Markosh. Before long, they had left the ruined town behind them and were crossing back into the wild once more. The air grew clean and fresh as they swapped mud and ashes for grasslands, and the sight of blackened wooden structures gave way to the green and yellow hues of trees swaying in the soft afternoon breeze.

Agnaz spat on the fertile ground in disgust. "These lands are a foul and loathsome companion," he said to Malgorth as he shook his head in revulsion.

"You are not wrong, scout. But we must hold our course south and bear what we must bear for the might of Aclevion," replied the commander with only mild reproach in his tone.

"Of course, Commander. I did not mean to speak out of turn," replied Agnaz with confidence. Malgorth grinned; lesser orrecs would have cowered at his words and pleaded for forgiveness. The scout was not so easily intimidated, and had so far proven himself loyal and capable. Malgorth liked Agnaz, and determined that he would reward the scout upon their return to Elgiroth.

As the night drew closer and the air turned cold, the two orrecs increased their pace as familiar scents began to announce themselves on the air. Maintaining their newfound pace, they made good time, and at length they came to a sudden stop, as Agnaz held up his fist to halt his commander.

"Here," he said, "this is the place."

Malgorth walked past the scout slowly, all senses alert and information assaulting him from every direction. He could now see the shallow grave in which the charred remains of his fellow orrecs lay. He noted the unmistakable scent of man, of elf, and of... *something else*. He turned to consider the trees which hemmed in this small clearing on one side, and again to take in the bushes and scrublands opposite. It was here he beheld an orrec slumped against a tree, its head nearly cloven in two. Had he not also glimpsed the intricately decorated, silver-tipped arrow which was still stuck fast in the tree trunk, he would have sworn that the axe of a dwarf had been responsible for the death of this orrec. He continued to survey the scene, gathering information, building his own picture of what had happened here, and only tangentially aware of Agnaz's own commentary as he pointed here and there and gestured toward things unseen. Malgorth walked up to the arrow and easily extricated it from the tree. He held it close to his eyes, looking up and down the accursed thing from silver tip to delicate fletching, taking in the carvings of vines and leaves which adorned it. Even an orrec commander could not deny the craftsmanship which must have gone into creating something so delicate yet so unmistakably deadly. Agnaz came up to join his commander and cast his own eyes over the arrow.

"Filthy elves," he offered. "Good riddance to Keya and the rest of her haughty kin." Malgorth continued to study the arrow, then sniffed at the fletching. He narrowed his eyes in suspicion then licked the silver tip, blood, splinters and all.

"No," he said to Agnaz. "Not Keya; not the elves."

"Commander?" the scout asked, clearly not taking Malgorth's meaning. Malgorth snapped the arrow in two across his knee, and cast the pieces onto the ground. He placed the silver tip into a pocket, and patted at it as if to assure himself of its location.

"When we reach Adeniron, we must find ourselves a raven or an owl; a messenger - anything we can use to send word to Aclevion and the ears of our prince. The barrens of Ehronia have ventured forth, my friend; we may need to teach them their place."

Chapter Thirteen

Xeb looked to the sky and assessed the quality of the daylight. He judged it to be around late morning as he continued his way east across the open ground which led away from Vitrius and the crones' hidden grove. His mind was racing with plans and ideas, swirling with thoughts of hopes fulfilled, and of dreams shattered. He played out scenarios in his head, and sought to lay contingency upon contingency in case of betrayal and double-cross. He had so far only made one plea for help, and while he did not hold out much hope that the crones would indeed come to his aid, theirs was the help he coveted the most – even if he would not yet bring himself to admit that. Still, he saw encouraging signs, and recognised good omens when they showed themselves. There were many towns, cities, communities, and encampments yet before him, and he knew deep down that not all men, dwarves, elves or the other many and varied denizens of Gibrion were likely to be of a unified mind. Some would prove sympathetic and would stand resolutely at his side; others would react with open hostility, violence even. Others still would be reluctant to act for good or ill, regardless of their feelings or political leanings. He had to believe he would find the help he sought; that he would find the numbers to challenge Prince Vinadan. On he walked, lost in his thoughts, through dense trees and over areas of open grasslands which gave way at intervals to rocky terrain he pushed.

"I know you are there," he said out loud, grinning. "You can tell the good ladies that they do not need to spy on me. Anything they wish to know, I will gladly tell them." He cast his gaze upwards, squinting a little at the increasingly bright sunlight. He was aware that the magpie had been following him for a number of hours now, circling high overhead but never straying too far; he finally resolved to address it directly.

"The legend of your masters' existence proved true indeed, my friend." He did not shout nor raise his voice; he did not have to. "That being the case," he continued, "you must be Branwen, no? Well, Branwen, you can tell the good ladies of Vitrius that I have no reason to deceive them nor seek to hide my intentions. I am headed to Frostpeak. There I hope to simply rest and take on food, maybe ale. *Definitely* ale." It amused Xeb to find himself addressing a bird in so casual a tone, but this was no mere bird, at least not as mortal men knew them.

"I have nothing to hide from you or your masters, Branwen. I spoke as truly in their presence as I speak now. Come with me to Frostpeak, if you must further satisfy your suspicions; I'll buy you a drink. Do magpies drink ale?" Xeb chuckled under his breath. He found that he was quite enjoying this conversation, one-sided as it was. Branwen, Lady Yilmé's familiar, turned and wheeled away toward the cover of the woods, hopefully satisfied that Xeb was indeed holding his present course, and not racing north into the lap of his dark master to report on the existence of the crones. And hold his course he did, for mile after mile he moved east toward the mountains after whose snowy summits the human town which sat ever in their shadow was named.

As the light began to fade and the late afternoon threatened to succumb to the evening dark, Xeb found himself at last among the stone buildings and cobbled streets of Frostpeak. The home of millers, smiths, armourers, and merchants, this was. No garrison of soldiers nor any suggestion of a barracks were to be found here; the human occupants of Frostpeak were a devout and superstitious people, unaccustomed to taking up arms in battle.

The sight of so many wounded and bandaged men, each with blood-stained swords or axes in their hands, therefore came as something of a surprise to Xeb. He passed taverns, stores, and apothecaries; he walked by tailors and food stalls, the usual fare for a market town such as this. But upon each face he read weariness. In each stance he saw exhaustion. In each eye, no matter how bright and welcoming on the surface, he saw horror and grief etched as if in stone. His first instinct was to seek out someone in authority, the ruling council or Mayor, perhaps, but Xeb had always found the unfiltered and unguarded speech of common folk of far greater worth than the practised, pristine word of politicians. Hemera knows he spent enough time around such beings in the capital. No, he would not yet present himself in any official capacity.

And he really *did* want that ale...

He ruminated on this as he walked, until, at length, the squeak and rattle of a wooden sign which hung from chains and blew in the wind caught his attention, and brought him back to his wits. He looked up, and beheld the source of the piercing sound, and decided that, since he was here, The Cold Shoulder Inn was as good a place as any. He entered the inn, and was immediately warmed by the roaring open fire, around which sat a group of men talking amongst themselves in hushed tones, each more dishevelled and weary-looking than the last. Sparing them but a momentary, casual glance, Xeb made his way to the bar and took a seat upon a vacant stool, acutely aware that virtually every eye in the place was now fixed pointedly upon his back. The apparent proprietor – himself as unkempt and bedraggled as his patrons – walked over to Xeb and tilted his head in appraisal of the newcomer.

"Ale please, barkeep," said Xeb, hoping to forestall the questions he knew were virtually inevitable. To his gratitude, the man obliged and produced a large, frothy tankard from which Xeb drank deep, draining half of the contents in one long gulp. He placed the tankard onto the bar and wiped his lips with the back of his hand.

"Impressive. I have always meant to sample the famous Frostpeak ale. The stories do not do it justice, my good man." The barkeep continued to stare at Xeb, clearly sizing him up and trying to figure something out. When he finally spoke, it was not to Xeb, but to all of the other patrons of the inn at once.

"Aether be blessed… We're saved! He heard our call! Our glorious Prince has sent us a saviour!" the barkeep announced, both arms open wide in Xeb's direction.

"Aether be blessed! Prince Vinadan has heard our pleas!" came another voice from a corner. Soon, all of the tired, injured, and clearly desperate men in The Cold Shoulder were crowding around to get a better look at Xeb, thanking Prince Vinadan and praising Aether aloud.

"Stop! All of you!" Xeb tried to make himself heard over the jubilation. Finally, he stood up from his stool and put some of his considerable magic into his voice.

"I said *stop*." This time the din ceased, and the men cowered a little in their boots.

"What happened here? I thought the men of Frostpeak were a proud and resourceful folk. But here I find you cowering like wounded animals. Well? Someone explain what is going on here!" It was the barkeep who accepted the invitation.

"Forgive us my lord, but you *are* a brother of the Asarlai, are you not?" At Xeb's reluctant nod he continued.

"It's those accursed hoblins, my lord. For months they have attacked us as we sleep, stealing our supplies and murdering our people. We have tried to fight them, my lord, but… We are merchants and smiths. Our strength is in coin, not blades. We *create*, but they only destroy. Thank Aether you have arrived at last!"

"What has this got to do with me?" Xeb asked the barkeep. Now it was *his* turn to look confused.

"Why, Prince Vinadan, my lord. Prince Vinadan has heard our prayers and sent you to free us from the hoblin scourge. Has he not?"

"No. I am but a mere traveller in these lands; I am here only for food and a room for the night. I mean to move on at first light and knew nothing of your troubles before I arrived here." The barkeep looked crestfallen, but an idea struck him, and a spark returned to his eyes.

"But you are here now; you can still help us!" he said, but Xeb was already shaking his head.

"No, no, no… I have pressing business elsewhere – I cannot help you. Actually, I should leave. I am clearly proving a distraction here. Barkeep, how much for the ale?" he said, reaching into his cloak.

"Nothing, my lord. Nothing for that one nor any others you might like. No mullions do you owe me for whatever food you might fancy, nor a single kreon for our finest bed."

Xeb sighed deeply and momentarily lowered his head in acceptance. And defeat.

"If I agree to help you," he concluded.

The barkeep – and most of his customers – nodded.

"Fine," said Xeb, more to himself than the patrons. He could already feel the beginnings of a headache coming on. "I will embark at first light tomorrow."

"Thank Aether!" went up the cry once more from all corners of The Cold Shoulder.

Thank Aether, indeed, thought Xeb. *The men and women of Frostpeak once called out to the daylight, sent their most private pleas and confided their deepest desires to Hemera. But oh, how easily Prince Vinadan can poison the well and watch the masses kneel in the dirt to lap up the tainted waters. How deftly he can offer a dagger as if it were a gemstone, and stand back victorious while the weak-minded trample each other to be the first to impale themselves upon the gilded blade.*

He speaks for the night, and the people of Gibrion turn their backs upon the day.

Thank Aether, indeed.

Chapter Fourteen

The orrecs stood guard, one either side of the door to Prince Vinadan's private chambers. Upon hearing movement within, they each stood a little straighter, raised their chins, and tightened their grips on the large pikes they held. The door opened, and a beautiful woman emerged, her brown eyes the perfect complement to her chestnut hair. She was dressed simply, in loose-fitting brown trousers and a sleeveless tunic, and her small feet padded softly on the cold floor as she made her way from the Dark Lord's chambers. She threw a playful wink at one of the orrecs as she passed on her way and, once she was beyond the hallway and – the orrecs assumed - both sight and earshot, they relaxed a little. The smaller orrec chuckled quietly; he motioned with his head in the general direction the young woman had left in.

"No surprise he chose *that one*," he said to his companion.

"The prince *does* like to hunt," the other said, grinning.

The young woman continued through the fortress, treading lightly on polished marble floors, passing through long, tall corridors adorned with portraits of great kings and queens of old, and tapestries depicting legendary battles and betrayals from Gibrion's long history. She edged beyond the inner-chambers and into the communal areas. She passed orrecs and servants, members of Vinadan's council, and brothers of Asarlai in turn. As she passed she averted her gaze, proceeding toward the enormous double doors which led away from the grand entrance chamber and out into the city of Aclevion itself. The unseasonal mid-morning sunshine warmed her skin, and the smell of freshly baked bread and pastries of all shapes and flavours assaulted her senses and set her stomach rumbling.

Market day, she realised with a smile.

She stood at the top of the great marble steps which led down from the citadel and into the main square, from which the residential streets and avenues split off like the silken strands of a spider web. She passed between two large marble statues, images of Gibrion's former lords – Vinadan's kin – as she descended the steps, and presently found herself standing before a large, ornately decorated fountain which sat at the centre of the main square. At its centre were towering likenesses of the three goddesses, each with pure, glistening water cascading down from their heads or tips of their upraised fingers, to fall at their marble feet. As the heat continued to bear down on her and the day began to take shape, the young lady ran her fingers in the fountain's clear waters as she passed it, and followed the smell of warm bread toward the bustling market stalls.

So busy was it that she found herself having to nudge and cajole her way toward the aroma which had so enticed her, but eventually she found herself at the front of the queue. Arrayed before her were all manner of sweet and savoury bakes, and the merchant on the other side of the counter looked proud as he watched her peruse his offerings.

And well he should, she thought, selecting a hot bread roll which had been twisted and folded into the likeness of a raven.

"Will that be all, my good lady... erm...?" he asked awkwardly, unable to match a name to her face.

"*Suleyne*, sir," she offered, bowing slightly in deference.

"My lady Suleyne; I do not believe I have seen your face before, but then I am no longer as young as I once was. I forget, see?"

"No, good sir, you are quite correct. I have only recently arrived in the capital. I hail from Aillen, originally."

"Ah!" said the merchant, raising a finger. "I thought I recognised a touch of the north in your accent".

She smiled politely in response and reached inside her dress for her coin purse.

"And here I thought I had trained out my northern accent. How much do I owe for the pastry, good merchant?"

He frowned and waved away her coin.

"No, no, no; I couldn't possibly. It's on me, lady Suleyne – a *welcome to the capital*, if you will. For the might of Aclevion and the glory of our prince!"

"Oh no, sir, I couldn't. Please, let me pay my way," Suleyne protested, thrusting a handful of kreons and mullions the merchant's way. He closed his hand around hers, and gently pushed her offer away.

"Next time, my lady, certainly next time, but for today, consider it my treat." She inclined her head and stowed her coin.

"You are a kind and noble man. Our great Prince would be glad of more from your stock, I'm certain. Your name?"

"Garrie, my lady," he offered, inclining his head. They exchanged one final kindly smile and the old baker set about serving his next customer in a bid to make a dent in the long line which had started to form behind Suleyne. She continued deeper into the market; as she went, taking her time, she passed stall after stall, each busy and crowded. The din of trade, conversation, and the chinking of coins changing hands was a constant backdrop as she wandered. Here, she passed a sour-faced old lady sitting behind a wicker basket full of trinkets and tomes; there, she passed a handsome young bard offering crude and colourful rhymes for a mullion apiece. She stopped to peruse an alchemist's wares, which were – in their own way – just as enticing as the baker's treats. On she went, smiling in apology as she nudged her way through the crowds. Now a different kind of smell found its way to her, a sweeter smell which reminded her of a man she once knew...

Spiced wine.

Despite the intensifying late morning heat, she determined there and then that a cup of hot, sweet wine was exactly what she wanted. She turned so that the warmth of the morning was no longer upon her face, but now caressed the back of her neck and shoulders, and stepped with a silent grace toward the bearded man standing amongst the assortment of barrels, gourds, and cups. This time she did not have long to wait, as the fancy for a hot drink on a warm day had taken but a handful of the market crowd. She raised a finger to indicate a single cup, and the winemaker nodded obligingly and turned away to make her drink. He returned in short order and held a cup of hot red wine out toward Suleyne; the aroma of cinnamon and berries was as intoxicating as the drink itself, and it called to mind a hundred memories at once. She accepted it with a nod and paid the seven mullion price willingly.

"Enjoy, miss," said the winemaker with a curt nod and a mirthless smile, lacking even half of the cordiality displayed earlier by the baker. Suleyne closed her eyes and breathed in deeply, lost in the heady scent of the warm drink in her hands. She barely even registered the contingent of orrec guards who had passed by close behind her, and she took a long, satisfying drink from her cup.

"Unbelievable…" The sound of the winemaker's deep, dour voice brought Suleyne back to herself.

"I'm sorry?" she said. The winemaker caught her eye, and nodded his head toward the orrecs.

"Them," he said through gritted teeth. "What do they think this is, a battlefield? It's an Aether-damned *market*. *Scum.*" He shook his head slowly, his eyes boring holes into the orrecs' backs. His countenance betrayed his bitterness, but Suleyne's face showed only confusion.

"I don't understand," she replied, "I may be new to the city, but I thought the prince's guards were her to keep us safe?" The winemaker snorted and shook his head cynically.

"Safe? Safe from what? The only threat around here is *our good prince* himself. Everyone knows the stories." Suleyne straightened and fixed the man with a pointed stare.

"What stories, my good man?" What do the people say about our wise and powerful lord?"

"*Wise and powerful?*" the merchant replied with sarcasm dripping like honey from his words. "You really *must* be new around here. The man is nothing but a sorcerer and a coward. You don't believe me? Go and ask an elf or a dwarf, if you can find one who's still breathing." Suleyne stood rigid before the winemaker, unaware of the vein beginning to show at her temple as she fixed him with a singular gaze.

"Vinadan, provides for us. Were it not for the prince and his loyal guard, war would ravage all the lands of Gibrion. He is wise, fair, and just," she said through increasingly clenched teeth in an increasingly loud voice.

"*Just?*" repeated the winemaker, "*Just a murderer*, more like." The merchant flinched as Suleyne's cup smashed into pieces upon the ground.

"What in the name of-"

"Guards!" screamed Suleyne, a look of rage etched upon her face and spittle playing upon her lips. The nearby orrecs turned around at the call, and hurried over to the spiced wine stall.

"What's goin' on 'ere?" demanded the orrec captain, surveying the peculiar scene. Suleyne turned toward the orrecs, and the fury upon her face began to morph into a deathly smile. As surely as her expression changed, so too did her appearance; her dark hair turned white, and the soft, pink skin of her face became ashen and flecked with lazy stubble. Her formerly delicate hands turned to large, trembling fists, and the thin, bare arms grew larger and rippled with muscle. Those passers-by who had curiously gathered to witness the scene unfold now stared in shock and cowered in fear.

"Arrest this man and bring him to the throne room at once," commanded Prince Vinadan, turning on his heel and striding triumphantly back toward the citadel of Ondellion.

The prince likes to hunt, indeed, he thought, as the sea of people parted before him. He took the great marble steps two at a time, and had not so much as a glance to spare for the statues of his ancestors as he passed.

*

Vinadan's leg bounced with nervous energy and his face rested upon his clenched fist as he stared down at the shackled winemaker who knelt before him at the foot of the dais. It was not voluntarily that the man kneeled; rather, he had been unceremoniously shoved to the ground by the orrec guard at his back.

"Talimarc Garron, you are charged with sedition and conspiracy to commit high treason," announced Alma, resplendent in his red robes standing beside the occupied throne.

"Treason?" replied the stunned merchant. "I have done nothing wrong! I have done nothing at all besides speak the truth!" Though he was entirely at the mercy of Prince Vinadan and his underlings, the winemaker Talimarc Garron had not surrendered his defiance.

"You deny the charges?" asked Alma.

"Deny them? Of course I fucking deny them! This is a farce; this whole thing is nonsense! What? Nothing to say, my *lord*?" This he directed at Vinadan, who remained in place upon his throne, silent; his leg still bouncing up and down in an outward expression of his simmering rage.

"You would do well to refrain from addressing your lord in such a tone again, merchant," warned Alma, but the winemaker was undeterred.

"What's the point, Asarlai? We both know I'm not walking away from this sham; you know as well as I that your precious prince has already decided my fate."

Now Vinadan stirred. His leg ceased to bounce, and he raised his head to meet Talimarc's defiant gaze.

"How much coin have you made today, merchant?" he asked. The merchant could not hide his confusion.

"Coin? What are you talking about?"

"Coin. Sales. Profit. How much have you made today? A fair amount I should wager, given the quality of your wares and the prices you ask. No, don't look at me like that, your wine is excellent, and I would not be so crass as to pretend otherwise." He stood from his throne and began to walk toward his kneeling captive.

"But why is that, I wonder? How are you able to create a product of such quality? How are you able to make such a profit? Is it, perhaps, because by my grace you can source your ingredients from across all of Gibrion? Is it because I open my city gates to travellers, merchants, clerics, and any other who wishes to live well and free? I am a just and generous lord. I am beloved by my people; the strongest military in this wide world guards us and protects our way of life. We live well here; we are all lords and ladies in Aclevion," he thrust out his right hand and grabbed Talimarc by the face, "*because I. Make. It. So*," he continued, enunciating each word for emphasis. "And you call me *murderer*."

The merchant was unmoved by Vinadan's words. He smiled as he locked eyes with the prince of Aclevion.

"We live well, do we? We live in *fear*. In fear of a tyrant with the temper of a child! And as for *lords* and *ladies*, why don't you ask your brother what he thinks about-"

Talimarc Garron would not finish his sentence. Vinadan closed the distance between himself and the winemaker in two strides, snarling in rage as he bore down on the man. He seemed to glow, as every inch of exposed skin burned white hot at the sudden emergence of fiery ancient runes. Talimarc was lifted high into the air under the strength of some invisible force, and more than one throat in the chamber swallowed hard with dread, as all in attendance beheld the look upon Vinadan's countenance.

"You *dare* talk to me of my filthy, traitor brother? You dare to talk back to your prince? You dare to even stand in my presence, you worthless dog?"

The merchant could not move, and could barely breathe as he was held, suspended in the air by Vinadan's dark magic.

"Your.. your…" Talimarc sputtered, trying to force his words out through his clenched and squeezed throat. "Your brother was a *hero*," he spat defiantly.

"Talimarc Garron, master winemaker of Aclevion. I declare you guilty of sedition and high treason," Vinadan said, his voice suddenly and surprisingly distant and devoid of its previous fire. "Let all present bear witness as I deliver your sentence." The prince clapped his hands together and the merchant's body was obliterated mid-air. As Vinadan opened his hands anew, what remained of Talimarc Garron's mangled corpse fell to the marble floor with a sickening, wet thud. All was silent for a long drawn out moment, and then Vinadan spoke.

"You, servant – clean up that mess and send word for the remainder of the merchant's stock to be brought into the citadel. Tonight, all shall drink for free." The serving girl nodded and raised a fist to her forehead.

"For the might of Aclevion, my prince." As she scuttled away to begin her gruesome work, Vinadan turned and strode away from the main hall and in the direction of his private chambers, his eyes vacant and his demeanour brooding. He motioned for Alma to follow and the Asarlai fell in step beside his master.

"My lord?"

"This is getting out of hand, Orderman. Today it is mere whispers; tomorrow it will be open rebellion. I will not have it. These peasants must learn their place."

"Yes, my Lord. You are of course correct. But do not allow the spite of one merchant to unsettle you; the people do love you, my prince, and Xebus is out there right now spreading tidings of your glory across all the lands of Gibrion. I have no doubt that, upon his return, he will have thousands with him, and all will march through the city gates with your name upon their lips, ready to toil and prosper for the might of Aclevion."

Vinadan's festering anger seemed to cool at the older man's soothing words. They continued deeper into the citadel.

"Yes, Xebus. He, at least, is loyal to me. But when he does return, he had better do so with nothing short of an army at his back." At his approach, the orrec guards opened the door to Vinadan's private chamber, and Vinadan dismissed Alma with a mere wave of his hand.

An army at his back, indeed, thought Alma. *Where are you, Xeb?*

Chapter Fifteen

Hoblins; when one crypt closes, another opens just as surely. Frostpeak is a loyalist realm beyond any doubt; there is no help to be found there among the merchants and millers. But as for the hoblins… I wonder.

Xeb could no longer make out the details of Frostpeak as he cast a look over his shoulder; it was far behind him now, and his present path took him in a new, albeit less defined direction. Grass crunched under his feet and he imagined that he could feel the dampness even through his heavy boots. He found himself more or less half-way between two mountain ranges, the one beneath which Frostpeak lay loomed far behind him, and the towering presence of the foremost Undonian range was yet ahead. Further west, the high, foreboding peaks of the Dinannian mountains seemed a constant backdrop as he inched ever onward. He felt exposed out in the open like this, and could hardly help but to cast furtive glances left and right whenever he passed boulders, crags, or other natural features which could cloak potential threats. He was in the wild lands now, and he knew it. At length, he found a patch of rocky ground which made for a good location to rest a moment. He sat down on the smoothest rock he could find, and leaned back against an adjacent boulder. He allowed himself a few pieces of bread and chicken which the barkeep had given him for the journey – the *least* he could do under the circumstances, to Xeb's mind - and took a few gulps from his waterskin. He sighed deeply and arched his back, feeling a satisfying *click* from his spine.

What am I doing? I'm getting too old for adventures and quests; my place in the monastery with a book in hand, not in the battlefield clutching a sword.

He dismissed these doubts with a shake of his head and stood up, determined to forge ahead and find the –

Hoblins, he registered with a start.

Whether it was their high-pitched voices or distinct aroma which first alerted Xeb to their presence he did not know, but the fact remained that they were close. He quickly stowed his waterskin and stood alert, head cocked to the side and breath held in anticipation. He turned and slowly peered around the large boulder and beheld three hoblins.

Only three? They must be scouts, he thought. *This may be my best chance.*

He took a deep, steadying breath and stepped out from around the boulder with his hood lowered and a somewhat-forced smile on his face.

"Greetings, my friends!" he shouted, catching the hoblin trio's attention. They spun on their heels and turned to face the source of the exclamation, surprise etched onto their green-skinned faces, alarm quite apparent in their large, sickly-yellow eyes.

"Get him!" cried one of the hoblins, and all three reached for their weapons. Xeb held up his hands, palms outwards, to forestall their attack.

"No, no, no, wait!" he said. "I am no threat to you! I seek an audience with-"

Too late. Xeb heard the tell-tale *twang* of the bowstring before he saw the dark, iron arrow flying toward him. Instinct took over, and as the rune for *Control* burned to life on the back of his right hand, its sister *Balance* likewise on his left, a shield of pure flame was born to his hands and the arrow was incinerated upon contact. Surprise turned to panic, and the hoblins charged at Xeb with curved, serrated blades raised wildly above their heads. Xeb planted his right foot firmly behind him and held fast to his burning shield.

"Please, stop this! I only want to talk!" Xeb shouted to the oncoming hoblin trio. They did not heed his words. He sidestepped the first with ease, and brought the shield down hard on the back of the passing hoblin's head and shoulders, forcing him to the cold ground already burning. The next came at Xeb from behind, aiming a heavy, two-handed overhead swing at the back of his head. Again, Xeb spun on his heel and easily blocked the blow with his shield raised in defence. Kicking out behind him, he caught the third hoblin hard in the stomach. He shoved forward, disengaging from the lead hoblin and buying himself some space to breathe. Sparing a quick glance downward, he registered that the hoblin he had knocked to the ground with his fiery shield had not regained its feet, and indeed never would.

Hemera curse this day, thought Xeb. *This was not supposed to happen.* With a hoblin now approaching slowly from both his left and right flanks, Xeb decided a new tactic was required. He extinguished his shield to nothingness, and the runes on his hands faded in turn; he held out his palms to the hoblins once more.

"Stop, please! I only want to speak to you! I have an offer for you; who is in charge here?"

"Speak to us? You killed Saald, red cloak! And as for who's in charge, well, it's not you, human," snarled the left-most hoblin. The two remaining hoblins shared a quick look and a nod, then charged as one.

I tried, thought Xeb with a sigh and shake of the head. He half-turned to the right and summoned to life a broadsword of pure blue flame. The hoblins faltered slightly upon its ignition, but continued in their charge. Blue fire was reflected in Xeb's eyes, and every inch of exposed skin burned with the rune which represented *Anger;* the hoblins had finally annoyed him. Xeb was a blur of motion as he dodged, parried, slashed, countered, turned, spun, and parried once more. A studious and learned order were the Asarlai, and they had garnered a reputation over decades for only resorting to combat as an absolute last resort, but once they had committed to it, there were few in all of Gibrion who could match their prowess.

Except Vinadan, of course. The lord of Aclevion, with the power of the Souls of Aether and Hemera coursing through his veins – now *there* was the exception.

Xeb caught a vicious, low swing upon his mystic blade, and pushed back hard, sending the hoblin tumbling away to the dirt as his partner advanced, aiming high. Xeb feigned to block but instead shifted his weight to the other foot and spun in a fast arc, breezing by the onrushing hoblin and cleaving him nearly in two with his flaming blade.

Two down.

He wasted no time in advancing on the final hoblin, who was down but trying to scramble to his feet. Xeb closed the distance to the frightened creature in two mammoth strides, and pointed his weapon downwards, its tip mere inches from the hoblin's terrified face.

"Stop! Stay down," he commanded. "I did not want this; I tried to warn you! I seek only an audience with your leader. I have a message and an offer." Long moments passed as man and hoblin stared at each other from opposite ends of the blue flaming sword, both panting heavily but slowly regaining their breath.

"An offer?" the hoblin said at last.

"Yes, I have an offer which you might be very interested in, if you can keep from trying to kill me long enough so that I might deliver it to your masters." The hoblin nodded, slowly at first, then faster with a little more certainty.

"Ugnor."

Xeb could not hide his confusion.

"Ug – what?"

"*Ugnor*; you need to speak to Ugnor. He leads us."

"Ugnor, okay. Excellent." Xeb extinguished his sword and held out his hand to the hoblin. The hoblin looked even more frightened at this gesture than he had moments earlier with a flaming sword inches from his face.

"W…what are…?" he stammered. Xeb couldn't help the muscles in his cheeks from twitching as he fought off a roguish grin.

"Well come on then, get up. You cannot lead me to Ugnor if you're sat arse-deep in the dirt." The hoblin hesitated a few moments longer, then cautiously took Xeb's hand. Xeb hauled him onto his feet and picked the hoblin's sword up from the ground.

"Can I trust that you will not stab me in the back if I hand this back to you?" he said, drawing forth a touch of his power so that his skin glowed with a faint outline of fire. The tactic worked a treat, as the hoblin backed away a step or two and stammered a reply.

"Y... yes, yes, thank you... Forgive and forget?"

Xeb nodded his agreement. "Of course." he said, handing the sword to the hoblin and allowing his flames to recede. "And I *am* sorry about your friends – I did not embark on this quest with death on my mind."

"Brothers," said the hoblin, more to the ground than to Xeb.

"What?"

The hoblin raised his chin and met Xeb's gaze.

"Usk and Saald – they were not my *friends*; they were my *brothers*."

"Usk and Saald," replied Xeb, quietly. "I am sorry. And your name?"

"Fennet."

"Fennet, okay. I am Xebus. Come now, let us give your brothers a proper burial, and we will be on our way." Fennet tilted his head and looked from Xeb to his fallen kin.

"Thank you, but that would take time. Couldn't you just… *you know*…?" Fennet gestured with his hands and, while Xeb didn't entirely understand, he got the gist of the hoblin's meaning.

"If you're sure?" he replied. The hoblin nodded in response, and Xeb could not help feeling like the hoblin just wanted to see another display of the Asarlai's power.

"Well, okay then." Xeb arched an eyebrow at Fennet and clicked his fingers; immediately his skin was aglow with countless reproductions of the rune for *Nature*, and the fallen bodies of Usk and Saald were reduced to ashes in a pair of brief but intense conflagrations.

"Now," said Xeb, wiping his hands on his robe for dramatic effect; he could see plainly how enamoured Fennet was of his powers, "take me to Ugnor."

*

"…and ever since then, Saald and I have barely spoken and I've hardly been able to look a chicken in the beak, let alone visit my cousin. So there's no harm done, really."

It had been a long walk from the ambush site to the promised meeting with the hoblin leader, but Fennet had done his best to show Xeb that he was no threat, and that the killing of his brothers was all water under the bridge as far as he was concerned. Xeb smiled in spite of himself as Fennet finished his long and disturbing tale; he was actually starting to warm to the hoblin. Thankful that his grin was hidden within the shadows of his hood, Xeb nodded along dutifully and, before too long, Fennet held up a hand and brought them to a halt.

"What is it, Fennet? Are we here?" Xeb asked, casting a dubious glance at their immediate surroundings. There seemed to be nothing around for as far as Xeb could see in all directions. The nearest town, Undon, was at least another ten or twelve miles to the west. There were no obvious signs of a camp or temporary domicile of any kind, just wide-open grasslands at the foot of the mountain, and…

The foot of the mountain, Xeb realised with a sigh. "Are you serious?" he asked Fennet, who shrugged innocently in reply. "Why do I get the feeling I'm walking into another ambush?" he said, forcing a little of his arcane fire into his voice.

"No, no ambush! This is where we live! Come on. I'll take you to Ugnor," said Fennet, already making for an inconspicuous looking crack in the face of the rock ahead of them.

A cave; of course they live in a cave, Xeb thought as he followed his hoblin companion into the dark crevasse. Deeper and deeper they went in near total darkness, leaving the meagre light from the outside world further and further behind them. Xeb's eyes had almost fully adjusted to the blackness within a minute or two, and he was guided more by instinct than by Fennet's directions, relying on his hearing and the feel of the cold rock walls to build a picture of the meandering natural tunnel system. Slowly at first, but increasing in intensity, Xeb became aware of a faint, orange glow up ahead. A few dozen steps more and he was met by the welcome sight of flaming torches ensconced upon the walls in iron brackets, and he could now make out their destination – a large chamber, as wide as it was tall, full to bursting with hoblins. Before he had fully reconciled his new surroundings, a booming voice rang out and reverberated around the rotunda.

"Where are your brothers, Fennet? Where are the supplies you were supposed to bring back? *And who is that?*"

Xeb tracked the voice to its source, and beheld a hoblin not too dissimilar to Fennet and his late brothers, nor much different to any one of the hoblins currently encroaching for a closer look – and the occasional jab and poke – at Xeb. The speaker sat upon a rickety wooden chair which sat upon a boulder so that he was at least a head's height above the rest of the hoblins. Xeb noted with interest that it was not a throne, necessarily, and the hoblins were not behaving like servants or subjects. No, Ugnor was respected and deferred to, to be sure, but he did not *rule*. He was not so different from the rest. Not so different but for the grey in his scraggly, dank hair, and the arrow shaft which protruded from his neck, the skin having long since fused around the wound.

"Great Ugnor! This is my friend Xeb, of the Asarlai from Aclevion. He comes with an offer." The room hummed with whispers and gasps at the introduction, but Ugnor appeared unmoved. He motioned for silence and slowly gained his feet.

"Aclevion, you say? *Hmph*," he snorted, and walked toward his visitor, the crowd of enraptured hoblins making way as he advanced. He reached the human and looked him up and down, sizing him up, judging him.

"Take down your hood," he snarled, and Xeb obliged. Without taking his eyes off Xeb, Ugnor spoke once more to Fennet.

"I will ask you once more; where are your brothers?"

"They… they did not survive the mission," said Fennet cryptically. A great murmur spread around the chamber, but Ugnor held up a forestalling hand.

"How, Fennet? What happened?" he asked, his eyes still boring into Xeb's own.

"Ah, well," Fennet began, nervously. "The thing about that, sire, is…. Well, you see…"

"I killed them," said Xeb, his even voice echoing around the cavern. A collective gasp issued from the hoblin horde, but Ugnor silenced them anew. He continued to stare at Xeb, and a knowing grin began to spread from his thin lips. He had already guessed the answer before Xeb had offered it

"You killed them," he said, nodding slowly to himself.

"I did, War Chief Ugnor, but I did so in self-defence. I did not seek a confrontation and did all I could to prevent bloodshed."

Ugnor continued to grin, which set the hairs on the back of Xeb's neck on end.

"You did all you could, did you? How noble. *Hmph*. Do not take me for a fool, Human.m I know what you think of us, it is written all over your face. The disgust, the pity, the revulsion; but, despite what you may think, we hoblins are not an infestation; we are not raiders, murderers, or thieves. We are not mindless, we do not lack for wisdom."

"Ugnor, if I-" began Xeb, but the hoblin had not finished.

"Silence! I know who you are. Rather, I know *what* you are. I have not always lived in a cave, Asarlai. I know of your order, I know of your powers, your runes, your Soul. If you had truly wanted to avoid bloodshed, you could have simply *compelled* young Usk and young Saald to stay their hands; your kind command the power to influence, do they not?"

"*Influence,*" answered Xeb, reddening slightly in the cheeks. "Yes, well, I've actually always struggled with that particular rune. But that is not the point. Fennet will confirm that, not only did I merely act to protect myself from harm, but I spared his life. I bring you an offer, all of you!" Xeb's voice carried in the chamber, and a tentative quiet fell over the crowd.

"An offer, you say?" asked Ugnor. "What do you know of hoblins, Asarlai, and speak only the truth here."

Xeb took a breath and composed himself; he knew he had to choose his words carefully.

"I know more about your kind – and of your plight – than most, though that is probably not entirely surprising considering where I come from."

Ugnor nodded at this, his dark grin turning into a cruel smile.

He does not mean to let me leave here alive, Xeb realised, as he continued. "I know that the people of Gibrion consider you a scourge; marauders travelling across the lands to kill and pillage, before moving on and raiding anew. And while this is true to a certain extent, I – unlike most – know why."

Ugnor had nodded along slowly, neither interrupting Xeb to object nor correct so far, but did so now. "Yes, you know exactly why. Yet you still hire them, work with them, dine with them, and drink with them. We were once a proud race, we once had land and homes, we bothered no-one, but then the orrecs came along; orrecs in vast numbers; orrecs with armour on their backs and weapons in their hands. Orrecs with the power of Prince Vinadan on their side," Ugnor drew a long, barbed dagger, whose golden pommel was fashioned into a rough approximation of a skull, and held its tip to Xeb's throat.

"Orrecs who murder *for the might of Aclevion*," he snarled; a look of fury mingled with determination in his eyes.

This is it, thought Xeb, but it was Fennet who intervened, knocking the dagger aside and standing between Ugnor and Xeb.

"Wait! Ugnor, stop! Please, hear him out! He can help us!" Long moments passed in tense silence, and Ugnor finally relented, sliding the mean-looking dagger back into its sheath.

"If only for my own amusement before I slit your pink throat: speak."

Xeb dabbed at his throat and cast a glance down at the blood now smeared on his fingertips. "I know you have been wronged; I know how many hoblins were killed by Vinadan's orrecs. You raid, you kill, and you steal, yes, but I know that you only do so to *survive*." The room was silent. *Good, they're listening.*

"Prince Vinadan has grown mad with power. He wishes to kill or enslave all those who do not openly worship him, and he has the power and the numbers to do it. We must fight back. My order are advisors to the capital, and we have power of our own, but not all think as I do. I cannot turn the Asarlai loose on Vinadan, so I must look to other means. And now I look to you. *Help me*; join me in my fight against Vinadan and his orrecs, and I promise you I will see to it that you once again have lands you can call your own. You can live free, raise your young; you will no longer have to live as travellers, hiding in caves and seeking shelter of the trees when the rain falls. You will have a home again."

Xeb had not exactly been expecting a round of voracious applause or cheers of exultation, but the long, uncomfortable silence which followed his words was deafening. Ugnor broke it at last.

"You mean to turn against your own? You would destroy your own brothers?"

"My hope is that it does not come to that," Xeb replied firmly, "but should any of my order stand alongside Vinadan in the war to come, and should I be forced to weigh up personal loyalties against the freedom of all men, elves, dwarves, and hoblins in Gibrion, then they will die just as surely as their master."

A murmur ran through the cavernous hall, and many of the hoblins turned and whispered among themselves. There were more than a few nods, Xeb noted.

"Where?" said Ugnor.

"What?" asked a nonplussed Xeb.

"Where are we to go? Where do you propose to take us once this war you mention is over?"

"I have thought about that, and my suggestions would be the islands of Grior or Skellt, due east of Adeniron, or perhaps the Dinannian cluster off the western shores."

"You mean to send us across the water? We hoblins are not a seafaring race, Asarlai; we have no means to journey across the open waters," replied Ugnor, shaking his head. Xeb smiled openly.

"You need not worry about that, my lord Ugnor. If a boat is all you need, I know a man. He's a talker, but he's cheap. Anyway, do we have an agreement?" Xeb asked, holding out his hand to the hoblin elder. Ugnor studied the hand as if it were a weapon pointed his way, so unaccustomed he had become to displays of respect or courtesy these long years past. At length he nodded, and took Xeb's hand in his own.

"Yes. Agreed. We will fight. But understand, Asarlai, that if you do not keep your word, if this is a trap, or if you betray us, I will rend you limb from limb and feed you to my children."

"Fair enough," replied Xeb, secure as he was in his intent. "Now, I really must be getting back to Frostpeak; the fools await my *triumphant return*. They expect me to bring back your head, I think, but I only promised I would bring an end to the raids," Xeb said pointedly, and Ugnor nodded his agreement. "Still, I must take back evidence of some sort if I am to rest and feast for free. War Chief Ugnor, is there perhaps something I could-" but the old hoblin was already unsheathing his dagger once more. He held it out to Xeb.

"Here, take this. This should do the trick." This time Ugnor's smile displayed genuine amusement, and he was not the only hoblin within the cavern to chuckle at the gesture.

"Why do I get the feeling there's a private joke I'm not privy to, here?" Xeb asked with one eyebrow raised. "Why the dagger?"

"Well, because they'll be sure to recognise it, that's why," said Ugnor. "It belonged to the previous Mayor; I took it from him, used it to kill his wife, then slit his throat with it."

"Oh," replied Xeb, "that *should* do the trick."

Chapter Sixteen

Adeniron nestled within the eastern shadow of the great Torimarian mountain range, and was surrounded on all sides by lush, verdant woods. A place of relative prosperity, it was a shining jewel in Gibrion's crown, home to artists, scholars, bards, and renowned alchemists. Fine silks were woven here in compliment to the gleaming, silver swords and axes which were produced in impressive numbers by master smiths. The ruling council of dwarves and humans had always endeavoured to keep their city beyond the gaze of Vinadan and Aclevion, paying their taxes and playing their parts with an overt and arguably cynical deference to the crown. But they were wise enough to know that they could not hope to remain unspoiled forever; they knew that the conflict and darkness which had spread inexorably throughout all of Gibrion's realms of late would reach their lands before too long, and the fine weaponry they produced and quietly stockpiled was a testament to their foresight and the inherent caution of the city leaders.

While Tyan fit in comfortably with the human and dwarf population, were one to overlook the dirt and viscera he had not entirely managed to rid his clothes of, Gael and Ruli made for a conspicuous duo indeed as they followed Tyan through the cobbled streets with hoods raised and keen eyes and senses on full alert.

"We need to get out of the open, Tyan, and quickly," Gael cautioned through clenched teeth.

"Relax, we're perfectly safe here. Don't worry," the human replied, not settling Gael's nerves one bit. "I've been here once or twice over the years. Adenironians aren't known for starting fights."

"I thought they were loyal to Vinadan," said Ruli in little more than a whisper. Tyan flashed a knowing smile in the barren's direction.

"Well, they are *officially,* but… Come on, keep up; there's someone I'd like you to meet." Ruli and Gael both trusted Tyan; he had come through for them time and again. He had saved each of their lives on more than one occasion these last months, and they were going to have to trust him again. They had left their forces camped within the shelter of the woods. The mountains stood as silent, dark guardians watching over their forces, and there they remained whilst their captains entered the city as a trio. Later, the men and women huddled among the trees would no doubt light fires and pass round skins of elven wine while they awaited the return of their captains. For now, Tyan, Gael, and Ruli pressed on into the city to seek shelter, food, and – with the luck of the Goddesses on their side – allies.

Ruli dared to raise his eyes and his head a little higher, risking a better look at his surroundings. Even beneath his hood he could clearly hear the mingled sounds of laughter, bartering, and the occasional spot of questionable street poetry. To their left, a trio of human men who looked as if they could be brothers entertained a small but growing crowd. One played the lute with both skill and showmanship; one beat an elaborate looking drum, while the third performed a curious dance which Ruli could only assume was a human peculiarity. The melodious cadence of market vendors peddling their wares filled the air and assaulted the senses. It was busy in Adeniron, but it was pleasant too, lacking the urgency, ruggedness, and undercurrent of danger which beset many market towns. The cobbles underfoot were of a pinkish hue, and as he looked up, Ruli noticed that most of the buildings which hemmed them in on both sides were of a similar colour and texture. The architecture was impressive to behold, and the skill and passion which had been poured into both the design and construction of the shops, libraries, guild halls, and homesteads was clear. Whether it was the pleasantness of his surroundings, the intoxicating mixture of voices and music, or the tantalising aroma of spices and freshly baked bread swirling in the air, Ruli lowered his hood and shook out his hair. Rather than the stares, frowns, and physical abuse he had been expecting, the sight of a barren in these parts was met instead with smiles, nods of greeting, and even the occasional suggestive wink. Gael, on the other hand, was not so quick to lower her guard, and she nudged Ruli hard in the ribs to get his attention.

"Cover yourself, Ruli. We are not safe here, despite what Tyan says."

"Hey, leave him alone, Gael, and try to relax," said Tyan, turning back and stopping to stare at the elves. "We're far safer here than we were out in the wild. There are *numbers* here - and weapons. Most importantly, unlike Markosh or even Torimar now, there are no orrecs. Okay?"

Gael sighed deeply, and blew out her frustration in a calming breath.

"Okay. Yes, I'm sorry. You know what they say: *once a soldier, always a soldier.*" She smiled and lowered her own hood, and was immediately soothed by the feel of the sun on the back of her neck.

"Okay, good. Now come on, it'll soon be midday and we have a lot to do; I just hope she's still here," said Tyan, the last part more to himself than to his companions.

"Who, Tyan? Who are we looking for?" asked Ruli, following closely at Tyan's heels.

"Pilmer," Tyan replied with a grin, as he pointed upwards at a wooden sign hanging above the doorway to a busy, bustling inn.

"*Pilmer's Anvil*?" Tyan, I'm not sure about this," said Gael, the look on her face saying more than her words. But Tyan was already heading inside, with Ruli in close attendance. Gael shook her head in resignation and followed them in. To Gael's surprise, it was actually quite pleasant inside. Her keen elven eyes did not need long to adjust from the sunlight outside to the more muted ambient light inside, but once they had done so she noticed at first how clean and tidy everything was. The floors, seating, tables, and bar were all of a deep, dark wood, very old but well maintained by the looks of it, and the air did not share that same sticky, bitter taste that pervaded most of the taverns and inns she had visited during her long years. The clientele, too, were cut from a different cloth than the usual assortment of thugs and scoundrels she had come to associate with inns. Their clothes were bright and their smiles genuine, and rather than greedy, furtive glances and hostile glares she sensed only welcome and courtesy here.

And it unsettled her for reasons she could not quite put her finger on.

Tyan and Ruli were already at the bar, and Gael could almost feel Tyan's excitement and relief as the human barkeep handed him a large, cold, frothy beer. She watched in mild amusement as Tyan paid the man and took his first, long gulp, before wiping the froth from his stubble with the back of his hand. She joined her companions at the bar and ordered a small glass of red wine, the same as Ruli's. Taking her first sip, she had to admit it tasted wonderful, and she felt good to be doing something so... *normal*. None of the trio spoke as they sat and savoured their drinks. In their own way, they each revelled in this chance to relax, to let their guard down for even a brief moment; to just *enjoy* something.

How long has it been? Seven, eight months? Maybe longer, Gael thought as she sipped her wine. Ever since the murder of Lady Keya and the massacre at Eonis, Gael had known only conflict, fear, death, and suspicion. Vinadan's shape-shift had fooled them all, and Keya had allowed him to walk straight into the orb chamber…

Montagor indeed, she thought, clenching her teeth and gripping her glass a little too tightly. *No, stop it*, she shook her head and banished her regret. She turned to see Ruli staring pointedly at her, the question of whether she was okay not needing to be given voice. She gave a curt nod and cleared her throat.

"So, what's the plan?" she asked.

"Well, first I'm going to finish this beer, order another, and then go and speak to Pilmer," Tyan replied.

"Is she here?" asked Ruli, casting a glance around the inn. He saw a tall, red haired woman sitting in the corner speaking to a dwarf whose back was turned. Off to the left, another human female in a floral yellow dress sipped an orange drink from a tumbler as she laughed with a handsome young man. To the right sat a group of four: two male dwarves and two human women. From the way they spoke to one another, Ruli got the impression they were more likely colleagues than close friends. A party of dwarves took up a whole table in the centre of the room, and they paid no mind to Ruli, Gael, and Tyan. They busied themselves with an elaborate game involving decks of beautifully illustrated cards, dice of varying colours, shapes, and denominations, and an intricately crafted pewter dragon. This coveted figurine currently sat in the centre of the table, but it was occasionally claimed by one of the players at the roll of a die or the playing of a particular card.

"Yes, she's been here the whole time," said Tyan. "Please, just be patient. And don't worry, I know what I'm doing."

Gael nodded and took another drink, reminding herself once again to trust in Tyan. *And try to relax*. The thought came quite unbidden, as if it originated from the mind of another. Her train of thought was interrupted by a loud cheer, and the trio turned as one to see one of the dwarves at the main table holding the pewter dragon in the air, as his friends shook their heads and threw their cards down onto the table in anger.

"Another game?" the victorious dwarf asked his companions, placing the dragon back into the centre of the table.

"I'm glad you're having fun, lads, but do try to keep the noise down; Here, I thought *Dragon's Destiny* was a gentleman's game," said the dwarf sitting in the corner opposite the red-haired human lady, in a playfully admonishing tone. Ruli was surprised to hear a wholly feminine voice issue from the bearded dwarven face, and both her shape and the grace with which she moved left little doubt as to her gender as she walked across the room to collect the dwarven gamers' empty glasses.

"Sorry, Pilmer," said one dwarf.

"Yeah, sorry Pilmer; just got a bit carried away," added another.

"It's okay, lads," Pilmer smiled; "same again?"

The dwarven proprietor made her way back behind the bar and set the glasses down with a rattle. Looking up, she noticed her three newest patrons for the first time, and let out a resigned – and intentionally melodramatic - sigh.

"Well shave my chinstrap and tell me I'm a hoblin; if it isn't Tyan of Markosh. To what do I owe this unexpected pleasure?

Tyan looked up and gestured toward Pilmer, as if noticing her for the first time. "Oh, Pilmer! I didn't see you there," he said, utterly unconvincingly, "how've you been?" Pilmer merely shook her head and let out a small snort of derision. "You didn't see me, huh? Okay… Let's go with that. What can I do for you Tyan?" she asked, already filling the other dwarves' glasses anew. Tyan took a breath and adopted an altogether more serious tone, and his change in demeanour gave pause to Pilmer's banter.

"We need a place to stay tonight, in truth. And there might be one or two other things I'll need to ask for, old friend."

Pilmer set the glass she had just finished refilling onto the bartop, and folded her arms. She fixed Tyan with a stare, not a playful or a dramatic stare, but one of ruefulness and concern.

"I heard what happened at Markosh, Tyan. It's good to see you're okay." The human merely nodded in gratitude but did not speak in reply.

"So few made it out, I heard," Pilmer continued, "Callie?"

A short, curt shake of the head was the answer she received this time.

"*Curses*," Pilmer spat through gritted teeth, slamming her fist down onto the bar and sending one or two of the glasses rattling to the floor. "Aether spit! Those fucking…" she took a deep breath, trying to swallow her anger. "I'm so sorry, Tyan. Those orrecs…"

She trailed off, lost for words, and instead turned to get a better look at Gael and Ruli, and learned all that she needed to know by their slumped shoulders and the distant looks in their tired eyes.

"Where have you been?" Pilmer asked the trio. "What are you doing? You look... Well, you don't look great, I have to say."

"Honestly? We've just been trying to survive out there," replied Tyan with a slow shake of his head. "We've been on the road for months, just trying to do *what* we can *where* we can. We ran into an orrec raiding party heading south from Elgiroth. We tried to find out where they were headed, but ran into a bit of a dead end. We think they had the Ears in mind, so we mean to press on toward Earon, maybe Eldon if we can get across the water."

"Just the three of you?" said Pilmer, failing to keep incredulity from her voice.

"No, there are more of us. Men and elves. They're not here, but they're not far. I thought it might be okay if we used the barn tonight."

Pilmer bit down on the friendly jibe which rose so naturally to her lips, and merely nodded in response.

"I was hoping you had rooms here, too. Two would be fine; Ruli and I can flip a kreon to see who takes the bed and who takes the floor." Again, Pilmer nodded her assent.

"Are you hungry?" asked the dwarf. "You all look like you could use a good meal."

"I'd love to," replied Tyan, "but I can't stay. See to it that these two get whatever they need, and just add it to my tab." He winked, trying to break the tension which had arisen so precipitously.

"*Tab*. Right," Pilmer said with a wry grin. "Where are you going?" Tyan stood and drained his beer in one long gulp, then placed his hands on his hips and exhaled heavily. "I think it's time I paid Gracen a visit." Pilmer's eyebrows shot up in surprise.

"Gracen? Do you think that's a good idea?" she asked.

"No, of course not. In fact I'd go so far as to say it's a terrible idea, but what choice do I have?"

*

As the tall and imposing trees came more clearly into view, Malgorth held up a fist to halt Agnaz. He stood for a moment and shuddered in disgust at the warm prickle of the midday sun on his shoulders.

"What is it, Commander?" asked his companion.

"Can you not smell that, Agnaz? Ignore the vegetation, and go beyond the stream," Malgorth instructed the scout, all the while sniffing intently at the air. Agnaz dutifully obeyed his commander. He closed his eyes and joined Malgorth in sniffing first at the air, and then at the wet grass underfoot, picking up the occasional rock or stone for inspection and scrutiny. His eyes suddenly sprung open in realisation.

"Elves, Commander…. And men!"

"Well done, Agnaz, but there is more. Go deeper, though you may not be accustomed to this particular scent." Agnaz resumed his sniffing, and licked at a pebble or two for good measure, until he did indeed nod in agreement with his commander.

"There *is* something else, my commander, but to my shame I can't place it."

"There is no shame to bear, Agnaz. It is a rare orrec indeed who would recognise the scent of an Ehronian."

"Ehronian, Commander?"

"*Barrens*, Agnaz. It would seem that elves, men, and barrens await us in Adeniron." Malgorth smiled, and the pair resumed their march, redoubling their pace as they headed toward the tall and imposing trees.

*

Tyan was quite sure that Ruli and Gael were in the process of being regaled with embarrassing tales of fist fights and drunken flirtation; Pilmer had never let him forget one or two of his more questionable moments, and he knew that a good laugh at Tyan's expense would be the dwarf's way of breaking the ice and making the elven pair feel welcome and a little more at ease. The sun was high in the sky and Tyan savoured its warmth. He knew all too well that each step on the bright, cobbled streets led him inexorably toward an altogether colder reception.

He had not seen Gracen in years, not since he was last in Adeniron enjoying Pilmer's hospitality to its fullest. He was a different man, back then; his days full of foolishness and drinking with equally foolish men. Everything changed with Leandra, and everything changed *again* with Callie.

Callie, who looked so much like the mother she never really knew.mCallie, who would smile and laugh as she played with the family dogs.

Callie… No. Not now. Get your head in the game, Tyan.

His knuckles were white, and a vein stood out against his temple as he clenched his teeth and forcibly evicted the memories which had bubbled unbidden to the surface of his consciousness. He wasn't even aware of the tear which had escaped his eye, and he wiped it away in anger as he pressed on through the pleasant and familiar streets. He half hoped Gracen would not be in the city hall at all today, and that the ugly scene which was bound to ensue with the man would be avoided. But Tyan knew deep down that Gracen would be there.

He always is, Tyan thought. *Honourable and dutiful to the last, that one.*

It wasn't long before he reached the front doors of the city hall; as the seat of governance in Adeniron, the building was even more lavish than the rest of the uniformly impressive city. The two guards stood stoically at the top of the steps which elevated the hall – somewhat symbolically - just a little bit above the rest of the city. As Tyan approached, he forced a polite and genial expression as he bade good day to the guards and made to simply walk past them into the municipal building.

"Halt; who are you?" said one of the guards, his outstretched palm barring Tyan's way.

"I have business inside today," replied Tyan, as conversationally as he could.

"I don't recognise you. What business do you have here?" the guard countered, assessing Tyan top to toe. Tyan suddenly became aware once more of the dirt and blood upon his clothes, and the altogether dishevelled appearance he was presenting amongst the finely clothed and majestically adorned denizens. He dropped the forced display of joviality and sighed.

"Look, I must speak with Alderman Gracen; it is very important that I see him, and now."

"The alderman is not taking visitors today, especially unannounced visitors of such *vulgarity*." Tyan allowed himself a wry smile at the slight, but did not rise to the bait.

"I'll tell you what," said Tyan, trying to inject an edge of venom into his tone, "I'll wait here with one of you fine gentlemen, while the other goes inside and speaks to Alderman Gracen. Tell him Ty- no, wait; tell him *it's about Callie.*"

The guards exchanged a quick glance before the one to Tyan's right shook his head in resignation and disappeared indoors. It was not so much a blatant staring contest as it was an awkward mutual appraisal as Tyan and the remaining guard stood facing each other in silence for what seemed like an hour, but what couldn't have been any more than three or four minutes. The door was eventually - and somewhat abruptly - thrown open, and the returning guard motioned for Tyan to follow him. In Tyan went, passing down a long corridor adorned with portraits of Adeniron's former leaders, and with grand tapestries telling stories of Gibrion's past. To Tyan's left, he beheld an intricate and stunningly beautiful tapestry depicting three Goddesses, each standing before a sphere which seemed to glow, despite being captured in this instance in silks and cottons. The Goddesses appeared to be descending toward the land below, drawing ever closer to the figures beneath them; figures on their knees with their arms outstretched and their heads lowered to the very earth in deference. Tyan had heard the tales, and marvelled now at the depiction of the Goddesses and the ancient Souls which some still believed to be the last vestiges, the actual physical remains of the Goddesses themselves. To his right hung a tapestry of an altogether different sort. Here he beheld a scene equally exquisite in its execution, but which elicited a deep dread in the pit of Tyan's stomach. He was not expecting to flinch, but flinch he did as he beheld the representation of the bright streets, the fountain, the grand steps flanked by towering, kingly statues, and the white marble citadel of Ondellion. Tyan had never been to Aclevion, but recognised the iconography immediately. Even were he not to, the figure which stood at the top of the steps with its arms raised high above his head, outstretched toward the glowing Soul so delicately recreated in thread, and seeming to cast its strange light onto his long white hair, even in such a facsimile as this, would have given away the location of this scene at once.

Vinadan. The thought struck like a poison arrow through his heart. An arrow not dissimilar to the one that…

"Hurry up. This way," commanded the guard, turning left down another corridor which terminated in a grand door of varnished walnut; it too was flanked by a pair of guards. Upon a nod from Tyan's escort, the door was opened and Tyan was led inside. The man sitting behind a desk almost as impressive as the walnut door, was of grim countenance, and his sigh did nothing to lighten the tension as he laid down his quill with more than a touch of melodrama.

"Guard; leave us," he said without looking up.

"But, my lord-" the guard protested, his eyes flicking between his master and the bedraggled visitor – or *prisoner*, depending on how you looked at it.

"I will not say it again," Gracen's voice was firm now as he met the guard's eyes; a barely-contained fury burned behind his own.

"Very good, my lord." The guard bowed low and left the room, but not without one last, very pointed glare in Tyan's direction. Once the door was closed and the two men were alone, the room fell silent but for the sound of their steady breathing. For a while the stalemate ensued, but the alderman finally broke the silence.

"*It's about Callie*, my guard told me. At first, I thought he must have made a mistake; I thought he must have misheard, but when he described the bearer of the message, well, I had to see for myself." Tyan did not reply as he knew from experience that Gracen was not yet finished, and that his pause was simply for dramatic effect. .."*It's about Callie*. You are a disgrace, Tyan; you are truly a disgrace, and in that much you have not changed a bit." Tyan was not fazed by the other's words, and met the alderman's gaze with a stern look of his own.

"Oh, come now Gracen," he said, "is that any way to greet your little brother?"

"Brother? No, Tyan. You gave up the right to call me that a long time ago. And now you come here, to *my* place of work, to *my* town, and use your daughter - my niece - as what? Some sort of password to gain access? A bargaining chip? Or were you merely attempting to get a rise out of me?" Gracen leaned back in his seat and appraised Tyan with narrowed eyes.

"I heard about Markosh, Tyan," he continued, his voice a little softer now, "I have eyes and ears across all of Gibrion. I know that only a handful made it out alive, and I also know that no children were among the fortunate. I *know* Callie is dead, and I curse you for using her name so cheaply in order to gain access to my offices." Tyan did not rise to the bait, but stood stoic and resolute before the alderman; before Gracen; before his older brother.

"Callie *is* dead, Gracen," he said at length, "you are quite right. She died, like so many others, at the hands of orrecs - Vinadan's orrecs - who came south from Elgiroth with nothing in mind but slaughter." His eyes became glassy as he spoke, and his voice betrayed a quiver despite his best efforts to keep his fraught emotions in check.

"I tried, Gracen," he continued, steeling himself, wrapping his heart in armour more splendid than that of the elves, and more reliant than that of the dwarves. "I held her in my arms as her lifeblood ebbed from her broken body, and her eyes darkened. I stroked her hair and touched her face; I told her everything was going to be okay, that *she* was going to be okay. I told her that she would be running around the yard, laughing, chasing the dogs before the sun set and the stars shone bright." He paused to wipe away the tears which now fell openly upon his ashen face.

"She was already missing an arm by this point, brother, and I tried in vain to keep her gaze fixed on me, and away from the two barbed arrows which had pierced her through. She died not with hope in her heart, not with dreams of happiness and laughter, not even with resolve or acceptance; no, she died with terror in her eyes and horror etched upon her soft, beautiful face. I can only thank Hemera that Leandra did not live to see her daughter carved into pieces upon the ground."

Tears now traced their glistening lines down Gracen's cheeks.

"Tyan, I -" he began.

"And you know the worst part?" Tyan continued, not letting his brother interject. "We couldn't even bury the dead. We had to leave; we got out of there as fast as we could, and we could not look back. Some, I saw, made for the cover of the trees, hoping the evening shade would offer some small protection from orrec arrows and bolts. I don't know if they made it. I try not to think of what became of all those poor souls who died where they fell. They are likely hanging from the city gates right now, if they were not simply left to rot."

Tyan snorted a mirthless laugh. "Do you think it's too much to hope that even orrecs show compassion to the dead? So yes, Gracen, *brother*: this *is* about Callie."

The men once again shared a long, sorrowful silence, staring into each other's bloodshot eyes as if trying to work out a puzzle or solve some abstract riddle. At length, Gracen exhaled heavily and spoke.

"What are you doing here, Tyan? Why did you come to me?"

"Honestly? I'm not entirely certain. Is it too far-fetched to imagine that I just wanted to see my brother?" He tried to keep his bottom lip from quivering; he would not allow Gracen that victory. This time it was Gracen's turn to snort in derision.

"Frankly, Tyan; *yes*. Yes, that is rather hard to believe."

"Look, Gracen. I am not alone here – though you probably already knew that before I even arrived at your pretty door." Gracen merely inclined his head in confirmation of Tyan's suspicions. "We have numbers, and weapons. We mean to head south toward Earon, maybe Eldon. We can't be sure, but we think The Three Ears may have been the orrecs' ultimate target in the south. We have to warn the elves, reinforce them even, if it comes to that. We need your help."

"Why?" Gracen replied, simply.

"Why *what*?"

"Why do you feel the need to warn the elves? What concern is it of yours? I should think that, having barely escaped one massacre, marching willingly into another would be the furthest thing from even *your* mind. And - more to the point - how in the name of Hemera does it concern *me*?"

Tyan could not hide his confusion. "Of course I want to warn them! If they are in danger, they must know!"

"But you don't know for certain that the orrecs were even heading toward The Three Ears in the first place?"

"Well, no but… What else can we do, Gracen? Stay here and do nothing? Sit behind a grand desk in a majestic hall, surrounded by guards, meeting with artisans and troubadours, commissioning new tapestries and portraits? What's next, Gracen, a full-sized statue of Vinadan cast in solid gold in the city square? If you would but send a messenger south to warn the-"

Gracen had heard enough, and nearly knocked over his inkwell as he stood up to his full height and slammed his hands down onto his desk.

"Fool! Ever you act the fool, Tyan; *brother-mine*. Do you think me blind? Do you think me idle? Do you consider me a loyalist? A zealot? I know exactly what Vinadan is, what he has done. I know his spite, his vile armies, his devotees. But I also know of his power, and I know of his fury. Would you have Adeniron be the next Eonis? The next Markosh? These artists and minstrels you speak of; the poets and the pipers you openly mock; would you see them suffer the same fate as Lord Thyrus and the dwarves of Torimar? No, Tyan; we are not blind, we are not idle, but neither are we so eager to court open war as you. We have peace here, Tyan; we have a good and rare thing which I, for one, mean to preserve. I do not labour under the illusion that Adeniron will be free and prosperous forever. I know that we will likely face occupation by Vinadan's orrecs one day. We may even need to take up arms and defend ourselves. *One day*, maybe. But not today, Tyan." He sat back down and folded his arms across his chest; a gesture of finality if ever Tyan had seen one.

"I will not help you," Gracen said simply, quietly, "this meeting is over." He rang a single chime from the small bell which sat upon his desk and, taking the quill back out of the inkwell, continued his work with not so much as another glance to spare at Tyan. The guards – all three, Tyan noted – entered the room within seconds and made no pretence of cordiality as they jostled him out of the room and practically marched him out of the building and practically threw him back out onto the streets of Adeniron once more. Tyan stood for a long moment, his hands firmly planted upon his hips. He felt some small comfort at the prickling of the sun's heat upon his face, and he remained in place, struggling to quiet his mind and calm his breathing. At length, the multitude of passers-by became a single, formless mass as he allowed his focus to falter, and the world around him seemed to shift, subtly, into a kaleidoscope of colour and sound as he let his eyes blur.

Fearing he would be lost forever in this dream-state if he did not put one foot in front of the other, he blew out a breath and blinked his eyes back into focus .

I need a drink; *a very big drink*, he thought as he turned and set off once more in the direction of Pilmer's Anvil.

Chapter Seventeen

Though it was still bright and warm, the trees provided much-needed cool and shade as Malgorth and Agnaz slowly picked their way through the woods; their keen senses were on full alert as they strode purposefully toward Adeniron. Neither orrec spoke as they moved; they turned west initially, then abruptly halted at Malgorth's signal and headed north for a time. Both orrecs sniffed the air and picked up seemingly random pieces of foliage which would have seemed nondescript to others, but which told a very clear story to the orrecs. Malgorth once more held up a fist to stall their progress and signalled for Agnaz to keep low as they traversed the next section of woods – the elves and men were close.

Agnaz cast a determined look to his commander; he gestured toward his weapons, then nodded eagerly in the general direction of the encampment, clearly spoiling for a fight. Malgorth answered Agnaz's expression with one of reproach; he shook his head, pointed to himself and then to Agnaz, and held up two fingers. He motioned next toward the encampment, then signalled his belief that there must be two-hundred men and elves hidden by the trees, not far from their current position. No, stealth would serve them best here, not a reckless assault against overwhelming odds. Malgorth did allow himself a fleeting grin at his companion's eagerness, foolhardy and strategically unwise though it may be.

We would probably run them close in all fairness, he thought, and they resumed their progress through the woods keeping a respectful distance from the encampment. It was not long before the trees began to thin and the assorted vegetation beneath their feet gave way to more uniform soft grasses. The orrecs cast glances to-and-fro as they crossed the small area of open land which terminated in the quaint and colourful structures of Adeniron. They had soon made their way onto the cobbled city streets, into the cacophony of voices and music in the marketplace, abandoning all pretence of stealth now that they had passed safely beyond the forces stationed in the woods. Their honed senses were assaulted by the aromas of bread and spices which almost – not quite, but *almost* – covered the scent of the man, elf, and barren they had tracked this far. Malgorth had to admit that the denizens of Adeniron were so far doing an impressive job of keeping both their surprise and fear from bubbling to the surface. Though men and dwarves alike openly turned and looked at the orrecs, they did so with a genial collective countenance, punctuated with the odd smile, nod, and one or two proclamations of "good day!" thrown in for good measure.

The orrecs knew this to be mere window dressing, a feigned cordiality which the very air betrayed. The scent of fear; the pheromones and perspiration which permeated each breath taken by the commander and the scout, confirmed what they had been expecting: the appearance of orrecs in Adeniron had sent a murmur of disquiet through the city like ripples upon the surface of a newly disturbed pond. Malgorth did not delight in this dissonance as his companion did; he had a purpose here, and inciting further panic would only serve to slow him down. He cast a cautioning glance at Agnaz, who immediately brought his grin under control. The orrecs strode purposefully along the cobbled streets toward the city centre, looking left and right as they went, surveying the scene and noting all possible points of ingress and egress - soldiers to the last. At length they arrived at the central marketplace and approached a small, quiet cobbler's stall.

"Good day, tradesman," said Malgorth with a sharp nod. To his credit, the cobbler did not flinch nor cower at the approach of the imposing and heavily armed orrecs.

"And a fine day it is, um…?" he replied, intoning for the orrecs to identify themselves.

"*Commander*. Commander Malgorth of Elgiroth, servant of Prince Vinadan. For the might of Aclevion."

"For the might of Aclevion, indeed, commander Malgorth. How can a lowly cobbler such as I be of assistance to one such as you?" The cobbler's smile appeared genuine. That's the funny thing about appearances…

"I must send a message," stated Malgorth, choosing to ignore the deftly-veiled slight; there would be time enough later to make an example of this fool. "You must point me in the direction of your leadership."

"Leadership, Commander? You'll need Alderman Gracen. He's based in the city hall. So, what you'll need to do is go down this main street, turn left…"

Once the cobbler had finished providing directions, Malgorth thanked him for his time and the orrecs resumed their journey through the town, more aware than ever of eyes on their backs and whispers trailing in their wake. The sight of a quick nudge in the ribs followed by a not-so-subtle nod in their direction was commonplace among the citizens as the orrecs departed the crowded market. The throngs began to thin as the orrecs moved against the general flow of foot traffic, and they soon found themselves at their destination. Climbing the steps without breaking stride, Malgorth and Agnaz were immediately stopped in their tracks by the outstretched palms of two guards.

"Halt there; state your business."

Malgorth could almost feel Agnaz's impatience bubbling to the surface. He flicked a warning glance at the scout, and stepped forward to speak to the guards, once again demonstrating diplomacy uncommon in his species.

"We seek an audience with Alderman Gracen, your master. We would be grateful if you were to allow us passage without further unnecessary delay." The guards were taken aback by the orrec's cordiality, and exchanged a brief glance which betrayed their bewilderment.

"Is the alderman expecting you?"

Malgorth snorted a mirthless laugh.

"Sooner or later, I don't doubt. Now step aside, good guardsmen."

The guards did not give way, and seemed to regain their wits and their courage in the face of the towering orrecs.

"Now hold on a moment; Alderman Gracen does not usually accept unsolicited visitors, especially-"

"Orrecs? Especially orrecs?" interjected Agnaz, not without a hint of menace in his tone.

"I will make this very simple, guardsmen," said Malgorth, "we will see the alderman – and now – or Prince Vinadan himself will learn of your disobedience. You *do* serve our glorious Prince, do you not?" Malgorth could smell the guards' emerging sweat, and could almost hear their hearts beating rapidly in their chests.

"Y…Yes, of course. For the might of Aclevion," one of the guards stammered. "Permit me to announce your arrival; who do I have the pleasure of introducing to the alderman?"

"Commander Malgorth, and Scout Captain Agnaz; emissaries of Elgiroth.

"Very good, Commander; follow me."

At length the orrecs were shown to Alderman Gracen's office and found the man red-faced and agitated. He stood at their entry and offered a short, curt nod.

"Greetings, Commander Malgorth, Captain Agnaz. I must say I was surprised to hear of your unexpected arrival. How may I be of assistance?"

"You seem a little on edge, Alderman," said Malgorth, "are we inconveniencing you?"

"No, not at all Commander. I'm just a little distracted today - family troubles, you know the type."

"No, I do not."

"Well…. Never mind that," Gracen replied, his cheeks turning as red as his hair, "what brings you to Adeniron?"

"What brings us to Adeniron, and what brings us to *you* are quite different matters, Alderman. I require you to send a message. Do you still use birds for such tasks?"

"We use birds, mainly. But we do have runners if the message is of a particularly sensitive or urgent nature."

"A runner it is then, Alderman. I would not trust a bird with a message destined for Aclevion, much less one which is to be placed into the hand of Prince Vinadan himself. Too many spies around, you see. Spies; malcontents; rebels."

It was all Gracen could do to keep the fear from announcing itself upon his face, and he held his emotions in check by the skin of his teeth.

"A message to Prince Vinadan, you say? Of course, Commander. For the might of Aclevion." Gracen took a fresh piece of parchment from his desk drawer and dipped his quill into the dark inkwell. "What would you like the message to say?" he asked, trying to appear as unconcerned as possible. Malgorth grinned and waved a finger in Gracen's direction.

"Oh, I think not, Alderman. Hand me the quill and parchment."

Gracen did not immediately do as instructed. "Now, hold on one moment, Commander," Gracen said, rediscovering some of his courage. "This is my office, and you are in my city. If a message is to be sent to the capital from within my walls, I have a right to know of its contents." A moment, mere seconds in truth, stretched out to an eternity between Gracen and Malgorth in deathly silence. Not even Agnaz dared to breathe too loudly lest he trample upon the silent battle of wills unfolding before him. At last, it was Malgorth who broke the deadlock.

"Indeed, Alderman, indeed. You are of course quite correct. Perhaps you *should* hear what I deem so urgent that from my lips to the Prince's own ear must it go. I will dictate, you will scribe."

Malgorth clutched his hands together behind his back and commenced pacing back and forth in front of Gracen's desk. He cleared his throat dramatically, and gave voice to his intended message.

My Prince, I write from Adeniron with urgent tidings.

Though the campaign in Markosh was a resounding success, the southbound party are slain. Myself and Scout Captain Agnaz came upon them following a brief sojourn with the Markosh garrison, and have determined an ambush.

While the confirmation of elves and men is unlikely to surprise your Lordship, I can also confirm a third interest among the number of the murdering traitors.

It would appear that the barrens of Ehronia have come forth, and are now allied with the elves and men. Of dwarves I have as yet discovered no trace, but their involvement in this act of treason cannot be wholly discounted at this stage.

If it pleases my Lord, I request that a legion be sent south from the capital to march on Ehronia, reinforced by a contingent from Elgiroth who will make all haste to join them without delay.

If, in your infinite and unparalleled wisdom, you see fit to spare a number of brothers from the great and powerful order of the Asarlai, their presence in

Ehronia would undoubtedly serve to quell any and all acts of open rebellion against the crown.

Scout Captain Agnaz and I will make for Ehronia at once to perform what reconnaissance we can, and we must assume the local garrison betrayed and eliminated.

I would also request a battalion be sent to Adeniron to stand in stewardship of the city, as I cannot rule out Alderman Gracen and the ruling council as sympathisers and collaborators.

For the might of Aclevion.

Gracen had lost all of his former colour and appeared as white as a spectre as he looked up at Malgorth; his shaking hand dropped small flecks of ink onto the parchment below.

"Now, wait just one-" he began, but was not permitted to finish his sentence.

"Alderman Gracen, we have travelled far and have seen much. We fight, we kill, we bleed, we claim… and we *track*. I have not spoken a dishonest word in your presence, and would not be so foolish as to lie to Prince Vinadan. We did discover our kin slain, we did confirm the involvement of your kind in the ambush. More importantly, there was one particular scent which we have tracked to this city; this building; *this very office.* And judging by your present demeanour and your earlier reference to *family troubles*, my only conclusion must be that at least one of the traitors is not only of your kind, but of your very *bloodline*."

Gracen stood up and looked Malgorth in the eye, his heart bursting with a newfound fire and resolve.

"I will see to it that your message reaches the capital unspoiled," he said through gritted teeth. "Was there anything else, *Commander*?" He held the orrec's gaze, unwavering in the face of the towering orrec.

"No," Malgorth replied simply. "That will be all, Alderman. It is unlikely you and I will cross paths again, but you should know this: defy Aclevion, take up arms against my kin, or utter so much as a black whisper against your Prince, and I will have your head - I will *personally* have your head."

The door slammed shut behind the orrecs, and Gracen fell into his chair and slammed his fist into his desk, breaking the skin and spraying blood across his assorted papers.

"Guard!" he called, and one of his men entered at once.

"Yes, Alderman?"

"The man who was here earlier, my brother; find him at once! Send a man - no, two men - to every inn, pub, gambling den, and bath house within our borders. Find him, and deliver him a message."

"Yes, my lord. What is the message?"

"It is quite simple," Gracen said with fury in his voice.

"They know. Get out."

Chapter Eighteen

Xeb had considered whether his decision had been made based on some misguided sense of guilt or obligation, or perhaps to allay his own suspicions. Deep down, however, he knew that he had allowed Fennet to accompany him back to Frostpeak because he had actually started to grow fond of the hoblin.

And I could use the company, he admitted to himself. The unlikely pair had left Ugnor and the hoblin enclave on foot and were making good time across the open lands, heading north-east toward the mountains and the promise of bed and board at The Cold Shoulder Inn. For Xeb, at least.

"Fennet, you do understand that I cannot allow you to accompany me into Frostpeak itself, yes? They would kill us both before we could utter a word of explanation."

"Yes, Master Xebus; of course," the little hoblin replied, nodding enthusiastically. "I'll just wait outside," he added with neither a hint of irony nor a flicker of sarcasm in his tone.

"Please, Fennet, don't call me that – *Xeb* is fine. And you'll 'wait outside' will you? All night? In the rain? Do not be foolish. I spotted a small farm on the outskirts; there was a barn, I seem to remember. You would have to make certain not to be seen by the owners, but the barn should serve you better than simply *waiting outside*."

"If you are sure, Mas - erm; if you are sure, Xeb."

"Yes I'm sure. I will come to you at daybreak; with a little luck and a Frostpeak ale or two inside my belly, I should have our next move planned before you wake."

"What are our options?"

Xeb smiled at the hoblin, not failing to notice the use of the word "our" nor the earnest expression Fennet wore.

"I am troubled, in truth," said Xeb, shaking his head. "Gibrion is wide, and at Frostpeak we sit upon a nexus of opportunities, each one a potentially pivotal thread in the web of fate we seek to cast about us. Our path will - or will not - present itself, for good or ill, at the mere roll of the dice."

"So what you're saying is that you have no idea where to go next," replied Fennet. It was not a question. This time Xeb allowed himself to laugh a little.

"Yes, Fennet, that forms the crux of my conundrum. The south-east is the domain of the elves, who have already suffered terribly at the hands of Prince Vinadan. Eonis licks its wounds and attempts to rebuild, relying heavily on the ports at Olon, Earon, and Eldon for materials and food. I cannot discount these lands as potential targets for Vinadan and his armies. Further inland we must consider Jo'Thuun, Haneth, Undon, even the barrens of Ehronia are not to be overlooked, especially after… well, never mind that." Xeb trailed off and resumed his ruminations in silence for a while. Fennet did not interrupt him as they continued to traverse the vast open plains which lay between the mountain ranges which towered east and west. Onward to Frostpeak and The Cold Shoulder.

The sun was just beginning to fade, and their way was now lit not by brilliant golden sunlight, but by a hazy glow which contrasted lazily with the deep shadows inevitably born in its wake. It was within one such shadow, cast by a large rock formation, that Xeb registered a flicker of movement and, careful only to glance out of the corner of his eye, identified a cat.

A scruffy-looking brown cat.

A cat he had crossed paths with before.

An uneasiness began to twist and writhe within his stomach at once. It troubled him to be followed and watched so closely by first the magpie and now the cat. Despite his wisdom and for all his power, he could not say with any certainty whether this sustained interest in his movements was a sign of good or ill.

Still, he thought, trying to be rational in the face of his unease, *the crones have not remained hidden this long by throwing caution to the wind and taking unnecessary risks. Had I suffered as they did, I daresay I would be the same. Go then, Danu, make your report. Tell your masters that I travel north with a hoblin in tow. Let's see what they make of that.*

Fennet's words cut into Xeb's thoughts.

"I'm sorry, Fennet, what did you say?"

"I said *I think I can see the barn.* Look," said Fennet, pointing off a short distance to the east. And he was right. By the light of the receding sun they beheld the farmhouse and the adjacent barn which was to make for Fennet's quarters tonight.

"Excellent," said Xeb, casting a fleeting look back over his shoulder. The cat was nowhere to be seen.

Rather than comfort him, Xeb felt a disquiet at the disappearance of the familiar; he shook the thought free of his head and continued on to stealthily secrete Fennet within the old barn. Before long, Xeb found himself back inside The Cold Shoulder, and was struck by the large number of patrons it now housed.

"He's here; he's back!" went up the call from the bartender, and the best part of fifty heads turned as one to behold the tired and dirty Asarlai as he closed the door behind him with a creak. Word of Xeb's quest had spread quickly, and had even reached the ears of the Mayor who now sat at the bar, nursing a tall, frothy ale. He stood and made his way toward Xeb, offering his outstretched hand in greeting. Xeb could not fail to notice the large golden chain he wore around his neck; a symbol of his office.

"Xebus, of the Asarlai," the man said with a forced exuberance. "What a pleasure it is to make your acquaintance. I am Mayor Ornick." Xeb shook the offered hand and muttered a cordial, if somewhat rote reply.

"How was your expedition? Did you find the hoblins?" Fifty voices began muttering, and fifty heads began nodding.

"Please, gentlefolk," said Xeb, wearily, "at least allow me a seat and a drink first." At his words, all but the elderly and infirm stood and offered their seats, while the barkeep busied himself pouring him a large Frostpeak ale. Xeb accepted a tall stool at the bar, and took the drink without a word of thanks. He drained the ale in one long gulp and practically slammed the tankard down onto the bar; a mere flash of his eyes in the barkeep's direction was enough to see the man scurrying to refill it. Drink replenished and weary legs now free of their burden, Xeb reached beneath his cloak and took out the long, barbed dagger with a golden, skull-shaped pommel. He spun and twirled it theatrically in one hand, and drove the tip down hard into the bartop beside his drink. A collective gasp went up around the room as all gazed upon the blade which had killed the previous mayor and his family; the blade which - until now - had resided upon the belt of a hoblin war chief named Ugnor.

"I found the hoblins," said Xeb to the room at large.

"They will not bother you again."

Mayor Ornick could not bear to look upon the blade which had seen the end of his predecessor any longer.

He swooned, and fainted with a thump.

*

Morning came with neither joy nor the memory of a restful bliss for Xeb, but instead it deigned to cast a long shadow upon him. Sleep had come in fits and starts for the troubled Asarlai, and he had sought guidance from sources other than his own wits. It was early, cold, and dark as he left The Cold Shoulder, and frost crunched underfoot as he made his way toward the barn, wrapped tight in his thick cloak. He approached with caution, employing both stealth and a touch of arcane power to ensure his passage went unnoticed by any but the waiting Fennet. As Xeb entered the barn, he found his hoblin companion wide awake, already prepared for departure, and deep in conversation with a horse.

"…which is why turnips are *infinitely* better than gravel; much less chafing and far fewer infections…"

"Fennet?" Xeb whispered.

"Oh! Master Xebus! Did everything go as planned?" The hoblin's enthusiasm had not faltered despite his night in the barn.

"More or less," Xeb replied cryptically. "Come, we must leave at once." He gestured for Fennet to follow him, but the hoblin's expression gave him pause.

"What is it? What's wrong?" Xeb asked.

"N…nothing is wrong. It's just… it's Florian," stuttered the hoblin, avoiding Xeb's gaze.

"Florian?" replied Xeb, utterly at a loss. "Who in the name of Hemera is Florian?"

"Him!" said Fennet, pointing to the horse. "Can we keep him?"

"What? No, Fennet, we absolutely, categorically cannot keep him. Would you draw attention by stealing a horse from under its owner's noses?"

"Well… no. No, that wouldn't actually help us, would it?" replied the hoblin, wearing a crestfallen expression upon his leathery countenance. He took a deep breath to regain some measure of composure and turned to face the horse.

"Well, Florian, this is it," Fennet said dramatically, a tear forming in one of his beady little eyes. "Goodbye, old friend." The hoblin placed a gentle hand against the horse's face; a gesture which entirely belied the commonly held view that hoblins were mindless, murderous vermin. He turned on his heel with more than a touch of dramatic flair, and followed Xeb out of the barn without looking back at Florian. Before long they were making good time across the open land, with the slowly rising sun just beginning to light their way.

"So, where are we going?" asked Fennet. "Did you decide?" Xeb halted and turned to face his companion.

"Even one such as I cannot entirely predict Vinadan's next move. He is slippery and deceitful to his very bones, and does not follow the rules of ordinary men. Add to that the unpredictable and volatile nature of his orrecs, and we were left with a difficult conundrum, my friend."

"So you still have no idea where we're going," said Fennet, deadpan as ever. Again, it was not a question.

"Ah, now come, Fennet; you give me no credit. I said we *were* left with a conundrum. Sleep did not come easily, even upon a soft bed with food and ale in my belly – I have brought some for you, by the way – so I took another path: I consulted the goddesses."

"Goddesses? You… I don't understand."

"I read the cards; I cast the runestones; I divined the shapes and patterns in fires of my own making." He held out a hand and brought forth a fire which burned within his palm, as the rune for *wisdom* announced itself upon his skin.

"You see? Can you see it?" he asked the hoblin.

"All I can see is a future trip to a healer if you're not careful, master Xeb."

Xeb grinned, and extinguished his flame. "All the signs, all the portents; every whisper, every half-truth and vague, formless future I can discern.. They all point to one place…." Xeb trailed off, his voice growing quiet and his eyes losing focus, as he became enmeshed in his own thoughts; images, feeling, smells, tastes, sounds… all played out like flashes of lightning before his eyes, propelled by the ancient powers of which he was master.

"….which is…?" prompted a hitherto-patient Fennet. Xeb blinked and shook his head, coming back to himself, anchoring his consciousness in the moment once more.

"*Ehronia*, master hoblin. We journey to Ehronia, the land of the barrens."

Chapter Nineteen

"Do they just sit there and play all day?" asked Tyan, pointing his ale in the direction of the dwarves who busied themselves setting up another round of *Dragon's Destiny*. He had not spoken much since his return from Gracen's office, preferring instead to drown his sorrows back at Pilmer's Anvil in as close to a brooding silence as he could get away with. So far, neither Pilmer, Ruli, nor Gael had pressed him much on the details of his clearly unsuccessful meeting with his brother, but all were itching to hear more once Tyan was a little more.... *lubricated*.

"Yes, for the most part," replied Pilmer. "They've - *we've* - had it tough of late. They work hard; they graft, they sweat, and they toil. Many of them lost fathers, sons, brothers, or friends when Vinadan destroyed Thyrus' host on the borders of Eonis. They work hard to rebuild after Thyrus died, to make Torimar strong. They keep busy and do their best to comfort those left behind. Many died that day, but we also lost something else... The scales fell away from our eyes. We know we are vulnerable, now." Pilmer turned sad eyes toward Tyan, Gael, and Ruli, but there was determination there, too; a fiery anger which would burn away her sorrow should it stray too close to the surface. "So yes, I let them stay for as long as they want. They sit at the same table every day, they play a few games, drink a few ales. They're family - each other's, and mine."

"I'm sorry Pilmer, I didn't…" stuttered Tyan, embarrassed at having brought up the subject.

"No, it's fine. If anyone here knows what it's like to lose their kin, it's you, and you," Pilmer added, nodding in Gael's direction. The elf lowered her eyes without replying. "But do not think you can distract me and avoid answering the question, Tyan," continued Pilmer, adding a touch of her famed dwarven resolve to her voice. "What happened in there?"

Tyan took a long, deep breath, and placed his tankard down onto the table. He closed his eyes and lowered his head for a moment, composing himself.

"He will not help us," he began. "My own brother, and he will not lift a finger to help us. Our people, his own flesh and blood lay dead in the streets of Markosh, defiled and spoiled by Vinadan's orrecs, and he busies himself with his papers and his meetings. He is a jester in his own court. We are on our own."

"Why?" asked Gael. "What cause could he possibly hold so dear that he would turn away his own family? He is an appointed official and he refuses aid to the decimated and displaced. *Why*, Tyan?"

Tyan closed his eyes. "Leandra." he said softly.

"What?"

"Leandra, my wife. Callie's mother. Gracen loved her, we both did, but she loved *me*. He will not go to war, will not rouse Adeniron to oppose the Prince Vinadan, will not offer shelter nor provisions to those in need, and will not so much as answer his own brother's request to send a message south, out of pure spite."

"Anger and hatred are flames which are not so easy to extinguish," offered Ruli into the silence which hung thick in the air, before turning his attention once more to his golden wine.

"I always thought the barrens a gentle folk; what do you know of anger and hatred?" asked Pilmer.

"My part in this tale and my place in this company are born of them, Ma'am." replied Ruli. "Ehronia has ever been a land of agriculture, of crops, of harvest. We work to provide food and materials for the rest of Gibrion, and we have made our living that way for as long as I know. What we lack in the arcane arts, we more than make up for in our skill with the scythe and our knowledge of the very soil under our feet." He took a long, slow drink from his wine glass before continuing.

"When Vinadan learned of this, he sent his orrecs to govern and command us. We still work for the same landmasters, but they now answer to the capital and live in constant fear of the orrecs. It's ironic when you think about it; we would have done the work anyway, and done it well, freely, for the prosperity of all, but we are now commanded to do it at the business end of the whip. We suffer, we scramble to save what few kreons are thrown into the dirt before us, whilst the dragon's share heads north to Aclevion." He laughed a little at his own words, as they reminded him of a friend…

"Still, we have each other; faced with such relentless torment, it falls on our friends to keep us on our feet - sometimes quite literally." He drained the last of his wine, and Pilmer motioned to one of her dwarven patrons to pass her the jug which stood on the bar. He did so at once and Pilmer refilled Ruli's glass. Nobody had yet spoken a word to interrupt the young barren.

"There were four of us; myself, Miseldi, Gerdan, and Horith. We would meet every morning on our way to the fields, and then again most every night to drink away the memory of the day. One day, not quite a year ago, I saw Horith sneaking away across the river, away from Ehronia, right under the noses of the orrecs." Ruli smiled at the memory, but his countenance quickly grew stern once more.

"And he was not alone. With him was, as far as I could tell at that time, a mage - human, old and frail he seemed. I had not the slightest idea how their paths might have crossed, nor in which direction their road now lay. But I was pleased, despite my misgivings. Horith was always a rebellious soul and he did not take the oppression of Aclevion lightly. I could only wonder what sort of adventures he might be setting out on in the company of a sorcerer, venturing forth under the cover of the trees."

"Is it Horith you now seek? Is this how your path crossed with theirs?" asked Pilmer, motioning to Tyan and Gael.

"Yes… and no," replied Ruli, inviting an inquisitive look from the dwarf.

"It is indeed how our paths crossed, yes, but I was not entirely honest about my motivations nor my ultimate goal, at first. When I came across Gael and

Tyan's forces, I told them I was looking for a friend, last seen heading north-east into the wildlands. Only later when I revealed Horith's name did Lady Gael tell me of what had befallen at Eonis. In truth, I did not seek Horith. I was not looking for my friend. That he was dead, and had been dead for a good while, I was already certain. It is vengeance I sought. I set out under the cover of night, as he did, and followed Horith's lead across the river and into the wild not to seek a reunion, but to avenge him."

"How, Ruli?" asked Gael, digesting this new information, "how could you possibly have known?"

"I knew, Lady Gael, because I heard him. He spoke my name with his final breath. I heard him as plainly as I hear you now. He called out to me, and there was no hope to be found in his voice; no joy or happiness was there upon the wind which carried his words to my ear. There was only pain, longing, and fear. In that moment, I knew Horith was dead, and I knew at whose black hand he fell."

"Ruli," said Gael slowly as she struggled to reconcile the young barren's words, "what you are saying does not make any sense. Such power has never before been witnessed in your kind. You must be mistaken. A dream, perhaps."

"I cannot explain it, Lady Gael, nor do I seek to; I am merely telling you what I heard and what I felt." A moment of silence played out between the two, before Gael picked up her glass and took a large gulp of her wine.

"I was there that day," she said to Pilmer. "Though I was not on duty when the company entered the throne room, one of our number was right at the centre of it, and he was lucky to escape with his life. I took up arms in the aftermath; I did what I could, but he was too powerful. Our people..." she shook her head, fighting away the tears which threatened to spill forth. Pilmer scratched her beard and offered a puzzled look.

"Forgive me, but I do not understand. Your friend - Horith, was it? Your friend entered Eonis, and I know that our own Lord Thyrus was with him; what I don't understand is what happened next? What of the third member? Who was he?"

"A mage," answered Tyan, "a human mage."

"A mage walked *in*," said Ruli, "but someone entirely different walked out."

"Vinadan," said Gael. Pilmer's eyes went wide as the elf continued. "He used his skill with the shape-shifting rune to trick his way into the Soul Chamber;

there he revealed his true form, and turned his dark powers toward the destruction of my people."

"And the Soul?" asked Pilmer, eagerly.

"Gone," Gael replied simply.

"If you would pardon my interruption," said one of the dwarves from the gaming table, who was now making his way toward the group, ale in hand.

"I am Brindo, my lady and lords," said the dwarf, bowing low. "Please forgive me, for I did not mean to eavesdrop. It's just the mention of Thyrus," he paused, as if seeking permission to join the conversation.

"Sit, Brindo; please join us," said Gael, gesturing toward an empty chair.

"Thank you, my lady. I was there - Torimar, that is," said Brindo, looking crestfallen and ashamed. "I was there the day they arrived. I sat in the same hall as they ate our bread and drank our wine. I did wonder at the time why a human and an elf - a barren, my apologies - would be within our halls, but I thought nothing further of it. I am no warrior; I work in the mines. I set out eastwards with my pickaxe and hard hat upon the very same morn' that their host ventured south. Had I known… Had I the slightest notion that… that…"

Gael reached across the table and placed her soft, pale hand upon the coarse, weatherbeaten hand of the dwarven miner. "He deceived us all, Brindo. He took us all for fools. That is his way; malice, betrayal, cruelty. You could not have known."

"And you could not have stopped him, even if you did," added Tyan, without a hint of reproach or mockery. Brindo nodded and seemed to regain some of his former resolve.

"Aye," said Brindo, simply, before downing his ale in one mighty gulp. The ensuing, rueful silence was broken by the sound of the front door of being thrown open, and one of Gracen's guardsmen rushed into the Anvil, red faced and short of breath. He cast his gaze quickly around the inn, taking in patrons of all races and genders until his eyes fell upon…

"You! In the corner!" he pointed at Tyan and made his way to their table with haste.

"Me? What have I…" began Tyan, but he was cut off by the Guard.

"Please be silent; I have an urgent message from the alderman - from your brother."

"Well?" demanded Tyan, wondering why the man was standing on ceremony, "spit it out, man."

"The alderman said to tell you: *They know. Get out.*" At the guard's words, Tyan, Gael, Ruli, and Pilmer all stood at once, and even the dwarves at the next table had all but forgotten their game.

"What does he mean? *Who* knows?" asked Tyan, quickly.

"Shortly after you left, the alderman received more unexpected visitors, but of an altogether different kind: an orrec commander and his captain."

"Orrecs? In Adeniron?" asked Pilmer.

"Yes, Ma'am. They commanded the alderman to dispatch a message to the capital, declaring Aderniron sympathetic to rebels and requesting that Prince Vinadan send an occupying force here." Shock and horror were etched plainly upon the faces of all and sundry inside the Anvil, and Pilmer's own countenance was one of ill-concealed rage.

"There is no way the alderman will actually send that message," she said, shaking her head.

"He already has," the guard confirmed, "and there's more; in addition to sending orrecs here, the commander has instructed that an entire legion should head south from the capital, reinforced by Elgiroth. He means to make war." The young Guard could not keep the fear out of his voice as he relayed the information to the now rapt inn, and Tyan stepped forward and took the man gently by the shoulders, looking him straight in the eye.

"Where, my friend; to where are they bound?"

"Ehronia. They mean to make an example of the barrens."

Ruli moved with lightning speed at the guard's mention of his homeland and his people, heading straight for the door, but Pilmer caught him by the arm in a gentle but firm grip.

"No, lad; not like that," she said in a tone which brooked no argument.

"But my people! I have to help them!" he protested, trying in vain to pull free of the dwarf's grip.

"Think, Ruli. Calm down. It will be days before the message reaches the capital, and maybe a week more before their forces are upon your borders. We have time; we have to plan." Pilmer's words seemed to have the desired effect, and Ruli relaxed somewhat in her grasp. She let him go and he slumped back into his seat with his head in his hands.

"Why Ehronia? It doesn't make any sense?" he asked the room at large.

"From what I can gather - and it isn't much - the orrecs believe the barrens to be responsible for an ambush, north-east of here toward the wetlands."

Ruli did not even try to keep the confusion from his face. "What? What could possibly lead them to think that barrens were…." he stopped mid-sentence and closed his eyes. "My arrows," he said softly, almost under his breath. He covered his face with his hands and was still - very still - for a long moment as the realisation dawned heavily upon him.

"This is not of your making, Ruli," said Gael, placing a hand on the barren's slumped shoulder. It was Tyan who spoke next.

"Snap out of it, all of you. We don't have time for this. You, guard - send word back to my brother. Tell him we are making for the barn on Pilmer's farm - she'll give you the directions - and tell him to meet us there after dark. What is your name?"

"Trissan."

"Trissan, my brother cannot say *no* to my request. Whatever has befallen us thus far is as nothing compared to what now heads our way - their way," he added pointedly, motioning toward the crestfallen Ruli. "Not only does the doom of Ehronia ride south on a black wind, but the end of Adeniron as we know it is now upon us. I am counting on you as a servant of this city and a guard of the alderman and the ruling council, but I am also counting on you as a free man. Trissan, *he cannot say no.*"

*

The atmosphere in the barn was tense. Men, elves, a single barren, and even a few dwarves who had followed Pilmer here from the Anvil having firmly allied themselves to Gael, Tyan, and Ruli's cause, barely spoke as they checked their weapons and otherwise busied themselves while they waited. The barn was spacious, lofty, and held a chill which lingered in the still night air. The aromas of almost two hundred beings, the occasional chicken, and the sweet smell of hay and straw stood in stark contrast to the baskets of bread, and jugs of wine and ale which were being handed around, courtesy of the group's dwarven host. It was a large structure indeed, but it was still a tight squeeze to fit them all inside. At length, there came a loud rapping on the wooden door. Gael unsheathed a dagger and moved silently to stand to one side of the entrance, alert and ready, while Tyan moved to open it and admit their visitor. Gael relaxed her stance and stowed her weapon as Tyan announced it was his brother at the threshold, as planned. Trissan was with the alderman, and he exchanged a curt nod with Tyan upon entering the barn.

"Gracen-" began Tyan, but his older sibling did not allow him to finish.

"You have really done it this time, Tyan; you have brought war down upon us, and you've barely been in Adeniron a single day."

"War with Aclevion is inevitable, brother," replied Tyan with steel in his voice. "Whether the orrecs arrive tomorrow, next month, or a year from now, they will come, and they will kill any and all who even think about opposing them and the will of their master." Gracen closed his eyes momentarily and inhaled deeply, before exhaling his frustration and fixing Tyan with a penetrating stare.

"What are we doing, Tyan? What's the plan here?"

"We don't have many options, in truth. But Ruli's people are in danger, and if the orrecs march on Ehronia in numbers with death on their minds, the barrens will be slaughtered." Tyan tried to avoid looking at Ruli as he laid their case before his brother. Gracen chewed at his lip and shook his head in frustration, but did not immediately object.

"Go on," he prompted.

"We mean to set out for Ehronia at first light; we don't have great numbers but we are strong and organised. Gael and her people alone are more than a match for the orrecs, and Ruli's skill with a bow is unrivalled. We will do what we can to disrupt and dissuade, but we know that we can't defeat Vinadan's forces with our current numbers."

Gracen raised an eyebrow. "A sacrifice, then? A noble last stand?"

Tyan did not flinch as he answered his brother. "What else is left to us? For months we have struck, raided, harried, and turned back the orrecs. From Markosh and the wetlands, south to the borders of Eonis, and as far west as Jo'Thuun, we have tried to keep them at bay. We are just rebels, now; insurgents,making nuisances of ourselves and trying to keep the capital off balance however and wherever we can. But in Ehronia we have the chance to actually make a difference; we have the chance to save an entire people from annihilation."

"And I suppose you want me and my guards to go with you, is that it?"

"No, brother," Tyan replied. "I want you - I *need* you - to send whatever forces you can spare south. I need your men to make for the Three Ears. Olon,

Eldon, and Earon must be warned of Vinadan's movements."

"Ever you are determined to court the favour of elves, Tyan. It does not become you - no offence," added Gracen, turning in the direction of Gael and her retinue.

"It is not their favour that I seek but their safety. The Three Ears is a region of commerce, Gracen. The elves there are fisherfolk, weavers, merchants, and smiths. They have a small force of guards and soldiers to defend them from raiders and pirates, but they could not hold back Vinadan's orrecs, let alone his own dark magic. And were he to send the Asarlai, it would be a massacre. *Another* massacre. All of Gibrion relies on their goods and their trade; we cannot leave them to their fate."

"Tyan, we don't even know that Vinadan means to attack the Ears; it is a fool's errand."

"You're right, we do not know for certain. But are you willing to take that chance when so much is at stake?" The brothers had reached an impasse, and both stood, hands on hips, unblinking in the face of one another's stubbornness.

"I will accompany your men, Alderman," came a voice from within the elven ranks. Gracen turned toward the source, glad of an excuse to break free of his sibling's gaze.

"And you are?" asked Gracen, barely concealing his scorn toward the tired and dishevelled-looking elf who emerged from the crowd. He was tall, physically powerful, and had an air of authority about him, to be sure. But there was a look in his one remaining eye which spoke of horror and nervous shock. The left side of his face was burned and blackened; his scalp was bare upon that side, and the empty eye socket spoke volumes about the hardship he had clearly endured.

"Thalnon Meldreth, my lord," announced the elf with a low bow in Gracen's direction. "I was one of Lady Keya's most senior guards, Alderman. I was there the day Vinadan destroyed Eonis and took the Soul. I was there the day he murdered Lady Keya and decimated our people with his foul arts. Not only was I there…" he paused, as if composing himself, "I invited him in. I survived, though not wholly unscathed, while my brothers and sisters were torn apart before me. Lady Keya trusted me, but I could not save her; allow me this chance to regain my honour and avenge my kin."

Gracen met the elf's intense gaze, and nodded.

"To have faced Vinadan and survived must surely have taken courage beyond measure, Thalnon Meldreth. My men would surely be glad to have you among their ranks."

Thalnon returned Gracen's nod. "I know of others who will likely aid us if I entreat them; others who survived that dark day. I will establish contact and rally more to our cause."

"And what of you, mistress dwarf? Are you to accompany my brother to the land of the barrens?" asked Gracen of Pilmer.

"No, Alderman," replied the dwarf. "Much like you, I must remain in Adeniron for the sake of normality. The orrecs will come, and soon I'd wager, and when they do, it would not bode well for them to find an abandoned city. Appearances must be maintained. Eyes must remain sharp and ears must remain close to the ground. No, I will go back to the Anvil, I will serve drinks, and I will rap the knuckles of drunken troublemakers. And I will watch, listen, and report." A wave of nodding confirmed the credit Pilmer's decision held.

"*A spy in the camp* would indeed prove valuable," offered Gael. "And with the alderman in situ to maintain a semblance of order and obedience - at least for the moment - our movements may remain unnoticed by the capital a while longer."

Gracen sighed and turned to the barn at large, every inch the politician and experienced public speaker. "So be it. I will send men south to Earon, and from there they will make the crossing to Eldon and Olon to warn the elves of Vinadan's black schemes. Thalnon Meldreth, you will speak to your kin and rouse a force of elves to accompany my men on the road to the elven lands."

"I already have, Alderman," replied Thalnon, winking, though with only one remaining eye it could also have been a blink.

"Ah, yes, of course," stammered Gracen, embarrassed at his ignorance of the elves' natural telepathic abilities. "I place you in joint command, Trissan. Master Meldreth here will be your right hand, and you will be his left eye. Go: warn, observe, and plan - but do not engage the enemy needlessly. Remember, we are trying to prevent open warfare, not initiate it."

"And we will head west toward Ehronia and Ruli's people," said Gael, moving to stand beside Gracen, looking every bit the elven noble. "It is a long road from Adeniron to the barren lands, and we will likely have to forgo rest and comfort along the way. The lands are open and wild between here and our destination, and we cannot risk unnecessary attention by stopping at Undon, Jo'Thuun, or Haneth, nor any of the smaller settlements which stand between us and our destination. So sharpen your swords and axes, and string your bows tight. Sleep well tonight, and fill your stomachs before we depart at first light. We must be prepared and ready for what lies ahead." She cast her stern gaze around the barn.

"There's no telling who we might meet on the road."

Chapter Twenty

A layer of dust still coated the spine of the book, and as Prince Vinadan opened it up and inhaled the scent of the centuries-old pages, he felt conflicting waves of calm and excitement battling for control of his wits. As the mustiness of the book filled his nostrils, he imagined he could almost see hands beyond count poring over the enormous pages; eyes beyond measure greedily absorbing the mysteries within across centuries and cycles. The book, Vinadan knew, was a rare and much-coveted prize. Written by Daedan Asarlai himself, it held secrets and incantations which had proven beyond the skills of even the most learned and powerful scholars and mages throughout its long history. Now it resided in Vinadan's private library, high in the mountains above the capital.

In his youth, Vinadan had attempted to learn the secrets of this particular tome - for tome it was, requiring two hands to turn the pages and weighing as much as the very bricks which built his city - but his magical abilities and proficiency with runes was sorely lacking back then. But now he was stronger, far more powerful; his magic had multiplied exponentially, and he had mastered more runes than anyone in living memory.

Except, perhaps, those accursed hags in Vitrius, he thought. He had always been studious, and had always favoured mind over muscle. Even as his brother Valahir rode off to war on an armoured horse, and stood tall and proud, parading in front of the adoring masses, Vinadan would watch from the shadows. Valahir would wave and smile, revelling in the scent of the flowers as they were thrown at his feet following upon his return from another glorious victory against all manner of skirmishers, raiders, and myriad other threats to their father's kingdom. Vinadan, however, preferred the company of books, and the wisdom of those long dead, in whose timeless hand they were written. The brothers of Asarlai had allowed him access to their trove of books, tomes, scrolls, carvings, and countless other repositories of ancient, arcane lore when he was still a young man, though they did so grudgingly. Had he not been the son of King Entallion, such a request would surely have been denied.

Above all, this particular text was the one he had coveted the most, and he was only ever allowed to view it in the presence of one of the Asarlai, and even then his time with the book was severely restricted. To the present day, his advisors among the Asarlai continued to caution him against the uncovering of its secrets. Even among their own order there were few who would risk death or madness by attempting to gain control over the particular rune that Vinadan was now deep in the study of.

Some runes he had mastered early; *Persuasion, Influence, Defence*; these came naturally to the young prince of Aclevion. But others took much longer to learn, and Vinadan had turned to the dark powers of the night goddess Aether to syphon the power he needed to fully wrestle their control unto himself.

If *Obedience* and *Domination* were wild beasts to tame, then the rune for *Necromancy* was a veritable demon to forcibly enslave. He was lost in his thoughts; his brow furrowed and his hands frozen in the act of turning one of the ancient pages. At length, Vinadan snapped himself out of his revelry and completed the turn, his eyes feasting on the dark knowledge here written, as he might savour an iced wine on a hot day. The words were not new to him, the pages neither foreign nor surprising in their heft and scent. He had read these first pages before, of course, but had never gotten very far given the limitations of his youth. But now he had the power of the twin Souls coursing through his veins, and this both pleased and distracted him. The power of men and elves mingled and merged within him, a chimaera which answered to his will alone. He was both light and darkness, ice and fire; he was hard-forged iron and the finest woven silk.

He was day and night, Hemera and Aether. As his mind wandered, a smile tugged at the corner of his mouth. His skin burned bright with runes of all denominations, though he was too distracted to notice. At length, he took a deep breath and attempted to quiet his mind. The runes upon his skin lost their incandescence and began to fade. He had to focus, he knew, if he was to finally understand the dark and dangerous knowledge which reached out to him invitingly from the past, whispered by sorcerers, necromancers, witches, and demonologists long-dead. All around him was silent as he read and read, with only the sound of his own breathing breaking the sanctity of the void in which he sat, engrossed.

Minutes turned to hours, and Vinadan read and read with increasing vigour and speed. His eyes grew larger by increments as words, phrases, incantations, and revelations quickened in his mind. Clarity and understanding dawned where previously there had only been confusion and frustration.

Suddenly, he stood up, mouth open and eyes wide in frenzy. He reached forward and slammed the book shut, pulling his hands away as if the very pages were molten steel at his fingers. Walking - stumbling - over to the side table, he picked up his jug of wine and, disregarding the goblet which stood beside it, drank long and deep directly from the source. He replaced the jug and stood with his palms flat on the table, bracing himself against it for support while he regained control of his wits. He turned and looked over his shoulder, unblinking, and jaw hanging low in shock and horror.

Slowly, he turned to face the hastily closed book and simply stood and stared at the dusty cover for what seemed like an eternity, until he finally allowed himself to slide unceremoniously to the ground to land clumsily on the cold stone floor. All was silent. Vinadan merely sat, slowly shaking his head, eyes unfocused and seeming to see objects and places other than the old study in which he sat.

He ran a hand through his hair and blew out a long breath to steady himself. And he laughed.

Prince Vinadan, lord of Aclevion, threw his head back and laughed like a child; he roared and chuckled; he giggled and guffawed until he could barely breathe.

His eyes were bloodshot and filled with tears, and his face was flushed to a deep crimson. He stood up, poured himself a goblet of the vintage 270 red, and returned to his chair. Before he reopened the book, he took a handful of candles from a nearby drawer and set one upon an ornate pewter girandole. At a click of his fingers, the wick burst into flame.

He took a sip of his wine and reopened the book with a genuine, unguarded smile upon his face.

He understood it, now; it all made sense. He had done what nobody else in history - save perhaps Asarlai himself - had been able to accomplish.

The impossible rune…

He clicked his neck left and right, stretched his back, and cracked his knuckles. It was going to be a long night.

Chapter Twenty-One

Xeb had travelled far and wide during his decades in service among the Asarlai, so Ehronia was not entirely unknown to him. Still, he felt uneasy at the thought of his inevitable arrival among the barren elves and their orrec masters. He had nothing to fear, in truth, for dressed as he was in the accoutrements of his order, he would be hailed among Vinadan's vile servants as a master, a figure of esteem and authority. Fennet, he had decided, could be explained away simply as a servant, and the orrecs in their arrogance would not deign to question the arrangement. The road was long, however, and there would be plenty of time for Xeb to ruminate on his vague, formless unease which gnawed at him as he and Fennet pressed on southwards.

Frostpeak had all-but receded from view at their rear, and the respective peaks of the Undonian and Dinannian mountains were in view, though they were shrouded in the early morning fog which seemed to rise from the damp grasses like a wraith from a nameless tomb. They pressed on, and found themselves approaching a narrow lane with no obvious route around. Though Xeb would prefer that he and Fennet remain hidden from the sight of the general populace - such an odd and memorable pairing as they were - he was wise enough to recognise that they must occasionally shun the more difficult wild lands and seek safer, more travelled roads. Hesitating for but a moment, Xeb opened the wooden gate which allowed passage onto the lane, and - as instructed by the sign upon the gate - closed it behind him. The lane consisted of a narrow dirt road, with trees rising high on either side. The trickle of water could be heard off in the distance, though neither Xeb nor Fennet could immediately discern the source.

Xeb's heart began to beat a little faster as he beheld two shapes off in the distance, moving toward them on the lane. Within a minute or two, the shapes had resolved themselves into two humans, each holding the other by the hand. With a polite "good morning" exchanged all round, the couple continued and paid no further mind to Xeb and Fennet, at least not openly.

The sound of running water intensified, and the Asarlai and the hoblin soon found themselves crossing a small stone bridge, underneath which a stream ran fast, east to west. Another Xeb in another time may have remarked upon the quaintness of the bridge, or would at least have smiled at the peaceful scene, revelling in the simplicity of the beauty around him. As it was, Xeb barely even registered it as he led Fennet over the bridge and away from the crossing, looking over his shoulder as he did so. The strain which the recent weeks of travel and toil had placed on Xeb's body was matched only by the dark cloud which enveloped his mind of late.

What am I even doing? he thought as he trudged on. *Can I seriously hope to raise an army strong enough to oppose Vinadan? In my haste, I left Acelvion behind and am now committed to a fool's errand. Hoblins, witches, barrens... None have the strength of numbers nor the discipline necessary to challenge the prince, let alone overthrow him. Still, my course is set. The die has been cast and the rest will play out as Hemera wills it. I march inexorably onwards to defeat and death - that much I may deserve - but what darkness will my rash actions bring to the innocent beings who will be caught in the crossfire?*

Xeb shook his head, but did not give voice to his ruminations as he and Fennet walked on in silence, exiting the covered country lane and emerging into a wider area of rolling hills and rocky outcroppings. At length, Xeb became aware of a faint sound coming from a little further ahead. As it grew in intensity, he began to recognise it as the sound of hooves and of rolling wheels. It did not take long for his eyes to confirm what his ears suspected, and three covered carriages, each pulled by a pair of large, powerful looking horses, came into view from behind the cover of a hillock. Unease clenched tightly around Xeb's stomach, and he was instantly on high alert as the carriages abruptly altered their course and turned toward him and Fennet.

"Be on your guard Fennet, but do nothing to provoke them. With luck, they will pay us no mind and simply continue on their way. If they do stop, follow my lead; play along if you have to. We don't need trouble here."

The hoblin nodded his understanding and, almost imperceptibly, loosened his sword in its sheath a little. It did not take long for the newcomers to reach Xeb and Fennet, pulled along as they were by beasts of obvious physical prowess. A call of "Ho!" from the driver of the lead carriage, and the accompanying raising of a fist into the air signalled their halt and brought the company to a stop just short of the unlikely human and hoblin companions.

"Greetings and salutations, travellers," said a balding man in mismatched leathers as he alighted from the carriage. His companions likewise disembarked their own vehicles, and Xeb, via the merest flick of his eyes, left to right, clocked eight assorted men and women, each one armed and armoured to varying degrees.

"Good morning, friends," responded Xeb with a cordial smile. He spread his hands wide to take in the group and their horses. "What magnificent beasts you have there."

"You know much about horses?" replied the lead human through missing teeth.

"Sadly no, but I recognise strength when I see it," said Xeb, still smiling.

"A man and a hoblin, eh? What business do you have here, in the middle of the wild?"

"Oh, I am but a scholar, travelling abroad in search of knowledge. This hoblin is my servant. We are simply performing field research for a new book I am writing."

"Servant, eh? Slave, I'd wager. All *their* kind's good for," replied the balding man with vitriol. His companions each laughed along in turn, and Xeb felt the knot in his stomach tightening further.

"Erm, yes, yes, that's right!" interjected Fennet. "I am just a lowly servant." He lowered his head for three heartbeats. "In fact, I've already received three separate beatings from my master just this morning. It's okay though, I deserved *at least* two of them."

"Ha, my colleague jokes, of course," said Xeb, internally cursing Fennet. "Now, we must be off; farewell, and safe travels to you all." He took Fennet gently but purposefully by the shoulder and made to leave, but a sword blade across his chest stalled any forward momentum.

"Now hold on a second," said the tall, blonde haired woman at the other end of the outstretched sword. "Aren't you going to inspect our wares?" Xeb swallowed hard and tried to force what modicum of cordiality he could muster into his response.

"Oh, you are merchants? I see. Then, of course; my friend and I would be glad to see what you have for sale, but I must warn you that the life of a travelling scholar is not a lucrative one, so we do not have a great deal of money - at least not until I find a publisher for my book." Xeb added with a smile in an attempt to break some of the mounting tension. He and Fennet were led to one of the carriages, and the tall woman opened the back to reveal the goods within. Xeb wasn't quite sure what he had been expecting, but he had to admit his surprise at the contents of the carriage.

"Well, I must say, this is a rather fine collection you have here," he said as he scratched at his bearded chin. The floor of the cart was laid out neatly with fine silver swords and daggers of obvious elven smithing, golden battle-axes which could only have come from Toraleth, and vicious-looking, spike-topped maces often favoured by Fennet's people and their orrecish cousins. In addition to the weapons were poultices and salves of all colours and purposes, vials of potions, and bottles of tonics, all of which, thought Xeb, ruefully, would actually be of great use to them in their quest.

"Sadly, my good lady, as I stated a moment ago, we have little enough coin to cover the cost of such fine items. We must therefore bid you goodbye, with thanks." Xeb turned to Fennet and motioned with his eyes for the hoblin to start moving, but a hand on his shoulder and a blade placed at the small of his back stopped Xeb in his tracks.

"You can drop the act," said the bald man with the missing teeth. "We may not know *who* you are, but we know *what* you are."

"Please, there's clearly been a misunderstanding here-" Xeb began, but was cut off by the tall woman.

"The way you speak, your robes, the very way you carry yourself; you are from Aclevion. You are one of the Asarlai."

Xeb kept his voice level and his hands up as he turned slowly to face the tall woman - the leader of the group, he now understood.

"Even if I were of the Asarlai, what difference would that make here?"

"What difference?" the woman replied. "The only difference we care about: kreons and mullions. Your pockets must be overflowing with gold underneath those red robes. How else would you have paid for your hoblin slave?" Her companions laughed among themselves, mirthless laughs with neither warmth nor humour at their heart. Xeb closed his eyes and took a deep, calming breath.

"He is not my slave, he is my friend. And truth be told: *yes*; I do actually have more gold about my person than I may have admitted." Xeb's eyes were unblinking and fixed upon the group leader. He forced an edge of cold steel into his voice as he continued, "but you will never see a coin of it."

"Is that so?" she replied, placing her face inches from Xeb's. "I would have thought someone of your ilk would have learned how to count. Look around you. We are taking your coin, and your lives. You're not even armed. You're the easiest sport we've had for weeks," she laughed, and her companions did likewise. Xeb shook his head slowly and fixed the leader with a pitying stare.

"So, not merchants after all. Bandits. That explains the elvish blades, at least. I was rather hoping it wouldn't go this way, and I just want you - all of you - to know that you brought this on yourselves." He turned his head and winked at Fennet, and the little hoblin - knowing exactly what was about to happen - dived for cover behind the cart.

Xeb's eyes blazed with violent flames of red and orange, and every inch of his skin was set aflame with burning runes. The arcane markings which represented *Death, Anger*, and *Sorrow* repeated themselves in sequence, and the very air around Xeb crackled and sizzled in answer to his terrifying display of power. Xeb did not enjoy taking lives, but he had long since reconciled the necessity to do so should fate steal away all other options.

The bandits did not have chance to do so much as raise a shield in defence, and they were all-but obliterated in seconds by Xeb's pyromancy. Where eight grinning, cocky bandits had stood mere moments before, now only charred bones and the smell of burning flesh remained. Fennet slowly stood and peered around the side of the carriage, taking in the scene and watching in awe as the runes slowly faded from Xeb's skin and the flames in his eyes receded once more.

"Well," said the hoblin, rubbing his hands together as he tiptoed his way through the burning remains. "That went well. Are we taking the horses as well as the axes, or…?"

"What?" asked Xeb, not quite taking Fennet's meaning.

"The horses; we have a long way to go, and it would be a shame to leave them here alone." Xeb had to admit there was merit in the hoblin's words.

"You might have a point there, my friend. We shall take one, and set the others loose. I suppose there is no sense in leaving the potions and tonics behind. Here," he said, reaching into his robes and pulling out a hessian bag, "take this. Fill it with as many of the ointments and poultices as you can carry. And I suppose you could help yourself to a sword or two," he added with a smile. Fennet returned the smile with interest, and immediately set about rifling through the contents of the bandits' carriage. Xeb, requiring only the weapons of his own making, busied himself instead with untethering the horses from the conveyances they pulled. They did not immediately try to run away, and remained in place but for the odd step or two toward each other. Xeb selected the one he and Fennet would take, a large, powerful looking friesian whose coat was as black as the night sky. He shooed the others away, and they slowly began to make their way across the open plains, away from the carriages and smouldering remains of their former masters.

"I'm ready," said Fennet from behind Xeb. He had dutifully filled the bag with potions and concoctions of all varieties, and had an axe and a mace stowed at his back, crossed at their centres and handles within reach over his shoulders. His own hoblin-made sword had been unceremoniously discarded, and in his hands he held an immaculate elvish blade. Its hilt was carved ivory, inlaid with the finest silver, and the blade was a thing of rare beauty. It was etched deep with characters of an ancient elvish dialect which neither Fennet nor even Xeb could translate, and as it caught the rays of the sun it reflected them like pure starlight, as if a galaxy had been plucked from the night sky and forged within the steel and silver.

They mounted the horse, Xeb riding and Fennet behind, and secured the newly-filled bag to the saddle. Xeb turned and looked over his shoulder at the hoblin, who was already holding on tight despite the fact they had not yet started moving.

"What shall we call him?" Xeb asked.

"Hmm… Let me see," replied Fennet, holding his chin as he gave the matter some serious thought. "*Trumpet*," he said at length.

"Trumpet?" replied Xeb. "That's a strange name for a horse."

"Well, what can I say? He's a strange horse," replied Fennet, deadpan as ever. Xeb laughed and shook his head in a mixture of amusement and bewilderment. "Fair enough; *Trumpet* it is."

With that, he kicked his heels into Trumpet's side and off they went, resuming their journey toward Ehronia once more. Xeb still wore an amused grin, and Fennet held tightly to the Asarlai's waist with one hand.

In the other he carried an elvish blade; a blade from the pages of legend, long since lost to the annals of time.

A blade wielded in battle, centuries ago, by *Ealdris the Unworthy*, the traitorous elven king.

Chapter Twenty-Two

"Keep your eyes sharp and your guard up, Scout; we are walking into the unknown here," said commander Malgorth, as he and Agnaz crouched low amidst the bushes which littered the treeline on the outskirts of Ehronia. "We know that at least one barren was responsible for the deaths of our brothers in the north-east, so we must assume that the garrison here is destroyed."

"But, Commander, they're just barrens; they're no match for either of us - let alone both," replied Agnaz, eliciting a reproachful glance from his superior.

"While they are no match for us in single combat, or even in modest groups, if the entire population has indeed turned on our kin and have taken back their lands, what good are two orrecs against a thousand elves - barren or otherwise? What about ten thousand?"

"Yes Commander; of course. So what should we do?"

"We will use stealth to our advantage as we move closer to the main population centres. We lack information, so that should be our first priority." They moved slowly and quietly through the trees and bushes, keeping low, stopping now and then as a bird flew overhead or a beast ambled by. They could see structures in the distance, structures made of wood and brick, and could smell the smoke rising from chimneys in the town directly ahead. As they inched inexorably closer to the town, exposed, lacking immediate cover behind which to hide, they were on full alert, ears pricked and muscles taut with anticipation.

"Come on, get a move on you scum!" came a cry from up ahead, appearing to come from behind the building closest to Malgorth and Agnaz, though nobody could yet be seen. Malgorth gave a quick, decisive gesture with his hand, and he and Agnaz sprinted for the building, placing their backs flat against the east-facing wall. The crack of a whip rang out in the air, followed immediately by a grunt of pain and a low whimper. Malgorth bade Agnaz stay put, and he crouched low and peered around the corner of the wall toward the source of the unexpected sounds. Stepping out from behind the opposite wall and continuing forward came a procession of chained and manacled barrens - ten or eleven as far as Malgorth could see - led by an armed and snarling orrec captain whom Malgorth did not recognise. Malgorth stayed low and continued to survey the scene. As the column of barrens ended, two more orrecs came into sight at the rear. Malgorth raised his hand and issued two quick signals to Agnaz, indicating the number of orrecs and number of barrens, respectively, in his line of sight. Receiving a nod of comprehension from his companion, Malgorth broke cover and strode toward the procession.

"You there; situation report at once," he called out to one of the lead orrecs who nearly jumped out of his skin in surprise at the sudden booming voice.

"Commander Malgorth? Sir? What are you doing here?" stammered the orrec, bringing the column to a swift halt.

"Do not presume to question me, captain…?"

"Ishiig, Commander,"

"Captain Ishiig; what news from Ehronia?"

Ishiig dared to cast a glance at one of his colleagues, and registered the same confusion as was writ large upon his own countenance.

"Sir? Nothing to report, Commander. All is in hand. We are just leading this rabble to their place of work, as is customary." Malgorth raised the thick brow above the leftmost of his deep-set eyes.

"F.. .for the might of Aclevion, Commander," the orrec added hastily, eliciting a chorus of the same from his cohorts.

"Very good, Captain Ishiig. Very good." Malgorth stood in place for a moment, eyes locked with the captain. His expression remained neutral and his posture stoic and calm. "You can go about your business," he added finally. Malgorth could see the wave of relief flood over Ishiig and his companions. He gestured with his hand to indicate they should be on their way.

"Oh, one final question before you go," Malgorth added, his tone suggesting this was merely a casual afterthought.

"Y…Yes, Commander, of course," replied Ishiig.

"How many barrens have left these lands on your watch?"

"Commander?"

"It is not a difficult question, Ishiig. How many of them," he continued, pointing toward the column of bound barrens, "have left these lands," he pointed to the dirt at his feet, "in the last - say - six months?"

"Well, none, my lord. Of course; none are permitted to leave, Commander."

"Well I did not imagine for a moment that you wrote them permission slips, Ishiig, but I must ask again how many have left?"

"None, sir! None at all!"

"Okay. That is good to hear. Perhaps, however, you would care to explain this?" Malgorth reached into his pocket and took out the ornate silver arrowhead he had taken from the scene of the battle by the river. He held it up for Ishiig and his companions to see, and as one they failed to mask their shock, their disbelief, and their shared horror.

"My lord?" said a confused captain Ishiig.

"This was taken from the sight of an ambush in the riverlands due-east of Markosh. The blood of our kin was still slick upon its tip, and it is clearly barren-made."

"My lord, I assure you none have-" Malgorth reached out without warning like a striking snake, and took captain Ishiig by the throat.

"At best, you are an incompetent fool. At worst, you are a traitor. One thing I am sure of, though: you are lying to me," snarled Malgorth. "Scout!" he called over his shoulder, and Agnaz appeared at once, making his way toward the scene with fury in his eyes.

"Yes, Commander." he said upon reaching Malgorth.

"Do me the honour of demonstrating to this wretched creature why it is not advisable to displease me."

"With pleasure, my lord," Agnaz replied, cracking his knuckles and taking out a vicious-looking dagger. The grin upon his face was as wide as it was genuine.

"W…wait! My lord!" pleaded Ishiig, whose feet were struggling to maintain contact with the ground as Malgorth held him by the throat with one hand. Agnaz did not heed the stricken orrec's pleas, nor did he hesitate for a moment as he ran the dagger clean through the hapless Ishiig, pushing until his own hand ran warm with the other's blood and tissue. He pulled his hand free of Ishiig's newly-opened stomach, and wiped the dagger blade clean upon his coverings. Malgorth released the orrec, and the deathly silence which followed the dull, wet thud as Ishiig's body hit the ground seemed to stretch for an eternity. Ishiig's companions had each taken a few steps back away from Malgorth and Agnaz, and were pushing the barrens backwards in turn.

Malgorth fixed the terrified orrecs with an intense stare, then cast his gaze across the collection of barrens, still tethered and trying their best to remain unnoticed.

All but one.

"You," yelled Malgorth, stretching a large and muscular arm toward the assembled barren elves. His finger pointed to the the only one among their number who was openly smiling, and she made no attempt to avert her eyes from Malgorth and Agnaz.

"Come here at once," Malgorth commanded.

The barren looked at her orrec chaperones and raised her manacled wrists. One of the remaining orrecs looked at the cuffs, then turned and looked at Malgorth, then back to the cuffs. Noting the hesitation and confusion upon the orrec's face, Agnaz marched over and dealt a vicious backhanded blow to the dumbstruck orrec.

"Well untie her then, you bumbling idiot. Do as your commander orders!" The orrec wasted no time in obliging, and within moments the grinning barren was free of her bindings and was standing face to face with Malgorth, head tilted backward to take in the enormous orrec.

"I will give you once chance to explain to me exactly what it is you are smiling about, barren, or I will begin the systematic execution of each filthy, impotent, powerless half-elf in this group," said Malgorth, his voice little more than a whisper.

"You and your kind are not welcome here in Ehronia, amongst the trees and the streams. Your kind are a plague sent from the north to subjugate and to kill us. I will tell you no more than this, *Commander*," she replied. She spat at his feet, and raised her eyes once more. Malgorth stood silent and stoic as a statue, and finally he snorted a short, disdainful sound of derision mingled with just a touch of disbelief and amusement.

"You have heart, half-elf, even if you do not have magic. But you have already betrayed yourself and your kind." Malgorth once more removed the silver arrowhead from his pocket and held it up before the barren.

"You recognised this, didn't you?" he said. "You know who it was that ambushed and murdered my men in the northern territories." This was not a question but a statement of fact. "I will have that information from you, then you will die, along with your co-conspirators."

"I will never-" the barren began, but the sudden and unexpected splash of warm blood upon her face from the left stole the words from her lips.

"That is on you; your disobedience and your smart mouth has just cost the life of one of your kin. Think about that. Guard, put her back in chains and secure this group in a holding cell on my authority. Leave *that* there as a reminder of the might of Aclevion," barked Malgorth, issuing orders left and right. The barren was quickly manacled and chained once more, and was forcibly shoved back into line, blood still running warm down her face. Malgorth and Agnaz turned and moved away without further word, and the column of barrens was quickly led away by the orrec guards who were, each and every one, thankful for an excuse - any excuse - to be away from Malgorth.

"What are you doing?" hissed a panicked barren to the blood-soaked female, "you're going to get us all killed!"

"No, Gerdan," replied Miseldi, "I think help may be on the way."

As the column of barrens was led away by the orrecs, the headless corpse of the unlucky barren whose only crime was to be next in line to the defiant Miseldi, had already begun to attract the attention of the Ehronian tumble flies; great carrion-eating insects which dwelt in and around the fertile lands of the south west regions.

The head they would save for later. Striding with purpose away from the scene, and already planning his next move, Malgorth absentmindedly wiped his blade clean upon his coverings, and sheathed it once more upon his mighty belt.

Chapter Twenty-Three

"...which is why, ever since that day, I've never really trusted goats. *Or* dressmakers, for that matter," said Fennet, nodding slightly in agreement with himself. Xeb was quite sure that, given the chance, his hoblin companion would talk all the way to Ehronia, and probably all the way to Aclevion if they survived long enough to make it to the capital. The hoblin's grip on Xeb's waist had relaxed somewhat, and Trumpet was now in full stride. The sun was high in the air, and golden rays bathed the unlikely pair in an unseasonal heat.

"Oh, what I wouldn't give for a damp cave right now," said Fennet, squinting against the sunlight.

"I would enjoy the warmth of the sun while it lasts, my friend. I foresee that our path will be paved with nothing but darkness before too long."

"That's a metaphor," said Fennet.

"Indeed it is, but it doesn't make it any less likely." They fell into a ponderous silence as Trumpet carried them onwards, across fields of green and brown littered here and there with flashes of red, yellow, and white. At length, they crossed a small stream, the horse picking his way more intricately among the slippery rocks underfoot. Before long, they were back on dry land, and Xeb registered absently that their path would lead them through a small wood situated in the nook of a valley, whose steep sides rose up too high to climb without costing precious time.

"Are we going through the woods, master Xeb?" asked Fennet.

"Yes. I see no other way around."

"That's okay; it will be nice to be under the shade for a little while, anyway," said the hoblin. Xeb manipulated the reins and Trumpet dutifully slowed down as they approached the treeline. Though not a forest, the trees were many and the woods were dense with foliage of all kinds and colours. Xeb and Fennet were quiet as they made their crossing into the woods, and the very air around them was alive with the deep, hot breathing of their horse, and the myriad chirps, cheeps, and clicks of countless unseen animals and insects.

"Where are we?" asked Fennet, wide-eyed and a little awestruck. Xeb smiled at the hoblin's enthusiasm. *I don't suppose hoblins ever really spend much time in woodlands*, thought Xeb. *I can see why he may think them a little magical.*

"Unless I am mistaken, my friend, this is *Green Haven Wood*, meaning we are now less than two days from our destination." Fennet did not reply, but continued to look here and there, left and right, high and low. Looking closer, he now saw crickets among the leaves, and watched on as spiders spun their intricate webs among the trees. He saw a squirrel seemingly defy gravity as it ran effortlessly up the trunk of a mighty tree. A hedgehog poked its nose out of the undergrowth long enough to take in the man and hoblin astride the great black horse, then darted back out of sight. All the while, dragonflies zipped through the rays of sunlight which cascaded through the gas in the treetops, and butterflies fluttered aimlessly through the heady haze of falling pollen.

"What's *he* doing here?" asked Fennet, pointing to one animal among the wood's inhabitants which didn't quite belong. Xeb's gaze followed Fennet's outstretched finger and focused on the animal in question. The scruffy-looking cat was staring at them intently, sitting among the tall grasses but making no attempt to conceal its presence.

"*Danu*," said Xeb, noting the virtually imperceptible green glow in the cat's eyes which marked it out as something otherworldly; something quite apart from the average feline. At Xeb's word, the cat turned and ran deeper into the woods, leaving the man, the hoblin, and the horse far behind in moments. Xeb scowled and turned to look over his shoulder at Fennet.

"That the good ladies of Vitrius still seek to track us could be a blessing, my friend. They will come to view us true, and see that there is no lie nor malice in our intent. On the other hand, their watchfulness could just as easily be the blackest of curses, should they harbour malice of their own towards ourselves or our goals."

Fennet chewed Xeb's words in his mind for a moment, then nodded his agreement.

"Also," added the hoblin, thoughtfully, "that cat looked like he could do with a good long brushing." Xeb laughed out loud for what seemed like the first time in an age.

"Yes, Fennet, he really did. Come, Trumpet." Xeb pulled at the horse's reins anew, and the horse began a slow canter through the dense woodland.

"Oh, and another thing-" began Xeb, but his next words died in his throat as his attention was suddenly caught by the sudden *whoosh* which passed mere centimetres in front of his face, and by the intricate, silver-tipped arrow which was now fixed tightly into the tree trunk immediately to Xeb's right. He pulled hard on the reins and Trumpet stopped immediately in place.

"Move one muscle and you are dead, Aclevion filth," came the voice from somewhere amongst the trees. Rage, barely contained, fuelled each word. Xeb and Fennet did as instructed and remained motionless, though their hearts beat a little faster as they beheld the elves, men, and occasional dwarf emerging from the treeline, weapons drawn, with hatred etched unmistakably upon each and every countenance. Xeb and Fennet found themselves surrounded, and as the retinue stood on guard with weapons ready and muscles taut to react, the final member of the new group came into view, bow drawn taut and fury in his eyes.

"Oh look, master Xeb," said Fennet, "a barren!"

"Stand down, Ruli," came a gentle yet firm voice which momentarily drew Xeb's attention away from the barren whose arrow was nocked and ready, aimed directly between Xeb's eyes. He turned to behold a tall and elegant female elf, fully armed and armoured, extending her arm out to the young barren, signalling that he should lower his bow. The barren hesitated for a moment, then grudgingly did as instructed, lowering his weapon but never taking his eyes off Xeb.

"Greetings, friends-" Xeb began cordially.

"Who are you? What are you doing in these lands, so far from the capital? You *are* of the Asarlai, are you not?" interjected the elf. Xeb took a deep breath, and noted that Fennet, still sitting behind him and clutching his waist, was uncharacteristically quiet.

"My name is Xebus, and this is my companion, Fennet. I am, as you say, Asarlai, and I have no reason to deny that, my lady." Xeb offered no more, and a tense silence fell between the mounted duo and the assorted militia by whom they were now utterly surrounded. At length, the elf exhaled and gestured to her two most immediate companions.

"I am Gael of Eonis; this is Tyan of Markosh, and - well - you've already met Ruli."

"A pleasure, my lady," said Xeb, lowering his head in deference. "But I do of course wonder why you and your company saw fit to surround us like this; we mean you no harm." Ruli raised his bow in anger and drew back the string. "He's lying! We should take off his head and leave him in the dirt; let the flies do the rest."

"I do not believe we have met, master barren, so I must ask why you show such hostility to a stranger such as I?" Ruli pushed past Gael and Tyan and stared up at Xeb, who was still sitting astride Trumpet, hands raised, palms out, in front of him.

"You are Vinadan's lackey and a murderer! Your kind are little more than the lapdogs of a tyrant who deceived and killed my friend." Ruli spat on the ground at Trumpet's feet, and the prominence of the muscle in the young barren's jaw and the bulging of the vein at his temple told Xeb that the young half-elf was quite sincere in his fury.

"I assure you, master Ruli, that I did not kill your friend. I have taken many lives - more than I care to acknowledge - but your kin are not among the dead who walk silently behind me." Ruli was not placated by Xeb's words.

"You willingly serve a murderer, so you are just as guilty of Horith's death as your dark master."

Horith? Thought Xeb, and the realisation caused his heart to sink. He rubbed at his forehead to soothe the ache which was threatening to burst into life there.

"*Horith*," he repeated. "Of course. Horith of house Nindrius, I believe."

"How dare you speak his name!" shouted Ruli. The barren had murder in his eyes and made to lunge for Xeb, but Tyan reached forward and grabbed Ruli around the middle, restraining him.

The fools, thought Xeb, and he added a touch of authority to his voice as he spoke. "Master barren, my good lady Gael; you are unlikely to believe this, but my companion and I are not your enemy, indeed we are about the closest thing to allies you are going to find in these parts."

"Liar!" shouted Ruli, but Gael once again gestured for the barren to contain his anger.

"Let him speak," she said, narrowing her eyes as she looked pointedly in Xeb's direction. "What do you mean, Asarlai? What is a man of the capital doing so far south, and in the company of a hoblin no less?"

Okay, thought Xeb. *The elf is in charge; she is the one to convince, here.*

"May we be permitted to dismount the horse?" Xeb asked, and received a nod in reply. He and Fennet climbed down from Trumpet and tethered the horse to the nearest tree. Palms still raised in front of him, Xeb began.

"Ruli, I did not know your friend Horith, but I know *of* him. You are correct that I served Prince Vinadan, and indeed I am - was - one of his inner circle, one of his most trusted advisors. You know, clearly, that your friend is dead, but you may not know why. Vinadan himself, disguised as an old mage, recruited your friend and played him for a fool, all to gain access to the Soul chamber in Eonis. He counted on your friend's passion and rebellious spirit - the same fire I see in you - and weaved an elaborate ruse in the pursuit of even greater power."

"We know this, Asarlai," Gael said impatiently.

"But there is much you know not," Xeb replied, raising a finger. He looked around the group, and realised that they were all - men, elves, dwarves and the barren - listening. No one spoke to interrupt him, so Xeb continued.

"Vinadan now has in his possession both Aether and the Hemera; the day and the night; the Soul of Aclevion, and its elven sister. He is now as dangerous as he is powerful, and he is drunk with both. He grows ever more impatient, petulant, vengeful, and arrogant with the dawning of each new day. He kills any who dare to question him, any who speak a word against him, even those among his own citizens in Aclevion. He is both their saviour and executioner - a demon masked as an angel - and he must be stopped."

Gael raised her eyebrows at Xeb's final exclamation.

"Stopped?" she asked, "You mean to overthrow your master?"

"Why else do you think I would be so far from the capital, my lady? And with a hoblin in tow, no less. Employing a ruse of my own, the prince granted me leave to journey across the lands of Gibrion to spread the word, to weave tales of his glory and return with loyalists with which to flood the capital. He means to surround himself with yes-men and fawning admirers, so I massaged his vanity to my own ends, and have journeyed far and wide these last weeks with my *real* goal in mind."

"You're building an army," said Tyan, nodding and scratching at his chin.

"Indeed, Tyan of Markosh. I am in every way a traitor - to the prince and to my own order. Many among the Asarlai revere and deify Vinadan, and I see in their hearts and their methods that they are just as intoxicated by the power of the unified Souls as he is. There are still some who remain loyal to the old ways, however; some who wish to see the prince in chains, and there are others still who wish to see him in the ground."

"You cannot possibly believe any of this?" said an incredulous Ruli, looking from Gael to Tyan, then to the wider company. "He is lying through his teeth, taking us for fools, just like his master!" Ruli's eyes flicked downwards toward the dagger at his belt, and that single moment of inattention was all it took. The barren froze in place and raised his hands in surrender as he felt the cold, sharp tip of Fennet's elven blade at his throat.

"Master Xebus speaks the truth," said Fennet, projecting strength into his voice. "I have seen it first hand, and we hoblins have already pledged ourselves to fight alongside him. He is an honourable man, and does not lie. Think about it; he could have burned you all where you stand with as little as a wink, so why didn't he?" The hoblin had an intense look in his eyes which Xeb had never seen before. For all his quirks and his general good nature, Xeb was now reminded that Fennet was still a hoblin, and had been raised to fight with rage and resilience. He looked every bit the warrior as he held the sword to Ruli's throat. Neither hoblin nor barren blinked for a long time as they held each other's gaze at opposite ends of the sword. With a sigh, Fennet lowered the blade and sheathed the sword once more. Ruli put his fingers to his throat to check for blood, and found that there was none.

"We are on a quest," continued Fennett, "and our next stop is Ehronia."

"Ehronia?" said Gael. "It seems we share a common destination."

"You also make for the barren lands?" asked Xeb.

"We do. Tyan's brother is the alderman of Adeniron. An orrec commander paid him a visit and spoke of an army heading south from the capital to march on Ruli's people. We set off with all haste and abandoned all thought of sleep, but I fear that even now we may be too late."

The expression on Xeb's face spoke of his concern. "It all makes sense now," he said, more to himself than to anybody else. He looked at each of the company leaders in turn, and allowed his gaze to fall finally on Ruli. "I read the portents, studied the cards, and deciphered the runestones, and all pointed me to Ehronia, though I knew not why until now. If Vinadan is sending a battalion south it can mean only one thing."

"Which is?" asked Ruli.

"Think, Ruli. Your kin are already shackled in servitude, so there is only one logical outcome which the arrival of a fighting force would signal."

Ruli's face was impassive and his voice strong as he spoke the words. "He means to annihilate us."

"That is my conclusion, master barren." The only sounds to be heard for a long, tense moment were the chirping of birds and the fluttering of flying insects as men, elves, dwarves and a single barren looked at each other, lost in their own doubt and dread. It was Gael who broke the impasse.

"Okay, well you two had better mount up if we mean to make it to Ehronia before all is lost," she said, checking her armour and weapons.

"We?" asked Xeb, one eyebrow raised.

"It seems we share a common purpose, as well as a common destination. We march to Ehronia to aid the barrens. Our numbers may be modest, but our hearts are as brave as our blades are sharp," she said.

"You're not seriously suggesting we take them with us?" asked Ruli.

"Yes, I am," replied Gael definitively. "I believe him, and you know the power the Asarlai wield. We will need that strength if we are to succeed here."

"She's right, Ruli," said Tyan, moving to stand beside Gael. "We need them now, and will need them even more for what comes after."

"After?" asked Xeb, though he knew in his heart what Tyan was thinking. He thought it too, and could see in the hundreds of faces amassed around them that they all thought it, though it was Gael who put voice to their collective thoughts.

"We have allies; with a strong wind and the favour of Hemera, more of my kin may join us soon enough. Alderman Gracen may yet rally more men to our cause; add to our strength the ferocity of the hoblins, and we may just stand a chance. We must make haste to Ehronia, and then we strike north."

"Aclevion," said Xeb.

"Aclevion," Gael confirmed. "We march on the capital; we kill Vinadan."

The company moved away on Gael's command, and soon the Green Haven Wood was quiet once more save the sounds of the myriad creatures which called it home. It was as if the woods had reset upon the departure of the loud, trampling company; returned immediately to their former state and restored their natural equilibrium. Where elves had recently stood, spiders now skittered. The trees against which men had just been resting were once again crawling with squirrels and burrowing insects. The company was out of sight and beyond earshot when a dark shape rose from the tree canopy, and spread its wings wide as it took to the sky.

We kill Vinadan, squawked the mynah bird. *We kill Vinadan. We kill Vinadan.*

It took a moment to bask in the sunshine, gliding upon the warm currents above Green Haven, then turned and headed north. It was a good servant, and had never failed to please its master.

Chapter Twenty-Four

It was somehow wetter and colder inside the cell than it was outside in the open air, and Miseldi shivered in the corner. She pulled the meagre and soiled blanket around her shoulders for the scant warmth it offered, and hugged her legs tightly to her chest. It was dark inside, too, and even her sharp eyes struggled to make out more than the faintest of silhouettes and shadows. The barrens had heard rumours that the orrecs had built dungeons below the town hall, but none who had seen them first hand had yet lived to spread the word of their true existence. Now, huddled and shivering, bruised, beaten, and exhausted, Miseldi could indeed confirm there were dungeons beneath Ehronia.

The orrecs had tried to break her; they had tried every foul means of coercion they could think of to get her to talk. Her cuts, bruises, sprains, and fractures were testament to the orrecs' perseverance, but Miseldi's spirit was far stronger than the orrecs had expected, and her lips - though now cut, swollen, and bloodied - had remained sealed.

"Miseldi," came a small voice from the next cell. "Miseldi? Are you awake?" The voice was coloured with fear and concern.

"I'm here, Gerdan; I'm okay," she replied, trying in vain to inject strength and poise into her own.

"We need to get out of here! Somehow, we need to free ourselves or they're going to kill us," said Gerdan. Miseldi sighed, and felt a sharp pain in her ribcage as she exhaled.

"He'll come. He'll rescue us. I can feel it in the air, and I know it in my heart." Miseldi did not see Gerdan place a tired and bloodied hand upon his temple, nor did she see her friend slowly shake his head in resignation.

"Ruli is dead, Miseldi. You must know this. Just like Horith," he said softly.

"He is not, Gerdan. I believe that Horith is gone, yes; but Ruli still lives. He is out there somewhere, fighting, and I know we will see him again. And soon."

"How? How could you possibly know this, Miseldi? He's been gone for *months*, and all you have to go on is a silver arrow tip which could have been fashioned by any elf - barren or otherwise."

Now it was Miseldi's turn to close her eyes and shake her head. "I cannot say, my friend. Just a feeling, I suppose."

"Well, I-" began Gerdan, but his next words died in his throat, and both he and Miseldi turned their heads and pointed ears toward the sound which had so suddenly cut into their conversation.

Rrrrooooooooooom, went the mighty horn, a little way off to the east.

"What was that?" asked Gerdan with an edge of panic.

"A war horn," said Miseldi, more to herself than to Gerdan. "The orrecs have sent reinforcements."

*

Malgorth noted at first how their red robes stood in stark contrast to the more utilitarian browns, blacks, and greys of the orrec armour, and was even further removed from the sandy coloured fur of the huge wolves they rode upon. He and Agnaz, flanked by a dozen or so armed and imposing orrecs, stood unmoving as the battalion approached, led by the two mounted Asarlai.

"How many have come, Commander?" asked Agnaz.

"As far as I can tell, Scout, our good prince has seen fit to send a force some five hundred strong. Orrecs, of course; I also see mountain wolves, two of the Asarlai, and I believe I even see a northern fire troll at the back of the procession."

"That's embarrassing," said Agnaz.

"Not at all, Scout," replied Malgorth. "Just because we did not find the open rebellion we had expected, the arrival of this fighting force will send a message to all lands who oppose Prince Vinadan. Besides, a public display of force is always a perfect tonic to any seeds of sedition which remain within these elves."

"*Public*, Commander?" asked Agnaz. Malgorth flashed his companion a menacing grin.

"Oh yes; if our captives will not talk, then perhaps a public execution or two will serve to loosen the lips of their friends and co-conspirators."

The two mounted Asarlai halted their wolves a few feet from Malgorth and Agnaz, and climbed down to meet the orrec leaders.

"Welcome, my lords," said Malgorth.

"For the might of Aclevion, commander Malgorth," replied the first of the Asarlai. "I am Balus, and this is Temmon," said the brother, indicating his companion. Malgorth offered a curt nod of his head.

"Commander Malgorth, And scout captain Agnaz," he replied.

"So," said Temmon, a bearded and serious man with dark skin and darker eyes, "what is the situation here?" It was Agnaz who replied.

"One or more of the barrens have escaped their homelands and have engaged in acts of sedition and rebellion against the capital."

"Your proof?" asked Temmon. Malgorth reached inside his armour and took out the silver arrow head.

"When I showed this to the incumbent orrecs," he said, holding the item up for the Asarlai to see, and sending small rays of light into their faces as the sun reflected off the tip, "there was a stirring among the barrens; they recognized it as one of their own."

"And where did you get this?" asked Balus, reaching out his hand and taking the arrow head from Malgorth.

"We pulled it from the head of one of our soldiers, just outside of Markosh."

"Markosh?" asked Balus, his eyebrows furrowing in what Agnaz took to either be surprise or disbelief.

"That is correct," replied Malgorth, "as my companion states." Balus turned the arrow head over in his hands then held it up to the light, squinting one eye shut as he scrutinised the item. Presently, he handed it to Temmon, and he in turn inspected the relic.

"This is most troubling, indeed," said Temmon, handing the arrow head back to Malgorth, "but it does not explain your request for our presence here." He turned and spread his arms wide, indicating the battalion at his back.

"Brother Temmon," said Malgorth, "we expected to find an uprising upon our arrival. We believed that the barrens had turned on their handlers and attempted a coup. Frankly, the fact that they have not is a moot point."

"How so?"

"If they have not already turned against the capital, they soon will. The barrens have a predisposition to mischief, and the spark of hope burns within them all. I suppose any race which has been told, generation after generation, that they are little more than a worthless, accidental offshoot of greater and more powerful kin will grow rebellious by their very nature."

"So what do you propose?" asked Balus.

"Oh, nothing much," replied Malgorth. "Just the public execution of a handful of insurgents, and if the rest do indeed rebel, then the systematic extermination of these barren vermin would serve as a solid *Plan B.*"

Balus and Temmon exchanged glances, allowing unspoken words to pass between them, told only in their eyes and expressions. Long moments passed, and the only sounds to be heard were the deep, rumbling breaths of the wolves and the restless crackling of the fire troll's burning skin, vividly juxtaposed against the whistling of the birds in the trees, and the low chirping and clicking of the insects, unseen among the reeds and grasses. At length, Balus nodded.

"Very well, Commander. Prince Vinadan will not suffer open rebellion; we approve of your plan. Now, we are hungry and weary from our journey south from the capital. The infantry need rest, and the wolves will require water; lead the way," said Balus, already moving in the direction of the main town square.

"As you wish," replied Malgorth with a slight incline of his head. "For the might of Aclevion."

The sound of the birds and insects was drowned out a moment later by the din of five hundred assorted orrecs, mountain wolves, and one enormous northern fire troll marching into Ehronia, past pair after pair of terrified barren eyes.

Chapter Twenty-Five

The sun broke through the clouds early the following morning, and the greens and blues of Ehronia were cast in a pale grey light which seemed to bring a chill, rather than the warmth of the burgeoning sun, to the damp and muddy streets. There was something dark about the day, and all seemed to sense it; not even the birds had taken up their morning chorus, and all was silent. At length, the sun forced its way more decisively through the dawn clouds, and the muted tones of the barren lands were transformed into vibrant hues by the light of the new day. But still, all remained quiet. Even as the early risers cast open their windows and doors to begin anew their daily routines, they did so with trepidation. The arrival of the Asarlai with a battalion of orrecs in tow had sent all of Ehronia into a disquiet, and everywhere there were whispers; rumours had begun to spread about the reason for the sudden arrival of this fighting force from the capital.

"They're just here to relieve the others," said one elderly barren to her partner whilst they prepared for the day ahead.

"Perhaps they've come to free us," said a younger barren on the other side of town, already queuing outside the inn to make the most of his sole day off.

"I'd wager my good ear that they're here to kill us," said a grizzled and sullen barren, though nobody but the rats were around to hear him in the dark and gloomy alley in which he had become accustomed to sleeping.

As the day began to hit its stride and the barrens were led to their fields, mills, smithies, and looms by their orrec guards, the air was thick with a potent mix of tension and fear. A few kilometers short of the most south-westerly point of Ehronia, where lush greenery eventually gave way to a sandy shore, a procession of barrens were being led to their field under armed orrec guard. They passed through the wooden gate and onto the dirt road upon which stood a large equipment storage shed, and one by one the barrens collected their scythes, ploughs, and pitchforks, and secreted various small trowels and other, more exotic farming equipment about their persons for the hard day's labour ahead. Once prepared, the contingent of barrens trudged down the dirt road until their boots found grass once more, and they took up their positions and began their work. From the main building behind which the field was located, came the sound of voices growing increasingly loud and curt with each exchange.

"No, I will not do it," said Merund, the land owner, slamming his palms down onto the oak desk and spilling some of the fragrant tea from his terracotta mug. "We can barely afford to eat as it is," he continued, "so I can only imagine how difficult it must be for the workers to make ends meet."

The orrec captain with whom Merund was remonstrating stood, grinning, with his hands crossed at the small of his back.

"You'll do as you're told, half-elf, or should I take your head as well as your farm?"

Merund scoffed and shook his head, refusing to be goaded by the orrec.

"You put us in an impossible position, Captain. Those of us who own lands or mills, or whatever else, already send far too much north. We're left with little to show for our loyalty to the prince. As for our workers, they earn next to nothing and call us *blood traitors*." Merund blew out a long breath and placed his hands over his face in exasperation.

"Prince Vinadan is your lord," said the orrec, entirely unmoved by Merund's words, "and *he* raised your tax, not me. There's no negotiating here; you'll pay or you'll die. Should I go and fetch commander Malgorth? I'm sure he'd be more than happy to hear your arguments."

Merund's eyes widened a little at the mention of Malgorth, but he was quick to dampen his reaction and regain his poise.

"No, that will not be necessary," he said, looking at his own silken shoes rather than meeting the orrec's gaze. "Tell your master that it will be done."

The orrec did not reply as he turned on his heel and left the office, passing barren after barren on his way to report back to Malgorth. Merund picked up his mug and spilled a few more drops of his tea onto the papers which covered his desk as his hands shook with nervous energy and a suppressed fury. *Blood traitor indeed,* he thought, as he took out his quill and reached for his stack of parchment. He sat down behind his desk and covered his face with his hands as he collected his thoughts. At length he nodded, dipped the quill into his ink pot, and began to write as quickly as he could. A minute or so later, he picked up the parchment, read it back to himself and, satisfied, rolled it up tight and bound it with string. Setting it aside, he took another piece of parchment and reapplied the ink to the quill. He repeated the contents of the previous letter, and rolled this one just as tightly as the last. Again and again, he wrote, rolled up, and tied the parchments until at last he had a pile of messages small enough to go unnoticed by the orrecs, or so he hoped. He scooped them up and placed them inside his robes.

It was a warm day, but the heat of the morning sun did little to warm the chill which ran through Merund's veins as he passed orrec after orrec, nodding dutifully at each one in turn. He made his way down the dirt road, through the gate, and away from his farm. He tried as hard as he could to appear calm and casual - just a simple landowner going about his business. Should any of the orrecs challenge him, he would simply say he was off to continue his discussion of the new tax arrangements with the captain. Luckily, he was not stopped as he went on his way, he began to notice the heat of the sun upon the back of his neck.

He was in open ground now, his farm far behind him and the main city centre still some way off. The treeline stood around two hundred metres to his right, and once he was sure that he was not being watched by orrecs, he turned and darted in that direction. It seemed to Merund that it took a lifetime to cover the distance, and his every sense was on alert for the sight, sound, or smell of orrec. He broke through the treeline at a sprint and felt a wave of relief wash over him at the feel of leaves and branches at his back, hopefully obscuring him from prying eyes or wandering gazes.

Merund pressed on through the dense trees until the soil at his feet began to include the odd speck of sand here and there, and eventually he found himself on the beach, the trees now behind him. He felt exposed, but knew this was more than a little irrational as the orrecs had no love of the open water, and he could not see another soul in any direction along the shoreline. Still, he tried to be as fast and discreet as possible; it was dangerous for him to be away from his farm for too long as the orrecs would soon start asking questions. He ran along the beach as fast as his ageing legs could carry him, and he deftly hopped over small rock pools and dunes until he arrived at his destination.

Where others may have hesitated, Merund did not so much as break stride he entered the small, dark cave which stood, open-mouthed and ominous, in the base of the white cliff wall. He inched his way carefully through the cave, relying on his sharp vision and keen hearing to navigate his way through the darkness. Eventually he came to a spot where a natural crack, high upon the ceiling of the cave let in a single ray of pure white sunlight, illuminating a small section of cave and setting it in stark contrast to the deep blackness at its edges. The sight seemed to Merund like something from a childhood story; indeed, the first time he had ventured into this place he had half-expected the single point of light to terminate upon a pile of treasure, a gleaming jewel, or an ancient and powerful sword.

  A ruffling of feathers, a beating of wings, and a crescendo of high pitched calls snapped him out of his revelry, and he grinned as he withdrew the handful of tightly-bound scrolls.

  "Good morning, my friends," he said aloud amid the cacophony of shrieks and squawks.

  The fools, he thought, as he set about his work. His hands worked deftly as he set about his work in the darkness. *They underestimate us, and that will be their undoing. Go ahead if you must; destroy the ravens, cage the owls, and eat the pigeons. What we lack in magic, we make up for in our affinity with nature, Hemera be blessed. There are other ways to get a message out.*

  Moments later, Merund stood and turned to follow the creatures back toward the cave mouth, and he smiled as they flew out of the cave and high into the air. The reward was worth the great risk he was taking. The orrecs, he knew, remained blissfully unaware of the existence of the Ehronian black gulls. Up they flew, higher and higher, turning graceful circles in a coordinated dance. At once, they snapped out of their spiralling climb and broke formation, each of the great birds extending their wings to the fullest of their gargantuan spans. Some turned east, whilst others turned north; some climbed higher still, whilst one or two others descended, meaning to seek a more clandestine altitude from which to approach their eventual destination. It was to these destinations that Merund's thoughts and hopes now turned.

Olon, Eldon, Earon, Eonis, Haneth, Jo'Thuun, Torimar...

Chapter Twenty-Six

The hours all seemed to blend into one nameless, shapeless stasis after a while, and Miseldi no longer had any concept of the time of day - nor of the day itself - as she lay dozing on the cold hard floor. Day after day the orrecs had tried to extract information from her, and day after day she had resisted and defied them. The more she resisted, the more invasive the orrecs' methods had become, but still she had held firm.

  She raised her head slightly at the sound of a key turning a little way off in the distance, and she heard Gerdan groaning and whimpering in his sleep, one cell over. Having failed to extract any information from Miseldi, the orrecs had - only the day before - turned to Gerdan. Miseldi had feared for more than just the life of her friend as she heard his tortured cries, she had feared for the lives of all her kin. Gerdan, she knew, was a loyal friend and a good person, but she knew in her heart that he would not be able to hold out as long as her. He was a gentle soul, and he lacked the fire which Miseldi held within her heart - the same fire which had burned so strongly in Horith.

No, she had thought, listening intently, with pointed ears alert and attuned for any word she might have discerned through the walls, *he will talk eventually; they will break him, and he will talk.*

But he had not.

As he was dragged back to his cell by two orrecs, bloodied and bruised, his feet trailing along the cold, hard floor before being unceremoniously deposited to the ground with a sickening thud, he did not speak.

"Gerdan," she had whispered once the orrecs had left. "Gerdan? Are you okay?"

He did not answer her. The only sound which had issued from his cell was a small, barely perceptible, muffled whimpering. Had Miseldi been able to see into her friend's cell, she would have beheld a broken and defeated barren, curled up in the corner, his face buried deep within bloodstained coveralls, his chest rising and falling rhythmically as he wept. But they had not broken him, and Miseldi loved him for that.

The creak of an opening door and the sudden intensifying of the ambient light brought Miseldi back to the present, and she came fully awake with every nerve and sense on alert. Malgorth entered the room, flanked by two powerful looking men in hooded red robes. They moved to the far end of the dungeon, and Miseldi strained her neck trying in vain to peer through the bars to get a better look at what was going on.

Click, creak; click, creak; click, creak, went cell door after cell door as they were unlocked and opened, with barren captive after barren captive dragged out and pushed up against the damp brick wall. Miseldi's countenance was grim but defiant as one of the red-robed men unlocked her cell, dragged her out, and shoved her up against the wall.

"What is this?" she demanded, casting a quick glance in the direction of Gerdan, whose eyes were staring absently at the ground beneath his feet. "What's going on?"

Malgorth smiled and walked over to her, lowering his head and bending his knees in order to stand eye to eye with Miseldi. She felt the warmth of his foul breath against her skin, but she stared unwaveringly into his bloodshot eyes.

"I see we have ourselves a ringleader," Malgorth said over his shoulder to Balus and Temmon.

"Good," replied Balus, "that saves us the trouble of deciding who goes first."

"On the contrary, Asarlai," said Malgorth, not taking his eyes off Miseldi for a moment. "This one shall go last, so she can watch her friends die first." The group of barrens were hastily shackled, their hands bound behind their backs, then dragged out of the dungeon and up the staircase. Their eyes adjusted to the growing light quickly, but still stung and watered given how long they had been in the darkness of the dungeon. They were cajoled and bullied as they were led away from the dungeon and back into the city hall proper, where a cadre of armed and grinning orrecs met them with further jeers and insults. Soiled, damp hoods were placed over the barrens' heads and they were pushed outside into the midday sun.

Miseldi felt the warmth of the day upon her skin, but took no comfort from it. Her senses suggested to her that there was a large crowd gathered, though no murmuring nor chanting met her ears to confirm this. All she could hear was the sound of her own breathing, deafening inside the thick black hood covering her face. Her breath was warm and damp inside the hood, and she felt disoriented as she was pushed and pulled this way and that. Her feet found wooden steps, and up these she was led. One, two, three, and then level ground once more, the wooden boards giving way just a little underfoot as she walked.

She had lived in Ehronia her entire life, and knew these lands like she knew the lines of her own face, so whatever this structure was, with its wooden steps and boarded floors, it was new, she had no doubt of that. She was taken by the shoulders and marched forwards, struggling to keep her feet under the power of the orrec behind her. The short march was over in seconds, and she winced in pain as her legs were forcefully kicked out from underneath her. She landed on her knees, hands still tied at the small of her back.

She instinctively closed her eyes as the hood was yanked from her head and blinding sunlight flooded in. A moment or two later, she opened them, and feared her heart may stop at the sight she beheld. She steeled herself and hardened her heart, lest it be rent it two right there upon the makeshift platform. She, Gerdan, and the other prisoners were lined up side by side, all upon their knees on the hastily-erected wooden platform in the central square. They were around four feet above ground level, and she was forced to look out onto the terrified, horrified faces of hundreds upon hundreds of her kin, all facing the platform, surrounded on all sides by exultant orrecs. There was even, she noted somewhat abstractly, as if in a dream, a fire troll at the back of the crowd; its black and red skin sparking and crackling like the embers of a dying campfire. At the far right end of the platform stood a large orrec with an even larger axe and, at his feet, a heavy wooden block.

A heavy wooden block with a wicker basket positioned ominously in front of it.

So this is it; this is what it has come to, thought Miseldi, *we are to be publicly executed.* But there were no cheers or chants from the crowd, such as would be expected of such a spectacle in the wilder lands of Gibrion; no snarls of bloodlust or exclamations of justice to be served were to be heard among the captive barren audience. There were only solemn faces, slow shakes of downcast heads, and tears. Miseldi watched as one of the red-robed men walked to the centre of the platform and removed his hood, needlessly raising his hand for a silence which already held sway in the town square. He took a deep breath as if savouring the moment, and the midday sun beat down upon his dark skin, drawing forth beads of sweat from his brow. He looked at the gathered faces of the barrens, then at the army of orrecs which encircled them. He blew out the breath he was not aware he had been holding, and looked past the crowd toward the wooden buildings which made up the ramshackle city centre, and the lush green trees which served as a natural backdrop to the scene, as they did in all of verdant Ehronia. Then he smiled. A small, intricate rune burned to life on the side of his neck, and was replicated upon the backs of his hands. He opened his mouth to speak, and the power of the rune amplified his voice, projecting it loud enough to be heard clearly by all in attendance.

"Prince Vinadan, lord of Aclevion, and ruler of all the lands of Gibrion is your rightful master. Through his power and wisdom are opportunities provided for all, and prosperity to those with the guile to seize it." Here, he gestured to a group of barren land and business owners - the so-called *blood traitors* - who averted their eyes and flushed crimson at the Asarlai's words.

"Alas, where there is balance, there will always be those who seek to upset it. Where there is harmony, there will be those seeking to sow discord." His eyes narrowed and his voice took on an edge of dark menace. "And where there is peace, there will inevitably be those who court war. Before you," he gestured toward Miseldi and her fellow captives, " is a group of such dissidents; traitors; malcontents." Each of the bound and kneeling barrens shuffled nervously, eyes silently pleading with the crowd for help.

"And this," Temmon continued, raising his arm and pointing toward the huge orrec with his razor sharp axe, "is the price of treason. For the might of Aclevion." He turned on his heel and walked away, taking up his former position beside Balus. At this signal, the orrec hefted the axe from the ground and slung it menacingly over his shoulder, the blade edge catching the sunlight and reflecting back its blinding light. He took up position beside the wooden block and shifted the axe, taking it in two hands, flexing and readjusting his fingers until he found the optimal grip. Malgorth, standing with the Asarlai, nodded to Agnaz, and the scout heaved the first barren to his feet and marched him to the block.

"Please, don't do this!" pleaded the barren. "I'm just a tailor, I don't know anything! I didn't do any-" a swift punch to the gut from Agnaz choked the tailor's words off in his throat, and he doubled over in pain, unable to bring his bound hands to his wounded abdomen.

"On your knees, you barren scum," said Agnaz, forcing the tailor onto his knees, and pinning his head to the block with a mighty hand.

"No!", "Stop it!, "Leave him alone!" came the cries from the line of barrens who were destined to follow their kinsman to the chopping block.

"Silence!" said Balus, stepping forward, eyes burning with angry crimson fire. The sight of the Asarlai's power was enough to quell the vocal rebellion, and he turned to the orrec at the block and nodded for him to continue. The very air around the city centre was thick with horror, remorse, and anticipation. The silence screamed into a thousand pointed ears, as not a single one among the captive audience dared to utter so much as a word in protest.

A bird chirped somewhere off in the distance; a lazy gust of wind rustled the leaves of the surrounding trees, and the pulses of a thousand rapidly beating hearts reverberated against finely tuned eardrums as the orrec raised his axe high above his head.

The tailor held his breath and squeezed his eyes shut, but Miseldi forced herself to keep hers open. She needed to see this. It would break her heart and quicken the molten rage within her veins. A piece of her - some intangible, innocent vestige of her - would die with the tailor, but she needed to see this.

As the sunlight bounced off the rapidly falling axe blade, she did not flinch nor cry out as she watched, but simply swallowed hard as the axe found its mark and the tailor's head fell into the waiting basket with a sickening wet thump.

A cheer rose up from the orrecs, sending the first real murmur throughout the barren crowd in response. Malgorth raised a hand for silence and received it almost immediately. Order having been restored by his commander, Agnaz strolled casually to the wooden block, where the blood was still pouring from the headless corpse of the barren tailor. He kicked the body hard, and it slumped off the block, rolling over the edge of the platform and falling the few feet to the ground below. With the block now available for the next barren neck, Agnaz turned once more toward the line of prisoners and took the next barren - a female - by the shoulders, and dragged her kicking and screaming to the block.

"No! Please no!" she cried in terror, "I'm just a librarian! I have children! I'm not a traitor! No!" She continued to plead and beg through tears and mucus even as Agnaz held her head firmly in place on the block, only moving his hand out of the way at the last minute as the orrec brought the axe to bear. The barren's wriggling and struggling, however, ensured it was not a clean strike, and her head somehow remained attached to her body. Worse, the stroke of the axe did not kill her outright, and even now she tried in vain to escape her doom, acting on sheer instinct rather than upon any semblance of conscious thought. A swift heft and a second swing from the headsman's blade put paid to both her meagre ambitions and her life, and the wicker basket claimed a second trophy.

Again there came a cheer from the orrecs in attendance, and again Agnaz disposed of the body with as little grace as dignity. Another murmur passed through the crowd; another burgeoning whisper of discontent. Where before the barrens stared at the ground and avoided drawing unnecessary attention to themselves, a growing contingent now grew restless and defiant. Perhaps they had hoped - maybe even truly believed - that this was all just for show; an elaborate charade with the sole intention of scaring any lingering spark of defiance from the barrens. But that hope, that belief, had died upon the stroke of the headsman's axe, and a dark cloud had gathered over the collective hearts of the barrens. The encircling orrecs made a show of pushing and shoving the more vocal back into submission, but the seed had now been planted.

The barrens, perhaps more than any other race in all of Gibrion, knew that from but a single seed, many a mighty thing may grow.

"Next," announced Malgorth, not requiring the power of the Asarlai rune to make himself heard above the growing clamour. Agnaz nodded in obedience and dragged the next captive barren to his feet, before depositing him to his knees with his head on a wooden block now grown slick with the blood of its first two occupants.

"Gerdan," Miseldi called out, her creaking voice betraying her devastation, "be brave." Gerdan managed to turn his head far enough in her direction to make eye contact with her, just for a moment, before Agnaz forcibly turned it in the other direction to make the headsman's job that bit easier. Miseldi's will was breaking; the walls of her world were rent and crumbling; she felt that her heart would break apart right there and then, and there would be no need for the orrec's axe to add her blood to its gilt edge. She would willingly die, right here and now, once the evil act had been carried out upon her helpless friend.

Gerdan, the best of us; meek of spirit yet resolute of heart, she thought as she watched through tear-soaked eyes as the headsman adjusted his grip on the axe's handle and lifted it to his shoulder.

They did not break him. They tried, but they did not break him.

At a nod from Agnaz, the headsman raised his mighty axe high above his head; sunlight reflected off the blade once the orrec's lift had reached the apex of its arc.

The next thing Miseldi was aware of was the din of chaos erupting all around her. She blinked away the blur of her tears, and could not immediately reconcile the sight in front of her. The orrec headsman was dead, his head split almost in two by an arrow - a finely crafted arrow with a distinctive silver tip, clearly fired with great precision.

All around her, orrecs were unsheathing their weapons and barking orders as hundreds of men, elves, and even the occasional dwarf, emerged running from the trees and from behind the ramshackle buildings. Last to emerge from the cover of the trees was another man, robed in red, his eyes burning like the very fires of Aether's pit; he held a burning sword of pure crimson flame in a defensive stance in front of his face as he marched with purpose toward the unfolding scene. Beside the man was a being Miseldi could not possibly have expected to see: a hoblin, armoured and snarling, with a look of determination and purpose on his face, and a shining elvish blade held high above his head as he broke cover and ran into the mire.

Everything was motion and noise, and already the sound of steel clashing upon steel permeated the air. Miseldi found herself free, though she did not see who it was who had cut her bonds and set her loose. She ran to Gerdan and dragged him to the back of the platform, touching his neck, chest, and torso, checking for injuries.

"I'm okay," he said, though he did not understand how; his eyes were wide and wild with confusion. "Miseldi, what's happening?" he asked. Miseldi flashed her friend a genuine and heartfelt smile as she untied Gerdan's bonds.

"He's come, and he's brought help," she said.

"Who, Miseldi?" asked Gerdan, "who has come?"

"Me, my friend," said Ruli as he moved into view. He threw his arms around his friends in a tight embrace, even as the sounds of battle rang out in the air around them, and arrows pinged and zipped in every direction.

"But come," he said, handing each of them a sword, "we have a battle to win."

*

It was dark inside his chambers despite the sunshine outside. He had drawn the heavy drapes and was reading now by candlelight alone. He did not fully understand why he did this, but it was a habit he had formed as a child, when his father, King Entallion, had allowed to study with the Asarlai.

Even when he did not *allow me*, he thought, suddenly recalling his father in the candlelight. He remembered the look on Entallion's face the last time he saw him alive, and he smiled at the memory. But there was no love nor warmth in his smile, only contempt; he relished the memory as one might look back on a fine meal sampled long ago in some exotic land, or as one might recall with longing the intoxicating warmth of a summer's day upon exposed shoulders. Dust blew up from the ancient pages as Vinadan closed the book upon his desk, and he coughed a little as ancient particles entered his lungs. He blew out the candle and stood, resolving to make his way to the Soul Chamber. His chair creaked as he slid it backwards, and he made his way over to the heavy velvet drapes, throwing them open and flooding the room with blinding natural daylight once more.

It's a good thing I'm not of the haemori, he thought, absentmindedly as the sunlight poured in. His brow furrowed as he looked again at the book upon his desk. *I should finish my research,* he thought, still standing haloed against the tall, bright window. *This is important - quite literally life or death. The Souls are not going anywhere; they can wait a day longer.* He continued to stand, torn between the book and the Souls, between theory and practice. At length, he put one foot in front of the other and strode away from the window, past the dusty book upon his desk, and toward the door.

The Souls are my prize, my victory. I must tame them, and continue to assimilate them, he thought, resolving at last to leave his studies there for the day.

Tap, tap, tap, tap, tap.

Vinadan spun on his heel to face the source of the sound. He looked here and there, high and low.

Tap, tap, tap, tap, tap.

The window.

On alert now, the rune for *Destruction* blazed to life all over his skin, the better to put a swift end to any threat. He walked over to the window, his senses alert, and he immediately relaxed when he discovered the identity of the perpetrator. The runes upon his skin began to fade at once, and he reached out to open a small window set into the frame of the larger main window of his quarters. He extended his arm outside in invitation, and smiled a little as a woodland mynah bird hopped onto his arm with perfect poise. Vinadan had no love for his fellow men; no love for orrecs or hoblins, and he was openly hostile to elves, dwarves, and barrens like the fool Horith of house Nindrius, but animals he liked; he respected the birds and the beasts of Gibrion, and even employed them as spies from time to time. He leaned in close as the mynah walked up his arm and hopped onto his shoulder. It, in turn, placed its beak close to his ear, and delivered its report.

Vinadan's face was unreadable, impassive, but a vein stood out against the skin of his neck, betraying his anger at the mynah's message.

"Thank you, my friend," he said to the bird. He watched it jump down from his shoulder and onto the window frame before it soared away into the skies once more, quickly becoming little more than a dark dot on the horizon. He turned and walked slowly back to his desk, sitting down in his chair and sliding it back into position with another telltale creak. He sat for long moments pondering the bird's message.

"Guards," he called over his shoulder, and two armed orrecs immediately entered the room on high alert, eyes darting left and right for any sign of danger to their master.

"Yes, my lord?" said one of the orrecs to the back of Vinadan's golden head.

"Where is Elder Alma?" asked Vinadan, still facing the window, the orrecs at his back. The orrecs exchanged a look and shrugged as one.

"I expect he's in his chambers, my lord. Or maybe he's in the monastery."

"Find him, and bring him to me," said Vinadan, his voice soft and even, barely rising above a conversational tone.

"Yes my lord, at once, sire."

"Oh, and one more thing," said Vindan, turning to look over his shoulder at the orrecs. "Bring a bottle of the '270 red with you - take one from my own personal stores; I hear it's his favourite, you see. And two glasses - the good ones."

"Yes, yes my lord, as you wish. For the might of Aclevion." The orrecs hurried away about their duties, closing the door behind them with a thud.

"He will like that," Vinadan said to the empty room, "plus, it's only good manners."

He opened the dusty book and resumed his research.

Chapter Twenty-Seven

Xeb's burning eyes were focused solely on his Asarlai brothers as he strode through ranks of orrecs, cutting them down with his burning blade, or incinerating them with the merest of gestures. Fennet, he saw in his periphery, was like a whirlwind; ducking, slicing, spinning, parrying, more than holding his own against the orrecs. A quick look to his left informed Xeb that Tyan and Gael were running toward the fire troll which was causing mayhem in the city square, stomping and slamming men, elves, and barrens in all directions, and burning anyone foolish enough to come into direct contact with it. But still Xeb pressed on through the chaos, seeking out his fellow Asarlai who, even now, were deploying their own rune arts against a group of Tyan's men. One by one they fell, burned black by Balus' flaming mace and Temmon's arcane longbow.

He closed the distance, and sent the remaining men from Markosh away with little more than a look. He turned, sidestepping away from the main battle, leading Temmon and Balus toward the execution platform.

"Traitor!" shouted Balus, pointing his burning mace at Xeb, who had now climbed the three steps and stood on the platform, a few feet off the ground.

"No, brother; it is Vinadan who is the traitor. Traitor to all who breathe free air and would choose not to live in fear of a tyrant," Xeb replied, his own flaming sword held out in front of him, pointing at the two Asarlai.

"You have betrayed us all, Xebus," said Temmon, moving slowly toward the steps, "and have thrown in your lot with rebels and insurgents." He summoned a flaming arrow which materialised from nothing to appear upright in the palm of his hand. He nocked it and pulled back the burning crimson string, and took aim at Xeb. He did not immediately loose the arrow, but continued to train it on Xeb as he gained the platform.

"No, brothers. I have chosen freedom over oppression, which is what our order has done for centuries; what we stand for," Xeb replied, backing slowly away from Temmon, noting out of the corner of his eye that Balus had now climbed up onto the platform from the opposite end; they were flanking him.

"Is our order not a check against corruption? Do we not advise the capital for the sake of the greater good? Come, brothers, join me; we do not have to fight," Xeb continued, though he did not extinguish his sword. Temmon made the first move, bending his knees in a lightning quick movement, and releasing the burning arrow as he did so. It screeched through the air toward Xeb's stomach, but was knocked off its course via a well timed swing from Xeb's fiery blade.

Balus came next, swinging his mace in a strong overhand arc aiming straight for Xeb's head. Again, Xeb was able to parry, spinning on his heels as he did so, opening up a little more room for himself on the crowded and creaking platform.

*

"Tyan, flank left," commanded Gael, as she approached the enormous, lumbering fire troll. She could feel the heat emanating from its hide, and could hear the crackling and snapping of the embers which glowed both inside and outside of the creature's very bones. She drew her sword, an elvish blade so silver it was indistinguishable from moonlight as it moved, and she swung hard for the troll's legs. The blade found its mark, and great sparks flew from the wound. Tyan, on the other side, jabbed with his own sword, meaning to sever the troll's foot. But it was no use, his man-made sword barely left a mark, and Tyan's arm reverberated with the impact shock of steel upon the troll's thick, smouldering hide. He took his sword in two hands and tried again, swinging in a wide, horizontal arc at the troll's leg. Again, his only reward was a dull thud. Gael, on the other hand, was ducking, spinning, and leaping out of the way of the troll's slow, lumbering blows, and replying to its assault with attacks of her own. Here she cut; there she sliced; again and again her blade found its mark and hurt the troll, cutting deep and sending sparks flying.

"It's okay, Tyan," she called out as she jumped, flipped, and landed with the grace of her kind, "I can handle this." Tyan nodded and left her to face the troll. His eyes scanned the battle field, watching with a mix of pride and horror as his men fought with everything they had against the army of orrecs. He saw some of their dwarven allies in fierce combat with a pack of wolves. He saw a pair of Gael's elves exchange blow after blow, parry after parry with a group of six orrecs. All were more than holding their own, and if not for the barrens, the battle may well have been over before too long.

But the barrens were not warriors, and they were both unarmed and terrified. Tyan watched in horror as a large, powerful orrec picked up a frightened barren elder by the head and squeezed hard. The barren's struggle ended with a sickening crunch and explosion of crimson. The orrec tossed the broken body to the ground, wiped his hand on his armour, and laughed.

You're mine, thought Tyan. He ran toward the orrec, pushing and shoving others out of his way as he did so, and he soon found himself face to face with the imposing orrec.

"You'll pay for that, filth!" he spat at the orrec, and he held his sword, two handed, in a defensive stance in front of him. He planted his left foot, and turned his body slightly, placing his right foot behind him for balance.

"And what do we have here?" said the orrec. "Are you in charge of this rabble?"

"I am Tyan, captain of Markosh, and mine is the last face you'll ever see."

"Well if we're doing introductions," said the orrec, drawing its own sword, pointing its black, serrated blade at Tyan, "I am Scout Captain Agnaz of Elgiroth. Markosh, you say? I have passed through Markosh recently," Agnaz continued as he sidestepped, circling Tyan. "The streets were lined with corpses, and we feasted upon your young. And as for your women - well…" Agnaz bared his teeth as he laughed.

Tyan gave a mighty yell and charged at Agnaz, swinging his blade wildly toward the orrec's head. Agnaz blocked the strike easily with a single hand upon the sword's hilt. He punched Tyan hard with his free hand, sending blood flying from his mouth, and Agnaz thought he had heard the sound of bone breaking. Tyan shook his head clear and regained his composure. He circled Agnaz, never taking his eyes off the orrec despite the cries and the chaos all around them. He aimed a swing high toward the orrec's head once more, but pulled short at the last minute, pirouetting on his heel and bringing the sword down in a low backhanded strike at the orrec's leading leg. Agnaz managed to readjust his position and caught the blow upon his own blade, but he was half a second too slow, and the edge of Tyan's blade caught flesh, opening up an angry laceration on the orrec's leg.

Agnaz cried out in pain and frustration, and took his sword in two hands, throwing overhand strike after overhand strike at Tyan, beating him down. Tyan raised his sword in defence and blocked the incoming barrage, but he was breathing hard. He began to see spots at the periphery of his vision, and his legs betrayed him with a slight wobble. Agnaz continued his assault, and Tyan kicked out at the orrec, landing hard upon the orrec's knee. Agnaz growled in pain as his knee buckled, the leg now bent at an unnatural angle. He fell to his good knee, but still held his sword firm in one hand, using the other for balance.

Tyan took a moment to catch his breath and clear his head, then raised his sword as he moved in to put an end to the contest, and to the orrec. He ran at Agnaz, swinging his blade in a large overhand arc as he went. Agnaz waited until Tyan was almost upon him, his sword held, one handed, in a high defensive position. He saw the man's eyes flick to the raised sword, just for a moment. But a moment was all he needed.

In one swift motion, Agnaz reached with his free hand to pull his dagger out from the back of his belt, and brought it to bear, hard and fast.

Tyan's momentum carried him forward, and he stopped with a jerk, dropping his sword to the blood soaked, muddy ground. He looked down at his torso, and could not quite understand what he was seeing. The orrec's outstretched hand was pressed directly to his solar plexus, stained with blood, and he felt a sharp, cold pain from the direction of his spine. His legs gave out, but still he remained in place, dangling upon Agnaz's blade like an animal caught in a snare. Agnaz pulled Tyan close until they were practically nose to nose.

"Now I will burn down your world, vermin," he snarled through clenched teeth.

"*For the might of Agnaz.*" He pulled his dagger free of Tyan's body and watched the man fall to the ground, limp and unmoving.

Tyan's eyes began to darken, and the sounds of battle, of cries, of weapons clashing and arrows flying faded, until all he could hear was his own heartbeat, slowing and slowing to a crawl.

Then to a whimper.

Then to nothing.

The last thing he saw was Callie, running through the green fields of Markosh on a warm summer's day. Her arms were spread wide, and she wore yellow ribbons in her hair.

"Daddy!" she smiled as she ran to him.

And then she was gone.

And then *he* was gone.

*

Xeb was overmatched; he parried left and dodged right, ducking flaming arrows and deflecting wild swings of a fiery mace. He backed away as he fought, yielding ground, and now jumped from the execution platform and back to the ground. Balus and Temmon were quick to follow, landing with poise and immediately bringing their weapons to bear. Again Xeb parried, and once more he deflected and dodged, spinning and turning to keep his weapon between himself and his adversaries; his *brothers*.

I cannot keep this up much longer, he thought as he crouched low to duck a vicious backhand swing from Balus' mace. Temmon extinguished his fiery longbow, and Xeb watched as the conjured weapon disappeared into nothingness only to be replaced by an axe, also born of the Asarlai's arcane powers. Temmon turned the axe over in his hands, gauging the heft of the fiery weapon. Xeb's attention was absolute and unbroken, so he did not miss the quick glance shared for but a moment between his Asarlai opponents. They advanced as one, Balus swinging high, Temmon swinging low. Xeb knew he would not survive this fight much longer. Somewhere within himself he reconciled the fact that he would not be able to talk his brothers down; he could not reason with them any more than he could defeat the two of them in open combat. He jumped backwards, and the mace and axe found empty air where their prey had stood but a moment before. Xeb turned and made for the treeline at a run, extinguishing his sword as he went.

"What is he doing?" asked Balus.

"I don't know, brother, but we must not let him escape," replied Temmon, taking off at a run with his flaming axe held low by his side, Balus only a step behind him. They broke through the outer line of trees and found themselves inside a dense wood, the sounds of battle still audible though muffled and abstract behind them.

"Xebus," called Temmon. "Show yourself. You're only making things worse. Surrender, and Prince Vinadan will grant you a quick and honourable death. Keep this up, and… well; you'll find out."

Tortured and executed as a traitor, Xeb thought as he crouched low in the undergrowth, not far from the other Asarlai, but remaining out of sight. *No, I have to end this.*

He closed his eyes and reached into the deep well of his powers, and the rune for *Nature* burned to life upon the back of his hand. He gestured ahead of the two slowly advancing Asarlai, and the branches of a tree in the distance ruffled and swayed under the power of his will.

"There!" hissed Balus, nudging Temmon and indicating the sudden movement up ahead. They quickened their pace and headed for the site of the disturbance. "Last chance, Xebus. Show yourself right now. Do not drag this out unnecessarily. We will destroy you, one way or another," shouted Temmon, raising his ethereal axe.

"I'm here," said Xeb from behind his fellow Asarlai, his voice little more than a whisper.

Temmon and Balus spun around in surprise to see Xeb standing there, his eyes burning with the fire of a thousand suns, and every inch of his skin smouldering with the ancient runes of their order.

Domination, Control, Destruction, Anger, Death, Balance; Xeb had never before poured so much into a single incantation. Before his brothers could register that they had been tricked, Xeb raised both hands in front of him, arms extended in their direction.

Temmon and Balus did not even have time to scream. With a single blinding flash, they were reduced to little more than ashes, smoking upon the ground among the leaves and branches. Xeb slumped to his knees, exhausted. His shoulders and chest heaved in, out, up, down, as he struggled to catch his breath even as the runes faded from his skin. He looked up at the two burning piles on the ground in front of him, and shook his head with grief and regret.

Damn you, Vinadan. Damn you.

*

"Ruli!" called Gael over the din of battle. Blow after blow from her elven sword had landed upon the fire troll, and the great beast was labouring in pain, off balance and hurting from its wounds. But still it would not go down, and like the literal wounded animal it was, it lashed out wildly, taking down men, elves, barrens, and even some of the orrecs and wolves on its own side as it tried to defend itself from Gael's onslaught.

Ruli heard his name, and looked around for the source. He saw the troll before he saw Gael, but immediately he recognised the blur of blonde hair and silver blade as his commander. He ran to her, taking down orrec after orrecs as he went, his bow a flurry of activity and his long knife brought to bear when it became necessary to bloody his hands. As he drew closer to Gael and the lumbering fire troll, his keen eyes noted that his commander's defensive movements were starting to slow a fraction, her counter attacks lacking a shade of their former finesse.

She's tiring, maybe injured, Ruli thought. *Perhaps both.*

One final orrec stood between Ruli and Gael, and the young barren did not have time to slow his pace and engage the foul creature. Instead, without breaking stride, he leapt high and somersaulted over the orrec's head, landing directly behind the creature and moving swiftly on without looking back. The orrec did not so much as glimpse the arrow which Ruli had driven through its skull at the apex of his leap.

He joined Gael and fell immediately in step with her, warding off blow after wild blow from the fire troll, turning, spinning, ducking, and pirouetting to keep himself and Gael covered. His arrival bought Gael a precious moment's reprieve, and she bent forward, hands on her thighs, and took a long, steadying breath. Some of her strength recovered, she shifted into a ready stance, half-turning to place her left flank toward the troll, left foot extended outwards and right leg, knee bent, bracing her weight behind her. She held her silver sword in a two-handed grip, high beside her right shoulder, and flourished the blade in a figure-eight arc as she narrowed her eyes and planned her next move; timing would be everything.

"Ruli," she called, and the barren immediately cast a glance in her direction.

Now I find out for certain if I'm right, she thought, swallowing hard. *If not, we both die here and now.*

She blew out a calming breath, and crystalised the plan inside her mind. She sought for Ruli inside the abstract, cloudy plane in which she could feel the minds of her elven kin, lighting up corners of the murky grey curtain with intermittent flashes of diffuse colour. She saw the familiar greens and blues of her Eonian company inside her mind, shining in their own unique hues as torches illuminate the fog, and she continued to look deeper.

Green, blue, hazel, cyan… Deeper… Further…

She pushed and pushed with her mind, further and deeper into the web.

More blue, more green, some fading, others suddenly blinking out of existence. And then…

Gael's eyes snapped open at the sudden blinding pain in her head. She had never before felt a light shine so brightly among elven minds, let alone in such a bright yellow flash - and certainly not from a barren. She knew that she had found Ruli's mind among the mists, and dismissing the shocking implications as a conversation for another time - a time when they were not in imminent mortal danger - she let her plan flow through the mental stream, pouring her intent toward the shining yellow beacon in her mind.

Without waiting for any form of acknowledgement from her Ehronian cousin, Gael pivoted on her leading foot, and swung her blade in a wide, two-handed, upwards arc, putting her full weight behind the attack. As she had hoped, the ferocity of her strike staggered the fire troll backward, and it called out in pain as sparks flew from a deep cut from its stomach to the base of its throat. In delivering her blow, she only felt rather than heard Ruli backflip away from the troll to land directly behind her, crouching low, arrow drawn as far back as the bowstring would allow; one eye closed in immense concentration, the accuracy of his aim being the only thought currently occupying his mind.

Exactly as Gael had planned.

Gael spun to the left, taking herself out of Ruli's line of sight, and as she came to a stop, completely unaware she was holding her breath, she watched as if in slow motion as the bright silver tip of Ruli's arrow flew through the air at immense velocity to find its mark directly through the pupil of the fire troll's right eye. The creature's roars and bellows ended abruptly as the arrow travelled deeper to pierce its brain. It did not fall forwards, dramatically grasping at the arrow shaft as such creatures did in the old stories Ruli's parents used to read to him as a child; instead, it simply buckled and collapsed to the ground, its legs bent at an unnatural angle as its bulk landed on top of them. Ruli and Gael each took a step forward, coming closer to the dead troll, and watched, mesmerised, as the former oranges and reds of its flaming hide cooled and rescinded, until its hue was not so different to that of the orrecs.

The orrecs, thought Gael, and she gently spun Ruli around by the arm, leading him away from the troll and back toward the battle at large.

*

Should bards ever sing of The Battle of Ehronia, they will surely devote at least a verse or two to '*The Hoblin and the Dwarf,*' such was the ferocity and effectiveness with which Fennet and Brindo moved through the ranks of orrecs and wolves which besieged the square.. Side by side, elven blade and dwarven axe were a singular blur of motion, and the pair, though small in stature, were mighty in battle. Orrec upon orrec, and wolf upon wolf had already fallen by their hands.

"There," said Fennet, pointing ahead with the tip of his appropriated elven blade. Brindo narrowed his eyes and followed the bead of the sword toward a towering orrec who, even now, was casually breaking and rending barrens, elves, and men with little effort expended.

"Malgorth," said Brindo through gritted teeth. He spat on the ground as if to rid his palate of so foul a name. "Are you sure about this?" the dwarf asked his hoblin companion, readjusting his grip on his axe.

"What choice do we have?" replied Fennet evenly, his countenance a mask of resigned determination. Brindo nodded gravely, and he and Fennet turned and ran towards commander Malgorth.

*

At the sound of mingled hoblin and dwarven battle cries rapidly approaching from the left, Malgorth spun, casually tossing aside the human he had just choked the life from. The sight which greeted him was enough to elicit a snort of derision and amusement.

"Really?" he asked, arms spread wide and a sword in each hand, "are you two stunted rats so eager to die?"

Fennet and Brindo stopped a few feet short of Malgorth, and held their respective weapons in high defensive positions.

"The only one who will die here is you, orrec," snarled Fennet. Malgorth merely laughed.

"You dare to threaten me, you filthy hoblin vermin? I thought we had purged the pestilence of your species from every nook and cranny in Gibrion; clearly Aether has seen fit to leave me one more of your kind to crush. You and your *pet*," he added, nodding in Brindo's direction. Fennet and Brindo exchanged a quick glance, and then they moved as one; Fennet swinging high from the left, Brindo hacking low from the right. Battle had been joined with the most formidable opponent on the battlefield. They were committed, now; there would be no running from this fight.

*

Miseldi's wrists still stung where they had been tied, but she was glad to be free of her restraints amidst the chaos unfolding around her. All was motion and colour, as men, elves, orrecs, and barrens fell on all sides, the formerly picturesque square now a slick and deadly mass of carrion. She shook her head to dispel her shock, and grabbed Gerdan by the sleeve, pulling her friend along at her side with her free hand, the other clutching the sword Ruli had given her.

"Come on," she said, ducking low and moving quickly amongst the chaos.

"Miseldi!" called Gerdan, pointing ahead with a shaking finger, his own sword held loosely by his side. Miseldi looked ahead toward the indicated point, and could only watch in horror as an orrec, who she recognised as one of those in command, stood unsteadily on a badly wounded leg, wiping down the blade he had just pulled from the torso of one of Ruli's companions.

"Come on, he's wounded. We can do it," replied Miseldi, giving her sword a quick twirl in anticipation of what was to come. She started toward the orrec, but Gerdan grabbed her sleeve, tugging her back.

"No! You can't; he'll kill you!" Gerdan pleaded, tears already tracing clean lines in the dirt which covered his face.

"We must, Gerdan; you and I together. He's badly injured; we can take him off the board." She pulled free of Gerdan's desperate grasp, and ran full speed at the orrec, leaping over Tyan's body and aiming a mid-air swing directly at the orrec's neck. Her feet hit the ground as her blade met Agnaz's, and her shoulder reverberated with the impact of his defensive stroke. Their blades were locked together for a moment, as each pushed against the other, unwilling to concede so much as an inch of ground. Though Agnaz was injured, his leg bleeding and shaky beneath his weight, he was still a large and powerful warrior. Releasing one hand from the hilt of his sword, he planted a fist squarely onto Miseldi's jaw, sending her tumbling away to the ground. The orrec pressed his advantage, swinging a one-handed stroke overhead toward a prone and stunned Miselsdi, but the barren was able to raise her arm at the last moment and send his stroke skittering along the edge of her own blade to land safely in the dirt beside her. Miseldi regained her feet and spun on her heel, putting a sword's length between herself and her opponent. She took a deep breath and looked Agnaz in the eye. Working her jaw, she spat out a mouthful of blood and teeth onto the ground between them.

"Good," Agnaz laughed, "you, I see, are tougher than most of your filthy, impotent kin. Tougher too, I would say, than *him*," Agnaz inclined his head toward Tyan's body. Miseldi flicked her eyes toward Tyan for a heartbeat; though she understood he was one of Ruli's companions, she did not know him and felt little at his passing.

Her momentary lapse of concentration was all it took. Agnaz advanced, swinging wildly, cut after cut, thrust after thrust, his injured and bleeding leg hardly slowing him a step; it was all Miseldi could do to parry and dodge, and she cursed herself for falling for the distraction. Agnaz pressed his attack, and a low, backhand swing snuck through Miseldi's defences, cutting into the meat of her thigh. Miseldi staggered back with a cry of pain, but did not fall. She tightened her two-handed grip on her sword, and put her left foot forward, meaning to arrest Agnaz's advance and initiate a counter attack. The big orrec swung high for Miseldi's head - a finishing blow - but Miseldi ducked under the blade and brought her own to bear, slicing deep across Agnaz's abdomen. But orrec hides are tough, and Agnaz only clutched at the wound in anger. He brought his hand up to his face and registered the blood, then turned and screamed at Miseldi, a sound of pure rage and vitriol.

  He charged forward, but did not swing his sword. At the last moment, he turned his shoulder and barged into Miseldi, knocking the wind out of her and sending her sword flying to land harmlessly, ten feet away in the dirt. Miseldi opened her eyes, registering a sharp pain in her lungs, and found she was struggling to breathe. She could not see her sword, and found that she lacked the strength to even stand, let alone to fight.

A shadow loomed over her. She squinted, and raised a hand to shield her eyes from the sunlight. The realisation that Agnaz was standing over her, crouching low to straddle her chest, unsheathing his ebony-bladed dagger as he did so did not send Miseldi into a blind panic; she did not whimper, cry, nor beg for mercy. She took as deep a breath as her broken ribs would allow, and tried to calm her mind.

"You're a tough one, I'll grant you that, half-elf," said Agnaz as he settled into position, one knee either side of Miseldi's prone and badly injured body.

"I hope that's some consolation," Agnaz continued, his words soft and at odds with the malice written upon his face.

"But now," he continued, "it's time to-"

The look of shock mingled with horror etched upon Agnaz's face was one Miseldi would never forget. The orrec dropped his dagger, and placed both hands around the blade which had run him through, back to front, and now protruded out through his chest, slick with his own blood. The hands upon the hilt were shaking, but did not let go and continued to push the sword further and further through the orrec's back. Miseldi was quick to recover her senses, and leaned to the left in an attempt to identify her saviour. To her shame, she had not expected it to be Gerdan.

"Gerdan!" she exclaimed, overcome with love and pride for her friend.

"Miseldi! Look! I-"

Once again, they had underestimated the strength of will possessed by the orrecs of Elgiroth, and neither barren could do a thing to stop Agnaz reclaiming his dagger from the dirt, turning it over in his hand, and ramming it high above his right shoulder and straight through Gerdan's eye. The last of the orrec's strength now spent, he toppled, dead, and landed next to Miseldi on the ground. She could only watch, open mouthed and wide-eyed, as Gerdan, too, crumpled like a rag-doll to take his place among the dirt and carrion.

*

Hoblin and dwarf alike fought for more than just their own lives and the liberation of the barrens. Having been driven underground, long ago, by the self-proclaimed superior race of orrecs, hoblins, Fennet knew, were viewed as little more than vermin by most. So as he swung high and low with his elvish blade; as he spun and ducked, in tandem with Brindo against the vicious onslaught of Malgorth, his heart was filled with both molten rage at his enemy, and a deep, burning love for his kin.

Brindo was much the same; as he spun and twirled his mighty axe, blocking Malgorth's powerful blows and redoubling his own counter attack against the orrec's legs and midsection, his mind was focused on his guilt and shame at his inability to prevent the massacre of Lord Thyrus and his men at Vinadan's hands, and his steadfast determination to ensure that not a single dwarf in all of Gibrion would suffer that fate again.

But in Malgorth, they had chosen a fierce and unforgiving opponent, and the orrec did not seem to tire as he threw blow after blow - high from the left; low from the right; a spinning back-hand with both blades extended - at Fennet and Brindo. He drove them backwards, grinning as he watched hoblin and dwarf slip and falter on the blood-drenched ground, slick with the sticky remains which littered the battlefield. Fennet stumbled on the body of an elf and nearly lost his footing entirely, but managed to bring his weight to bear at the last moment and remained upright. His momentary stumble, however, provided Malgorth with an opportunity, and the big orrec thrust his right-hand blade forward, catching

Fennet along his left flank and opening up a pink flesh wound which stood in stark contrast to his grey-green skin.

Fennet gave a grunt of pain but did not go down. He tightened his grip upon the hilt of his sword and focused his attention entirely on his enemy, ignoring the pain in his side and the blood which he felt trickling down his hip. He hopped up and down on his feet with nervous energy, and cast a sideways glance at Brindo. The dwarf's countenance betrayed his concern for Fennet following his wound, but the hoblin merely winked at his companion to show he was okay.

At least I hope I am, thought Fennet, not daring to inspect his wound, lest its severity lessen his confidence. He twirled his blade in front of him in a figure-of-eight motion and took a large step forward, bringing the blade down in a powerful overhead arc aimed squarely between Malgorth's eyes. The orrec commander pivoted to the left, letting Fennet's swing land harmlessly in the dirt. A strong kick to the hoblin's gut sent Fennet tumbling away to the ground, and Malgorth had enough time to cross his swords in front of his chest, catching Brindo's axe where the blades met. He turned his shoulders in a quick circular motion, and sent Brindo's axe flying away out of the dwarf's hands to land a few feet away. Malgorth stepped to the right, placing his imposing frame between Brindo and his weapon.

The distance between dwarf and axe might as well have been a mile; Brindo had no way to retrieve his weapon, and nowhere to run. He was unarmed, and at the mercy of a grinning Malgorth, who turned his dual blades over in his hands as he advanced, cutting arcs in the air between he and Brindo.

"I'm not afraid of you, orrec filth," Brindo said through gritted teeth. He balled his fists and raised them in a defensive stance, which seemed to do little but amuse Malgorth.

"You would face me hand-to-hand, dwarf?" said the commander, who stood a good four feet higher than Brindo.

"You scared?" spat the dwarf, flashing Malgorth a taunting grin. Malgorth considered this question, though not for long.

"No," he answered, having seemingly given the question some serious thought. He was far too quick for Brindo, and before the dwarf could even register what had happened, two bloodied blades were protruding out through his back, and he found that he could not breathe.

Malgorth pulled his blades free of Brindo's chest and watched the dwarf slump to his knees. He slid his left-hand sword into his belt, and took up a two-handed grip on his remaining weapon. He pulled his arms back, then delivered a powerful blow, right to left, and let his momentum spin him one hundred and eighty degrees to face away from Brindo. He strode away in Fennet's direction, and did not so much as glance backward as Brindo's head landed in the dirt beside his still-kneeling body. Fennet looked upwards from his prone position, and saw that Malgorth was striding toward him with a terrifying smile on his face and murder in his eyes. The orrec, Fennet saw, was wiping his sword clean of blood as he came, and the hoblin could see no sign of Brindo.

No, he thought, and shook the thought from his head. He was dazed, and found the simple act of breathing to be a labour. The pain in his side was now a dull throbbing, and he did his best to ignore it.

Get up, Fennet, he told himself. *Get up or you're dead.*

He ran a mental inventory, noting the laceration earned at the tip of Malgorth's blade, possible broken ribs, and a slight concussion. Malgorth was close now, almost upon him. Fennet pushed as hard as he could into the ground, and his arms shook with fatigue as he heaved himself up, first to his elbows, then to his knees. He retrieved his sword and used it as a crutch, dragging himself to his feet. He pulled the sword tip out of the mire and held it out toward Malgorth, now mere feet away. The towering orrec came to a dead stop.

"Do you really want to end up like your friend over there?" Malgorth gestured over his shoulder, and Fennet now saw what remained of Brindo. Waves of anguish and hatred battled for control of Fennet's senses. He looked away from Brindo's corpse and returned his gaze to the still-grinning Malgorth. The orrec commander matched Fennet's stare, and fancied that the very fires of the Asarlai were burning somewhere just behind the little hoblin's eyes.

"You will die for that," said Fennet, his words coming out quieter and calmer than he had expected.

"We will see, *vermin*."

Orrec and hoblin alike swung as one, and the echo of their clashing blades could be heard all across the battlefield. Back and forth they went, blows raining down on each other; most were parried, however narrowly, while others went wide of their mark. On and on the orrec and hoblin fought, blades coming together in a violent onslaught which took them halfway across the town square as they each took their turn advancing, pressing their attack, before a punch, a kick, or a headbutt would turn the tide and see the aggressor turn defender once more.

Malgorth registered in his periphery that the wider battle was starting to wind down; the crowd was thinning, and the sound of his and Fennet's clashing blades became the dominant sound among the din. Small pockets of survivors began to group together, looking to Malgorth like little galaxies drawn together by some macabre gravity to form their own little clusters in the grand expanse of the battlefield. The survivors, the commander noted, were predominantly men, elves, and barrens. Though some orrecs remained among the living, Malgorth saw that they were being shackled and shoved to their knees en masse by the rebel fighters. He snapped his head back just in time to avoid being seriously hurt by the hoblin, but still took a nasty cut to the face as the price of his distraction. This momentary lapse had nearly cost him, and his rage nearly choked him as he roared in a black fury.

A crowd had begun to gather around Fenent and Malgorth; a circle of men, elves, and barrens was closing in around them, watching the duel unfold but not daring to interfere. All but one.

"Fennet," said Ruli, more to himself than to his companion. He reached over his shoulder and pulled an arrow. As he made to nock it, he felt a strong hand take his arm.

"No," said Gael, "this is his fight."

"But he is overmatched," protested Ruli, trying to pull loose of Gael's grasp. Gael narrowed her eyes as she observed the fight between orrec and hoblin, paying particular attention to the sword in Fennet's hands. A small grin tugged at the corners of her mouth.

"I wouldn't be too sure of that, my friend," she replied. She was right.

Fennet, far from being forced on the defensive, was starting to press his attack. His silver elvish blade swung high and low, cutting shining arcs in the air and staggering Malgorth backwards. The big orrec had lost one of his own swords, and now held a two handed grip on his remaining weapon, parrying and blocking Fennet's blows. But the occasional strike got through Malgorth's defences, and the orrec was bleeding from a few small but deep cuts. The orrec was ceding ground, moving backwards under Fennet's relentless assault, and the circle of rebels was almost at his back.

Fennet pressed and pressed, trying with every fibre of his being to ignore the pain in his side, to push past his fatigue and end his foe. He swung a low backhand slice toward Malgorth's shin, and took immense satisfaction from the orrec's resulting roar of pain as another wound opened. But Fennet was exhausted, and he was still losing blood. His view of Malgorth was momentarily obscured by a darkness pulsing around at the edges of his vision, and he lost his footing as he swooned. He took a deep breath and squeezed his eyes shut in an attempt to focus his mind. He did not remember falling to his knees, and his every sense and instinct screamed at him that he was suddenly in very real danger. From his kneeling position, he turned to see Malgorth charging toward him with his sword drawn back over his shoulder, ready to take advantage of Fennet's stumble and end the fight once and for all.

Fennet tried to stand, but his legs were like straw. He was done. He had fought with all his might, but he had nothing left to give. But he did not cower in the face of his own annihilation; he did not beg for mercy nor ask for quarter. He remained kneeling, but stared undaunted into Malgorth's wild eyes.

He felt the heat before he saw the flame, and did not immediately understand what had happened. Malgorth groaned in pain as he lay in a heap some ten feet away, having been flung backwards by a powerful fireball cast from somewhere behind Fennet. The hoblin turned toward the source to see

Xeb struggling toward him, the fire in his eyes and the runes upon his skin already starting to fade.

"Are you okay?" Xeb asked, betraying some of the panic he felt. Fennet noted the dark patches under Xeb's eyes, and saw how his shoulders slumped as he walked.

"Are *you*?" the hoblin asked in return.

"I'm fine," replied Xeb. I just need rest. Maybe an ale." He winked at Fennet and continued to advance, eyes fixed on the prone and moaning orrec commander on the ground.

"Now to finish this," he said, and picked up Fennet's dropped sword.

"No," said Fennet, holding out a hand to stop Xeb, "Do not; I have to do this."

Xeb stared into Fennet's eyes for a few heartbeats, then nodded. He held out his hand and Fennet took it. He hauled the little hoblin to his feet and handed him the elvish blade. Fennet accepted his weapon, and took a few long, deep breaths. He blinked, and shook his head to clear his vision, then turned and paced over to the stricken orrec commander. Malgorth was cut, burned, and beaten, but he was still dangerous; a wounded animal, cornered and acting on pure instinct.

"You will die for this, Asarlai traitor," he screamed at Xeb.

"No," said Fennet, his voice quiet and steady. "Only you will die today. The rest of your kind will die tomorrow, and your master will die the day after that."

"Fool!" shouted Malgorth, "You have no idea of the power-"

A lightning-fast backhand slice separated Malgorth's head from his neck and left his sentence eternally unfinished. Fennet did not cheer or gloat; he did not spit upon Malgorth's body or offer a witty remark. He slid his sword into its sheath, and walked back toward Xeb.

"I am injured, master Xebus. Can you help-" Fennet's own sentence would remain incomplete as he collapsed into Xeb's arms.

Chapter Twenty-Eight

The sun was almost down, and the sky was a beautiful swirl of oranges and purples; an image which not even the greatest artisans among elves or men could ever hope to recreate. There was a chill in the air now, and the sound of the waves encroaching and receding from the shoreline seemed like a heartbeat; the steady, rhythmic beat of nature's drum. Gael felt a shiver run the length of her spine, and she clutched at the exposed flesh of her arms feeling goosebumps rising to the surface. The mood was sombre on the beach, and not man, woman, or child of any race spoke as the crowd of hundreds stood stoically in a mass gathering, not unlike the gathering in the doomed square three days before.

Only this time, they were there by choice.

About half a mile to the south stood a smouldering and smoking mass of bones and charred meat. The survivors of the battle of Ehronia had piled and set aflame the bodies of their orrec tormentors; the image and stench of spoiled and burning flesh was like an indelible scar on the Ehronian landscape. Even the black gulls, so fierce and cunning a species as they were, gave that area of the beach a wide berth and grew wary and restless in its vicinity.

Gael looked around at the gathered and silent faces. Some she knew, most she did not. Ruli stood to her right, his friend Miseldi beside him. Gael and Miseldi had been introduced, though briefly, in the days after the battle, and in Miseldi Gael recognised the same strength of will that she saw in Ruli. She liked the young barren, and knew that Ruli loved her like a sister. To Gael's left stood Xeb; he looked better now, rested and recovered. To his eyes had returned that spark of determination, though the elf also thought that she detected a great sadness behind them. The deaths of his fellow Asarlai at his own hand weighed heavily on Xeb, and she fancied that he had both surprised and frightened himself at the display of power he had been forced to produce to finally defeat his brothers.

Next to Xeb was Fennet, still sporting a bandage wrapped all the way around his torso. He, too, looked stronger now, thanks to his days of convalescence and the employment of Xeb's healing arts. It was to Fennet that Gael made her way. Placing a gentle hand on his shoulder, she led him away from the main group. A number of eyes followed them, but the pair were out of earshot.

"My lady," Fennet said, bowing low, when they had come to a halt beside a rock pool. A small crab skittered away from them into the safety of a nearby crevice.

"Master Fennet," Gael replied, "you look to be on the mend."

"Yes, my lady; I feel much better now. I am at your service."

"Hand me your sword," said Gael, extending her hand to Fennet. The hoblin flinched a little and felt his heart skip a beat.

"I… I did not steal it," he said.

Gael laughed and shook her head, sending her golden ponytail dancing across her shoulders.

"No, Fennet, you did not. Please, do not misinterpret my intentions. Hand me your blade."

Fennet did as he was bade, and pulled the sword from its sheath. He had cleaned it after the battle, and it now shone like a star in the light of the burgeoning moon. Gael took it from Fennet with a nod of thanks, and turned it over in her hands, examining the intricate markings along its blade, noting the runes carved into the hilt. She held it up in front of her face, and turned her head. She placed an ear to the blade and closed her eyes. After a long moment, she opened her eyes and smiled at Fennet. But it was not a joyous smile, full of humour; rather, it was a sad smile, one which wore mirth as a mask to hide its melancholy. She handed the sword back to Fennet.

"It is as I thought when I saw you take on the orrec," she said.

"My lady?" replied Fennet.

"This," said Gael, pointing to the sword, "is *Enarhaedon,* known as *The Traitor's Blade* to the non-elven."

"Traitor's blade?" asked a confused Fennet.

"Yes," replied Gael, "it once belonged to the elven king Ealdris, a very long time ago."

"I'm sorry, my Lady, we hoblins do not have tales of great elven kings."

Gael laughed once more at the little hoblin's forthrightness.

"No, I don't expect you do. Well, he was a king, to be sure, but he was not great," Gael said. "Ealdris was a traitor; when his people - my people - needed him most, he turned on them. He killed many of his own kin before he fled, and he left the rest of his people to die. An entire town, destroyed overnight."

Fennet was enraptured by Gael's words and did not interrupt.

"So they cursed him. His sword - *this* sword - had already taken so many lives, what was one more? He died upon his own blade, and his spirit, like those of the countless he murdered, are bound to this weapon."

Fennet looked at the sword with wide eyes, as if he might see the souls Gael spoke of.

"It is old magic, dark magic; an archaic elven device now outlawed as necromancy," Gael said. Fennet held the sword out on open palms and offered it to Gael.

"My lady, I…if you want to take it…"

"No, my friend," she interrupted, "that's exactly the point."

Fennet tilted his head to one side in confusion. Gael smiled warmly at the hoblin and knelt down to look him in the eye.

"This sword is an ancient elven relic, believed long since lost to time and decay; it is famous - perhaps *infamous* is a better word - among my people. Some fear it, others covet it. All elves know of Enarhaedon, the sword of the Ealdris the Unworthy. My ancestor."

Fennet's eyes widened further.

"Your ancestor? Then it *is* yours; it belongs to you my lady!" said Fennet, trying once again to hand Enarhaedon to Gael.

"I suppose you are right," she considered. "It is truly mine. In that case, I hereby officially bequeath it to you, master Fennet."

"Are…are you sure, my lady?"

"Of course," replied Gael. "I long to see it do some good in this world. I wish to see it wielded by one with love, not greed, in his heart."

"You honour me, Lady Gael," said Fennet, bowing low.

"The honour is mine, my friend," said Gael, gesturing for Fennet to rise.

"Besides," she added, "it seems to have taken a liking to you. Maybe one day you will rename it."

Fennet returned Gael's smile, and the pair headed back to join the others beneath the moonlight.

*

The boats were full, and the line of archers was ready with bows drawn. They held their positions, and not a single arm wavered. A group of the strongest men, elves, and barrens marched solemnly forward, the gentle crunch of sand beneath their feet giving way to the sloshing of water as they stepped into the sea. They waded out toward the waiting boats which bobbed up and down in concert with the waves. On the count of three, the volunteers pushed, sending the boats along a new trajectory, south and west away from the shore, destined to be carried into the waiting arms of whichever goddess their occupants held dearest in life.

Xeb walked in front of the archers, standing between the bows in front and the laden boats behind. He raised a hand, drawing on the *Sorrow* and *Nature* runes for his power, and at the flick of his wrist, a hundred gleaming arrow heads burst into flame, casting an otherworldly orange and yellow glow in challenge to the silver light of the moon. A command from the lead barren signalled the loosing of the arrows, and Xeb tracked their arc as they flew over his head to land with precision among the boats which immediately burst into flame, returning the dead, wrapped and shrouded within them, to the oblivion of centuries.

Gael stepped forward; the bright glow of the burning boats cast fiery shapes across her face, and the flames in the distance were reflected in the tears which rolled openly down her cheeks. The only sounds to be heard were the gentle rise and fall of the waves, and the crackling, snapping sounds of the burning boats.

She took a deep breath and began to sing.

By waves and by trees, by darkness, by light,
Return, my friend, to eternal night.
By pain and by love, by wrong and by right,
Return, my friend, to eternal night.

Oh sing to the chorus of the eternal night,
Sing to the chorus of the eternal night
Oh, to Hemera by day, and to Aether by night,
Sing to the chorus of the eternal night,

By the gull, by the sparrow, by the eagles in flight,
Return, my friend, to eternal night.

By the tears of the fallen, and the stars burning bright,

Return, my friend, to eternal night.

Oh sing to the chorus of the eternal night,

Sing to the chorus of the eternal night

Oh, to Hemera by day, and to Aether by night,

Sing to the chorus of the eternal night.

All was still as Gael fell silent; the sound of the burning boats growing distant as the waves carried them away. Gael turned to the crowd at her back, and was overwhelmed at the sight of so many men, elves, and barrens; families, friends, lovers, brothers in arms - everyone hugged the one closest to them, and all let the tears flow openly, not fighting the grief and the pain, but welcoming it; a fitting send-off for the brave fallen.

Gael relinquished the walls she held high around her heart, and fell to her knees upon the sand. Her shoulders heaved as she wept openly for the dead, silver moonlight haloing her golden hair.

Goodbye, Tyan. Be with Callie; be at peace. Leave this war behind, my friend.

Chapter Twenty-Nine

Though it was really not that long ago when measured against the lives of the elves and the age of the mountains, Ruli could hardly remember the last time he had stepped foot inside The Broken Staves inn. Horith had been there, that much he knew, but he could recall little besides. Though barely a year had passed, so much had happened to Ruli and to the world around him that he simply no longer felt like the same barren who had decided to leave his home behind in search of his friend. The same barren who had packed weapons and scant provisions and had snuck across the borders of Ehronia under the cover of night. The same barren who had so nearly been caught by a patrolling orrec. The same barren who had performed his first kill as he silenced the orrec before it could raise the alarm. The sound of his arrow shattering the orrec's skull was one that Ruli would never forget.

And now, as he sat among fellow barrens, a contingent of elves and men, a handful of dwarves, and an unlikely pairing of an Asarlai and a hoblin, Ruli drifted out of the conversation around him and slipped deeper and deeper into his own mind. A melancholy lay on him, and despite their victory over the orrecs, Ruli was deeply troubled.

"We need to talk," said Gael.

Ruli looked up and saw the elf in deep conversation with Xeb and another of his own kin. But as Ruli raised his gaze to her, Gael flicked her eyes in his direction whilst continuing to speak and gesticulate to the others.

"I am at your service, my lady," Ruli said without moving his mouth; his mind projecting the words directly into Gael's own.

"I see it now, master barren," she replied directly into his mind as she sipped her wine. "A power has awakened in the barren race," she continued, "and you are the spearhead, my friend."

"Spearhead?" Ruli replied silently.

"The *arrow head*, then, if you prefer," she grinned at the young barren. "Somehow, your telepathy is more than equal to that of many of my woodland kin, but that power has been absent in your kind for centuries," Gael explained, whilst simultaneously conferring with the Asarlai.

"I don't really know what to say, my lady. I have not studied the art. I am just…. *me*; I have always been so."

Gael nodded almost imperceptibly to signal the end of their brief mind-meld, and she sent a wave of support and reassurance to Ruli, sensing the disquiet which lay upon him.

"So what are we to do, then?" said Fennet, snapping Ruli's mind back to the here and now.

"Firstly," said Gael, "we need to ensure the injured and infirm have all the supplies they need as they recover. The city hall is full to bursting, this is true, but more and more recover each day thanks to the doctors and the volunteers."

"Yes," said Xeb, "their work is commendable, and whilst we must do what we can to aid them, do not forget that our business lies to the north."

"And the sooner the better," added Ruli, now back amongst the conversation. All eyes turned to him.

"Would you care to explain?" asked the elder barren who sat at their table, a large, frothy ale in hand.

Merund, Ruli realised, *one of the land owners.*

"Vinadan's orrecs may have been defeated, but do you really think he will not have learned of our victory?" Ruli replied.

"How?" asked Merund. "We left none alive."

Ruli allowed a snort of laughter to escape his lips.

"How, indeed?" he said. "Vinadan has spies everywhere; orrecs, men, mercenaries from the western isles... Perhaps even one or two blood-traitor slavers, hey Merund?"

The older barren slammed his ale down onto the table and waved his finger at Ruli.

"Now, listen here, *boy*. You have no idea how hard it was for us. Do you think we enjoyed watching our own kin worked half to death for a pittance? It was all we could do to keep them from killing you if you so much as dropped your Aether-damned pitchforks!"

"Now, gentlefolk, let us not bicker amongst ourselves," said Xeb, raising his palms and calling for calm. Ruli continued to stare pointedly at Merund, who scoffed, and picked up his ale, taking a large swig before wiping his mouth with the back of his hand.

"Anyway," Merund continued, "we're just thankful you arrived when you did. I don't know how much longer we were going to last. The orrecs were growing bolder whilst some of our folk - not unlike our young master Ruli here - were growing restless. Ehronia had become a tinderbox; it only needed a spark - an orrec making a play for power, perhaps, or a plucky barren answering back - and the whole thing would have gone up like the Wicker Elf on Gibrion Day." He took another large gulp of his ale and set it down, shaking his head.

"It is still a wonder that you arrived so soon; with an army, at that. I had heard tales of the swiftness of the black gulls, but I never thought they would marshall such aid so quickly."

Xeb, Fennet, Gael, and Ruli exchanged a confused glance.

"The black gulls?" asked Fennet, "are they a band?"

Merund threw back his head and laughed heartily.

"No, master hoblin. The black gulls are quite literal birds; huge, black birds which can carry messages for leagues and leagues. But of course you should know this," Merund continued, narrowing his eyes, "you received my message, no?"

"No," answered Xeb. "We received no message, and certainly did not look upon the gulls; though I have encountered them before on my travels."

"Then how came you to be here, and in such numbers?" asked Merund, not shy about letting his confusion show.

"It is a long story," said Gael, "but suffice it to say we already had business in Ehronia."

"Well, we are all thankful that Hemera saw fit to guide you here. We only grieve the blood that was spilled before you arrived. And after," said Merund, his eyes downcast. The rest of the table followed suit, and a moment of brief silence ensued as the dead were recalled. Those who fell in battle; those who were executed as Xeb's party approached; those who were shot in the back with orrecish arrows, or torn asunder by the wolves of Acelvion as they tried to flee the besieged square; all were remembered in that moment.

"Still," said Merund, raising both his head and his tankard, "I sent the gulls to every corner of Gibrion. Swift are their wings and sharp are their minds, they will not fail to deliver the messages. They never do." Merund's pride was obvious; he clearly had great affection for the birds.

"And where, master Merund, were they dispatched to?" asked Gael.

"Where *weren't* they dispatched to?" laughed Merund. "Haneth, Torimar, Ideenion, Jo'Thuun, Skellt, the Ears, Adeniron… Someone may yet heed our call to arms."

"That was a bold move," said Xeb, "and risky. Vinadan has spies in all of the major cities, and likely among the smaller townships. If one of the gulls is intercepted-"

"It won't matter," said Ruli with finality. "We need to leave here as soon as we can. At first light if possible."

"You have only just arrived," said Merund.

"I fear the boy is right," said Xeb. "As much as we would like to stay here longer - rest, recuperate, rebuild, tend to the wounded - we must not waste the advantage we find ourselves with. I must admit I did not anticipate leaving so soon, but I believe young Ruli is correct. Vinadan will surely learn of this defeat, and soon. Whether by words or by wings, he is never kept in the dark for long." Those around the table grew silent once more, pensive and brooding, as all considered the implications of taking up arms again so soon, and making the perilous journey north to the capital. Xeb drained the last of his ale, and placed his tankard down firmly, jolting all and sundry from their thoughts. He looked at Fennet, and his countenance spoke of gravity; a hint of concern lining his weathered features.

"Fennet, my friend," Xeb began, "I know you are not yet fully healed, but I must ask you to prove your worth once more."

Fennet set his jaw and nodded. "Of course, master Xebus. What do you need?"

"It is time for you to return home. Take Trumpet, so that you might cover the distance with all haste. You must entreat Ugnor to keep to his word; you must rally the hoblins and meet us in Rainwater Wood, east of Dinann, three days from now."

Fennet nodded gravely and drained the last of his own ale. He did not find it as palatable as the hoblin-brewed equivalent, but it would do. He stood and nodded to Xeb, then turned to nod at Ruli, Merund, and Gael in turn.

"I will leave at once," he said to Xeb. "I won't fail; you can count on my kin and I to do our part."

Xeb stood and placed a firm hand on the hoblin's shoulder. "Ride fast, and fare well my friend," he said. Those around the table would later wonder whether they had truly detected an undertone of great sadness in Xeb's voice. Perhaps it was merely pride. Maybe it was just the ale. Fennet turned to leave, but Gael called his name.

"Yes, my lady?" he answered, lowering his head in deference. Gael pointed to the sword upon Fennet's back.

"*Enarhaedon*," she said, "it serves you now. Trust it." Fennet did not respond, but bowed, low and long, before turning on his heels and leaving The Broken Staves, making for the stables to the saddled and waiting Trumpet. Back inside, their table had grown quiet as each dwelt on their thoughts following Fennet's portentous departure. The sound of barrens, elves, and men encroached on their collective silence as if it were the first time they had really heard it. All around, in every corner of the inn, groups conversed and drank, some laughing, others weeping. All were united by a common grief; it just chose to express itself differently from being to being.

Ruli looked around and a warmth began to fill his heart. Drop by drop, flame by flame, the molten fires of rebellion were announcing themselves in his throat and his chest as he observed those around. All present, he realised, were united by more than just grief, loss, and suffering. They had a common purpose; a common enemy, and whether they called the forests of the south or the cities of the north their home, all knew, deep down, that they could never go back to the old ways; that they would have to fight, bleed, and die, if they wanted to be free of Vinadan's evil.

He inhaled deeply, then blew out a long, steadying breath. He stood, and instinctively checked the straps and buckles of his armour and weapons. Taking Ruli's lead, Xeb, Gael, and Merund also stood and pushed their chairs back under the table.

The room fell silent, and all eyes turned to the quartet. Ruli met the collective gaze of his fellow barrens, and raised his chin.

"Many of you already know me," he began, "my friends and I have been coming here for years. Horith Nindrius is dead; murdered at the hand of Vinadan himself. Gerdan Draioch is dead; killed in battle by the orrecs. Miseldi Mykani is badly wounded; even now she is tended to by our healers."

He looked around the room, and he knew he had struck a chord. All eyes were on him, and all voices were silent.

"All have suffered, and all have lost," he continued, "not only our kin, but all free races have felt the bitter sting of grief by the machinations of our so-called prince. I do not ask you to join us; I would not expect anyone to trade their life for mine, but we," he gestured toward Xeb and Gael, "travel north, and soon. We make for Aclevion in arms, and I do not truly expect that we should return."

The ensuing silence was deafening, yet all eyes remained on Ruli.

"We leave at first light. We mean to gather what forces we can, and kill Prince Vinadan. Any who would volunteer to come with us-"

He did not even get to finish the sentence before the silence was broken by the sound of chair legs scraping backwards across the floor of the inn. Every barren who was able was on their feet, heads held high, and the unmistakable look of fiery determination etched upon their faces. Xeb permitted himself a wry grin.

Well done, Ruli, he thought, and could have sworn that the young barren acknowledged the thought with a wink.

Chapter Thirty

The air was warm and carried the taste and smell of saltwater along the breeze. Thalnon could see for miles out to sea, and as he sat at the edge of an old wooden pier, he savoured the moment. The mewing of seagulls and the sweet smell of fish, crab, and lobster permeated this place, and as the setting sun painted the sea in a beautiful golden hue, Thalnon felt at peace for the first time since the massacre at Eonis.

"Here," said Trissan, handing Thalnon a tall, cold glass of wine, "a gift from Lord Driador."

Thalnon had not even heard Trissan approach and was momentarily startled by the man's words. "Thank you, my friend," he said, as Trissan sat down beside him, his feet joining Thalnon's in dangling lazily from the edge of the wooden pier. Thalnon sipped the honey-coloured wine, and Trissan followed suit. Thalnon closed his eye and savoured the warmth of the elven wine as it slid down his throat. Trissan coughed slightly and made a face as he drank.

"Elven wine is strong, Trissan," Thalnon said with a smile.

"You're not kidding," replied Trissan, his eyes beginning to water slightly. "How are you feeling about today?" Trissan asked, as a fish broke the surface of the water a few metres below them, then just as quickly returned under. Thalnon sighed, and rubbed at his temples.

"Much as you would perhaps expect," he replied. "Our mission was to warn my kin of an impending attack from the orrecs of the north. That attack has not happened and, if I am honest, I no longer believe it will." He took another sip of his wine.

"Vinadan's attention lies elsewhere," said Trissan, nodding slowly to himself. Thalnon turned to face him and nodded his agreement. "It would perhaps be too much to say that our journey has been a waste of time," said the elf, "but I had hoped to impress the danger upon the three lords. Instead, Driador, Akeen, and Magos seem satisfied that there is no immediate threat to their lands or to their people." He shook his head in what Trissan took to be mild exasperation. "Had they been there, in Eonis… Had they seen what I…"

"Don't do this, my friend," said Trissan, placing a hand on Thalnon's shoulder, "please; carry this guilt no longer. Let it go, if you can find the strength. I see it in you, but you must be the one to recognise it."

"I do not know if I can," said Thalnon softly. A boat passed close, and Thalnon's gaze settled indifferently upon the mesh-covered boxes of crab and lobster which the elves onboard were filling, tying, and securing. One of the elves looked their way and nodded at the pair, and Trissan returned the gesture. Thalnon was momentarily lost in his thoughts, so Trissan took another drink and looked around. The pier they were sitting on extended around one hundred feet from the beach. Craning his neck to look back over his shoulder, Trissan could make out the tops of the tallest trees of the forest a way off in the distance. Earon's main trade was in fish and seafood, though the forests also provided an abundance of wood for the manufacture of the exquisite furniture which adorned the homes of only the wealthiest across Gibrion. Trissan had never been to Earon - nor Olon or Eldon for that matter - and there was something about the sound of the waves, the calling of the seagulls, and the ubiquitous aroma of saltwater and crab which warmed his heart.

Lord Driador, master of Earon, had been their latest and final host on the mission, and Trissan had found him to be a polite and well-mannered elf, but not without an undercurrent of strength which one could not fail to recognise in his bearing. As Akeen of Olon, and Magos of Eldon had done before him, Driador had welcomed Trissan, Thalnon, and their men to their lands with warmth and grace. As Akeen and Magos had also done before him, Driador had ultimately thanked Trissan and Thalnon for their concern and warning, but had refused to increase their watch, let alone muster their forces.

Trissan, like Thalnon, had been left frustrated by their actions, but as he sat upon the pier watching the sun set over the bay, wine in hand, the smell of saltwater intoxicating his senses, he too felt at peace.

Thalnon looked up and scanned the orange and red skies as a sound, almost imperceptible at first, began to grow louder. He looked around and Trissan, whose human ears registered the sound only after Thalnon's keen elf ears, did likewise. At last, Thalnon located the source of the mewing, calling sound, and he raised his eyebrows as he beheld, standing in stark contrast to the pastel skies, a large black gull heading their way.

So the legends are true, he thought as he placed his glass down upon the pier and stood.

Chapter Thirty-One

All were in silence; a sullen procession they presented as they rode north with grim countenance and heavy heart; trepidation and the twisting ache of shredded nerves following hot on their heels like some snarling and snapping predator.

Like the war dogs of Aclevion, Xeb mused, unable to keep their destination from the forefront of his thoughts. He glanced to his right, feeling a drop of perspiration run down his neck and into his clothing. He looked at Gael; her eyes were unfocused and unblinking as they stared lazily ahead, but in them Xeb read balance, poise, and determination.

And anger.

He had not know Gael, Ruli, and their men long, but in the elf he saw a leader - a ruler, perhaps, one day - but he also saw the shadow of grief which cast her flawless features and lily-white hair in darker hues; like a rain cloud whispering a terrible secret to a bright spring morning. Xeb had come to know all which Gael had lost since Vinadan had hatched his plan to seize the Soul of Hemera from Eonis.

Many of her family and friends had perished at the hands of the prince, as he so emphatically cast off the guise of Montagor. Her leader - her friend - Lady Keya, deceived and butchered inside her own sanctuary. Gael had befriended and allied herself with the man Tyan of Markosh, whose body was cast to sea to burn, even as Gael sang to the waves. All of this, Xeb knew, fuelled the fires he could practically see burning within her.

Xeb glanced further to the right and saw Ruli riding beside Gael, the female Miseldi seemingly asleep in the pillion position, her arms wrapped tight around Ruli's waist, fingers interlocked at his abdomen.

As for the young one, he thought with a sympathetic shake of the head, *he was a close friend of Horith Nindrius, not to mention the barren Gerdan, slain by Agnaz. The female Miseldi completed their quartet, as I understand it, and it is a wonder she is able to accompany us on our journey, so grave were her injuries.*

Xeb slowed his horse and held up a hand, signalling for the rest to follow suit. He looked behind him and beheld their group, all pulling or drawing to a halt in turn as the message filtered back through their numbers.

Our numbers, he thought, feeling his jaw tighten.

Around three hundred men from Markosh who followed Atennos in Tyan's stead; a similar number - maybe a handful more - of Eonisian elves under Gael's command; six dwarves who now called Gorik their leader, and four, maybe five hundred barrens with Ruli and Miseldi in the lead.

A thousand swords, give or take, thought Xeb. *Not bad, but the barrens are not warriors. While they are undoubtedly stout of heart and hardy of spirit, I would not wager that there are many more like Ruli among their number. Still, I have faith that Fennet will muster his kin, and their hatred for the orrecs of the north will make each hoblin count for two or three again. And all the while, I still hold out hope for-*

"Xebus?"

Xeb had been so lost in his thoughts, he had not heard nor seen Gael ride up alongside him.

"My lady?" he asked.

"You brought us to heel, Xebus. What do you need?"

Xeb thought for a moment, and chewed at his lower lip.

"My lady, we are but an hour from Haneth to the east. It is a realm of men and barrens primarily, so my head tells me it should be a safe destination to take shelter, food, and rest."

"And your heart?" asked Gael, fearing she already knew the answer.

"My heart, Lady Gael, tells me that at this critical moment with our numbers so thin, we should not risk confrontation, exposure, or discovery by even one pair of unfriendly eyes; we must reserve trust only for those we see here at our side."

He turned and gestured at the array of elves, men, dwarves, and barrens; armed and armoured, unflinching in the downpour, and his heart swelled with pride and purpose. As far as Xeb knew from his lifelong study of the ancient texts in mastery of the ageless runes, elves could not read the thoughts of the Asarlai. But as Gael looked into his eyes, her own softened and she shared a warm smile with him.

"Those we see," she began, "and those we will soon see again."

She reached out and gently touched his cheek; her soft fingers like the silken wings of a butterfly as they caressed his dry and age-worn skin for the briefest of moments.

Xeb could have sworn that his heart stopped dead, and the swelling of emotion in his chest threatened to manifest itself as tears at her touch. Whether through intuition or the arts of her race, Gael had looked into his heart. There, she saw clearly the fear that Xeb had tried to bury, to dismiss as irrational. Xeb feared he had already looked for the last time upon Fennet.

"I agree," Gael said at last, snapping Xeb back to the present.

"You agree, my lady?" he asked.

"I agree. We cannot risk Haneth; nor can we risk Dinann or Undon. I suggest we make camp as we travel, and set a watch while we sleep in shifts."

"I concur,"

"I would, however," Gael continued, rubbing her chin as she pondered, "venture to suggest that we would be safe in Torimar, though whether we would be welcomed is not certain."

"Whether the dwarves would welcome our company or not," replied Xeb, "Torimar lies too far to the east to make it viable. We must press on, sticking as close to the western coast as we can."

Ruli rode up beside Gael and Xeb and slowed his horse to a stop.

"Is something wrong?" he asked quietly, trying not to make the dozing Miseldi who still clung tightly to his waist.

"No," said Gael, "there is no cause for alarm; Xebus and I were contemplating where - if anywhere - we may lay our heads tonight."

"If I may, my lady," Ruli replied, "I do not think we should risk exposing our numbers to anyone, whether we would consider them friendly or not; we should press on through the wild and make camp by night."

Xeb and Gael smiled and exchanged an approving glance.

"Then we are all in agreement," said Xeb, "Lady Gael and I arrived at the same conclusion, master barren." The company resumed their journey and pushed ahead. They crossed open plains and relied on the keen eyes of the elves and barrens to keep lookout for potential threats while they had little cover behind which to hide or defend. They crossed rivers and streams where they had no choice, they could ill-afford the time they would take to circumvent, or where seeking to go around would lead them too close to inhabited areas. Xeb felt rather than saw that night was beginning to draw in around them; the former lush greens and vivid blues of the open countryside had taken on a more muted hue, as if the canvas of the world had been stained in grey. The last of the light was fading as their way became slow and treacherous. The soft grasses and open fields had given way to rock and stone, and both man and best had to watch their footing as their path became an irregular, winding incline.

  The rock beneath their feet rose higher and higher around them on all sides as they pushed forward,, and here and there were old, decaying wooden signposts, long-since devoid of legible lettering. Behind the signposts, some distance back into the rock walls, were tall and broad openings, reinforced all around with wooden beams.

  Mines, thought Xeb; *this is the Bilgemouth Pass.* He had heard tales of these mines throughout the years; dwarven mines, once full of gold, jewels, precious metals, natural gases, and coal to feed the furnaces of Torimar. But these looked abandoned and desolate, a far cry from the bustling, prosperous places the old tales spoke of. Xeb felt stabs of unease poking and prodding his stomach and his throat; he had never seen the Bilgemouth Pass nor its mines for himself, and he had not known that they now lay in desolation. He could not decide whether he was saddened or rendered fearful by this grey and deathly place. The company moved on with caution, falling into a near single-file formation, with Xeb and Gael at the head. They rounded a natural corner, and Gael immediately threw up a hand to signal a sharp stop. Xeb knew not why Gael had called such an abrupt halt. He looked at her, and could not mistake the tilt of her head and narrowing of her eyes.

Listening; she hears something. Gael, still mounted, unsheathed her weapon, and one by one the rest of the company, barring Xeb, followed suit. Xeb's body prickled with energy, and early traces of runes announced themselves faintly upon his skin. A spark held sway in his eyes, threatening to become a flame at the merest sign of a threat. Tense moments passed, seeming to stretch out eternally until, at last, Xeb's ears picked up what Gael had heard. The sound of heavy, clunking boots was unmistakable, and the sound of gruff voices and raucous laughter confirmed Xeb's suspicions.

Dwarves, he realised. He exhaled and lowered his guard, dampening the burgeoning runes.

"Easy, my lady," he said to Gael. The expression he wore went some way to convincing the elf, who lowered her sword but did not sheath it.

"Gorik," called Xeb, waving the dwarf forward hurriedly, "quickly, to me, you and your kin."

Gorik did as Xeb bade, and he, along with his five

companions, hurried to the head of the company just in time for a contingent of dwarves to appear from around the corner. They stopped dead in their tracks at the sight of Xeb, Gael, and the armed host blocking their way, and the three in the lead immediately brandished their own weapons.

"My brothers!" exclaimed Gorik, spreading his arms wide and taking a step toward the new arrivals. He was unarmed, and the smile he wore as he greeted the dwarves did not quite make it to his eyes. His kin, they were undoubtedly; whether they were also his friends remained to be seen.

"I must admit," Gorik continued, "I did not hope to encounter our kind on this journey of ours," he indicated Xeb and the rest with a jerk of his thumb over his shoulder, "so the sight of your beards is an unexpected but very welcome gift!"

The leader of the dwarven company was unusual for one of their kind. His head was clean shaven, and his chin contained only a light red stubble in place of the more traditional beard. His companions were of a more traditional appearance, with one sporting a scraggly beard flecked through with grey which stood in stark contrast to the shock of raspberry red hair which stood in a mohawk upon his head, and the third wore a head of hair and full beard which were as dark as the look in his eyes. Behind these three stood, by Gorik's estimate, some three-hundred and fifty or so dwarves; all armed and armoured.

"I am Gorik, formerly of Torimar, latterly of Adeniron; and who might you be, friends?"

A single bead of sweat had announced itself upon Gorik's forehead, and was making its way slowly down his temple as he waited for one of the dwarves to speak - or at least to lower their axes. At length, the lead dwarf appeared to relax his grip on his axe, and his shoulders lost some of their tension.

"Well found, Gorik of Adeniron," he said, "I am Nil; these are my brothers: Cade and Zimmon; originally of Mid-Burrow, latterly of Bilgemouth."

"Well found indeed, Mid-Burrows," said Gorik, bowing low in response. "If I may enquire as to-"

"You may not," said Nil, "we have answered your question, now you must answer one of ours."

"Ask away, master Nil," said Xeb in a soothing tone.

"For starters," said Nil, placing the pommel of his axe at his feet and resting his hands across the top of its blades, "who in the name of the goddess are you lot?"

Xeb allowed himself a wry smile at Nil's tone; he recognised it immediately - gruff, impatient, and angry on the surface, but underneath there was warmth and a touch of humour to be found.

"Oh, where to begin?" said Xeb, spreading his arms wide, "my name is Xebus; this is Lady Gael of Eonis; Ruli and Miseldi of Ehronia; and you have met Gorik and his kin. Our company of elves, men, dwarves, and barrens are travelling north, and we have no quarrel with you or your company."

"North?" said the dark eyed Zimmon, "what's there in the north for such a party as yours?"

"Many things lie north," said Ruli before Xeb could answer, "each one of them less your business than the last."

Zimmon turned his gaze upon the young barren.

"Well, continue with that kind of attitude, *kid*, and you won't live long enough to *see* the fucking north."

Ruli bristled and shifted in his saddle, but Xeb moved quickly to calm the situation.

"Now, gentlefolk, there is no need for confrontation here. Indeed, I am fairly certain our causes are aligned, judging by the weapons and armour I see about your men, master dwarves."

"And what cause would that be, old man?" asked Cade.

"Oh no, it is once again your turn to answer a question."

Cade narrowed his eyes and grinned menacingly at Xeb. "Ask away," he said at length.

"What is your business in these parts?"

"Our business?" said Zimmon. He held his axe up in front of Xeb, and the Asarlai could see quite clearly that the edges were stained with blood. "*This is our business.*"

"Our company," said Nil "is made up of former mine workers, labourers, smiths, and merchants. And some former infantry who served alongside Lord Thyrus in the old wars."

"Like you three," observed Gael.

"Aye," Nil confirmed, "we used to offer our services to any for the right price; from Torundel and Lantess, as far as Grior, even Barkash on occasion. Now," his eyebrows furrowed and his countenance became stern, "now we hunt."

"Who do you hunt?" asked Gael.

"*Northerners,*" replied Zimmon, "orrecs, more specifically."

"You have quarrel with the orrecs?" asked Xeb, quickly, seizing upon this information.

"If you call seeking revenge for the countless dwarves they have killed, the villages they have destroyed, and the lives they have ruined," said Cade, "then yes; I suppose you could say we had quarrel with the Vinadan-damned bastards."

Nil, Zimmon, and a large contingent of their dwarven party spat emphatically on the ground at Cade's mention of Vinadan, and Xeb did not miss it.

"My lords," he began, climbing down from his horse and moving to stand toe to toe with the Mid-Burrow brothers, "our cause is truly one and the same. All here have suffered terribly at the hands of Vinadan and his foul armies; we have only recently left Ehronia where the pyres still smoulder in memory of the dead."

The dwarves listened to Xeb and did not interrupt.

"I would not reveal our quest unless I were certain of my audience: we march on the capital, and we mean to take the prince's head. Were you to join us; were you to ally your numbers to our own, we could end this. We could end *him*."

Nil, Cade, and Zimmon exchanged furtive, knowing glances, and then each turned and shared similar looks with those dwarves at their backs.

"Well," said Cade, "I must admit your offer is tempting. But there's one problem."

"Which is?" asked Xeb.

"*You*," answered Zimmon, pointing his axe directly at Xeb. "Your cloth, your bearing, your speechcraft… you are of the Asarlai."

"I am, at that," replied Xeb, nodding, "I do not seek to deny it. How else do you think I have been able to secure such staunch support? The very fact that I am of the prince's court is one of the most powerful cards in our deck. I assure you I have no love nor loyalty to Vinadan, and have seen first-hand the justice he dispenses upon the guilty and the innocent alike."

"So you're a turncoat, then; a traitor to your own," said Nil.

"Hold your tongue, dwarf, before I-" began Ruli.

"No," said Xeb, extending his palm to the young barren to quiet his protest, "he is correct, for the most part. I am a traitor to Vinadan and his followers. I am a traitor to Aclevion and perhaps all of Gibrion in turn. But I have not betrayed my order.

The Asarlai have ever been a check on the whims of the crown, a veto upon the corrupting influence of power and all of its trappings. But even I have to admit that there are those among our number who have grown fat and wealthy these past decades under Vinadan's rule; those who have gleaned his favour at the cost of their morals; they are the true traitors."

"Okay," said Cade, "I think I actually believe you, Xebus of the Asarlai."

"I thank you, Cade," Xeb replied.

"But there is yet a larger problem."

"Even if we add our number to your own," Zimmon said, taking Cade's lead, "if we align our causes, we don't have the numbers to launch a direct assault on the capital."

"I would not be too sure of that, master dwarf. You meet us, at this moment, as we make our way to a rendezvous with yet more loyal allies. We hope to see at least four, perhaps five hundred; all armed and ready to make war."

"Well…" replied Zimmon, "I mean… that's a start."

"More than this," Xeb continued, "the word is out amongst the allied realms that we are making a stand. More will yet heed our call, of this I am certain. Men, elves… perhaps others."

"We do not have time to linger here among the rocks," said Gael, "we must reach Rainwater Wood by nightfall."

Nil, Cade, and Zimmon stood stoic and silent, though the looks they exchanged spoke words enough for a thousand written volumes. Nil took a single step forward and placed himself directly in front of Gorik.

"You vouch for Asarlai? For men, and elves?" he asked.

"Yes," came the unhesitating response.

"You trust these beings to watch your back in a fight? To pull you from the dirt and heal your wounds?"

"By my body and my beard, I trust them implicitly," said Gorik, not flinching from Nil's direct and loaded questions, "they have, all of them, already proven their loyalty and skill in battle a hundred-fold."

Nil nodded almost imperceptibly and turned his gaze on Xeb. His eyes narrowed, just a touch, and he rubbed absently at his stubbled chin.

"Well it's a bit of a tight squeeze through this pass, so I suppose I'd better turn my men around," he said. He thrust his hand into the air, and made a quick one-two motion, signalling a full about-turn. As one, the dwarves spun on their heels and were now facing the direction they had come from.

"Rainwater Wood, you say? Well, follow us. And do try to keep up."

*

The usual clatter of noise - the clinking glasses, the roar of laughter, and the scraping of chair legs across the floor - had become more of a muted background hum of late; a nervous, precipitous wave, replete with forced smiles and feigned mirth. Workers still swigged their ale, washing away the stresses and exertions of the day; artisans still sipped at their sweet wines, composing their fledgling masterworks on parchment in darkened corners; but it was just not the same. A cloud now hung over Pilmer's Anvil, and the dwarf felt as if the weight of the world lay not on her shoulders, but heavy upon her chest, threatening to steal her breath and break her heart every time she glanced at the empty table which would usually - especially at this time of day - be full of her fellow dwarves, all drinking and laughing over yet another game of Dragon's Destiny. She stood behind the bar, absentmindedly drying a glass with a cloth, not realising that the glass had been bone-dry for a while now. She was simply going through the motions, afraid that at any minute a legion of orrecs would burst through the doors and arrest her.

Or worse, she thought with a slow shake of her head. The feeling was not new; it had lingered about her like a half-remembered dream ever since Tyan and his party had left Adeniron, weeks ago. She put the glass away under the bar, and placed her hands on the counter. She took a deep breath to settle her nerves and looked around the inn, taking in the faces and zoning in and out of the snippets of conversation gleaned from her patrons, trying in vain to distract and occupy her mind. The front door creaked open, allowing bright sunshine to spill in, carrying along with it the sound of a high-tempo lute composition and the collective cheer of the listening crowd.

A dark shape entered the inn, haloed and silhouetted by the bright sunshine. Pilmer felt a bitter wave of dread well up inside her throat, and she squinted to get a better look at the newcomer. As the figure came deeper into the inn, Pilmer's eyes flicked down toward the hatchet she kept under the bar, reassuring herself that it was indeed within reach.

Whoever - or whatever - this being was, they were wearing a floor-length black robe, heavy and hooded. Pilmer would have thought nothing of this in the winter months - Hemera be damned, it gets cold in Adeniron - but the choice of attire in the current sunshine and heat set Pilmer's every nerve on edge.

"What will it be, friend?" she asked the dark shape as it took a seat upon a barstool, forcing as much of an air of conviviality into her voice as she could muster.

"Wine, please; red, if you have it," the newcomer asked from beneath the dark hood.

"Coming right up," Pilmer replied. Though the voice was low, barely above a whisper, she felt she recognised it. She placed a large goblet of blood red wine in front of the robed figure. The newcomer reached a hand inside the robe and Pilmer stiffened in alarm. A pale hand, reddish brown hairs upon the wrist, handed a coinpurse to Pilmer.

"Thank you, Pilmer. Please, do keep the change."

The figure cast a furtive glance left, then right, then let out a long breath and lowered his hood. Pilmer weighed the coinpurse in her hand.

"Thank you, Alderman," she said, pocketing the payment. Gracen took a long, deep drink from the goblet, all-but draining it of its contents. He held up the golden receptacle and raised an approving eyebrow in Pilmer's direction. She had been serving drinks long enough to recognise the gesture, and immediately refilled the goblet.

"So," she said, watching Gracen take another satisfied swig, "to what do I owe this unexpected pleasure?"

Gracen met her eyes for a long moment, and Pilmer saw tiredness in his expression; his countenance one of exhaustion mingled with, as far as she could tell, turmoil.

"I wonder if we might speak," Gracen said, taking his goblet in hand and standing up from his stool, "in private."

Pilmer regarded the alderman for a moment, hands on hips. *Whatever this is,* she thought, *it can't be good.*

"Of course," she said, motioning toward the small anteroom behind the bar which served as her office, "Swann; watch the bar for me."

"Of course, Pilmer!" said Swann - one of her regulars - as he took up position behind the bar, straightening his hair and smoothing down his beard. He leaned on the counter to steady himself, already beginning to regret that last ale, never mind the four before it.

Chapter Thirty-Two

The market square was loud and busy, and the old man had to push his way past several groups gathered around various stalls. The sounds of offers being shouted and thanks being given were as ubiquitous as the aromas of sweet pastries and grilled, spicy meats.

  The old man's mouth watered as he revelled in the smells which permeated his senses, as the sun beat down upon his dark and weathered scalp. He raised his hood to keep the sun from burning his bald head, and continued on his way through the market. He did not mean to stop and make any purchases, despite the ache in his stomach for a pastry and a glass of spiced wine. He was heading away from the crowds, out of the market and toward the very gates of Aclevion. He had made this journey before, long ago, and it was not one he relished. He sought calm, solitude, and silence. He had to think, and there were things he had to say out loud where he could not risk being overheard. Besides, he was meeting someone, and had decided against an open and public rendezvous.

He made his way at last to the main gates, and could no longer hear the din of the market, now far behind him. One of the guards emerged from his station and approached the hooded man.

"State your business, citizen," demanded the guard.

The man raised his head, slowly, and stared at the guard from beneath his hood. The stern yet perpetually youthful face of Prince Vinadan glared out from beneath the hood, his dark eyes seeming to see both through and beyond the sentinel. The guard immediately knelt, and raised a fist to his forehead.

"My lord," he said, hurriedly, "for the might of Aclevion, sire."

Vinadan said nothing; he merely motioned for the guard to rise. Within seconds, the guard and his colleagues had opened the gates wide enough to allow passage, and the once-again-old, wizened man made his exit without a word uttered. Once outside of the capital, and having heard the gates slam shut behind him, the old man lowered his hood and straightened his arched and arthritic back. He stood tall, enjoying the clicking of his spine and the stretching of his muscles. He shook his dark, bald head, and long, white locks freed themselves to fall about his shoulders. He removed the robe and dropped it casually to the ground, revealing layered silver and crimson armour beneath. His chest plate displayed the sigil of house Daelectus, his kin, of whom he was the last. A sword was at his waist and a staff of ash, topped with an impressive red gemstone, was strapped to his back.

It had been a long time indeed since Vinadan had walked abroad so armed and armoured, but since Vitrius was long-since abandoned, and the thriving cities of Lantess and Tornudel lay many miles away to the south and to the east, he had felt no hesitation in ridding himself of the shape he had worn in order to leave the capital in secret. He walked in silence; slowly and with his head high. He had always preferred to be in his own company, and valued the sounds of birds and the chirping of insects; the hum of running rivers and the soft trickling of streams, to the din of court and the grating voices of his advisors. Now, as he made his way toward his destination, he felt at peace, despite the weapons he carried and the nature of his sojourn.

He continued east, following the line of the mountains, drawing calm and comfort from the blue skies above him and the green grasses beneath his boots. Though he had arranged the meeting, he felt in no rush to get there, and let his hands brush the branches of trees as he passed. So lost was he in his thoughts that he almost missed the turning. He stopped suddenly as he recognised the three rocks which sat at the foot of a great oak tree. He had placed them there himself, many years ago as a secret marker. He turned abruptly to his left, and pushed his way through thick, thorny bushes. The way was difficult, virtually impassable in places.

But that was the point.

Presently, he broke through to the other side of the bushes, and found himself in a small clearing. Trees surrounded it on all sides, and the meagre light which penetrated their canopies cast an eerie glow down upon the small clearing, painting it in a gloomy, diffuse light, despite the glory of the northern midday sunshine. At the centre of the small grove lay three more rocks, lined up horizontally, equidistant from each other. It was to the left-most rock he went, dropping to his knees and letting his hands fall to his sides, landing softly upon the grass.

"Brother," he said to the moss-covered rock.

"I am betrayed, and I will soon be tested as never before. Ever have I sought to rule with might, yes, but justly. I am not a monster, you see, Valahir, though many believe this to be true. It has come to my attention that there are those out there," he waved over his shoulder, "who will tell their children tales of me to frighten them into obedience; they would tell of a 'Dark Lord' who would steal them from their beds and burn down their homes, just to get them to go to sleep or eat their vegetables."

He shook his head, then pushed an errant strand of blonde hair from his eyes.

"It is a disgrace to my name - our name, brother. And so they move against me in the darkness; they lie, they plot, and they scheme. Even the Asarlai cannot be trusted, it seems, and I expect that they will soon seek to pit their powers against my own upon the battlefield."

He laughed without humour.

"A pity for them," he continued, "for as much as I respect - have always respected - their order, even their combined strength will be no match for mine, not now that I have tamed the Souls; not now that I have harnessed both Aether and Hemera; and not now that I have finally mastered the rune which none but Daedan Asarlai himself have ever harnessed before me. No, Valahir; I fear I must destroy them - I fear I must destroy them all."

He shifted, pulling his knees out from under himself, and sat on the grass, finding it damp despite the heat, and crossed his legs not unlike a child at story time.

"And the irony, my brother? I would not actually choose this unless I were forced, and make no mistake, they do force my hand. But in doing so, I will become the monster they tell tales of; I will become little more than a wolf in their eyes, perhaps I will be feared like the haemori," he chuckled at the comparison, shaking his head slightly.

"No, Valahir, I am not a monster. Not yet. They test me, truly, but I will be victorious - as I have always been. I will crush their uprising. I will stamp out the burgeoning fires of rebellion; I will enforce my will upon these ungrateful peasants and will ascend to true godly status. Whether by choice or the force of my divine will, they will worship me, and all will be mine,"

He stood, and grinned down at the rock at his feet.

"And you, Valahir; brother - you will remain in the ground, rotting in your shallow, traitor's grave where you belong." He spat upon the rock, and grinned as his saliva mingled with the moss to drip down to the dewy grass. He turned his head to the right to take in the other two rocks.

"Mother. Father," he said with a malicious grin. A sound from behind him caught his attention, and he turned on his heel with his hands clasped behind the small of his back.

"My lord," said the orrec at the edge of the clearing. He was tall and muscular, and held his helm in his hands in front of his barrel chest. He bowed his head in deference to Vinadan.

"Thank you for coming, Commander," said Vinadan walking toward the orrec.

"I did not wish to interrupt-"

"You did not, Commander Belliak; I am done here."

"How may I serve you, my master?" asked the orrec, whose eyes flicked left and right, taking in the bizarre location to which he had been summoned.

"Oh, do not worry, Commander," laughed Vinadan, noticing the orrec's hesitation, "if I wanted to kill you I would have simply walked up to you and slit your throat back in the capital. No, I have a mission for you which requires a conversation away from prying eyes and ears."

"If I may, my lord?"

"Yes, Belliak?"

"What is this place?"

"Oh," said Vinadan with a grin, "pay it no mind; just an old family picnic spot."

The orrec nodded slowly. "You said you have a mission, my lord,"

"Indeed; our enemies stir, Belliak. Many have turned against us and allied themselves with traitors and rebels. But for all of their plotting and scheming, we have one major advantage."

"We do?" Belliak asked.

"We do indeed. They believe us ignorant, Commander. They mean to catch us unawares, but they underestimate my reach. Your mission, Commander, is a very simple one: you will muster Elgiroth."

"Yes, my lord, of course. Which legions?"

"*All* legions, Belliak. We must assume that we are compromised, threatened by every town and city in all of Gibrion. From Aillen to Ideenion, we are betrayed, and so we must make war. You have four days."

"Yes, Prince Vinadan; it shall be done, my lord. Every orrec, armed and armoured."

"Every orrec, Belliak, and every wolf. Every troll, and every bat. Choose a second in command; send them east, only by night, to treat with the haemori. Baron Diaemus will send a force, I am sure of it.

And I need you to parley - personally, Belliak - with Dhruaghar."

The orrec's eyes went wide and wild.

"Dhruaghar, my lord?" he stammered.

"Yes, Belliak. Dhruaghar; is that going to be a problem for you?" asked Vinadan in a silky voice, allowing small sparks of fire to glow to life in his stare.

"N... No, my lord; of course not. Consider it done, my prince."

"Excellent!" said Vinadan, with a single clap of his hands.

"Be not afraid, Belliak," said Vinadan, placing a hand on the orrec's shoulder and leading him away from the grove, "if anything, I would urge you to enjoy the experience! After all," a twinkle came to Vinadan's eye, "it's not every day that one gets the chance to treat with a *dragon*."

Chapter Thirty-Three

Had any of the company harboured any doubts as to how Rainwater Wood acquired its name, they had most assuredly been alleviated upon entering the thick treeline at the foot of the Dinannian mountains. This part of Gibrion, close to the western shore, surrounded by mountains and towering trees, seemed to be inundated with incessant rainfall, serving to cast the lush, verdant surroundings in perpetual grey.

It occurred to Xeb that nobody had spoken since they had crossed into Dinannian country and the rain had begun to fall. A heavy rain it was, too; falling in perfect horizontal showers; not caught upon the whims of the wind and blown here and there, but unrepentant in its relentless downpour. Xeb chuckled without enthusiasm beneath his raised hood at the fleeting thought that his company's spirits were as damp as their clothing. Most of the company walked behind him at a steady pace, while others rode those Ehronian horses which could be spared for the journey. Of the new arrivals, Nil, Cade, Zimmon, and a handful of other dwarves whose names Xeb had not yet learned, fell in with Gorik and his companions, and it pleased Xeb to see that some of the previous tension had given way to banter and burgeoning brotherhood, so rare in these dark times.

Even among the Asarlai, he thought with no small amount of regret. Xeb could not point to a great many dealings with dwarves in his time, but he had always found them to be a loyal, hardy race - if a little rough around the edges - in those interactions he recalled. As happy as he was to have added such a fierce force as the dwarves to their numbers, Xeb turned his mind to the here-and-now, and focused all of his attention on their immediate surroundings. The time was right, the location was correct, but all was still and silent; the only sounds to be heard were the constant patter of rain upon the leaves overhead, the trickling of rainwater as it cascaded down all around them, and a low, almost cautious chittering and chirping of myriad unseen woodland creatures.

"He will be here," said Gael, moving up beside Xeb and offering her warmest smile.

"I know," Xeb replied, hoping his voice carried more certainty than he felt in his heart. He turned and met the elf's gaze evenly, shaking his head, allowing some of his doubt to bubble to the surface.

"I am troubled, in truth. Should we fail to win the support of the-"

"Hoblins!" came the cry from the ranks behind Xeb and Gael, and the metallic swish and clatter of drawn weapons echoed amongst the dense trees. Xeb and

Gael spun to see the new contingent of dwarves - axes, swords, and warhammers raised - bearing their teeth as they issued war cries to an approaching trio of hoblins whose leader brandished what looked like an ancient elven blade.

"Wait!" cried Xeb, Gael, Ruli, and many of the original company. Gorik, joined by Atennos of Markosh, rushed out from the ranks and placed themselves between the dwarves and the hoblins, palms raised to forestall the dwarven assault.

"Wait!" cried Gorik, "Lower your weapons; they're with us!"

Zimmon took a step forward and placed his face perilously close to Gorik's.

"What?" he demanded, "You ally yourselves with the enemy? What sort of nonsense is this?"

"They are not the enemy," said Atennos, "look," he added, pointing at the approaching Fennet.

"That's Fennet, ally of Xebus; Lady Gael gave him that sword. Lower your weapons and *look*!"

Xeb, Gael, and Ruli had arrived on foot now, and each also motioned for calm.

"It's okay, my good dwarves," said Xeb in his most placating voice, "Atennos and Gorik speak truly.

Fennet, here, is my companion; I tasked him with rallying the hoblins of the western wilds to our cause, and my hope is that he has returned with an army at his back."

Fennet held up a hand, signalling his two companions to hold their positions, and he moved to join Xeb, treading slowly, and maintaining his grip on Enarhaedon, though the blade remained sheathed.

"Fennet, meet our new friends," said Xeb, gesturing to the dwarves.

Fennet remained silent a moment longer, one eyebrow raised curiously in Xeb's general direction, before releasing his grip on his sword and clapping his hands together.

"Welcome to the company," the hoblin said enthusiastically, "you seem very angry; you'll fit right in! Come," he said, turning his back and gesturing for the dwarves, Xeb, and the others to follow him.

"Master Xebus; you remember Ugnor?" said Fennet, casually ignoring the fact that many of the dwarves had yet to lower their weapons.

"How could I forget?" replied Xeb, involuntarily flinching at the memory of his last encounter with the hoblin war chief.

"Well," continued Fennet, "he is with us, and he is very keen to help - hence his gift."

"What gift?" asked Xeb, not without a hint of suspicion.

"Oh, not much," said Fennet, dismissively waving a hand, "just a few barrels of hoblin wine."

The sound of swords, axes, and warhammers being sheathed en masse brought a grin to Fennet's face, though it was hidden from the dwarves as he continued to walk away from them, further into the wood.

"Hoblin wine?" asked Cade, jogging to catch up with Fennet and his guards.

"Oh yes; and one of our better reserves," replied Fennet, sticking his chest out in pride. Zimmon and Nil were not far behind. Xeb shook his head and laughed openly, increasing his own pace and following Fennet into the trees to meet with Ugnor. And to sample the hoblin wine, of course. Gael went with him, followed closely by Gorik, Atennos, Ruli, and Miseldi, who was now strong enough to walk unaided, though she remained close to Ruli.

The rain continued to pour, but by this point all were beyond the point of feeling it. How much wetter can sodden hair, clothing, and soggy armour possibly get? The deeper they went into the wood, the thicker the trees became, affording them some respite from the downpour. At length, Fennet and the company leaders emerged into a small clearing to find Ugnor sitting behind a roaring campfire, surrounded by hundreds of armed and armoured hoblins - far more than Xeb could possibly have hoped for. Behind them stood an enormous wooden cart, which looked to Xeb as if it would fall to pieces were it to encounter so much as a rock upon the road. Sitting flat on the ground and leaning up against the side of the cart were four muscular hoblins. They panted, and the sweat upon their bodies was indistinguishable from the rainfall barring the aroma; their appearance, plus the lack of horses or other traditional beasts of burden left Xeb in no doubt as to who had pulled the cart here. Upon the cart, conspicuous by their colour and size, were, by Xeb's count, twelve red barrels, each roughly the size of a dwarf.

"Fennet," said Xeb, pointing to the barrels, "is that the wine?"

"Oh yes, master Xebus," said the hoblin, "we didn't know how many would turn up, so we brought a few extra."

"Xebus of the Asarlai," came Ugnor's voice from behind the flames of the campfire, "come; sit. Your friends, too."

There was a calmness to the hoblin's voice which surprised Xeb, and he did as instructed, as did his companions. Ugnor nodded to a hoblin to his left, and the other immediately hurried to the cart, returning quickly with goblets of wine for all.

"I am pleased to find you here, War Chief," said Xeb, offering his goblet to Ugnor, who *clinked* his own against it in a gesture of good cheer.

"I was not planning to come," replied the hoblin leader. "When Fennet returned and put his case - *your* case - to me, I thought for a moment that I should exile him. Maybe even kill him." Ugnor drained his wine and shook his head slowly. Xeb read sadness in the hoblin's expression, and something else.

Tiredness, he realised. *Ugnor is old and weary of conflict.*

"What changed your mind?" asked Xeb. Ugnor met his gaze, unflinching.

"Freedom," he said, "your promise to my people," he jabbed a finger in Xeb's direction for emphasis.

"I have not forgotten my promise, Ugnor, nor do I intend to break it. Help me - help *us* - and I will ensure your people are given safe passage to a new land where you can start again."

Ugnor accepted a new goblet of wine from his faithful servant, and took a long gulp.

"I may rue these words, Asarlai, but I believe you; more, I trust you to keep your promise. This is why we have come, and this is why we make such an offering as this," he indicated the wine in his goblet, "Aether knows, it's all we have."

Ugnor, Xeb, and the rest drained their goblets and sat for a moment in silence, listening to the sound of the crackling flames of the campfire, and the hurried coming and going of hoblins refilling their goblets.

"So tonight, master Xebus; elves, dwarves, men - all present - tonight, we will drink; we will eat; we will laugh. It is likely that, come nightfall, when the stars shine above us, many will weep; some may even dance by the light of the moon."

A lump came to Xeb's throat as he listened, enraptured, to the hoblin's unlikely words.

"Yes," Ugnor continued, "tonight we will *live*, for our way is as uncertain as it is dangerous and, for many of us, this may be the last chance we will ever have to drink with friends under the stars."

Ruli felt Miseldi's hand close tightly around his own, and his mind filled with images of Horith and Gerdan. He reached out with his thoughts and allowed his mind to meld with hers. Miseldi laid her head upon Ruli's shoulder and wept openly for the first time since the battle of Ehronia. Ruli shared her grief and shed tears with his friend. They held one another by the warmth of the campfire. They drank, and they laughed. Later, as the stars burned so brightly that Miseldi could almost see the face of Gibrion herself in their radiance, they danced by the light of the late summer moon.

Chapter Thirty-Four

The road ahead was long, and the company was quiet as they inched cautiously northwards. The recent additions of the dwarves and hoblins had served to swell their ranks to over two thousand, which both pleased and troubled the company leaders. Though Xeb did not regret their decision to rely on stealth over speed and turn the horses loose, his aching feet served as a constant reminder of it. The rain had thankfully abated as the company advanced north beyond Dinann, leaving Rainwater Wood (and twelve empty red barrels) far behind them. The sun was high in the sky, and Xeb - no doubt the whole party - was soothed and comforted by its warmth.

Their path had taken them a short way east as they skirted the foot of the mountains, where they at least had the cover of the trees to shield them from unfriendly eyes. Once they had cleared the range and left the peaks in their wake, the way became far more perilous. While vast expanses of wide open, lush green plains replete with narrow streams and small bridges, farmhouses, stables, and even the occasional crumbling stone temple, would prove a most appealing backdrop to most, it presented great danger to such a company as theirs whose success would always rely as heavily on secrecy as it would upon strength of arms.

So far, they had encountered little in the way of life upon the open lands, and Xeb hoped beyond hope that their luck would hold a little longer. They were now within sight, though distant, of the town of Lantess, a human settlement unapologetic in its support for Aclevion and the rule of Vinadan. He called the other leaders to him, and they knelt upon the soft grass as they took counsel.

"Our approach will be seen a mile off," Xeb said, initiating the discussions.

"Do we not have friends there we can call on to aid us?" asked Atennos. Xeb stroked his beard and took a moment to consider.

"While there may indeed be some inside who would welcome our cause," said Xeb, "there will no doubt be many more who would see us jailed or hanged for high treason."

"We cannot risk discovery," added Gael. "To have come so far and lost so much, only to see our journey end here? No, we must move by night; slowly, and in silence."

"Agreed, ma'am," said Nil, leaning on his axe, "but night is yet hours away. What do we do until then? We are at risk even now, here in the wildlands."

"You are correct, my friend," replied Gael, "we must get out of sight, and quickly."

"I know a place," said Ugnor. All heads turned toward the hoblin. "What? Do you think this is the first time us hoblins have been forced to hide by day and move only under darkness? When you live as an exile, you get to learn a thing or two about caves." He indicated a spot a distance off to the south west; they would have to double back on themselves a little, but the alternative was far worse.

"Excellent, Ugnor," said Xeb, motioning for the group to stand. "We must turn back a ways, but lost time is better than lost lives. Lead on, Ugnor."

*

The drip, drip, drip of water, echoing from places unseen was a constant companion as the company hunkered down inside the cave. Though it was without question a tight fit, the cave was just about deep enough to allow shelter and cover for all. They waited, they watched, and they whispered in the semi-darkness, as the world beyond the cave mouth lost its colour; vibrant greens and pearlescent blues turning grey and dull as the hours ticked inexorably onward toward the darkness the company sought. The telltale sound of snoring and snoozing issued from the back of the cave, and Xeb felt a grin tug at the corners of his mouth.

Let them sleep, he thought. *There will be little enough time for it once we make our move.*

The sound of heavy breathing and shuffling feet snatched the Asarlai's attention away from the sleeping, and he turned toward the unmistakable silhouette of a dwarf approaching him rapidly, haloed by the last of the outside light.

"We may have a problem, Xebus; my lady," said Zimmon, kneeling in front of Xeb and Gael, sitting by his side.

"What is it, master dwarf?" said Gael, on full alert.

"Men," replied Zimmon, "a Lantessian patrol is headed this way."

Xeb felt rather than saw all in his immediate vicinity stiffen, sitting up or standing to attention at the news. Zimmon, too, recognised the burgeoning panic and moved quickly to allay it.

"It's okay," he said, raising his palms to instil calm, "I have an idea."

Gael stood and loosened her sword in its sheath. "What do you need us to do?" she asked. Zimmon smiled and bowed his head.

"I need you, Lady Gael, to stay here and keep out of sight. The same goes for you lot," he swept a finger across the group, indicating Xeb, Ruli, Miseldi, Gorik, and his brothers.

"Atennos," he said, turning to the leader of the men of Markosh, "I need two of yours, right now."

Zimmon's expression and the urgency in his voice was enough for Atennos to obey unquestioningly. "Ander; Herral - go with him, double-quick," commanded Atennos, who was pleased to see the discipline in his men as they stood and joined Zimmon within seconds. As the trio turned and headed toward the cave entrance, Zimmon threw a look over his shoulder.

"It'll be fine," he said, "just stay put, and do not interfere."

Xeb's heart sank as he watched them leave; he had a pretty good idea what the dwarf had in mind. But he would stay put, and not interfere.

The light from the patrolmen's torches was bright against the backdrop of the new nightfall, and insects buzzed and whirred as close to it as they dared before the men waved and swiped them away. They chatted idly as they approached within close proximity to the cave, and one of them threw a cursory glance in its direction. *They must have walked this route a thousand times,* Xeb thought as he watched on from the darkness, judging by the way they did not so much as stop to check their location nor direction of travel. The area was notorious for hoblin raids and skirmishes, so Xeb could not blame the Lantessians for widening the scope of their patrols beyond the immediate borders of their city.

The patrolmen chatted and joked as they walked their route, which was bringing them closer and closer to the cave entrance with each step. Without warning, one of the patrolmen pulled his sword from its sheath and nudged his partner to do the same.

"You there!" the man shouted, pointing with his sword toward a pair of newcomers; two human men had appeared from within a small wooded area and were stumbling, holding each other up, seemingly quite drunk. The patrolmen walked up to the pair cautiously, swords raised in defensive stances.

"You there; I said stop at once!"

"Who, us?" said one of the new arrivals, slurring his words as he held a hand up to shield his eyes from the glare of the torches.

"Yes, you," said the irritated patrolman, "do you see anyone else around?"

Herral and Ander looked around, left and right, feigning inebriation.

"Erm... No," said Ander, "No one; just a couple of guards... How are you this evening, office... Off...offices?"

The patrolmen looked at each other and shook their heads. They stowed their weapons and relaxed a little.

"Hemera-damned drunks," said one of the patrolmen with a sigh, "why is it always dru-"

Zimmon moved with a swiftness and silence which belied his stature, and before Ander and Herral could register what had happened, both patrolmen were on the ground, throats sliced open, ear to ear. Zimmon stood behind them with a bloodstained dagger in his hand and a look of determination etched upon his face.

"Well done, you two," he said, sheathing the dagger, "now help me drag these into the trees. We don't have time to bury them, but we'll be far away from here soon enough."

They were back inside the cave within a few minutes, having worked quickly to hide the bodies. Zimmon saw conflict written upon almost every face, even in the darkness. It was a conflict he too felt, but he did not apologise for his actions. It was Gael who spoke, as Zimmon, Ander, and Herral sat, gladly accepting the goblets of wine handed to them by the hoblins.

"It is unfortunate that they had to die," she said to everyone and no-one at once, "but we can take no risks. Our task is too important, and we cannot fail now. Thank you," she said, inclining her head to the trio who had just saved all of their lives.

*

They had filed out of the cave as soon as Zimmon, Ander, and Herral had caught their breaths and finished their wine, and the next stage of the company's journey north was thankfully uneventful. No movement nor sound had they seen barring the slinking of foxes among the grasses and the hooting of owls, unseen among the trees. A firefly here; a bat there, but no human patrols, and thankfully this far north, no orrecs. Their long, silent march brought them to the borders of Vitrius, and the trees loomed large and foreboding, like ghouls with splayed fingers that would snatch them all away in their sleep. Vitrius was a bad place - especially to men - and fear was thick in the air. Though it could not be heard out loud, Xeb fancied that many of the company swallowed anxiously and fought to maintain calm as they realised where they were, and where they were heading.

"Master Xebus," said Atennos, tugging gently on Xeb's sleeve, "surely we are not venturing further toward..." he nodded in ge direction of the gnarled and twisted trees, noting the absence of crickets, birds, beasts, or sound of any kind from within.

"We are indeed. But do not worry, we will be quite safe, captain Atennos," Xeb replied, placing a reassuring hand upon the man's shoulder.

"But Xebus," Atennos protested, "this is an evil place. The old tales say that it is haunted, that no man who ventures there ever returns. There is a darkness at work in this place, master Xebus, a darkness that I care not to see for myself." Atennos shook his head, and Xeb saw panic beginning to announce itself upon the young captain, and many of his men.

It is not so for the elves, barrens, hoblins, or dwarves, though, Xeb realised. *Curious…*

"Captain Atennos; men - all of you," he said, raising his voice to address the group of humans, "you have nothing to fear from these woods. I am living proof that a man may venture into Vitrius and come out unscathed."

There was a collective gasp from Xeb's audience, and Atennos put voice to their shock.

"You have walked the paths? You have journeyed through Vitrius?"

"I have. And recently, I might add."

"When?" asked Atennos, not even trying to hide his shock and incredulity. Xeb shook his head and scratched at his beard.

"Whilst it feels like a lifetime ago, it must only have been three, maybe four months ago in truth."

"What dark magic do you possess, to walk unmolested through this evil place?" Atennos backed away from Xeb, just a step, but enough for the Asarlai to realise that he must speak plainly to avoid losing control of the situation.

"I possess no darkness, Atennos. I assure you that there is nothing in these woods save stories and superstition. We will venture inside only as far as we need to in order to conceal our forces during the daylight hours. It is nearly two miles before we would reach the ruins of the old village, and I intend to rest only among the outer treeline. We will be perfectly safe, I give my word, such as it is."

*

Xeb was thankful that their long journey north by the light of the moon had taken a toll on most of the company, and as he looked around at the mass of sleeping eves, barrens, and dwarves, he too felt his eyelids become heavy. His breathing slowed, and his heart rate fell to a crawl, and before he knew it he was sound asleep.

Atennos, Ander, Herral, and a handful more of their kin sat huddled together, having volunteered to take first watch. Though the day would dawn before long, and outside of the Vitriusian woods the sound of early morning birdsong would be heard, here inside the woods, all was of darkness and silence.

The men had drawn their swords, and had laid them across their laps or upon the ground within easy reach. Although many of their fellow men now slept, comforted by the watchfulness of their brothers, many more could not. A restlessness hung like fog over and about the men, and a lingering, gnawing fear ate away at them to a man, inching its way to the fore from its birthplace in the darkest recesses of their minds.

None spoke out loud; some fidgeted, picking up and checking their weapons; one or two dared to whisper conspiratorially, glancing here and there as if the trees themselves would suddenly swallow them up.

At length, the woods grew misty; a swirl of fog rolled outwards from the heart of the woods, announcing itself inconspicuously among the camp. As the mist became thicker, rising higher from the dirt at their feet to claw at their chests and shoulders, and even the most alert of the men grew deathly tired. One by one, the formerly awake and fearful men fell into a deep sleep, and were soon snoring louder than the dwarves.

Atennos awoke with a start. For a split second, he did not know where he was, and the familiar sight of his sword on the ground by his side did nothing to warm the blood which had frozen in his veins. He looked left and right, eyes darting here and there in panic, and reached for his sword. It turned to ashes in his hands and fell harmlessly to the dirt. He quickly recognised his surroundings; he had not left the camp. His kin and their companions lay huddled and sleeping at his feet, and no amount of nudging, shaking, nor hissing at them to wake seemed to rouse them from their slumber.

Though he recognised that he was still within the camp, he registered on some unconscious level that things were not quite right; that everything was just a fraction... *off*. He narrowed his eyes and tried to concentrate, bringing the sickly purple trees, the burning red sky, and the bright blue grass into razor focus.

Perfectly normal. Nothing weird about that, he concluded. He looked again at his companions, sleeping on the ground. He noticed their black, dead eyes, swollen, lolling tongues, and the ruby-red slashes across their opened throats.

Again, perfectly normal, he shrugged, *exactly as they should be.*

He registered movement in the trees off to his left and he retreated in fear, putting his back against a tall and wide tree. A woman emerged from the treeline wearing a white silken nightgown so tight and so thin that it clung to every curve and every line of her young body. Her hair was raven black, and her eyes were the colour of freshly-spilled blood, vivid in her pallid blue face. Atennos was caught adrift somewhere between ice-cold terror and a deep, burning desire, and he temporarily lost his footing, allowing his back to slide painfully down the tree trunk until he was sitting on the dirt, his legs stretched out in front of him.

She advanced toward him, leaving the treeline in her wake and padding barefoot across the clearing. A wind blew through the woods, loosening the delicate nightgown at the left shoulder. Atennos felt his heart thump hard within his chest as the gown fell to reveal a small breast. The woman made no attempt to cover herself, but continued to walk silently toward Atennos, a burgeoning grin dawning upon her dead face. As she came closer, she knelt on the ground, and placed her hands flat on the dirt. She stalked toward him on all fours, like a predator moving in to deliver the killing blow to its wounded prey.

She was upon him now, and her coy grin blossomed into a full, maniacal smile; her mouth was wide, and her long, sharp fangs were bared. A snarl, full of hatred and torment, issued from somewhere deep within her, and she reached a small, soft hand toward Atennos.

Closer and closer came the hand toward his face, and as he looked closer, he beheld the pale and flaking skin which gave way to yellow, mangled nails. Gripped by a terror so absolute that he feared his heart may explode, Atennos squeezed his eyes shut.

As he felt the hand touch his shoulder and squeeze, he screamed out in horror and his arms flailed in terror.

"Whoa, whoa; easy," came Gael's soothing voice. Atennos opened his eyes wide, and was both confused and overjoyed to see Gael's kind, caring face. She was kneeling in front of him and her hand was upon his shoulder.

"I… I…the-"

"It's okay," said Gael, "you were having a nightmare, I think."

Atennos looked around, and saw that more of his men were being roused from their sleep by elves, dwarves, and barrens. To a man, each of his kin shared the same confused, terrified expression, and Atennos was quite sure that his nightmare was far from unique.

"Come on; on your feet," said Gael, standing. She offered Atennos her hand and pulled him up. As he regained his wits and steadied his breathing, he noticed stars shining overhead through the canopy of the trees.

"We have to move while we have cover," said Gael. Atennos nodded, and took a deep breath.

"You heard her," he said to his men, "gear up." And gear up they did, in silence; not one of them looking another in the eye, each with cheeks flushed red. As Atennos replaced his sword in its sheath and threw on his satchel, he could have sworn he heard a faint note of ghastly laughter, carried through the clearing on the breath of a lazy midnight breeze.

*

They were not long in their journey and no other living soul did they encounter, for the paths which led away from Vitrius were dark and seldom travelled. At once, Xeb raised a hand and brought the company to a halt. Not a sound could be heard save the cawing of some faraway bird, and the gentle purring of the wind as it blew in from the northern seas. Hearts were heavy, and minds sharp with a razor focus tinged with the sharp urgency of fear. Elf, barren, man, dwarf, and hoblin; all jaws were set, all eyebrows furrowed; breathing was deep and deliberate as all fought to calm their nerves and conquer their fear.

Through the golden haze of an early morning fog, the company looked at last upon the imposing capital realm, nestled between the mountains to the north and west, protected from assault on all sides save one. Xeb closed his eyes, and felt a deep sense of purpose mingled with an absolute dread which threatened to overwhelm him. He registered a single tear which ran openly down his left cheek, and made no move to wipe it away. Gael moved to stand in front of him, and placed a soft, warm hand upon his cheek.

"You have led us this far, Xebus; we trust you to see this through. The power of Vinadan may be a great and terrible thing," she continued, "but it is as nothing compared to the power of hope, belief, and loyalty."

Xeb opened his eyes and met her gaze. He saw the hope Gael spoke of shining in her eyes; she was resolute and determined, and not a hint of fear could he see upon her face. He drew strength and courage from the lady of Eonis; his breathing came rapidly as anger swelled up inside of him. Anger at the pain, the loss, and the suffering he had witnessed for far too long. Anger at the killing, the deaths of friends and strangers alike, and the vengeful ruthlessness of Vinadan's forces.

Runes of a hundred shapes and sizes blazed to life upon his skin, and his eyes burned bright with the fires of the goddesses. At this display of raw power, every elf, man, dwarf, barren, and hoblin bared their teeth and raised their weapons. The sound of their war cry echoed around the clearing at the foot of the mountains, but no sound was to be heard from the capital in reply. Though they were still some distance away, Xeb was troubled by the lack of movement from Aclevion. No guards patrolled the lands, no archers could be seen atop the towers or the perimeter walls, and no long line of traders filed in or out with laden carts, horses, or caravans conveying food, weapons, gems, or other luxuries only the people of the capital could afford.

All of this struck Xeb as both strange and alarming. But worse than the lack of activity, one thing stood out to Xeb as profoundly ominous.

The gates are open, he realised, tasting bile rising in his throat.

Chapter Thirty-Five

The wind kicked up a swirl of dust as it blew out through the open gates toward Xeb and his company, but still no word nor call was issued from within. They waited, and they watched; every eye and ear straining to pick up even the most scant stimulus which would let them know that somebody was there.

Anybody, thought Xeb; *any*where*, for that matter.*

He had lived both above and within Aclevion for as long as he could remember, and he had never seen it empty. The sun was rising higher in the sky now, and the lingering fog had begun to clear. Xeb could already feel burgeoning heat upon his weathered face.

It's going to be a nice day, he thought, and he took a long stride forward, followed by another. The company were quick to follow at his heel, and within minutes they were mere feet from the open and foreboding gates. From the gates, one could look straight ahead down the main city road, off of which branched streets and avenues beyond count. Beyond the waterfall which stood in the central courtyard, also visible from the gates though barely, rose a set of large marble steps. At the top of the steps the citadel of Ondellion rose high and imposing; its white walls and high towers gleaming like jewels in the morning sun.

Out of the citadel doors and down the white marble steps came a figure Xeb could not definitively identify at this distance, but in his gut he already knew exactly who it was. What Xeb's heart knew to be true, Gael's keen elven eyes quickly confirmed.

"It's him," she said, "and he carries something; a box."

Xeb turned and motioned to Ruli, Miseldi, Gorik, and Nil. "You four; to me, hurry." They did as instructed and were huddled around Xeb in moments.

"When this begins, and make no mistake, it *will*," he began, looking each of them in the eye in turn, "I need you four, and a small force of those you trust, to undertake an objective."

"Speak it, and it will be done," said Nil, whose leg bounced up and down with nervous energy; he was clearly spoiling for a fight.

"Do not enter the city; go around, past the outer walls. Behind the citadel lies a path up into the mountains; take this path with all haste. Do not look back, do not stay and fight on the ground. Take this path; it leads to the Asarlai monastery; my home. Once inside, push on into the mountain. Deep within you will find the Soul Chamber where the spheres of Hemera and Aether reside, suspended between two pillars."

"What would you have us do?" asked Ruli.

"Destroy them," said Xeb, "Destroy the pillars. I do not know what it will take to bring them down, so ancient are they and so little of them we understand, but I implore you to use whatever strength of arms or arts you possess to bring them down."

"Will it work? Will it stop Vinadan?" asked Miseldi.

"Stop him? No, it is unlikely that it will stop him. My hope, however, is that, should you succeed, it will weaken him, even temporarily; cutting him off from the source of his powers." Xeb swallowed hard, then continued.

"I do not expect that *all* of the Asarlai will take up arms against you, but neither am I so naive to think that you will not be faced with great danger. I am also aware that in order for you to succeed, many of my brothers will likely die. And for this, Hemera knows I am sorry."

The four looked at each other, and unspoken words passed between them; a bond; an agreement.

"It will be done," said Ruli. He took a step toward Xeb, hesitated for a moment, and then grasped him firmly by the shoulder.

"Thank you," said the young barren, "for everything."

With that, the four retreated back into their ranks and hurriedly roused their chosen companions for the mission Xeb had entrusted to them, and were soon out of sight.

Fennet marched up to Xeb and nudged him hard in the ribs. "Do you not trust me with a secret mission?" he asked.

"Trust you?" replied Xeb, "I trust you implicitly, my friend. But I need you by my side when battle is joined. If this is to be my end, then I can think of nobody I would rather be with than a hoblin wielding an elvish blade." Though he wore a grin, Xeb's words were full of regret and emotion. Fennet placed a hand on Xeb's shoulder, and the Asarlai fancied that he could see the beginnings of tears in the goblin's eyes. The look was short lived, as Fennet took a deep breath and unsheathed Enarhaedon, gripping the Traitor's Blade tightly with both hands. Xeb put one foot in front of the other and began the advance into the capital, his forces amassed behind him. Just before the first of the branching streets appeared to the left and right, he held up a hand to stall the company.

"You fear an ambush?" asked Gael.

"Fear? No, my lady. I *expect* an ambush."

Here they waited, as Vinadan continued to walk toward them; his gait and bearing were casual, nonchalant; as if he were merely addressing a nuisance caller at his door. As he came closer, Xeb recognised the look the prince wore on his pale face.

Smugness, Xeb thought, *satisfaction. Can he be forewarned?*

Vinadan advanced to within mere feet of Xeb, Gael, and their forces, and set the box down at his feet. He took three long strides backwards, leaving the box equidistant between him and the amassed forces before him.

"Hail, Xebus!" he began, raising his arms theatrically, "My most loyal and trusted advisor finally returns!" He brought his hands together in front of his stomach, interlocking his fingers. He tilted his head to the left and narrowed his eyes.

"And I can see that your mission was a roaring success; not only have you spread the word of my power and benevolence to the people of Gibrion, but you have brought back a veritable army of loyal followers; all armed and armoured, ready to join the royal guard."

Xeb said nothing, and he fought to keep his face neutral as a wave of alarm washed over him.

"Unless, of course," Vinadan continued, raising a hand to cover his mouth in an elaborate act of feigned shock, "you mean to overthrow me? Unless this was all an elaborate ruse, and you have been busy building an army to challenge me, all these long months you have been away."

"It's over, my lord," said Xeb, finding his voice at last.

"Yes, yes… That certainly does appear to be the case; I'm clearly done for," said a grinning Vinadan. "But before you destroy me, Xebus; a gift," he motioned toward the box.

"Xeb, don't," said Gael, "it's a trap."

"Oh, I assure you, *elf*," spat Vinadan, "the trap has not yet been sprung."

Vinadan and Gael locked gazes, and Xeb took a step forward, then another, and soon found himself standing over the ornate, gilded box. He knelt in the dirt and opened the lid. He did not react, did not shed a tear; he closed his eyes and shook his head solemnly. He did not see Vinadan's hungry grin, nor the amusement in his eyes as he revelled in Xeb's torment.

"Butcher," said Xeb, rising. He stepped away from the box, and set his feet into a fighting stance, left foot out, right leg braced behind him. Fire erupted in his eyes and the runes of his order blazed into being upon his skin.

"Your old master told me everything before I took his head," said Vinadan. He raised his left hand above his head, then took a long step backward as, from every alley, street, avenue, and building, Vinadan's orrecs swarmed into view and flooded the central promenade. Within seconds, the silence which had greeted Xeb and company on their arrival in Aclevion was replaced with a cacophony of war cries, the metallic ring of clashing weapons, and the screams of the injured and dying.

The final battle had begun.

*

"It can't be much further, surely," panted Gorik, as the party skirted the mountains which encircled the capital on three sides.

"Come on, we're almost there," replied Miseldi, though, in truth, she had no idea how much further they had left to go. They were running hard; each elf, man, dwarf, and barren, pushing themselves on and on despite the protests of their screaming lungs. They had a job to do, and each and every one among them was steadfast in their determination to see it done. At length, they rounded an outcropping, and Ruli shouted in surprise and delight.

"There; the stairs. Look!"

Sure enough, as the party followed the bead of his extended finger, they saw the stairs, hewn into the very mountain rock; leading inexorably upwards into the heart of the Asarlai monastery.

"Well spotted, kid," said Nil, "but there's one small problem." He did not have to explain the problem to his companions, as the orrecs at the foot of the stairs had already drawn their weapons and begun their charge, followed by a mountain troll who tried its best not to step on them as it pounded its way forward. Ruli loosed an arrow which struck the lead orrec directly between the eyes. He reached over his shoulder and pulled another arrow as his companions drew their weapons and charged at the orrecs.

*

Xeb and Fennet fought side by side; they pushed, cut, thrust, and burned their way through the enemy ranks, moving deeper into Aclevion in pursuit of the fleeing Vinadan who had spun on his heel as the battle began in earnest, and was now heading for his citadel. Orrec after orrec fell to Enarhaedon, or were all-but incinerated by the arcane weapons were brought to life in burning fire by Xeb. The Asarlai was aware of his companions all around him, fighting for their lives; many failed in the act. Gael was like a whirlwind as she pivoted here and pirouetted there, her elven blade a blur of motion as it cut through enemy after enemy. Her elves were arrayed around her, and their swords and arrows made short work of their foe. But still, the orrecs kept coming; whether on foot or atop great wolves, Vinadan's forces appeared endless.

The hoblins rallied to Ugnor, and a quick glance showed Xeb that the hoblin chief's main target was a mountain troll rapidly making its way down a side street toward the centre of the battle. Ugnor and his forces meant to prevent the troll's arrival, and worked hard to bottleneck the street, cutting off and hopefully cutting down the enormous troll.

Here and there, men, barrens, hoblins, elves, and dwarves charged at Vinadan's forces, only to retreat when the enemy ranks were reinforced. Still, it occurred to Xeb, his own company appeared to be gaining a foothold.

They may outnumber us, he realised, *but they are disorganised and lacking in finesse.* He saw from the corner of his eye that Fennet was overmatched; taking on three orrecs at once but somehow holding his own. The Asarlai's eyes burned and his skin was incandescent as he called to life a longbow of pure fire, and made short work of two of Fennet's assailants; Enarhaedon took care of the last.

"Come, Fennet," said Xeb, seizing upon the momentary respite, "follow me." The hoblin nodded and fell in step as Xeb turned and set off at a sprint toward the citadel.

I only hope the others are faring better, he thought as he ran.

*

"On your right" shouted Gorik; Cade spun away to his left, narrowly avoiding being bisected by an oversized axe which came crashing down to the ground with a deafening *thud*.

The red haired dwarf nodded his thanks to Gorik, and brought his own axe to bear on the wrist of the mountain troll as it tried to extract its weapon from the ground. Cade's strike drew blood, but it was not the severing blow he had hoped for, and he dodged a huge retaliatory fist and jumped backwards, putting some ground between himself and the troll.

"To me!" he shouted, daring to glance here and there to take stock of their predicament. Ruli, Miseldi, and a handful of barrens were driving the orrecs back toward the stair. Many lay dead on the ground, enemy and ally alike. Of his own kin, most still fought, but he could see at least three dwarves on the ground, unmoving and silent.

Gorik, Nil, and Zimmon rallied to Cade's side, facing the mighty troll. Its weapon was now back in hand, and the gouge it had hewn in the ground was deep.

"We end this," said Zimmon, and the four dwarves charged as one.

Cade swung low, driving the edge of his axe into the troll's right ankle, while Gorik aimed an overhand strike at its left knee. Zimmon and Nil circled the mountain troll and jumped, throwing vicious strikes at its lower back. But even surrounded and assailed, to bring down a mountain troll was no stroll in the meadow. It retaliated, lashing out in all directions with fist, foot, and blade. The dwarves were forced to concede ground to avoid being pummelled by the angry and injured creature. It stomped its feet and beat its chest in rage, releasing its anger and frustration to the world as it roared its challenge.

"This isn't working," said Gorik through gritted teeth, "we need a plan."

"Don't worry," said Zimmon, "my brothers and I have killed far worse than mountain trolls." He turned to his kin, "what do you think, boys; the old *Scarred Burrow shuffle?*"

"Are you mad?" said Cade, "are you forgetting what happened the last time? Do you remember Breyan, rest him?"

"No, he's right," said Nil, "besides, I always thought of Breyan as more of an artist than a fighter. So technically it was his own fault." He turned to Gorik, and placed a reassuring hand on his shoulder.

"Gorik," he began, "on the count of three, I need you to charge directly at the troll, and just before you get to it, drop your axe."

Gorik did not even pretend to consider the idea. "Oh, Aether-spit!" he exclaimed, "are you out of your rock-hewn mind?"

"Trust us, brother," said Zimmon, "but it must be now."

Gorik's eyes flashed from Zimmon, to Nil, then to Cade, then he shook his head and sighed.

"If I survive this madness," he said, jabbing a finger toward the Mid-Burrow brothers, "you three owe me drinks. *Many* drinks." He took a deep breath, jerked his head to the left, eliciting a satisfying *click*, and he charged at the troll. Just before he got to the huge creature, he dropped his axe.

The troll, not expecting the move, hesitated for a moment as the unarmed Gorik continued his charge, running directly between the troll's legs. Nil and Cade came next, axes raised; their razor sharp edges catching the golden rays of the morning sun. When they were almost upon the troll, they each spun; pirouetting a full three-hundred-and-sixty degrees, swinging their axes in mighty arcs and opening deep lacerations in the troll's legs as their momentum carried them forward. Damage done, the pair crouched in perfect synchronisation, and braced themselves. Zimmon came charging from behind them. He leapt, using his brothers' wide backs as stepping stones, and launched himself into the air, axe shining brightly as the blade was brought to bear.

The troll's head hit the dirt before Zimmon's feet did, and the brothers raised their weapons and roared in triumph, unaware that Gorik was still running as if the fires of Elgiroth were licking at his heels.

*

It's hard to believe there is usually a market here, thought Gael as she ran her blade clean through another of Vinadan's orrecs. They were relentless; coming like waves to crash against Gael and her elves. Her company had suffered losses, to be sure, but they were holding their own, reinforced by a strong contingent of barrens. They had pushed the orrecs backward, driving them from the gates into the city proper, and now every street, alley, and square resounded with the din of battle. She had lost sight of both Vinadan and Xeb as the battle began, but she was vaguely aware that the Asarlai was pursuing the prince as the latter made his retreat toward the citadel.

Coward, she thought, taking the head off an orrec with a vicious backhand swing. More orrecs came spilling out of every nook; some mounted on wolves, others shadowed by the monstrous bats which flew overhead. Gael set her jaw, took a deep breath, and pushed forward, unaware that the wide open space behind her, through the towering gates and out onto the plains beyond the walls of Aclevion, was starting to fill with orrec reinforcements.

*

"Do not relent, Fennet; we are almost upon him," cried Xeb, as he cut his way through orrec after orrec. He had drawn his actual sword, meaning to conserve his powers for the inevitable encounter with Vinadan. He had called upon his runes to summon arcane weapons of all shapes in his pursuit of the fleeing prince, and the strain had begun to show. Sweat spilled openly down his face, obscuring his vision and drenching his beard. Fennet was in the lead now, wielding Enarhaedon against Vinadan's legions, pressing his own assault and trying to cover

Xeb where he could to allow the Asarlai to catch his breath and recover his strength.

The pair went back to back; their blades a blur of motion as they parried, thrust, blocked, and cut away at the orrecs assailing them. They were close to the citadel now, and a quick look over his shoulder told Xeb that, in their haste to catch Vinadan, they had opened up a sizable gap between themselves and their army.

Come on, Ruli, he thought; *fail, and all will be lost.*

*

The stair seemed to go on forever; leading inexorably upward toward the looming door which marked the entrance to the Asarlai monastery. Ruli had no idea what to expect when they arrived inside; Xeb had not really told them anything about the layout, only that they should go deeper and deeper inside, and that they would eventually find the chamber.

And then what?

They pressed and pressed, feeling their thighs burning with the effort of the upward climb. At length, the path lost some of its steepness and began to level out, and the group took a moment to catch their breaths. Ahead stood not so much a door, but more of a huge opening in the rockface; an entrance hewn into the very side of the mountain. Inside, Ruli could make out the flickering of candles, casting strange shadows upon the inner walls as the Asarlai went about their business inside, barely paying them any mind.

"Come on. This is it; it's now or never," Ruli said to his companions. Cade shook his head and rolled his eyes.

"Any other cliches you'd like to waste your breath on, or are we fucking doing this?" said the red haired dwarf, with a wry grin. The group took up their march once more and crossed the threshold into the Asarlai monastery.

*

The sound of the deep, booming horn coming from behind caught the attention of most of the barrens, men, hoblins, and dwarves embattled within the city walls, but it was something else which drew Gael's eyes.

The skies have darkened, she realised. She looked up in time to see a great black cloud, moving with unnatural speed; it swept lazily into place above the gates and beyond, blocking out the sun, and rendering Aclevion as dark as a winter's night.

Her heart froze in her chest as she heard a high-pitched screeching; even above the bass drone of the orrec horn, it pierced her ears and froze the blood in her veins.

"No," she said aloud to nobody in particular. "Fall back!" she called to her companions as she began to concede ground and retreat deeper into the city.

"To me!" she called, louder this time, trying to keep the razor edge of panic out of her voice.

"My lady?" said elven captain Gerrin who moved up beside her, "What is it?"

"Heamori," she said. "Pull everyone back, Finn; pull them back at once; we make our stand at the citadel."

Her eyes did not leave the horde of dark shapes which moved through the gates and into the city. Even as she fought - blocking an orrec blade here, cutting down a wolf rider there - her keen eyes were fixed upon the newcomers. A mass of orrecs, dark, armoured, and spoiling for battle made up the bulk of the reinforcements, but in front, the one race in all of Gibrion Gael truly feared: the haemori.

She could not take her eyes away from the humanoids; their long, dark cloaks, billowing in the wind; their piercing yellow eyes and razor sharp fangs. They hated the sunlight, and advanced now, grinning, under the cover of a darkness their dark arts had manifested in the skies above the capital.

Smiling, hissing, snarling; the twenty or so haemori that Gael could see had murder in their eyes, and their bloodlust was tangible as it hung in the thick, dark air.

Gael could hear her blood pulsing in her ears, and knew that they could, too.

*

The moment they were afforded to catch their breath came as a welcome relief to Xeb and Fennet, but they were not permitted to savour it for long. Scores of dead orrecs, wolves, and bats lay at their feet, and the pair were not without injuries of their own though they were superficial for the moment. Xeb leaned against his sword, drawing deep breaths, willing the oxygen to rejuvenate his tired body.

Fennet, much to Xeb's relief, still carried the same look of determination in his eyes, and the adrenaline running through the hoblin's veins was as obvious to Xeb as the blade in his hand. The hoblin must have noticed Xeb's glance.

"Come, master Xebus," he said, "we end this together."

He, at least, has plenty of fight left in him, thought the Asarlai as he looked around. They were in the main square at the foot of the great marble steps which led into the citadel. The enormous water fountain, some thirty feet across, stood a little ahead of them, and the likenesses of the three goddesses which stood at its centre were as bright and impressive as ever.

"Congratulations," came an all-too-familiar voice from behind Xeb. The Asarlai closed his eyes and offered a silent plea to Hemera. He opened his eyes and turned.

"You have come far, and displayed some impressive skills," continued Vinadan, walking slowly down the marble steps toward Xeb and Fennet. He threw a quick glance to his left and then his right and, with a small shake of his head, instructed the orrecs which were emerging from narrow side streets to hold their ground.

"But now," he continued, "it is over. Your little insurrection was amusing, Xebus, but did you really think you ever actually had a chance of defeating me?"

"You are a tyrant, Vinadan," Xeb retorted, "a murderer; a spoiled brat of a child playing king."

Vinadan's eyes narrowed at the jibe, but he did not reply. Xeb continued, taking a step toward the prince. "You will stand down your armies, and you will surrender yourself to stand trial for your crimes. Fail to comply with our terms, and - make no mistake - you will die here today."

Vinadan remained impassive and unreadable as he stood on the marble steps, a few feet from ground level, eyeing Xeb and Fennet keenly. A moment more, then another, before Vinadan threw back his head in raucous laughter.

"Oh, Xebus," he said, wiping a tear from his eye with the back of his hand, "thank you for that; I haven't laughed like that since I was a boy. Turns out I *really needed* it," he descended the final few steps and found himself on ground level, mere feet from Xeb and Fennet. He spared a glance overhead and beheld the dark cloud creeping toward the citadel, plunging the gleaming city square into semidarkness.

"But make no mistake of your own, Asarlai," Vinadan continued, "*you* are the one who will die today. And, come to think of it, why wait?" he added casually.

Despite the world seeming to move in slow motion, Xeb had no time to react or even to call out as Vinadan's eyes blazed with a sickly crimson flame. The prince flicked out his right hand, extending his arm toward Xeb, and a blast of serpentine fire flashed from his fingertips toward the Asarlai.

If Vinadan was quick, however, Fennet was quicker.

Xeb felt as if his heart had been cleaved in two as he saw the hoblin throw himself sideways, placing himself between Vinadan and Xeb, and taking the full force of the prince's arcane attack. He was dead before he hit the ground.

"No!" cried Xeb; he immediately tried to force his grief down, bury it deep lest it swell and drown him. It would condemn him to his fate as surely as Vinadan's powers would if he lost his focus. Acting on pure instinct, he fired a blast of his own fire in return, his left hand ablaze with the rune for *Vengeance* as it spat a ball of red flame toward Vinadan, who blocked it with an open palm. With his other hand, Xeb reached down, claiming

Enarhaedon and he charged, covering the distance in seconds.

Vinadan grinned, interlaced his fingers, and cracked his knuckles. He drew his own sword and planted his right foot behind him.

The clash of their blades rang out and echoed around the courtyard.

*

"You should not be here," said a red-robed Asarlai, placing himself in front of Ruli, Gorik and the others, and holding up a stalling hand. Under his arm were tucked a number of old scrolls, and Ruli noticed that the Asarlai's fingertips were stained dark blue with ink, "go back, at once."

"We cannot do that," said Ruli, softly, but with some urgency, "we are in great haste. We have no wish for blood to be shed inside these hallowed halls, Loremaster. Now please, step aside."

The Asarlai did not move.

"This is a domain of study and knowledge; what business could you possibly have here, with your swords and your axes?"

"We don't have time for-" started Zimmon, pushing his way to the front.

"Peace," said Miseldi, holding out an arm to halt the dwarf's progress.

"Our only goal is peace," she continued, "Vinadan must be stopped, and we know how to stop him. Please, let us through."

"Stopped? Vinadan is the lord of all Gibrion; he has united the Souls of Aether and Hemera and he leads an army the likes of which have not been seen in centuries" the Asarlai replied, lowering his arm as he did so, "what makes you think he needs to be stopped, or that you can actually accomplish it?"

Gorik stepped forward.

"Do you know where your Elder - Alma, I think it was - do you know where Alma is right now?"

A small shake of the head and a look of confusion betrayed the Asarlai.

"We are under siege," he replied, "I expect the Elder is protecting the monastery from assault, or perhaps he guards prince Vinadan. Why do you ask?" an edge of concern crept into his voice.

"Because," said Ruli, without a hint or reproach or mockery, "Alma's head now rests in a box at the main gates; an offering from your prince."

More of the Asarlai had arrived now, gathering behind the loremaster. "You lie," came a deep voice from underneath one of the raised hoods.

"He does not," said Miseldi, stepping forward and placing her hands on the loremaster's own, "We saw it; Vinadan murdered Alma, and brought his head to the gate to mock your brother, Xebus."

"Xebus is nothing more than a traitor and insurgent," said a tall, pale skinned Asarlai who pushed his way to the front of the group, "he has raised an army of filthy malcontents - like you - and means to usurp our great and powerful prince."

"*Great and powerful?*" spat Cade, "Oh, okay, we understand; you're one of the ones whose pockets Vinadan has lined with gold," some of the other Asarlai turned and looked sharply at the newcomer.

"You lot didn't know?" continued Cade, sensing he had struck a chord, "your great and wonderful prince has made some of your traitor brothers stinking rich in return for their... *fealty.*"

"We are academics and advisors," said the loremaster, "not bows for hire."

"We know, Sir," said Miseldi, "but everyone has a price, it seems."

The pale Asarlai fixed Miseldi with a wicked stare, and the passageway in which a crowd now stood grew tense and silent. At once, the Asarlai's face bloomed into a maniacal grin, and his skin blazed to life in a melody of burning runes.

All scattered, diving left and right, drawing weapons and seeking cover as the fighting began. Asarlai on Asarlai; those loyal to their order deployed their arts upon those loyal to Vinadan.

Ruli and his group were caught in the crossfire; arrows flew, axes flashed, and swords blurred as they regained their feet and pressed on. They fought alongside the scholars and cut down the defectors. The powers of the Asarlai were many and strong, and barren after barren, dwarf after dwarf fell to the fires of their order. Ruli crouched low, dodging and weaving as he nocked arrow after arrow, their silver tips reflecting the burning orange light of the Asarlai fires as they flew to strike their targets.

He felt an urgent tug upon his shoulder, and turned to see Miseldi waving their group toward a small corridor which led off from the embattled entrance hallway. Ruli stood and wasted no time in sprinting after Miseldi and the others.

Though his heart was heavy, he did not glance back to count the dead.

*

Gael felt as though she was sleepwalking through a waking nightmare. At first she could not understand why the blade of her sword shook as she held it in a defensive stance in front of her face. She glanced down, and realised that it was her hands which were shaking. She spun and blocked a wild slash of an orrec blade, turning it aside and beheading the assailing orrec. She continued to concede ground, stepping backwards as she fought, as did her kin.

She looked to her left, and could only watch in horror as one of the haemori lunged at an archer and sank its teeth deep into the elf's neck. Gael's reeling mind noted absently that the blood looked almost black in the artificial darkness which had heralded the arrival of the creatures from the eastern isles. To her right, another of the parasitic, ageless creatures had finished gorging itself upon one of her kin and was wiping its wide, grinning mouth with the sleeve of its black robe. The elf which the creature had killed lay in the dirt, pale and gaunt, exsanguinated.

Then it opened its eyes and began to sit up.

It was all Gael could do to keep from losing the last vestiges of sanity which had already begun to wane at the arrival of the nightmare creatures. The fear she harboured toward the haemori was primal, and she physically shuddered as she gazed upon them.

"Full retreat!" she screamed, her voice breaking with strain and panic. One of the haemori, drawn by the sound of her voice, snapped its head in her direction and fixed her with a glowing yellow stare. Gael turned and ran deeper into the city, not daring to look back, keeping her eyes fixed on the towering pinnacle of the citadel in the distance.

*

Vinadan's forces held their positions, ceding the entire central courtyard to the two combatants. Xeb and Vinadan's blades clashed and sparked as they spun and moved, attacking high, blocking low. The swordplay was punctuated with fire as, with every advance and retreat, the physical assaults were reinforced and augmented by those of a more magical nature.

Vinadan spun backwards, turning a full circle and bringing his blade to bear in a vicious backhand swing. When his blade found only thin air, he called upon the rune for *Destruction* and sent a volley of fire at Xeb with his free hand.

Xeb, having crouched to avoid Vinadan's sword, threw his left arm high, calling upon the *Defence* rune to place a shield of pure flame between himself and the prince's attack. Both men were panting with exertion, and their respective attire was singed here and there, holes burnt through to blister the flesh below.

"Stand down," commanded Xeb, replacing a two-handed grip on Enarhaedon.

"Stand down?" replied Vinadan, "I am but toying with you, Xebus. This ends when I decide it ends, and not a moment before." Vinadan bared his teeth and renewed his assault. He charged at Xeb, spinning his sword in an overhand flourish before bringing it down in a powerful strike aimed directly at Xeb's head. Xeb strengthened his grip on the hilt and thrust his own blade upwards to block the attack, though barely in time. His arms reverberated with the force of the blow, and Vinadan seized advantage of his opponent's momentary weakness. He aimed a powerful kick at Xeb, catching the Asarlai in the ribs and sending him tumbling away to land uncveremoniously upon the ground.

The pain in Xeb's ribs was blinding as he tried to breathe.

Broken, he thought, bringing his hand to his side to assess the damage. Vinadan closed the gap between himself and the Asarlai, replacing his sword at his belt as he advanced. Xeb realised in a moment of horror that he was no longer holding Enarhaedon, and a panicked look around did not yield the sword's location.

"Well, well," said Vinadan, spreading his arms wide and eliciting a deafening cheer from the captive audience, "perhaps you are not as strong as I had given you credit for, Xebus of the Asarlai."

Xeb struggled to his knees, every breath bringing more pain from his shattered ribs and pierced lungs.

"I must admit, I had expected more of a challenge," continued Vinadan, "but one must take what practice one can get in these days of *peace* and *prosperity*." He smiled openly and balled his hands into fists. Xeb staggered to his feet and looked Vinadan straight in the eye.

"There will be peace; there will be prosperity," he wheezed, "once you are in the Aether-forsaken ground." nWhether it was his burning hatred for Vinadan, his grief for Fennet, or the final dying embers of hope which sustained him, Xeb drew on what little strength he had left and raised his hands, adopting an offensive stance.

One by one, the runes for *Hope, Love, Fear, Hatred, Vengeance, Justice*, and myriad others burned to life upon his skin, and his eyes spewed a living fire which clawed and reached toward the blackened skies. Xeb screamed at the top of his battered lungs, and his feet left the ground. He hovered a few inches above the ground; a creature of fire, now, barely human in his countenance.

Vinadan roared in anger and raised his arms. His left hand blazed to life in ruby red, and his right burned black with the fires of the night. Not unlike the spilling of ink into water, the whites of Vinadan's eyes blackened, until they were little more than voids, and his already pale skin whitened to a deathly pallor.

"This ends now," Vinadan said through gritted teeth, his voice a few octaves deeper than before. The prince and the Asarlai moved as one, casting their arcane fire magic upon one another, illuminating the darkness in violent reds and deep oranges.

As the remainder of Xeb's company - elves and barrens, men, dwarves, and hoblins - burst into the courtyard, Gael's mind flashed back to her childhood, so long ago. She remembered her father taking her to a pyromagic display upon the shore of the great lake Ideen on Aether's Eve; she remembered watching in awe as jets and streams of fire raced into the sky to burst into shapes and likenesses of animals, ships, and weapons. Such colours as Gael had never before seen captivated her mind and warmed her heart back then, but as she watched Xeb and Vinadan exchange fire beneath the canopy of arcane night, her blood ran cold and her heart sank with a deep fear for her friend. There was no relent to Gael's torment, and the screeching of the haemori and *thud, thud, thud* of advancing orrecs and trolls at their heels threatened to push her beyond the brink of despair.

Vinadan spared a glance at the newcomers as he poured crimson flames at Xeb with both hands, and he grinned. He doubled his efforts and intensified his barrage, but was frustrated that - somehow - the Asarlai was maintaining his defences, even now cocooned in a protective shield of fire.

Gael looked over her shoulder and saw that the orrec and haemori reinforcements had cut off the rear, and she noted the circle of orrecs maintaining their positions around the central courtyard.

We're trapped, she thought, *it is over.*

She took a deep breath, steadying her nerves, and tightened her grip upon her blade. She set her feet and adopted an offensive stance, turning to look one of the advancing haemori straight in the eye. The creature met her glance and snarled, opening its mouth wide to display fangs, dripping with a sickly combination of blood and toxins. It broke from the pack and charged at her.

At first, Gael fancied that she was somehow dreaming as she saw the gold-tipped arrow all-but sever the head from the haemori's body, but as the creature crumpled to the ground and more and more arrows rained down from the sky as if birthed by the evil cloud above their heads, her rational mind had no choice but to accept the evidence of her eyes. She glanced upward, tracing the trajectory of the arrows, and her heart leapt at the sight of Thalnon Meldreth and an army of elves crouched upon the city rooftops, pouring arrow after arrow down upon Vinadan's legions. From a side street, Trissan of Adeniron, followed by his own men, charged into the battle, coming at the orrecs from their rear. From another street on the opposite side of the courtyard, Alderman Gracen, flanked by the Adeniron city guard joined the fray, followed closely behind by Pilmer and scores of her hardy dwarven kin.

The orrecs abandoned their watchful perimeter and drew their weapons; the final battle for Aclevion had now truly begun.

*

"In the name of the goddess," whispered Ruli as he stared, wide eyed, at the enormous pillars. They had fought their way deeper into the mountain, and had stumbled, more by accident than design, into the huge room which Xeb had referred to as the Soul Chamber. The pillars were as thick as tree trunks; they were pale, a grey which only narrowly avoided being white. Into them were carved runes of all types in an angry blood red which stood in sharp contrast to the pristine pillars.

No, not carved, thought Ruli, *the runes are living things; I can feel them… They are as much a part of the pillars as my own blood is a part of me.*

Between the pillars, suspended some twenty feet above the ground, were the Souls of Hemera and Aether. To gaze upon them like this brought tears to Rulis eyes, and sent waves of alarm to shiver down his spine. The Souls were not united, not in harmony, neither were they suspended side by side; they orbited and repelled each other circling and rejecting each other in a violent dance. They reminded Ruli of two wolves fighting for dominance; they were discordant; lacking harmony. They were just…

Wrong, Ruli realised.

He knew what he had to do, though he knew not the source of this knowledge. But he was certain; as certain as he had ever been about anything before.

"Misedli, Gorik, my friends, all of you," he began, waving for the attention of those who remained.

"Ruli?" said Miseldi, "what is it?" she did not attempt to disguise the concern in her voice as she looked into her friend's eyes. She saw resignation there, and peace; purpose.

It's okay, my friend, Ruli said to Miseldi without moving his mouth. *Go.*

"Come on, lass," said Nil, taking Miseldi's arm, gently. He looked at Ruli.

"I hope you know what you're doing," he said. Ruli nodded.

"Hold them off, Nil; buy me as much time as you can."

The dwarf turned and led Miseldi and the others out of the Soul Chamber. Ruli put them out of mind and turned once more to face the mighty pillars. He closed his eyes, took a deep breath, and tried to centre himself, blocking out the arrhythmic pulsing of the Souls above, and the clash and cry of battle behind. He focused his mind. He thought of his home, of Ehronia itself. He thought of Miseldi, and of Gerdan. He thought of Tyan, and the scores of dead they had offered to the sea in purifying flames.

He thought of Horith, and recalled the fear, confusion, and loneliness his friend had felt at the end. He had felt it along with Horith. As the betrayed barren, Horith of house Nindrius, had spared his final thought for his friend, Ruli would now return the favour.

He focused on his pain, his rage, his love, his friends, and his home; he gathered them all to himself, visualising them as a pulsing orb of light, not dissimilar to those which still toiled and raged above him. He forced his mind to centre on the other part of him which he had always known had been there; the part of himself that should not exist, but did; the part of himself which Gael had recognised within him.

I'm the arrowhead, he thought with a grin. Eyes still squeezed shut, he drew every fibre of his being within himself for the briefest of moments, then let go.

*

Vinadan had abandoned all semblance of control, now; he was no longer toying with Xeb like a predator nudging and nosing its wounded prey. He was enraged; furious at the arrival of Xeb's reinforcements, and was being jostled and shoved by enemy and ally alike as the courtyard filled to bursting with combatants of all races and allegiances.

The gauntlets are off, he thought, as he harnessed the full power of the twin Souls. The prince of Aclevion was indiscriminate as he unleashed his furious arts on anyone in his path, casually destroying his own troops in the process as he advanced on Xeb. The Asarlai was on his last legs now, surviving on some heady mix of adrenaline and stubbornness as the battle raged all around him. He had lost Enarhaedon somewhere in the mire of bodies which littered the courtyard, and relied on his magic alone for both defence and attack. His vision had begun to blur, and he was so thirsty he feared that some primal panic may begin to set in at any moment if he did not take on water soon. He could see his companions fighting with every ounce of strength and bravery they could muster, killing and being killed by orrecs, wolves, haemori, trolls, or Vinadan's own dark arts.

The prince was advancing with purpose, and Xeb feared he lacked the strength to hold him off for much longer. The black cloud still held sway above their heads, and Xeb's ears rang with the clash of metal and the screams of the fallen. He looked to his left and saw Gael holding off three orrecs by herself, conceding ground with every parry. He raised a hand in her direction and summoned a spear of flame into existence. He threw it with all his might, and was relieved to see it skewer two of the orrecs, who burst into flame at the touch of the mystic weapon.

Gael turned and nodded her thanks; Xeb returned the gesture. The next thing he knew, he was on the ground, writhing in pain. Vinadan's fireball had caught him directly on his right flank, and had dumped him in a heap on the ground some ten feet away.

Xeb could not move; he could barely see.

This is it, he thought, and an image of Fennet came to mind, followed by Alma, Tyan, and more; the faces of the fallen hovered, unspeaking, unblinking, in the hazy space between his eyes and the world. He was vaguely aware of Vinadan strolling toward him with murder in his eyes and victory upon his ghastly countenance, but he found he could not focus on the prince, distracted as he was by a nibbling sound at his ear. He turned his head, wincing at the pain, and found himself face to face with a large brown hare. Behind it, utterly disinterested, sat a dishevelled cat, watching distractedly as a magpie circled above.

"Morrigan?" Xeb managed. The hare tilted its head to the side at the sound of its name, then bolted, darting out of sight as the ground began to shake.

Men and elves, orrecs and hoblins - all paused for a moment in confusion as the very ground beneath their feet began to rumble and shake violently, knocking many off balance and dumping them unceremoniously to the deck. Vinadan's face was a mask of rage as he sought the source of the unnatural quake, his head looking here and there for any sign of a culprit. Composure regained en masse, the battle was renewed all across the courtyard, and swords clashed in tandem with the deep rumbling below.

An ear-splitting, booming groan issued from the direction of the central fountain, and a vine some six feet across and monstrous in length erupted from the ground below, throwing rock and marble high into the air. Vinadan was knocked off his feet, and as he lay prone, covered in dust and stone, a ray of light broke through the dark cloud above.

Then another, and another. The breaks in the cloud widened and fused, giving way to glorious sunshine, and within seconds the dark canopy had been obliterated entirely. The remaining haemori were reduced to ashes as they took the sunlight head on.

Vinadan held a hand up to his face and squinted his eyes against the newfound glare. As his eyes adjusted, he beheld three silhouettes striding confidently into the battle, summoning vines, roots, and branches of ungodly proportions, and deploying them with devastating effect upon his forces. Left, right; high, low; the vines and branches decimated Vinadan's orrecs and armies, cutting them down or crushing them, even as they tried to get away.

Vinadan regained his feet and adopted a defensive stance.

"It is over, *Prince*," said Lady Karsha without a hint of deference in her voice. Yilmé and Grema flanked her, and their familiars were close.

"So," Vinadan said, forcing defiance into his voice, "the old tales are true; you live, *Crones*."

"Live?" replied Yilmé, "no, Vinadan; it has been many cycles since we truly lived. Now stand down, and you may yet live a little longer."

"Fools!" Vinadan spat, "Traitors! Pretenders! Do you know to whom you speak? I am no common criminal; no animal you have ensnared in your Gibrion-accursed webs. I am a god! I control the Souls; their power is mine to command! You - all of you - will kneel to me or be destroyed."

Neither of the three - nor any of the elves, men, barrens, hoblins, or dwarves who had rallied to them - were swayed by the prince's words.

"The Souls are sick, Vinadan," said Grema, "surely you feel it. They were not meant to be paired; they exist alone or as a trio; they cannot abide in any other state."

"And what would you know of these matters, hag?" Vinadan spat. He spared a glance around him, and noted with a gnawing dread that the arrival of the witches and the deployment of their magic had rendered his own forces virtually exhausted; the bulk of his orrecs either dead or fleeing in the face of their power.

"More than you could ever understand," said Karsha with more than a hint of sadness, "now surrender."

Gael had helped Xeb to his feet, and they moved to stand with the witches of Vitrius. Vinadan shook his head and laughed a low, inhuman laugh.

"Oh, we are not finished yet… *Dhruaghar*!" he shouted.

The dragon's roar was deafening, and for a moment it seemed as if the haemori's dark cloud had returned. The gust of wind generated by the dragon's wings was immense as it swooped overhead to land upon the citadel. It rested, perched upon the citadel as if the gleaming structure were a mere cushion beneath it. It bared its teeth and breathed in great warm huffs. It was impressive in its stature and terrifying in its countenance. Black and red scales, razor sharp teeth, claws like iron, and wings that blotted out the sun as they stretched to their full span. Its breath came in bursts from its huge nose, each exhalation like hot steam issuing from a burst pipe.

Xeb's alarm threatened to overwhelm him, and many of his company had fled into the side streets to seek cover from the giant firebreather. He did not blame them one bit.

"You see now the extent of my powers?" said Vinadan, gloating. He took a step forward, one hand held above his head as if he might issue Dhruaghar with a signal at any moment.

"No," said Karsha, "I see only a child breaking his toys; a false king with borrowed powers."

Vinadan abandoned all pretence and roared a command to Dhruaghar, lowering his arm to point at the company amassed before him. The dragon jumped down from the citadel to land in the courtyard with a ground-shaking crunch.

Karsha stood her ground, unflinching in the face of the monstrous dragon, and her sisters moved to stand by her side.

"Dhruaghar," she said softly, reaching out to touch the dragon's scaly face, "my friend; you were not always as you are now."

Vinadan watched on with a dawning horror as the dragon appeared to be listening to the witch instead of following his command and incinerating her.

"You know we can do it, Dhruaghar," Yilmé said.

"You need only ask," added Grema. The dragon stared at the witches for a long moment, then turned its attention to Vinadan, then back to the witches. The beginnings of a tear glistened in the dragon's huge eye, and then it nodded.

"What is this farce?" spat Vinadan, "I command you to-"

An almighty *boom* rang out around Aclevion, and a shower of rock rained down upon the courtyard. The witches raised their hands and uttered a single command, summoning a shield the colour of pure summer grasses above all their heads, and watched as the rock bounced harmlessly off their protective canopy to land elsewhere. They ceased their incantation as the rocks stopped falling, and all eyes now turned to the gaping hole in the side of the mountain above the capital.

Xeb looked at the rocks which were scattered all around the courtyard, and noticed with an unprecedented delight that interspersed among the dull brown boulders and stones were smooth, cylindrical pieces, light grey in hue, and covered in blood red runes of all denominations.

Vinadan was incandescent with rage; he raised both hands above his head, and brought them down, fast, aimed squarely at the witches, He loosed a blood curdling scream as he did so, meaning to unleash the full power of two Souls upon his enemies

The sputtering spark which issued from his shaking fingertips in answer was batted aside with ease by Lady Karsha. Vinadan looked down at his hands in horror, and then spun to stare at the hole in the mountain.

"No," he whispered, "no, no, no, no, no… NO!" He drew his sword and lunged at Karsha, and was immediately thrown backwards, crashing hard into a fallen boulder. None of those arrayed before the prince had seen it, but the silver tipped arrow which now protruded from Vinadan's chest was as real as the blood which flowed openly from his mouth.

All heads turned to see Ruli, bow in hand, leaning heavily on the bloodied and dirty Miseldi, followed by Gorik, Nil, Cade, Zimmon, and a handful of surviving dwarves and barrens.

Vinadan looked left and right as the group closed in around him, standing over him and blocking out the light of the last sun he would ever see.

"It did not have to be this way," said Xeb with some effort, "we gave you-"

Vinadan spat a mouthful of blood at the Asarlai. "Save it, filth," he said through clenched teeth. His face was pale and his breath came in shallow gasps, but still he grinned.

"Fools," he said, "you bunch of mewling, self-righteous, Aether-forsaken fools." He began to laugh, the sound mingled with the gurgling of blood in his throat.

"You think… you think you know power?" he raised a hand to point at Xeb, Gael, then the witches in turn. "You know nothing of *true* power… You'll see… you'll all see…"

He began to laugh again, a low, croaking laugh; a choking, rattling laugh.

It was the last sound Vinadan, prince of Aclevion ever made.

Chapter Thirty-Six

Long moments went by unwitnessed as Xeb, Gael, Ruli, and all in attendance looked upon the body of Vinadan, slumped against a fallen rock with an arrow in his heart. The loud, hot breathing from behind them reminded them that there was still a dragon in the courtyard to deal with. The huge creature, so fierce in appearance, was crouched low with its stomach on the ground. It waited, appearing to Xeb more like a faithful dog than a rampaging dragon. The sunlight which shone down upon the unlikely scene highlighted how the creature's black and red scales shimmered, displaying an array of hues as its hide moved in tandem with its breathing.

One by one, all heads turned to face Dhruaghar, but none save Karsha made any movement. She stepped close to the dragon, and placed her head forehead against its muzzle; her hair and clothing blown by its strong exhalations. The dragon closed its eyes, too, and the pair stood for a long moment in the silence of the courtyard, head to head.

Xeb's mind reeled at the juxtaposition of image and emotion he beheld; a dragon and a witch stood before him, but they displayed a tenderness he could not reconcile. At length, Karsha stepped away from the dragon and held her hands out to her sides. Grema and Yilmé stepped up beside her and took their sister by the offered hands.

Xeb considered himself a wise and learned man, skilled in the arts of the Asarlai, and witness to many wonders in his time, but he was not prepared for the sight he now beheld. The witches chanted to themselves in a language Xeb did not recognise, and as they repeated their charm, their bodies seemed to glow, to crackle with some unseen energy. Their bare feet left the ground, and the energy which engulfed them began to take on a sickly, poison hue; it strengthened, coalesced, until it bloomed brightly in a blinding flash of green the colour of the purest grass. There they hung, six or seven feet in the air, encircled in a web of green energy, chanting; louder and louder their words; stronger and stronger their resolve…

The ground began to rumble as if it were about to split open.

And then it did.

*

"No," said Xeb, "It… it cannot be."

A tear announced itself in his eye, and he allowed it to roll openly down his cheek. Gael threw herself to her knees, as did Thalnon and many of their kin. The dwarves removed their helmets, and many of the men placed their hands over their mouths in shock, perhaps fear.

From the gaping fissure the witches had opened in the ground emerged the Soul of Gibrion, resplendent, shining brighter than the sun, bathing the courtyard in its ancient emerald light.

"Are you ready?" Karsha asked. Dhruaghar nodded his mighty head, and Xeb fancied that he could read remorse in the dragon's face; remorse and resolve.

As one, the witches turned their hands toward the mighty dragon and poured the power of the Lost Soul into Dhruaghar. The dragon did not fight, claw, nor slash his way out of the reach of their blinding rays; he did not unleash his fire or his rage; he did not so much as flinch as the energy leached into him. One final exertion, one blinding flash, and it was over.

*

Xeb slowly lowered his hand from his eyes and dared to open them. He could see dancing spots of artificial colour where the blinding gare had obscured his vision, and it took him a few moments to blink those away. Of all the wonders he had seen on this day alone, he was now truly humbled.

Where Dhruaghar the Dread, dragon of the north; legend, tyrant, campfire fable; had stood moments earlier, now lay a man. He was naked and frail, curled like a baby on the courtyard floor, but he appeared to be alive. Karsha went to him, helping him to his feet and embracing him tightly. He tried to return the embrace, but his arms shook with the effort. His hair was as long and unkempt as his beard, and Xeb could see his veins beneath his thin, pale skin.

The veins appeared a purple so deep it was almost black, and the Asarlai traced their spider-like crawl up through the man's arms, torso, neck, face…

Poison, Xeb realised, *he is badly poisoned.*

*

"Dhru," said Karsha, holding the man at arm's length to take in the sight of him.

"Karsha," he replied weakly, "how long do I have?"

"Days," she replied through tears, "a little over a week, perhaps."

The man - Dhruaghar - nodded, and allowed Karsha to take his weight. Grema and Yilmé moved alongside her, and Karsha transferred the man to her sisters' care. Karsha turned to Xeb and the company, but it was Xeb who spoke first.

"My lady," he started, breaking away from the group and hobbling over to the witch, still struggling to breathe and still clutching his side. He reached her, but as he looked into her eyes his words escaped his grasp. He looked at Karsha, then to the Soul of Gibrion, still pulsing and undulating in the air above them, shining brightly as if it was unaware it had been missing for centuries beyond count. He looked back at Karsha, and gestured weakly to the Soul.

"How…?" was all he could manage. Karsha laughed without humour.

"First, Xebus of the Asarlai, allow me to assist you," she said. She reached out and placed a hand on his side, and Xeb's world lit up with emerald light and a brief, blinding pain. Within a moment the pain had abated, and he felt strong; stronger than he had in many a year.

"Thank you, Lady Karsha," he said, feeling vitality return to his body and mind.

"Think nothing of it, Xebus. Perhaps I misjudged you," she said. Xeb waved away her words.

"No, my lady; you were right to be wary, given your… history. Besides," he added with a smile, gesturing toward the witches' familiars, "Morrigan, Branwen, and Danu here were ever watchful. But I must know, Karsha - how?"

"The Soul of Gibrion was never truly lost, Xebus; more, it has been hiding in plain sight for many cycles." She reached down, and picked a handful of dirt, soil and rock from the ground.

"It was here," she said, holding out the dirt, "in the soil, the grass, the wind… Nature, Xebus; she is *Nature*."

Xeb nodded, though he did not truly understand.

"Now," Karsha continued, we must take our leave. But before we do, we must decide what to do with the others. Gael, I believe?"

Gael was startled by the sound of her name. She stepped forward.

"Yes, Lady Karsha?"

"You must protect Hemera. We will deliver her back to Eonis where she stood for centuries beyond measure, guarded and undisturbed; that is where she belongs."

"Me?" asked Gael, "why me?" Karsha laughed, this time with some genuine amusement.

"Let's just say that our kind have some small ability to divine future events; all will become clear soon enough. You must do this, and soon."

"I will see it done," said Gael.

"And what of the others?" asked Xeb.

"My sisters and I will tend to Girbrion, as we always have. Aether, however, presents something of a conundrum."

"How so?" asked Nil, stepping forward.

"The Soul of Aether," began Karsha, "is the Soul of the night; of darkness. Ever it has led those in whose vicinity it rests into the same darkness. Not at first, and not always - there have undoubtedly been some great and wise monarchs in the north these last centuries - but believe me when I tell you that Vinadan was but the latest in a long line of those corrupted by Aether's Soul. More than this, I tell you that the corrupted all have one thing in common: they were men; human men."

"Now hold on just a-" began Gracen, who had also managed to push his way to the front.

"The Soul of Aether cannot reside in Aclevion," Karsha continued, cutting Gracen off as if she had not heard him.

"Besides," added Grema, still holding onto Dhruaghar, "the pillars are destroyed. They must be remade anew."

"Anew, and elsewhere," added Yilmé.

"Where would you suggest, my ladies?" asked Xeb.

The witches exchanged looks, their glances speaking a thousand words. They turned to survey the crowd before them: elves, men, dwarves, barrens, hoblins…

"Ehronia," said Karsha, "perhaps even Tomirar. The barrens do not covet glory, and the dwarves are strong and hardy folk. Either would suffice."

"But you must decide now," said Yilmé.

"We would see that it is kept safe and guarded at all times," said Gorik. "Our walls are thick and our armour is strong."

"Aye," said Cade.

"Aye," said Zimmon, echoed by Nil and the rest of the dwarves.

"Hold on a moment," said Thalnon, "who speaks for the barrens? Surely they deserve a say in this?" All eyes turned to Ruli. He cleared his throat and stepped forward.

"Thank you, Lord Thalnon; I am of course happy to speak for my kin. We barrens are not a complicated race; we do not seek glory or covet riches. We are farmers for the most part, though we are not without great smiths and prosperous merchants. We do not seek solitude, but we welcome it nonetheless. Ehronia is now liberated from Vinadan's clutches, and we have some hope that we can rebuild our homes and our lives. We yearn for peace more than anything else in all of Gibrion, but we do not cower in the face of a threat. We too are strong, but strong in our own way." He turned to Gorik and the brothers.

"The Soul shall go to Torimar, where I know it will be in safe hands."

"So be it," said Karsha. She closed her eyes and slowly raised her arms at her sides, the very air around her crackling with energy as she did so.

"Wait!" called Xeb. Karsha ceased her incantation and opened her eyes.

"Please, if I may," said Xeb, holding up one finger to forestall their departure. He ran out of sight for a moment, and returned with Fennet in his arms. He laid the hoblin onto the ground before the witches, and raised his head, unashamed of the tears in his eyes.

"Is there nothing you can do for him?" he pleaded.

Karsha stepped toward Xeb, and crouched beside Fennet. She stroked the hoblin's ice cold cheek, and met Xeb's gaze.

"Xebus," she said, "we have survived for centuries unseen and untouched, we can summon the elements and employ the very whims of nature to our ends; we can brew potions that can freeze the heart of a giant, and can reduce mountains to ashes with a mere incantation," she looked over her shoulder and saw Dhru, still leaning heavily on her sisters, "we can even end a ceaseless curse," she placed her hand on Xeb's cheek and wiped away a tear, "but we cannot raise the dead."

Xeb let his head drop, and closed his eyes.

I'm sorry, my friend, he thought, *I'm so sorry. I will keep my promise to your kin. I will see you home.*

"I will do one thing for him, Xebus," said Karsha, standing, and motioning for Xeb to do the same.

"I will return him to the ground; to Gibrion herself."

She closed her eyes and extended her arms, palms down, over Fennet's body. Her hands glowed with a green fire, and a thousand runes of black fire blazed to life over every exposed inch of her skin. Vines and roots emerged from the ground around Fennet, encircling him until he was barely visible within. Slowly, gently, they pulled him down into the ground, which closed up behind them, a layer of fresh topsoil left behind where Fennet had lain.

"Here, Xebus," said Miseldi, coming up alongside the Asarlai, "we found this."

"Thank you, my lady," Xeb said as he accepted Enarhaedon from the young barren. He turned and met Karsha's gaze, nodding to Grema and Yilmé in turn.

"Go, with our deepest gratitude;" he said.

Karsha turned and joined her sisters, taking Dhruaghar under the arm as she did.

"Haem' y' Vandea," they called as one, and then they were gone, and the three Souls with them.

The courtyard, though still illuminated by the midday sun, seemed as dark as night in the absence of Gibrion's emerald glow.

*

Gracen's head was on a constant swivel as he went among the ranks. He imposed himself between the men, checking, looking, checking again. At length, he grew frustrated in his efforts and sought out Gael.

"My lady," he said, upon finding the elf, "where is my feckless brother? Where is Tyan? I want to see the look on his face when he realises-"

Gale placed a hand on Gracen's shoulder, and her face already spoke the words her mouth was about to utter.

"Your brother died liberating the people of Ehronia from Vinadan's forces. He was a hero; we cast his body to the western sea upon wind and flame."

She walked away without another word, leaving Gracen alone with only his ghosts for company.

*

Xeb stood stoically, one hand curled reassuringly around Enarhaedon's hilt as he looked up at the hole in the side on the mountain. He shook his head slowly, taking in the smoke and the ruin all around him. Although he drew his power, like the rest of the Asarlai, from the manipulation of the runes, he could almost feel the absence of the Soul of Hemera which had resided in the Asarlai monastery for centuries. Gael walked silently up beside him, and touched his arm. He turned to face her, wearing a smile he did not quite feel. Gael, too, looked up at the mountain, rising high above the citadel.

"What will you do now?" she asked. Xeb shook his head and allowed his chin to drop.

"I don't know, my lady. Vinadan may be dead, but I highly doubt his advisors and the ruling council will welcome me back with open arms; many were loyal to him." He ran a hand through his greying hair.

"There will be much debate and politics to come, here in the capital. Vinadan has no heirs; the Daelectus line is broken. The Asarlai have no wish to govern, so I would imagine the council will take charge for now and will look to elect a new leader in time. Though who, and how, I have no idea."

"But what about you, Xebus?" Gael asked again.

"In truth?" He looked Gael straight in the eyes, and the elf saw conflict and regret as plain as day in his countenance, "I have served the Asarlai since I was a boy. I have studied the lore, learned the runes; I have travelled across all of Gibrion in service of the crown for decades. Now, I simply wish to rest."

"You mean to accompany the hoblins," Gael said; it was not a question.

"I do, my lady," said Xeb, nodding, "the Asarlai will lick their wounds, but they will rebuild and endure. I will honour my promise and lead the hoblins to a new life on the western isles, and there I, too, will see out my days. What about you?"

Gael let out a small, involuntary laugh at Xeb's question.

"Well," she said, "if your friends the crones are to be believed, some great destiny awaits me in Eonis, so I believe I will go home." She pulled Xeb toward her and embraced him tightly. "Thank you, Xebus. You risked everything to help people you did not know. We will never forget that; you will always be welcome in Eonis."

"Thank *you*, my lady, for everything," Xeb replied, bowing in deference. He gestured over his shoulder to Vinadan's body. "What about him?" he asked.

"Him?" replied Gael. She winked at Xeb, and a mischievous grin tugged at her mouth, "burn him," she said.

Xeb's skin blazed to life with the runes of his order, and Vinadan's body was reduced to ashes.

*

Gael left Xeb and moved among the crowd, seeking Ruli, and finding the young barren in the company of Miseldi, Thalnon Meldreth, Cade, and Pilmer.

"My lady," the quartet said as one, lowering their heads at Gael's approach.

"It fills my heart with joy to see you, all of you," she spread her arms wide to encompass the group. "Though I must ask you, master Thalnon; mistress Pilmer, how did you come to be here in Aclevion?"

"The gulls," said Thalnon, simply, "the black gulls carried a call for aid, bidding all to come at once to Ehronia. Trissan and I were in Earon at the time, with Lord Driador's leave. When we arrived in the barren lands, Pilmer and Gracen's company were already there. We were informed that your own forces had already made for the north, so we followed with all haste."

"Well, it is a wonder that you did so, my friends; I do not think we would have survived if not for your arrival. Ruli," Gael continued, turning to the young barren, "I must know; what happened in there?" she gestured up to the mountains, where smoke still billowed lazily from the hole in the rock.

"In truth, I am not sure," Ruli began, "there is a power inside me, lady Gael, of that much you were correct. I think..." he paused, seeking the right words, "I think I finally accepted it."

Gael nodded along, but did not interrupt.

"No sword nor arrow was going to make a dent in the pillars, and I knew - somehow I *knew* - that it had to be me. I think perhaps Xebus knew it, too. I faced the pillars; I thought about my home, my friends, my companions; I thought about everything which would be lost if Vinadan won, and then I just.... let go."

"Well," said Gael, "this is no small thing, Ruli. Magic has awakened in the barrens for the first time in cycles. Will you accompany me to Eonis?"

Ruli's face betrayed his confusion and surprise. "My lady?" he asked.

"To Eonis, Ruli - you too, Miseldi, of course - will you accompany me to the great forests?"

"But, Lady Gael, barrens have not-"

"Do not worry about that," Gael interrupted, "you will be welcomed, and there we can untap your magic, we can learn exactly what you can do, and what this means for your kind. We can solve this mystery together."

"I... I would be honoured, my lady, Ruli replied with tears beginning to announce themselves in his eyes.

"As would I," added Miseldi, "if you would have me."

"Of course," replied Gael with a warm smile, "and you, lord Meldreth; you must make ready your men and journey with us back home."

"No," said Thalnon, quietly.

"Thalnon?" said Gael.

"My lady, I have seen enough of war for a lifetime. I have suffered injuries not just physical. If they will have me, I mean to return with the barrens to Ehronia and live out my days in peace. I will tend the land; I will raise crops. Maybe one day I might even have a family. I thank you, my lady, but no: I will not be returning to Eonis."

"If that is truly your wish, old friend," said Gael. Thalnon nodded.

Miseldi looked from Ruli, to Gael, to Thalnon, and back to Ruli. Spots of redness began to blossom upon her cheeks and her bottom lip quivered.

"Miseldi," said Ruli, "what is it?"

"Go with lady Gael," replied Miseldi, meekly, "I will accompany Thalnon and the others back home to Ehronia."

"But I need you by my side," Ruli protested, taking his friend by the hands.

"No, Ruli, you do not," Miseldi said through her tears, "you have a gift from the goddesses, and I would only slow you down; distract you."

"Miseldi I-"

"Go with lady Gael, Ruli, accomplish wonders, be who you were always meant to be. You can always visit," she added with a sniffle and a smile. Ruli nodded, shaking loose tears of his own, and he took Miseldi his arms and squeezed her tight in a long, loving embrace.

"For Horith and Gerdan," said Miseldi.

"For Ehronia," said Ruli.

Chapter Thirty-Seven

The runes upon the pillars had dulled to a muted grey in the year since Vinadan had so brazenly stolen the Soul of Hemera, spilling the blood of Horith and Keya in the act. Now, though the Soul Chamber was guarded day and night by a retinue of armed and armoured Eonisian elves, the chamber itself was dull, dusty, and cold. Elves avoided it, skirting the location entirely, or averting their eyes if forced to pass that way. There was a sombreness to the room, a disquiet, as if Hemera herself mourned within the high walls, and every elf in Eonis could feel it.

The throne still stood tall in the adjoining room, though this, not unlike the pillars, had remained empty these long months. The former queen's council of advisors had not yet selected a new monarch, and one or two within the cadre had suggested the dissolution of the system altogether, lobbying for the declaration of a republic to supersede centuries of monarchical rule. Elves were a long-lived race, so a single year or so without an elected leader was not a cause for concern among the council, though they were eager to resolve the matter of succession sooner rather than later.

A sudden, deep *boom*, and a colossal rumble in the ground heralded the arrival of something monumental in Eonis.

The two duty guards regained their feet and shook surprise out of their heads, recovering their poise immediately. They rushed into the Soul Chamber which had stood in a mournful darkness for months, and found themselves basking in a prodigious blue light. Six members of the ruling council followed on their heels and, in something of a first for a cabal of advisors, found themselves utterly speechless.

The Soul of Hemera had returned, and her pillars once again blazed brightly with runes of crimson fire. So awestruck and disbelieving were the elves by the sudden re-emergence of the Soul, that they did not hear the footsteps behind them.

"It's okay," said Gael, startling the council members out of their skins, "we can explain."

*

Lord Firvolg liked to wander the paths of Torimar just as the sun was rising. Here, far below ground level, the sky seemed impossibly far out of reach, and he had always marvelled at the colours it displayed at this time of the day. He had walked this route a thousand times as a child, trying to keep up with King Thyrus, his father, and he knew each step so well he could navigate his way around the kingdom and back inside to his throne room with his eyes closed. He was still young for a lord at only one-hundred and twenty, and was still finding his feet since inheriting the position upon his father's death. Round a corner he went; thirteen steps forward, ten to the right, then around another corner.

I could definitely do this with my eyes closed, he thought. He chuckled to himself, and shut his eyes. *Ten more steps forward, a slight incline, then turn left in three, two one, now. Fifteen steps forward, duck to avoid the outcropping. Slight turn to the right, and now it's straight ahead for another fifty steps.*

THUMP.

"Aether-spit!" shouted Firvolg, raising a hand to his forehead which sang with pain. He opened his eyes, and his jaw fell. Towering high above him were two almighty pillars of rock which, judging by the rubble at their bases, had recently sprung up out of the very rock of Torimar. Upon their surfaces were ruby red runes of an ancient kind; runes of a thousand denominations which Firvolg could not read.

Suspended between the mighty pillars was a huge, pulsating orb of pure red energy: the Soul of Aether. The dwarf lord placed his leather-gloved hand against the pillar tentatively, lest it injure him somehow. Satisfied that it was in fact real, he walked around the impressive structure - a structure which most assuredly had *not* been there yesterday.

Only now becoming aware how low his jaw was hanging, Firvolg closed his mouth and shook his head to bring his mind back into focus. He took two steps backwards, still staring at the Soul, basking in its crimson radiance, and he took a deep breath.

"Guaaaards!" he called at the top of his lungs.

*

The sun was high in the sky, and Xeb revelled in the feel of it upon his face. He walked a familiar path, and soon found himself staring at a dishevelled old boat. On the jetty alongside the vessel, a man slept with his hat over his face, blocking out the sunlight. As before - what now seemed to Xeb like a lifetime ago - the man could well have been mistaken for a corpse, but for the shallow rise and fall of his chest and gut.

"Imelda," said Xeb, and the man almost left the ground as he jumped out of his skin with fright at the unexpected voice. Xeb stifled a smile.

"What in the name of-" Imelda began, stopping as he recognised Xeb, "oh! My friend! You have returned from Vitrius safe and sound, I see." His eyes flicked left and right, and he tried his best to conceal his alarm at the sight of Xeb's companions.

"Indeed I have, good boatmaster," said Xeb. He gestured over his shoulder to the mass of hoblins at his heel. "My friends and I require safe passage west, to the shorelands, and I told them there is only one man for the job."

Imelda looked horrified for the briefest of moments, but forced a huge smile onto his face.

"Of course, m'lord, of course. To the shorelands, you say? Okay. One, two, three, four, five, six, seven…" he pointed behind Xeb, counting the individual hoblins.

"There are some three thousand of us, good boatmaster. But we will of course pay you handsomely." He waved Ugnor forward, and the war chief dropped a sack onto the ground at Imelda's feet, whilst two hoblins rolled a barrel toward him. Imelda's eyes lit up as he read the inscription upon the side of the barrel.

"Is this real?" he asked.

"I can assure you it is very real," said Xeb. "In fact, I still have the hangover to prove it."

Imelda knelt down and untied the sack. His eyes went wide as he beheld the gold within - more gold than he would make in ten years' ferrying strangers to lands far or near.

"I believe this will be sufficient, my friends," said Imelda, trying unsuccessfully to appear nonchalant. He looked at his boat, then at the hoblins. His mouth moved wordlessly as he weighed up how many of them he could ferry at a time. He looked back at the boat, then to the hoblins; then to the gold, the wine, then back at the hoblins, then back to the boat.

"Right lads," he said, clapping his hands together, "this is gonna take a few trips."

*

Xeb could taste the salt in the air, and took great pleasure in the feel of the water as it sprayed his face, cooling his skin and soothing his heart. He held a goblet of hoblin wine in hand, and he squinted as the sun's rays glinted off the waves. He had seen the sea before, of course, but now he felt that he was seeing it with fresh eyes, and it warmed him to behold the clear blue waters, tinted here and there with golden midday sunlight.

He raised his goblet and took a drink, spilling a little as the boat rose sharply upon a small wave. He wiped his mouth with this sleeve of his red robe. He paused, staring at the robe, then he placed his goblet gently upon the deck. He stood and took off the robe; a trapping of the Asarlai and an outward symbol of his work and service. He held it out in front of him, taking one last look at the robe itself and the memories held within the very fabric, then he cast it overboard.

He took Enarhaedon from its sheath and held it aloft, glittering in the sunlight. *Traitor's Blade no more, my friend*, he thought, recalling Fennet.

Enarhaedon no more. This sword I name Tir-Malahan; The Liberator. He sheathed the elvish weapon and said one final, silent goodbye to his friend.

The Imelda sailed on, heading due-west toward the shorelands, seeking a new home for the hoblins and a new start for Xebus.

The bright red cloak sat upon the surface of the sea, darkening as it took on water, and then it sank out of sight as the boat disappeared into the golden horizon.

PART III:
OF VINADAN AND VALAHIR

Chapter Thirty-Eight

Thirty-seven years earlier...

"Come on, Vindi; try to keep up!" said Prince Valahir of the King's Guard as he ran through the woods, dodging errant branches and hurdling logs and tree stumps with little difficulty. At twenty-three, Prince Valahir, son of King Entallion, was tall and lean, though his ungainly frame carried its share of muscle. He was strong, fast, and agile; a rising star among the King's Guard, he had already been given command of the king's most loyal and elite soldiers. He had seen battle on numerous occasions, and his left cheek carried a scar earned at the tip of an orrecish blade. Far from trying to hide the scar with makeup or growing his hair long to cover it with his raven black locks, however, Valahir wore it as a badge of honour; he felt it added some degree of 'roguish charm' to his fair countenance, and he harboured a suspicion that some of the ladies of the royal court agreed with his assessment.

The king had organised the hunting trip in celebration of another hard-won victory for his guard and the northern armies against an orrec incursion from Elgiroth. Though the battle was won, many of the king's men did not make it home alive, and Entallion felt a distraction would be good for morale. He also harboured some small hope that his younger son, Vinadan - a studious and shy thirteen-year-old - would perhaps learn a thing or two from his older brother.

Vinadan lagged behind and dragged his feet as his brother raced ahead; he picked his way through the trees with little enthusiasm, and the rhythmic knocking of his sheathed sword against his right calf punctuated his misery with each laboured step. His own black hair was plastered to his forehead with sweat, and his breathing was heavy as he forged his way through the woods at his brother's heels.

"I'm coming," he shouted in reply, "give me half a chance." Vinadan vaulted a fallen log, and came down awkwardly as his ankle overturned on a thick tangle of roots.

"Aether-spit!" he cursed under his breath. He tested the ankle and breathed a sigh of relief at this discovery that it was neither broken nor sprained.

"Come *on*, Vindi," came Valahir's shout; more insistent this time. Vinadan bent at the waist and placed his palms on his thighs. He closed his eyes and took a deep breath, adding a calming warmth to the cold edge of frustration which was beginning to creep over him. He opened his eyes and stood to his full height. He checked to make sure his sword was secure about his waist, and he ran, ignoring the lingering pain in his ankle. Before too long he caught up with his brother and, at his appearance, Valahir placed a finger over his own lips, gesturing for Vinadan to be silent. Valahir was crouched low behind a tree stump, and he waved Vinadan into a similar position. He directed his brother's eyes beyond their vantage point, indicating a small clearing between two trees, so small it would have been easy to overlook. Between the trees and idling, blissfully unaware of the presence of the Daelectus brothers, not to mention the thirty-or-so King's Guard similarly arrayed around them in various hidden vantage points, stood a wolf.

At least I think it's a wolf, thought Vinadan, as he narrowed his eyes for a better look. One thing he did know for certain was that the creature was huge, certainly bigger than any wolf he had ever seen. Its eyes were wild and unfocused, and saliva fell from its mouth in a constant flow. Its breathing could be heard from this distance without issue; as its ribs rose and fell, it huffed deep, loud breaths, and Vinadan realised with some amusement that his own breathing had fallen into sync with that of the beast he observed from cover.

"It's from Elgiroth," said Valahir, leaning close to Vinadan, "we captured it during Midhir's last incursion," he spat on the ground at the mention of the enemy.

"What is it?" asked Vinadan.

"I suppose you could call it a wolf," replied Valahir, "but different... *changed*. When Elgiroth spoiled, everything in that land became corrupted."

"I know the histories, Valahir," replied Vinadan, a little more sharply than he had perhaps intended. Valahir grinned and tousled his little brother's hair playfully.

"Alright, don't lose your britches," he said. "We captured it, and father thought it would make good sport. Now watch."

Valahir raised his head out of cover momentarily, and offered a series of hand signals to his men, still out of sight amidst the trees. Orders given, he took a few tentative steps out of cover, never once taking his eyes off the wolf; barely blinking in absolute focus. He slowly and silently unsheathed a dagger, and continued to pick his way toward the creature, crouching low as he made his approach. He was within twenty feet of the wolf now, and at a twitch of the beast's nostrils as it picked up his scent, Valahir went prone amongst the grasses, pressing his stomach to the wet soil.

  The wolf turned its head here and there, sniffing, trying to identify the source of the scent. Through gaps in the foliage, Valahir could still see the wolf from his position, and his dagger was still in hand. He waited, biding his time, hoping for an opportunity which was not long in coming. The wolf must have sensed that the scent it had identified was the herald of danger, and it turned its back on Valahir and company as it made to leave the clearing and head deeper into the woods. Valahir pushed up from the ground and sprang to his feet. In one fluid motion he broke cover and hurled his dagger at the wolf. The accompanying howl told him that his blade had found its mark, and he called for the men to advance on the wounded creature. Within seconds, the wolf was encircled on all sides by the King's Guard, and as its life ebbed away by virtue of the dagger which protruded from its thick neck, the men cheered.

  "Great shot, Commander!"

  "You got him, my Prince!"

"Take that, Elgirothan filth!"

"Crawl back to Midhir and tell that crazy bastard he's next!"

"Okay lads, okay, that's enough," said Valahir, though he secretly revelled in the adulation. "Vindi," he said, waving his brother forward, "come here."

Vinadan did as instructed and made his way slowly toward Valahir and the downed wolf. Rather than revel in the glory of the kill, however, Vinadan felt only revulsion and pity. He could see the fear in the dying creature's eyes as it beheld the crowd of cheering men surrounding it.

It cannot help what it is, he thought.

"Take out your sword, brother," said Valahir, calmly. Vinadan looked up at his brother with large, pleading eyes, and Valahir nodded his encouragement. Vinadan took out his sword - its blade immaculately clean - and held it tight in two shaking hands.

"Go on, little brother," said Valahir, at once encouraging and commanding his sibling.

Vinadan nodded his head repeatedly, more to assure himself than Valahir, and raised his sword high above his head. He looked the wolf in the eye and no longer saw fear; instead he read only resignation; acceptance.

"I…" he started.

"Vindi, it's fine. Do it," urged Valahir.

"I… I can't" said Vinadan, dropping his sword and looking upon the wolf through tear-blurred eyes. The men laughed, and nudged each other, whispering as they shook their heads.

"Enough," commanded Valahir, "do not forget that this is also the son of your king," he said, indicating his brother. The men ceased their laughter with mumbled apologies. Valahir placed his hands on his hips and turned to face Vinadan. The younger prince was pleased to see a certain warmth in Valahir's face, but it was underlined with something else… not anger, nor necessarily disappointment…

Embarrassment, Vinadan realised. Valahir turned away from his brother and, in one motion, drew his own sword and brought it down hard upon the wolf's neck, severing the head. He leaned down and retrieved his dagger whilst a chorus of cheers erupted from the King's Guard. Valahir stowed his weapons and held out a hand to Vinadan. The young prince was not even aware he had fallen to the ground, and as his brother pulled him back to his feet he felt his cheeks flush and his face grew warm.

"Come on," said Valahir, "let's get you home; I'm sure loremaster Tennatir has need of you in the library."

Chapter Thirty-Nine

The king's private study was dark, with only the light cast by a handful of candles and a roaring open fireplace to illuminate the large room. King Entallion preferred it this way once the sun had set, so the sconces along the walls remained devoid of torches. The king sat in his high-backed chair, and the fireplace was mere feet to his left. A long table ran the length of the study; it was currently laden with books, scrolls, maps, fresh parchment, and any number of other miscellaneous documents. Before the king sat a small table, upon which stood a bottle of a deep red wine and two goblets. The open fire cast the bottle's flickering shadow upon the surrounding walls.

"I thought you were saving this for the ceremony," said Valahir, sitting across from his father.

"Don't worry, Son; I've instructed them to make plenty," replied the king with a grin, as he filled the goblets. He took the first and handed the other to Valahir.

"Besides," the king continued, "though the dwarves are working hard and their foreman assures me they are on schedule, we do not anticipate that the work will be finished for the best part of a year."

Valahir whistled and raised his eyebrows. "That long?" he asked, rhetorically, "although, to be fair to the dwarves, it is no small task to rebuild half a citadel."

"Don't forget the new courtyard, Val," said the king, smiling.

"Ah, yes," said Valahir, raising a hand to his forehead, "how could I forget *that* particular extravagance? Are you certain you don't want the fountain to be any bigger?"

Father and son laughed heartily and raised their goblets.

"For the glory of the kingdom," said Entallion.

"For the glory of the kingdom," repeated Valahir. They each took a gulp of the wine, and smacked their respective lips in satisfaction.

"Aaah; that *really* hits the spot," said the king.

"It is a triumph, Father; you are to be commended."

Both men placed their goblets on the table, and Valahir leaned back in his chair, interlocking his fingers across his stomach.

"Turning back to our more immediate concerns," said Valahir, growing serious once more, "please do not be too hard on him, Father. He is young. He will learn soon enough."

The king let out a long sigh, and rubbed his temples. "How soon is soon enough, Valahir? Hmm? The boy needs to toughen up, and quickly, if he is to rule one day." Valahir nodded but did not interrupt, as he sensed his father was not yet finished.

"He is an intelligent boy, your brother - too intelligent for his own good, perhaps. But I fear his hands were made for the quill rather than the sword."

"Is that really so bad?" asked Valahir.

"In times of peace, no, of course not. But those times are not upon us," replied the king, "Take Midhir, for example-"

"Oh please, Father; Midhir has lost his mind - he is a mild annoyance at best."

King Entallion shook his head and waved an admonishing finger at Valahir.

"Do not be so quick to dismiss him, Son. As an individual, Midhir is quite insane - in that much you are correct - but a madman is one thing; a madman who commands legions is quite another."

"Forgive me, Father," said Valahir, reaching for his goblet and taking another drink.

"Elgiroth is loyal to him," the king continued, "he has shown the orrecs his power - power they cannot wield - and it has captivated them; perhaps it calls back to some primal instinct from before The Spoiling." The king took a moment, lost in his thoughts, before continuing.

"He commands their hearts and minds, while his own are fixated on me and my kingdom." Entallion shook his head and cursed under his breath. "And it is for that precise reason," the king continued, "that Vinadan must be pushed, no matter how harsh it may appear on the surface. His mind alone is nothing without strength to augment his wits, and all the books in the kingdom will do little to turn aside an orrecish blade."

Valahir continued to drink his wine; shadows danced across his face as the fire in the king's hearth was reflected in the young man's eyes.

"He is a good lad," he said at last, "and I have no doubt he will make a great leader one day."

"But…?" said the king, sensing some conflict in his eldest heir.

"*But*," Valahir continued, "I fear you are correct about his fortitude. We may have to push him harder, as you say." Both father and son sat in silence as the fire crackled beside them.

"Tomorrow," said the king, picking up his goblet, "he will go with you."

"On patrol?" said Valahir, raising his eyebrows and sitting forward slightly in his chair.

"Yes. He will shadow you; you will protect and instruct your brother."

Valahir opened his mouth to respond, but thought better of it and closed it again. He took an extra two or three heartbeats to process his father's words - his king's command.

"As you wish, Your Grace."

"Good lad," replied the king with a nod. He took a long gulp of his wine and placed his goblet back on the small table.

"Where is he, anyway?" Entallion asked. Valahir grinned and couldn't help but chuckle.

"Where do you *think* he is?"

*

"The scrolls you requested, my prince," said loremaster Tennatir.

"Thank you," Vinadan replied, taking the scrolls from the old man and spreading them out on the desk in front of himself as best he could given the number of books and documents already arrayed there. He had been in the library since he and Valahir returned from the hunting trip, and his fingers were stained black with ink as he made notes on parchment. The desk at which he sat was surrounded by candles and torches, and the old loremaster winced a little as the young prince opened out one of the ancient scrolls perilously close to a naked flame.

"Please, my prince," he said softly, "do be careful; this one is more than two thousand years old."

Vinadan could not keep the smile from his face as he looked upon the ancient scroll, written in the hand of Daedan Asarlai himself. He leaned close and sniffed the parchment, trying to imagine himself in Asarlai's position as he deciphered the very first rune, then another, then another…

"If I may, my prince?" said Tennatir.

"Go ahead, Loremaster."

"Why do they fascinate you so? The Asarlai, I mean."

Vinadan shook his head slowly, never taking his eyes off the scroll.

"I don't quite know," he admitted, "I have always found strange wonder in their order, and in their abilities."

"Do not be so quick to covet magical powers and shows of strength and pageantry," said the old librarian, unable to keep the scorn out of his tone.

"You do not approve of them?" asked Vinadan. The old man sighed, and took a seat next to the young prince. "Among their order," he began, "there are undoubtedly some good men and women; loyal to the crown, and devoted to the goddesses."

"Go on," said Vinadan, "you may speak plainly here, Loremaster."

"With your leave, my prince. It is perhaps just the cynicism of old age, but in my experience, the order has become bloated and self-important. Long have they advised kings and queens of our good land, but where the histories show us that this was often a matter of necessity, more and more I get the impression that the Asarlai have come to enjoy their position; behind the throne, in the shadows, whispering to the king from the heights of their monastery."

Vinadan looked the old man in the eye for a long moment, pondering his words, and feeling the other's experience of the Asarlai grating and scraping against his own image of the ancient order.

"I will be careful," he said at length. The old librarian nodded, satisfied at the young prince's response. He stood with a groan and bowed to Vinadan. "Now if you will excuse me, my prince, I must retire for the night."

"Of course," said Vinadan, "sleep well, librarian." He turned his attention once more to the books and scrolls on the candlelit desk before him. He picked up his quill and dipped it in his inkwell. His left index finger hovered over the ancient texts, while his right hand scribbled and scratched onto the parchment.

So enraptured was the young prince by his research that time all but got away from him entirely, and it was not until the first light of the early spring morning began to creep unannounced through the high windows that Vinadan realised that he had worked all through the night.

"Aether be damned!" he cursed, and quickly tidied away what books and papers he could, leaving his own notes on the desk. He pushed his chair back quickly and made to stand, only now realising that his left leg had gone quite numb as he had sat and worked. He winced at the discomfort as he made his way quickly toward the door, meaning to rush straight to his quarters to try to catch at least a few hours' sleep.

As he slammed the door behind him, the resulting draft blew the top few sheets of parchment from the desk and onto the floor. The pages were full from top to bottom, left to right, with notes, annotations, strange symbols, and meticulously recreated runes copied from Daedan Asarlai's own illustrations.

Under the runes, in Vinadan's own neat and ordered hand, were the translations: *Anger, Domination, Control, Fear…*

Chapter Forty

"You look tired," said Valahir as they walked in formation across the open lands. Behind them, the gates and walls of the capital were still visible. Above and around Acelvion, the mountains rose, tall and majestic, making the capital appear small as it nestled snugly, closed in on three sides. Secure. Defensible.

"I'm fine," replied Vinadan without meeting his brother's eyes.

"Did you get enough-"

"I said I'm fine, Valahir," Vinadan snapped. He quickened his pace and strode away from his older sibling.

"Hey," said Valahir, catching him by the shoulder, "slow down; don't get too far ahead."

"Oh please, Valahir, it's hardly as if there is any danger here. We've barely gone two miles - I can still see the city gates behind us."

"Do not be so quick to dismiss the threat, Vindi. Good and brave men have died much closer to the city than two miles. Besides, father said you had to stick by my side today. Your job is to watch and learn, brother. Now, back in formation."

The brothers were around twenty yards from the head of the column; there were thirty soldiers at their backs, and four scouts ahead of them. The king had requested that Valahir stay at the back of the group, just for today, while his brother was with him. Valahir would not entertain the idea, and after much debate the king had agreed to let his oldest son utilise his own judgement as to their position amongst the patrol. While Valahir was indeed his child, the king sometimes forgot that he was also a commander of the royal guard, and had seen his fair share of battles for a man of only twenty-three.

  Vinadan fell into step beside his brother, and the patrol resumed. It was a crisp morning and the grass crunched under their armoured feet as they marched. The heads and eyes of the men were constantly moving, alert for any sign of movement or of anything remotely out of the ordinary. Though the men did exchange occasional quiet words as they marched, the patrol was carried out in near silence, and the skill and discipline of the King's Guard was evident in their every movement. They pressed on further, putting another two miles between themselves and the capital. The cold morning had warmed up a little with every step taken by the King's Guard, but there was also moisture in the air. After another fifteen or so minutes of silent marching, the rain began to fall, and it fell heavily. The patrol had reached an area of woodland, and the formerly open grasslands were now littered with natural rock formations, trees, tall grasses, and an abundance of overgrown vegetation. The warmth in the air and the rain which beat down upon the scene mingled, drawing forth an array of sweet scents from the surrounding foliage.

The King's Guard did not complain nor curse the goddesses for their misfortune as the rain fell, but carried on with their patrol the same as they always had. Vinadan was not so accepting of his plight, however, and cursed under his breath and wiped his sodden black hair from his face. Valahir could not resist a smile as he spared his brother a glance.

He'd better get used to it.

Without warning, one of the scouts at the head of the patrol held up a fist to stall the company, and went immediately to one knee. He rubbed and poked at the ground, before bringing his hand up to his face to more closely study the grass and mud he had collected.

"Creze?" shouted Valahir, cupping his left hand beside his mouth, "What is it?" Little brother along for the ride or not, Valahir made no attempt to keep the concern out of his voice. The scout regained his feet and whispered something to one of his companions, before jogging back to join Valahir and Vinadan.

"I'm not sure, Commander. There are tracks, but given the rainfall I cannot be certain of their origin."

Valahir nodded his understanding. "Okay, Creze; bring your men back into formation. We proceed with swords drawn, and with caution."

"Very good my lord; I will tell-"

Vinadan squeezed his eyes shut involuntarily as his face was suddenly spattered with the scout's blood. He heard his brother barking commands to his men and the sound of blades being drawn as he wiped the blood from his eyes. As he opened them, he could not quite reconcile the man who had been speaking to them mere moments ago with the body at his feet. The blood-soaked arrowhead which now protruded at a grotesque angle from the man's obliterated face was obvious in origin, even to Vinadan.

"Orrecs," he said quietly, before he was pulled hard by the shoulder.

"Vindi, draw your weapon!" Valahir commanded, and it was then that the world came back into focus for Vinadan. Orrecs, around two hundred in number, were advancing toward the patrol from all sides.

It's an ambush, Vinadan realised with dawning horror.

"Vindi, behind me," shouted Valahir, and Vinadan fell in line. The orrecs were now upon them, and the clashing of steel mingled with the battle cries of orrecs and men alike was deafening. Vinadan had regained his wits, and with his sword clutched firmly in two hands, he set his feet as his brother had taught him, and steadied himself as the orrecs charged their position.

Vinadan did not see the blunt club, nor the orrec who swung it, before his world turned to black.

*

"They're retreating!" called one of the King's Guard, "They're turning back!"

Dozens of dead orrecs littered the ground, their blood virtually indistinguishable from the mud as the rain continued to beat down upon the grasslands. Seven of the King's Guard had been killed, and another ten had been wounded in the orrec ambush. Valahir clutched his left arm with his right hand, stemming the flow of blood from a flesh wound to his bicep. His eyes were wide and his face a mask of panic as he went up and down the line.

When his own search yielded no results, he grabbed one of his men by the shoulders and shouted in his face.

"Where is my brother?" he demanded, "Where is Vinadan?"

The soldier did not know; none of them did.

Vinadan was missing.

*

Vinadan felt as if his head had been cleaved in two. His left temple throbbed with a blinding pain, and he felt sick to the stomach with nausea. His mind rolled and twisted on waves and currents, as if it were swimming in the deep waters which lie somewhere between dreams and the waking world. He moved his arm, meaning to touch the side of his head and face to check for injuries, but found that he could not. The realisation jolted him fully awake, and the reality of his situation came crashing down upon him like a tidal wave.

Though he had opened his eyes, he could barely make out his surroundings. Torches hung sparingly upon the walls, casting a dim light upon this dark place. Vinadan realised that he was sitting with his back against a cold, rough wall. His hands were shackled above his head, held securely in place against the wall, but his feet were not bound.

I'm dry, he thought, *and warm, so I must have been here a while.*

He looked around the room - if it was a room - that held him, and tried to identify his location. The walls were a rough, natural stone, and the irregular ceiling was low. He could hear a faint trickling sound from somewhere off in the distance, and he could not help but register the mouldy dampness in the air.

A cave, he realised; *I'm in some sort of cave.*

He tested his restraints, pulling hard against the shackles at his wrists. It was no use, he was effectively bolted to the rock wall at his back; he was going nowhere. A shuffling, scratching sound caught his attention, and he opened his eyes wider in a bid to discern the source of the noise, only to close them tightly as a wedge of light burst into the room at the opening of a door which Vinadan had not even registered in the gloomy darkness.

Two orrecs entered the room with teeth bared and swords in hand. They stopped a few feet short of the sitting and shackled Vinadan, but kept the tips of their blades angled squarely in his direction. Vinadan did not speak, but fixed the orrecs - first one, then the other - with a pointed and defiant stare. Behind them, silhouetted by the light from outside the room, a third figure entered. Vinadan could not make out the being as it made its way toward him, but could tell it was no orrec. As the newcomer came within sight of Vinadan, he bowed, and the young prince did not discern a modicum of mockery or irony in the gesture.

As the man completed his bow and straightened his back, Vinadan could see him more clearly by the light of the torches. He was human, and old. That he had once been tall and strong, Vinadan could tell, but the man was now frail and small, though not without power, perhaps. His hair and beard were long and unkempt, and the young prince fancied that they had once been red. The man's face was grimy and his clothes dirty; he leaned heavily on an obsidian staff which was topped with three gleaming gemstones in the likeness of the Souls, set into a disc of copper. Though the man appeared old, frail, dishevelled, and entirely non-threatening, Vinadan knew better. The man's eyes were wild, and his smile held only the bitter sting of ice.

"My Prince," he said.

"Midhir," replied Vinadan.

Chapter Forty-one

"You were supposed to be watching him," said Queen Arianrhod. Though there was reproach and sorrow in her voice, the poise and stoicism with which she held herself stood in stark contrast to that of her eldest son. She stood by the window, looking out and down upon the capital. She could see all of Aclevion from here in the east tower; all of Gibrion, maybe.

"I know, mother," said a tearful Valahir, "and I was, but…" he turned his bloodshot eyes to his father, "but their numbers…"

"It's okay, Son," said the king, "from what you tell us of their assault, they must have been planning this for a while."

"Yes," said the queen, turning away from the window and facing her husband and her son, "it seems they knew exactly when to strike."

"But how did they know Vindi was going to be there?" asked Valahir.

"It is likely they didn't," replied the queen, "but they seized an opportunity which presented itself, unlooked for."

Valahir looked at his mother, then his father, and threw his hands into the air in exasperation.

"Well, all of that is great," he said, "but what about Vindi?"

"Had they wished him harm, they would not have taken him," said Arianrhod.

"Your mother is right," said the king, rising from his seat. He walked over to Valahir and placed a hand on the young prince's shoulder. "Look," he said, pointing to Valahir's injured arm, "they meant to kill; what does that tell you?"

Valahir looked from his father to his mother, and shook his head. "I don't know, father; what's your point?" he said.

"My point? Creze, Belfort, Lerond, Gannatine, Tyrolt, Profind, Altony: all dead; you and a dozen more are injured. What does this tell you, Valahir?"

The young commander took a deep breath and focused. "That if they wanted to kill Vinadan, they would have just done it," he said at last.

"Exactly," said the king.

"So he is alive," said Valahir, with the fire of hope beginning to kindle in his heart.

"This is my belief," confirmed the king. "Now," he added, moving toward the door, "alert the men, and ready Thunderfall."

"Thunderfall?"

"Yes, Valahir; ready my horse. Surely you do not think I intend to sit around idly whilst my son is missing?"

"You are coming with us?"

"No, Valahir," said the king, "*you* are coming with *me*."

"Find him. Bring him home," said Queen Arianrhod, looking between her husband and her son. The men nodded but did not speak in reply as they left her in her chambers. Only after the door closed behind them and the sound of their footsteps had receded did the queen allow herself to weep.

*

"Do you intend to ransom me?" asked Vinadan, as he looked up at the scruffy old mage.

"You?" replied the old man, still leaning on his staff, "I had not intended to do *anything* with you, my boy."

Vinadan's brows furrowed, but he did not speak.

"You see," Midhir continued, "when I commanded my orrecs to bring me the prince of Aclevion, I actually meant your insolent, narcissist brother. Imagine my surprise, then, to find *you* here upon my arrival."

"And where is 'here', exactly?" asked Vinadan. The old mage laughed, and the young prince inferred from the rattle in the man's lungs that this was the first time in many a year that he had done so.

"Nice try, my prince. But no, I shall not divulge our location so readily. At least, not yet."

"So what now? If you were expecting my brother, what happens next?"

"Well," the old man said, with a scratch of his beard and a tilt of his head, "I had quite intended to take his head, and send it back to the citadel in a box." Vinadan met the old man's eyes, but did not reply.

"But you…" Midhir continued, kneeling to look Vinadan in the eye, "I think not. It is no mere accident which brought us together, Vinadan; I sense something larger at work here." Midhir regained his full height with an audible click from his knees, and looked around the small cave; high and low, left and right.

"The goddesses work in ways that mortal men do not yet comprehend," Midhir continued, pacing around the chamber, "whilst some small proportion of their divine designs may indeed be discerned by the elves, they are far too pompous and arrogant a race to share their knowledge. As for dwarves, they are not so different from orrecs and hoblins, in my experience; quicker to the use of their hands than their wits." He turned, and fixed Vinadan with a stare which sent a shudder down the young prince's spine.

"But you, Vinadan… You are different. I have always known it."

"Always?" replied the prince, "what do you mean, always?"

"My boy," said Midhir, flamboyantly feigning offence, "you do me a great disservice. "Whatever your father and your brother may say about me, please do not take me for some wandering brigand; some marauding killer or cannibal, bent on pillaging and plundering. I am so much more than that."

"Really?" said Vinadan, not impressed by Midhir's

words, "because that's exactly what it looks like from where I'm sitting."

A flash of anger came to Midhir's eyes, but it evaporated just as quickly.

"My boy, I served as one of your father's closest advisors and healers for decades." As if to demonstrate his point, Midhir reached into his robes and took out a glistening red gemstone. He brandished it in front of Vinadan, as if expecting the boy to recognise the healing stone for what it was. He replaced it inside his robes and sighed, shaking his head wearily.

"I was by your mother's bedside the day your brother was born, and I myself pulled you - kicking and screaming - into this world. I hold you in great affection, Vinadan," he leaned in close, and grabbed the prince by his hair, "but do not test me." He let go, and resumed his pacing, the stale stink of decay and whiskey breath thick in the young prince's face.

"So if you were so well thought of, how come you now live in a cave?"

"Do not feign ignorance, my prince. You know as well as I do that your father cast me out of his service. And it was your brother who quite literally threw me out of the citadel."

"Why?" asked Vinadan.

"You mean to say they never told you? I would have imagined that all knew of my plight by now."

"To tell you the truth," said Vinadan, the light of the torches flickering upon his face in the darkness, "my father has never really mentioned you." Whether or not the young prince's words were strictly true, they had the desired effect; Midhir turned his staff on Vinadan in a moment of rage, and hit him hard across the face.

"Insolent pup!" he screamed, "I told you not to test me!"

Vinadan spat a mouthful of blood upon the old man's robes, and a devilish smile spread across the young man's face.

"See?" he said, turning his defiant gaze upon his captor, "nothing more than a common brigand after all."

"Is that right?" said Midhir, straightening his back and holding his arms out by his sides. He closed his eyes, and took a deep breath. As he exhaled, his skin blazed to life with hundreds of runes of all shapes and sizes, each one an inferno within the old man's very flesh. Vinadan watched in awe as the old man's feet left the ground. As he hung in the air, suspended by some force of magic, a circle of the flaming runes burst to life in the very air before the man. A wheel of ancient, arcane symbols turned slowly between Vinadan and the mage. Vinadan watched in wonder, and as the slowly revolving symbols were reflected in his eyes, he found himself captivated.

At length, Midhir extinguished the flames and returned his boots to the rocky ground. The runes upon his skin cooled and faded away into nothingness, and Vinadan found himself staring once more at a frail, dishevelled old man.

"You… you were of the Asarlai?" he asked.

"No, my boy, no. I was a healer by trade, though I had a mind for politics which placed me in your father's sights. I was loyal to the crown for decades, and my time within the walls of the citadel brought me into quite regular contact with the Asarlai. Though I am not, nor was I ever one of them, I did learn some small measure of their arts. As have you, I think, my prince."

Vinadan looked puzzled, though Midhir also gleaned some guilt in the boy's countenance.

"You are wondering right now how I know this," said Midhir. It was not a question.

"Whilst I am no mind-reader, it is as clear to me as the winter sky that you know of the runes. I can practically smell them on you, Vinadan. Plus, quite aside from what I am able to intuit, several of my orrecs now bear burns which were not given to them by any normal soldier of the King's Guard. No, these burns are of an altogether different kind."

"And what makes you think it was me?" replied Vinadan, "perhaps Valahir-"

"Oh please," said Midhir, cutting off the young prince, "your brother barely possesses wit enough to remember which side he buckled his sword on, let alone the intelligence to master the runes of the Asarlai. No, Vinadan, this was your doing. You forget that I was there as you were growing up; I know your interests were always of a more academic nature. Whilst your brother was in the yard, swinging a wooden training sword and attempting to decapitate straw men, you were always in the library. Your father and I even took you to the Asarlai monastery once, when you were but three years old, though you will not likely remember it now." A darkness fell over Midhir's face for a moment, and the old mage grew silent. It took Vinadan a moment or two to identify the look, and he found himself shocked at the realisation.

Regret, he realised; *regret and sadness.*

"Why were you expelled, Midhir?" asked Vinadan, softly. The old man looked at the prince for a long moment, before lowering himself to the ground to sit cross-legged, barely two feet away from Vinadan.

"The long and short of it," he began, "is that your father came to consider me dangerous. He decided I - or more specifically my beliefs - posed a threat to both his family and his kingdom. He denounced and excommunicated me, and left it to your brother to forcibly remove me from the citadel, and toss me bodily down the rough front steps."

"But why? What reason did you give my father to decide such a fate?"

Midhir sighed and bowed his head, letting his chin rest upon his chest. After a moment he raised his head and looked at Vinadan.

"The three Souls," he said, "or rather, the two that still exist."

"What of them?" asked Vinadan, not understanding the mage's meaning.

"You are a studious boy, Vinadan; what do you know of them?"

"Not much, truth be told," the prince answered. "Most believe them to be the actual, physical souls of Hemera, Aether, and Gibrion, though I do not put stock in this."

"Go on."

"I know that they… sort of… *power* the runes. Fuel them, like a furnace, I suppose."

"So many believe," agreed Midhir, "though it has never been definitively proven - how could it be? Many of the very wisest believe that magic as we know it would not exist without the Souls. Though the elves may have something to say about that."

Vinadan nodded, but did not reply.

"And what of the runes? What have you learned about those, my boy?"

"I am likely among a minority here," Vinadan began, "but I believe them to be the very language of the goddesses."

Midhir clapped his hands together and jumped to his feet.

"Exactly, my boy, *exactly*! When Daedan Asarlai translated the first rune, I doubt he fully understood exactly what it was he had accomplished. He had not merely deciphered a symbol, he had all but spoken to the goddesses themselves." The man's eyes were wide and wild, and the way he looked at Vinadan set the young prince on alert.

"But you still have not told me why you were banished from my father's court," said Vinadan.

"The Souls," said Midhir, "are separated; the Asarlai house Aether in the mountains above Aclevion, and Hemera resides with the elves in the south."

"And...?" prompted Vinadan as the old man trailed off, his eyes growing hazy and distant.

"And," said Midhir, coming back to himself, "I proposed that we unite them."

Vinadan could not keep the shock from his face. "Heresy," he said in little more than a whisper.

"Is it?" said Midhir, rounding on him, "Is it truly heresy to want to unite Hemera and Aether? As the old tales tell, they are sisters after all."

"But if one were to unite them-" began Vinadan.

"He would have the power to make or unmake the world as he saw fit!" said Midhir.

"So that's it, then. Power. I must confess you disappoint me, old man," said Vinadan, shaking his head.

"What else is there?" replied Midhir in genuine confusion, "Would anyone truly turn their back on ultimate power? Uniting the Souls would be dangerous, of course - some say they would repel each other like magnets; others believe they would decay, unable to bear each other's weight - but were someone like me to do it, someone good, and honest-"

Now it was Vinadan's turn to laugh aloud. "*Good and honest?*" he repeated, "You are a madman, Midhir, an enemy of the crown. You are a villain; a story parents tell their children at night: '*Don't misbehave, or the mad wizard will come and turn you into a frog*'."

Midhir's face was impassive and unreadable in the wake of Vinadan's mockery. The torchlight cast shadows across his face, and sent monsters dancing upon the walls of the small cave.

"I don't believe you," he said at last, "To many, I am a hero. To many, I represent the choice they are too weak and afraid to make. To many, I am the physical embodiment of their deepest and most secret desire."

"Which is?" supplied Vinandan. Midhir smirked.

"To burn Aclevion to the ground, and to place the heads of King Entallion, Queen Arianrhod, and

Prince Valahir in a box at the foot of the marble steps."

Vinadan could not help but swallow hard, his Adam's apple working as he gulped with nervous tension. "And what about me?" he asked. Midhir regarded the prince for a long moment, eyeing him, sizing him up.

"We will talk more tomorrow," he said, turning to leave. He stopped at the door and looked back over his shoulder.

"I suggest you rest, my prince; tomorrow your education truly begins."

The door slammed shut behind Midhir and his orrecs, and the prince heard the clicking of a lock and the jangling of keys. The sound of footsteps and the orrecs' heavy breathing subsided moments later, and Vinadan found himself alone and in silence once more. He took a deep breath and attempted to calm his reeling mind. His arms were throbbing as they hung above his head, and he had all but lost the feeling in his legs. There would be no rest for the prince that night, and as the flames from the torches burned out, Vinadan was plunged into total darkness as the chill of night set in.

Chapter Forty-Two

6 months later...

The knocking upon the door was respectful but insistent, and it seemed that the darkness of the hour only amplified the sound.

"Your Grace," came the voice of the guard as the door to the king and queen's private chamber was opened, "Forgive the intrusion, Your Grace." Entallion and Arianrhod were awake in an instant.

"What is it, Blissett?" asked the king, placing his bare feet on the cold stone floor.

"Forgive me, Your Highnesses, but you had better follow me. And quickly." The guard turned to leave, but paused at the sound of the queen's voice.

"Speak plainly, Blissett; what is going on?"

"Forgive me, my queen. It's Prince Vinandan; he's back."

*

The night was as cold as it was dark; a heavy, relentless rain pummelled the stone walls of the citadel, battering at the windows, shaking the tall, thin scaffolding which surrounded the eastern face of the stronghold, and drenching the ground by the meagre light of the fading winter moon. King Entallion, flanked by Queen Arianrhod and Prince Valahir raced to the city gates, surrounded by guards, despite the deluge. By the faltering light of the gatekeepers' torches, a single figure could be seen approaching the entrance to the city.

As the figure drew closer, it resolved itself into the form of Prince Vinadan. He was shirtless despite the freezing rain, and it appeared to the dumbstruck crowd that his raven black hair was now streaked through, here and there, with white. He carried something dark and vaguely round in his right hand, and his countenance was grim and unreadable.

"My son," said the king, taking a step towards Vinadan.

The young prince passed beneath the city gates, and as he reached his father, he tossed the thing in his hand down onto the ground at his father's feet. He did not slow his stride, nor stop to embrace his father or mother. His gaze was focused, fixed upon the citadel, and he shouldered his father and the guards out of his way as he continued, silent, in the direction of his home.

Neither Entallion, Arianrhod, nor Valahir could summon a word between them, such was the unreality of Vinadan's sudden reappearance. They watched him recede into the distance, bound for the citadel, and exchanged confused and disbelieving glances.

"My lord," said one of the guards, regaining the king's attention. He moved his torch, directing its light to reveal the item Vinadan had so casually thrown at the king's feet.

"In Aether's name…" said the king, looking in horror upon Midhir's charred, severed head.

*

Despite the lateness of the hour and the manner of Vinadan's sudden return, the young prince did not head to his chambers upon reentering the citadel, but to the kitchens. The ambient light was low, and as Valahir swung the door open and entered, followed by his mother and father, the sight of his brother sitting at a table, delving ravenously into plates full of bread, cold meats, pickled vegetables, and an assortment of nuts and grains, to say nothing of the carafes of wine and water either side of the young man, took on an otherworldly, almost dreamlike quality to the older heir.

Vinadan did not look up as they entered, but continued to gorge himself on the food and drink at hand. Crossing the room in three long strides, Queen Arianrhod grasped her youngest son by his bare shoulders and all-but dragged him out of his seat to pull him close in an embrace only a mother could provide.

"My son," she said, weeping, as she squeezed him tightly. Vinadan's eyes were glassy and unfocused as he stared over her shoulder, roughly in the direction of his brother and father.

"Please, Arian," said the king, "move." The queen released her vice-like grip on her son, and took a step back to look at him as best as the dim light allowed. He was gaunt, pale, and very still. His eyes were deep and hollow, and his hair was long and streaked with white.

"My boy," said the king, moving closer to the young prince, "how could you let this happen?" he snapped. Focus returned immediately to Vinadan's eyes.

"What?" he managed through his dry, cracked throat.

"You are the heir to the throne, not some lowly courtier to be bartered!" his father bellowed, "How could you let yourself be captured by a pack of mindless orrecs?"

"Entallion, I-" said the queen, placing a hand on her husband's forearm.

"No," said the king, shaking free of her grasp, "he has to learn. Ever your head is buried in books, maps, and scrolls, and look at what happens when you are finally tested out there in the real world!"

The king's face was red with anger, and his breath came fast and deep.

"Father," said Valahir, "it is as much my fault as his,"

"Fault?" said Vinadan, finding his voice, "you believe I am at *fault* here? You all believe that?" His features were unreadable and unflinching, betraying nothing of the simmering rage which threatened, even now, to overwhelm him.

"Where were you?" asked Valahir. Vinadan did not take his eyes from his father for a long, tense moment, then cast his gaze to his brother.

"Close," he said, "which you would have known had you bothered to look for me. Indeed I was not barterred like some lowly courtier, father; nor was I looked for, it would seem."

"Now, Vindi, that's not-"

"Please don't call me 'Vindi', Valahir. You gave up that right when you abandoned me for dead."

"That's not fair, Vinadan," said the queen, forestalling an outburst from King Entallion, "your father and brother were out on horseback every day looking for you."

"Really?" replied Vinadan, his tone emotionless, "I doubt father even realised I was gone."

"You insolent-" the king began, but Vinadan was not finished.

"Had you bothered to look - to really look - I would have been discovered with ease. But once again, 'Mighty King Entallion' and 'Valahir the Gallant' go bumbling in with their fists raised when they should have been using their goddess-given brains."

"Vin-"

"No, brother, you will not interrupt me. Do you believe Midhir to be a man of supreme intelligence?" When nothing but silence answered his question, he laughed and shook his head. "That was not a rhetorical question, so I will ask you again: do you believe Midhir to be a shrewd and intelligent man?"

"No," replied the king through clenched teeth, his anger at his son not yet abated. "He is skilled in the healing arts and knows the tricks and trappings of politics, but I would not deem him to possess a great intellect. Why do you ask?"

"And why did you expel him?"

"I don't know what nonsense he told you, but-"

"Answer the question."

The king took a deep breath to calm his own simmering anger.

"His views on the Souls and the runes were... extreme," said the king, and Vinadan nodded in mock encouragement.

"Good, father; very good. Would it be fair to say, then, that he is - *was* - a little obsessed with the work of Daedan Asarlai?" said Vinadan, like an adult talking a child through a simple mathematics problem.

The queen sighed - groaned would perhaps be a more accurate description - and placed a hand over her face.

"Entallion," she said, calmly and quietly, "please tell me that you extended your search north to Aillen."

The king's face grew red once more, though this time it was not anger which coloured his cheeks.

"Aillen? The north? Why would-" he stuttered, seeing the look on his wife's face. "Well, what you have to understand- "

"You *fool*," she hissed, "Of course Midhir would take him there. I cannot believe you - and you," she added, turning her wrath upon Valahir, "would be so blind as to…"

Vinadan did not hear the end of his mother's sentence. He returned to his seat, and poured himself a large goblet of red wine. He took a cold chicken leg from his plate and resumed his feast.

"Vind- Vinadan?" said Valahir once his mother had finished roundly chastising him and his father, "what happened? I mean, what really happened out there?"

Vinadan swallowed the piece of chicken he was busy chewing, and placed the stripped-clean bone onto his plate. He took a deep breath, and exhaled low and long. He picked up his wine and raised it to his lips, pausing before he drank. His gaze was fixed forward, boring a hole into the very brick wall.

"Leave me," he said at length, and his tone brooked no argument. He heard the door close shut behind them as his parents and brother left the room unseen, and only then did he allow a single tear to fall from his eye to land with a metallic ring onto the pewter plate before him.

Chapter Forty-Three

"Try as I might, I just cannot see where we went wrong with that boy," said King Entallion, as he and Queen Arianrhod walked. Winter had truly announced itself, and the feel of the snow crunching and compacting under his booted feet brought some semblance of calm to the king; a throwback to some disjointed childhood memory of frolicking in the thick snow with his own brothers. He must only have been around Vinadan's age, and…

He shook the thought from his mind.

"Do not be too harsh on him, my love," replied the queen, linking her right arm underneath his left, "he has been through a trying ordeal, one that would have broken lesser men."

"It *has* broken him, Arian, and he is not yet a man grown, but a mere boy."

"It has not been easy for him," the queen continued, "and we all process our emotions differently; you should know that better than most."

The king merely huffed under his breath, somewhat proving Arianrhod's point, and they continued to walk. They were not headed for anywhere in particular, but simply wanted to get out of the citadel and feel the cold air upon their cheeks, and enjoy the way their lungs seemed to chill as they inhaled the winter air. They were still within the walls of the capital, of course, and their wandering had led them through the city and back around toward home. As they made their way back toward the citadel, they were greeted with bows, nods of the head, and more proclamations of "Your Grace" than they could count. Even the dwarves, hard at work with hammer, chisel, axe, and pulley, ceased their construction efforts long enough to show deference to the king and queen.

"I know he is troubled," said the king, "Aether alone knows what torment he suffered at the hands of that mad bastard Midhir, but he will not talk to me; it's been weeks, Arian."

"He will open up to us in time, Entallion. Allow him the space he needs."

They said no more as they made their way back to the citadel, hoping to find a warm fire and a sharp brandy waiting for them inside. They climbed the rough stone steps, careful not to stumble where the well-trodden stone crumbled and cracked. The renovations which the dwarven crew worked so hard to complete could not come soon enough. The citadel had stood, proud and strong, for hundreds of years, protecting and sheltering kings and queens, princes and princesses - not to mention their courtiers and staff - from all manner of dangers and assault. But it was now showing its age, and was in dire need of repair.

The cracks are showing, and very soon it will break. The thought stuck with the king even as he made his way inside, and he could not quite shake the feeling that it was not the castle walls his head and heart were truly focused upon.

*

Vinadan was wrapped up tight against the cold weather. He wore heavy furs and a thick, black cloak with its hood raised. From within the shadow of the cloak, his intense eyes blazed behind locks of hair which blew across his face in the chill wind.

It was into those piercing eyes which Jannaforth of the Asarlai stared, as he held up a stalling hand to the young prince.

"I'm sorry, my prince, but I cannot permit you to enter the monastery," he said firmly. Vinadan looked back over his shoulder, watching as snow swirled and danced in the sky, set in contrast to the dark clouds and darker horizon. He could see all of

Aclevion from this height, and as he peered down on the capital, he felt the wind buffeting and battering him as he stood on the threshold to the Asarlai monastery. He turned his gaze back to Jannaforth, and raised his voice in order to be heard above the howling wind.

"You know who I am, Asarlai," said Vinadan, and the other simply nodded. It was not a question, after all. "I wish to gain entry to your library, and I order you to grant me passage."

"We do not take visitors, Prince Vinadan, nor do we allow *children* to enter, whatever their circumstances."

Vinadan felt his face flush despite the cold wind, and he fancied that his heart was beating faster than it had been prior to the Asarlai referring to him as a child.

"I will make this very easy for you, Asarlai," said Vinadan. "Move aside, allow me passage, or I will see to it that you will meet the headsman come morning."

"On what charge?"

"Charge?" said Vinadan with a grin," Oh, I'm sure I can think of something salacious and thoroughly convincing. Now stand aside, by order of the heir to the throne."

Jannaforth laughed a mirthless laugh, and though it could have been a trick of the light on this tempestuous day, Vinadan would later swear that he had seen a flicker of orange in the Asarlai's eyes; just a faint spark, and only for a moment."

"As you wish, *my prince*," said Jannaforth, stepping aside, "Enjoy your visit, and please take great care with our texts; some of them are worth more than all the gold in the kingdom."

They stepped inside, and the Asarlai swung the heavy door shut behind them, immediately silencing the whistling wind, and allowing Vinadan to feel the warmth which emanated from within the tunnels of the mountain. Torches lined the walls every few feet, and so bright and welcoming was it within that Vinadan all-but forgot he was inside the hollowed-out passageways of a mountain.

"The library is-" began Jannaforth, but Vinadan held up a hand.

"I know where it is," he said, not even looking at the man as he set off, making his way deeper into the mountain. He did not look back over his shoulder as he disappeared into the maze of tunnels.

"Arrogant brat," said Jannaforth, shaking his head.

Vinadan wandered the pathways of the Asarlai monastery, trying hard to keep his mouth from hanging open in awe as he beheld the carvings, tapestries, paintings, and sculptures which adorned the walls of this place. Here, an ancient tome which looked as if it would crumble at the slightest touch; there, a bronze statuette depicting Gibrion herself, with ornate flowers and vines carved into every inch of the immaculate piece. He continued toward the library, and soon found himself face to face with five Asarlai guards. Unlike Jannaforth at the entrance, these were armed and wore helmets beneath their crimson hoods. Behind them stood a pair of heavy, tall doors, and Vinadan did not have to guess what was housed within. He had reached the Soul Chamber. He nodded toward the guards who, upon recognising him, returned his gesture with a curt "My Prince," each. Vinadan continued past the chamber, but as he moved on he could not help but dwell on Midhir's words, and he felt a pull on his heart as if it were being dragged, weighted, to the bottom of the ocean. He had been here before, he had been told, with Midhir and his father, no less, but he did not remember it. Was it Midhir himself who first ignited Vinadan's curiosity? And if so, was it by accident or design?

Though it was not a conscious decision, Vinadan's pace increased, putting distance between himself and the Soul Chamber. He could not place the emotion, nor could he fully understand it, but he could not help feeling that his destiny was somehow linked - whether tenuously or intrinsically - to the Soul he had just left behind. He put it out of his mind as he rounded the final corner, and he found himself at last inside the Asarlai library.

Quite unexpectedly, he found that he shed a tear at the sight which met him, and he wiped his cheek with a furred sleeve.

The room was enormous, and glowed with an inviting orange courtesy of the torches which lined the walls. The colour of the flames, however, was slightly *off*; somewhat uncanny and discordant, and Vinadan knew in that moment that they burned with a fire made not by flint or kindling. Shelves which must have been thirty feet tall lined every wall, and each was full of books, scrolls, and tomes; letters, etchings, and notes. Vinadan felt that he could almost feel the energy pulsing from within the ancient texts. He felt as if the very room hummed and buzzed with a power he had not even dreamed could exist in this world.

He took a deep breath, savouring the scent of old parchment and leather mingled with dust and heat.

He shucked his backpack onto the floor and knelt beside it. He untied the strings and opened the bag, taking out clean parchment, ink, quills, and various other writing and sketching implements, and he moved to set them up on the nearest table. He removed his outer cloak and furs, savouring how warm it was inside the mountain.

Before he began in earnest, he turned and looked around the room, moving slowly through three-hundred-and-sixty degrees, head held high.

So much knowledge, he thought as he gazed in wonder at the myriad texts arrayed within the huge chamber. For a moment he considered trying to count the number of books he could see, but immediately thought better of it.

So much history. So much potential. So much power. So lost was he in his thoughts, that he did not notice that his skin had begun to turn red in places, and the faint outlines of runes had begun to announce themselves upon his exposed skin. He regained his wits, and watched as the runes receded, his skin returning to normal after a few moments. The fiery glint in his eyes could simply have been a reflection from the torches upon the walls; perhaps it *was*.

He grinned, and closed the doors.

Chapter Forty-Four

Vinadan slept long and deep that night, and his dreams were vivid and utterly bizarre. As he lay in his warm bed, covered with furs and blankets, the dying embers in the open fireplace adding their faltering heat to the room, his mind, too, was filled with fire. In his dreams, he walked. He left the citadel and Aclevion behind him, and found himself at length in the wider lands of Etian. From here, he pressed due-east, and dream-time propelled him inexorably to the country of Tol-Peregon, though it was nothing like the Tol-Peregon Vinadan knew. He knew all too well of its capital, Elgiroth, which to his mind was a hard place, full of fire, ash, and rock. He knew, also, that it had not always been that way. His teachers had taught him the basics of his histories but, ever the keen mind, Vinadan had conducted his own research into the Spoiling of Elgiroth. Though he did not yet fully understand it, he knew enough to know that it involved the third Soul, the soul of Gibrion, and that some great cataclysm had brought about the utter ruin of the once green and lush lands of Tol-Peregon, where men tended their farms and dwarves mined the hillsides, to say nothing of the devastation wrought upon its people.

Tens of thousands were killed when the land was brought to ruin, and those who survived were changed. When The Spoiling came, immeasurable cracks and fissures opened up in the very ground, but where men and dwarves fell in, creatures which later came to be known as orrecs and hoblins crawled out.

Vinadan saw it all as he slept.

From here, he ventured south into Skyoliin, taking in Markosh, Adeniron, and all of the smaller settlements which lay between. Further he pressed, moving south, not walking, nor really floating, but moving in a manner known only in the plain of dreams. He felt a heat at his back, and he turned to look over his shoulder. His entire field of vision was a curtain of fire which came on and on, inching closer and closer, pushing Vinadan to keep moving.

He found himself passing into the elven realm of Eirendollen, and his dream-self moved at an uncanny speed toward Eonis. He found himself face to face with an elven queen; she was beautiful, but sullen. Her dark skin and dark eyes seemed a jarring contrast to the vibrant green of nature which surrounded her. In further contrast to the ubiquitous green was the red which dripped from the dagger in his hand.

He felt his stomach lurch as he was pulled from Eonis; the green trees replaced at once with a grey-brown wall of rock, covered top to bottom with intricately carved representations of historical events. He did not recognise his immediate surroundings, but somehow knew that dwarven hands would have been responsible for the art he beheld. His dreaming mind turned him around and moved him back toward his home, back to the north, back to Aclevion. He saw tall spires, high walls, and a huge, gleaming fountain he did not recognise, and then everything turned to black.

He heard a scream somewhere off in the distance; a deep, horrifying scream, full of anguish, pain, and regret.

As he awoke, sitting bolt-upright in his bed, he could not shake the feeling that he recognised exactly who it was who had screamed, and could not help but feel the same anguish in his waking heart as his dreaming mind had registered.

It was only a dream, he thought, shaking his head to dispel the lingering disquiet. He turned over to face the wall and closed his eyes. Sleep found him again, and quickly, but this time he did not dream.

*

"Vinadan, here, come with me," said Valahir, finding his brother in the library. He was head to toe in armour, and carried two swords.

"I'm busy," came the younger man's droll reply.

"No, come on. Please, brother; king's orders," said Valahir, already turning and beckoning his brother to follow. With a deep sigh, Vinadan closed the book he was reading, and pushed his quill and parchment away as he stood. He followed Valahir through the citadel toward the still under construction eastern wing, and out into the training courtyard.

"Here," said Valahir, handing Vinadan a sword.

"What are we doing here, Valahir?" asked an impatient Vinadan.

"Father has instructed me to see to it that all of the men are ready to fight, and that includes you, brother."

"He wants me back out there?"

"Of course he does," replied Valahir, turning his own sword over in his hand, feeling the weight, and carving small circles into the air in front of him. "He knows it's been tough on you since you came back to us, brother, and he has tried to give you the space you need, but he's worried about you," said the older prince.

"You will perhaps forgive me if I don't believe you," said Vinadan, raising his own weapon in front of his face and setting his feet.

"By the goddess, Vindi, what is it going to take to convince you?"

"I don't need you to convince me of anything," said Vinadan, as he took a step forward and swung a horizontal cut toward Valahir's head. Valahir parried the strike with ease, and pirouetted away from his younger brother, "but what are we training for?"

"When you killed Midhir, you did more - far more - than you could ever know. Now his orrecs are rudderless and disorganised. Father plans to launch an assault on Aillen before long to finish the job."

"I think that unwise," said Vinadan, "the orrecs are no longer a threat."

"How can you say that?" asked Valahir, his brow furrowing, "they are a vile scourge on the north, and sworn enemies of the crown. They must be destroyed."

"And father wants me on the front lines?"

"Yes, he does. There is no conspiracy here, Vinadan," he said, thrusting his blade forward to be knocked aside by Vinadan's defensive stroke, "father just wants what's best for you; he just wants things to go back to the way they were before."

"Before?" spat Vinadan, "you mean before I was kidnapped by a madman from right under your nose?" He launched an assault on Valahir, aiming high and low, left and right; he spun, ducked, thrust, and parried in a furious dance with no heed given to the razor sharp swords they were using.

"I'm sorry, Vinadan, for Aether's sake, I'm sorry!" replied Valahir as he defended himself from his brother's onslaught. "What do I have to do to prove it to you?"

"What do you have to do?" How about you stay out of my way? How's that for a start?"

Vinadan dropped his sword onto the frozen ground, and balled his fists by his sides. Valahir watched with a dawning horror as he beheld fire burning in his brother's eyes, and looked aghast at the runes which blazed to life on Vinadan's skin, casting the gloomy, snow-filled courtyard in an unnatural orange and red glow. To Valahir, his brother was indistinguishable from a demon as he stood there, not six feet from him, wreathed in flame and shrouded in anger.

"By the goddess..." whispered Valahir.

"Not quite, brother," replied Vinadan, breathing heavily and grinning maniacally. Valahir brought himself back to his wits and marched over to his brother, seizing Vinadan by the shoulder and dragging him into one of the nearby stables, out of the reach of wandering eyes. The shock was enough to snap Vinadan out of his involuntary display of power; the runes faded quickly and the fire in his eyes was extinguished.

"Vindi; as your commander, as your brother, and as the closest ally you'll ever have, you tell me now: what did Midhir do to you?" Vinadan met his brother's gaze with his own unflinching stare.

"Nothing," he replied softly.

"Don't lie to me!" shouted Valahir, "For Aether's sake, Vinadan, I'm trying to help you, can't you see that? What happened out there? Did he experiment on you? Torture you? Tell me, please!"

"He did nothing, brother," replied Vinadan after a long moment, "I can honestly tell you that he truly did not lay a finger on me. I was not hurt, nor was I subjected to terrors the like of which you clearly imagine. He merely showed me the true way of things."

Valahir was not satisfied and did not let go of his brother's shoulders as he looked him straight in the eye.

"What does that mean, Vinadan? You're not making any sense. And that, out there... Where did you learn dark magic like that? You frighten me, brother; truly you do."

"Well," said Vinadan, shrugging free of his brother's grasp, "then I suggest you do as I say and leave me the fuck alone."

Valahir watched as his brother turned and walked away, back toward the citadel and no doubt the library. He did not even attempt to wipe away the tears which fell openly down his cheeks.

Such fear, such loss, and such grief as he felt in that moment, a fleeting moment of weakness though it may have been; at that moment Valahir wished that his brother had never returned.

Chapter Forty-Five

"Your Grace, allow me to present Thyrus, King of Toraleth; Lord of Torimar, and ally to the throne of Aclevion," came the high and nervous voice from the young courtier. His words echoed and reverberated around the throne room, and the young man barely recognised his own voice as it reached his ears a heartbeat later. The throne room was grand and imposing, with high ceilings and exquisite artwork adorning the walls. A long, deep green carpet ran the length of the room from door to throne, and white marble pillars stood either side of the walkway at regular intervals. It was down this carpet that a small contingent of dwarves now walked, heading toward the steps at the foot of King Entallion's throne.

The king stood; his grin was wide and his arms were spread wider.

"Thyrus, my friend," he said, moving to embrace the dwarven king, "it has been far too long."

"It definitely has, Entallion," replied Thyrus, "I extend my thanks and that of my retinue for your hospitality, as ever." Entallion waved this away and shook his head reproachfully.

"Oh, don't speak in that way; you know you are always welcome beneath my roof. Now come; let us leave these lofty halls and retire somewhere more comfortable, not to mention *warmer*. Ale?"

"Did you really just ask me that?" replied Thyrus with a wink.

*

"It is truly a rare blessing to be left alone for even a short time," said Entallion, as he and Thyrus drank a dark and bitter ale, gorging themselves on meat, breads, and assorted sweet cakes in one of the king's private rooms. Their respective aides, servants, and other assorted staff had been ordered to remain outside, allowing the kings to converse and relax alone.

"I would agree, wholeheartedly, my friend," said Thyrus, downing the last of his ale and helping himself to a top up, "too readily do they swarm and fuss; it's not like the old days."

"True, it is not, Thyrus, and I fear we will never again see a return to those days - at least not in our lifetime." They sat in silence for a moment, brooding on Entallion's words, each lamenting the passing of simpler times where the rule of common sense and a core council of able individuals was the prevailing model of governance, not the fussing and buzzing of a hundred nameless, faceless courtiers.

"Anyway," said Thyrus at length, "the good news is that the renovation of the east wing and the new courtyard are coming along ahead of schedule. We should be able to open in, say, three months; maybe two, if we really push it." Entallion waved away the dwarven lord's words and offered a small shake of his head.

"Please, there is no need, my friend. Hemera knows your people have already worked wonders to get to this point. No, three months is fine; it will take us beyond the bitter edge of the winter in any case. We may yet see the unveiling against the backdrop of a warm spring."

"That sounds good to me, Entallion," said Thyrus, raising his tankard to *clank* against Entallion's own.

"Cheers," they said as one.

"To other business, if I may," said Entallion, "I would do you the courtesy of letting you in on my plans."

"Oh?" replied Thyrus.

"Indeed. Now that Midhir is no longer in the picture, I am planning an assault on Aillen to clear out the last of the orrecs he had stationed there."

"Do you require soldiers?" asked Thyrus.

"No, my friend, but thank you. I plan to send the King's Guard only. My sons will lead the assault. From the little that Vinadan has told us, we believe their numbers to be small and their organisation lacking"

"A small force in return, then."

"Indeed. A full-scale assault on Elgiroth would require more men than we can spare, and I would certainly be taking you up on your offer in that case, but no; Aillen can be conquered by stealth and cunning in place of numbers and a show of overwhelming force. One man of the King's Guard is worth ten orrecs, at least. No, the dwarves shall sit this one out, my friend."

"As you command, my King," said Thyrus, with a deferential nod of the head. "When do you plan to make your move?" Entallion leaned back in his seat and absentmindedly stroked at his greying beard.

"Within a fortnight, I should say; a month at most. The men are ready, and Valahir has proven himself a worthy commander."

"That he certainly has, Entallion. You should be proud of the lad."

"I am, and he knows this," said the king, with an edge of pride sneaking into his voice. His head dropped but a little, almost imperceptibly, and he sighed deeply. "I do, however, have one final problem to solve."

"Is that so?" asked Thyrus, devouring a chicken leg. Entallion nodded, looking off into the distance past Thyrus' shoulder.

"Eat up, old friend," he said, pouring himself another ale and topping up Thyrus' tankard anew, "I must sadly call time on our meeting shortly. Vinadan and I are long overdue a conversation."

*

Vinadan sat cross-legged on his bed, staring absently out of his window at the clouds which gathered above the mountain tops, his attention caught at intervals by passing birds. He held a leather-bound book loosely in his hands, allowing it to rest upon his lap. His eyes had lost their focus, and the young prince felt as if he were in a daydream; the same way he had felt for much of the time since he had returned to the citadel. He was lost in his thoughts as he recalled his captivity, replaying Midhir's words in his head, and thinking hard about the lessons he had learned in those months. He absently raised a hand to the back of his neck and allowed it to rest there, touching the spot in which he bore a birthmark, and he allowed his head to loll to the side as he sat. A sad sight he would present to onlookers, but the young prince felt determination and resolve beginning to swell up inside him as he made his decision.

He blinked and shook his head, clearing the cobwebs, and bringing his attention back to the here and now. He put the book down as he jumped up off the bed, and walked toward the window. The sun was high in the sky, but its warmth eluded Vinadan and he shivered as he stood looking out over the capital from his high vantage point. On a clear day like this, he fancied that he could see not just all of Aclevion from his window, but all of Etain itself, maybe even to the border of Korrigand. He took a deep breath, and focused. He closed his eyes and balled his fists. Slowly, his skin began to turn pink, then red, as if he were burning from within. One by one, small but fully-formed runes began to announce themselves upon his skin.

Domination and *Influence*, repeated over and over again in strange patterns.

He stretched out with his mind, looking with eyes closed beyond the glass of his window, out into the cold winter air.

There, he thought, *I have you.*

He opened his eyes and smiled at the sight of a crow swooping down to land upon the ledge outside Vinadan's window. He closed his eyes once more and connected his mind with that of the bird. He shook with exertion, and sweat began to bead upon his forehead. With a gasp, he broke the connection and watched as the bird took to the skies. He was panting now, breathing hard, and the runes had begun to fade, returning his skin to its usual hue. He turned his back on the window and made his way back to his bed. He resumed his cross-legged position and picked up the leather book once more. He wet his sleeve with his mouth and tried to rub the red spatter marks from the cover of the journal - but only succeeded in smearing them further. He shrugged and opened the book, picking up where he had left off. His brow furrowed as he read the words, written in Midhir's neat hand, and he tried to make sense of the incantation. After a few moments he placed the book back down onto his sheets and his mouth fell open.

Surely not, he thought in genuine confusion, *surely it cannot be so simple… The old man clearly was not as smart as he thought. But I…*

He stood and marched to stand in front of the full-length mirror which stood on the far side of his room, next to his writing desk. He stared at himself for a while, noting every line and curve of his features, marking the way his hair, black, but now flecked through with white, hung around his face. He marked his height, his weight, his frame, his posture, mentally cataloguing everything which made him *himself*, physically, at least. He closed his eyes and forced his breathing to come in a steady rhythm. He brought his hands up in front of his chest as if he were praying to Aether herself, and then he balled his fists until his knuckles turned white; he forced his mind to work as he focused on the words and the symbols from the journal; he gritted his teeth and willed the incantation to work. He would not fail like Midhr did, like so many others had failed before him. He would succeed, here, he knew he would. His head hurt from the strain, and he feared he would pass out and fall if he persevered much longer. As the pain and the strain built to a crescendo, he screamed and opened his eyes.

He did not recognise the face staring back at him.

Eyes wide and jaw gaping, Vinadan touched his face. As he did so, his actions were duplicated by the dark skinned and wrinkled old man in the mirror. The young prince's reflection wore his clothes and stood with his gait, but the prince was gone, transformed into a dark and utterly unknown old man. If he were to guess, Vinadan thought the man looked to be from Skyoliin, but could not be any more specific than that. Why his subconscious chose this form for his first transformation, Vinadan would never know for sure. But it had worked, and all it had truly cost Vinadan was a headache. He looked at the journal on the bed and laughed.

Old fool, he thought, bringing Midhir to mind, *for decades you toiled, yet still died a failure.*

He stood a while longer, marvelling at his appearance in the mirror; so engrossed was he that he almost failed to register the sound of footsteps outside of his room.

"My prince," came the voice of the guard as he opened Vinadan's door, "I'm sorry to intrude."

"That's quite alright, Captain Jefree," said Vinadan, flicking his black and white hair out of his pale young face, "what is it?"

"The king awaits you, Prince Vinadan," replied Jefree, standing to the side of the door to demonstrate to the young prince that he was not to keep his father waiting.

"Of course," said Vinadan, walking to his bed and collecting a fur cloak which hung from a bedpost. As he placed it around his shoulders, he casually nudged Midhir's journal beneath the sheets and out of sight, "Lead on, Captain."

Chapter Forty-Six

"Why have you brought me here, Your Grace?"

"Please, Vinandan, we are alone; we can put aside our titles and simply be father and son." Vinadan's jaw tightened at his father's words. He cast his eyes around the glade, which was at once so familiar and yet, at this moment, unnervingly alien. He did not reply to his father's words, but folded his hands behind his back and took a step into the glade. It was lush and green; little more than a patch of grass upon which no trees grew by some natural fluke. All around the area, though, the trees stood tall and proud, enclosing and encircling the scene. Now, the grasses were dusted with white snow and ice, crunching underfoot as the king and prince made their way within.

"Do you remember it?" asked Entallion, spreading his arms wide and casting his gaze around the hidden grove. "Your mother and I used to bring you here - you and your brother - when you were young." He laughed at a fleeting memory. "When you were little more than a baby, you used to-"

"I remember, father," Vinadan replied curtly, "but you did not answer my question: why have you brought me here now?"

The king's shoulders slumped, and he sighed and rubbed at his temple. He quickly regained his composure and placed his hands on his hips. "By the goddesses, Vinadan, I just wanted to talk to you; like we used to, do you remember? When you were young, you barely left my side. You may not remember this, but I certainly do." The king's voice wavered slightly, and the beginnings of tears threatened to announce themselves in his eyes.

"Once," he continued, "I even had to have you escorted, kicking and screaming, from court because you would not let go of my leg."

Vinadan stood stoically and did not respond.

"What happened to that boy, Vinadan? That happy, care-free boy, full of wonder, who took joy in everything, small or grand, man or beast. I would give anything to see him again."

"Well, we do not always get what we want, father."

"Oh Aether be damned, Vinadan!" the king snapped, "What have I done to deserve such scorn from my own child? Such disrespect? Such cold indifference from my own blood."

Vinadan presented his father with a small, lop-sided grin, and took another step forward.

"Well, you left me to die at the hands of *your* enemy, for one."

Entallion could barely contain his fury and he jabbed a finger toward his son. "You know that is not true, and I curse you for speaking this falsehood!"

"Curse me? You cursed me the day you sired me, Your Grace. Ever have you favoured my brother. Ever have you looked upon me with naught but derision etched upon your righteous face. When you look at me, father, you see not a son, a prince, nor a king-in-waiting; you see a *disappointment*."

"How many times, and in how many ways do I have to tell you that you speak falsely, my son? I love you and your brother equally, and I could not be more proud of the men you are becoming. Look," he took a step toward his son, arms spread in a gesture of reconciliation, "I know you suffered a terrible ordeal-"

"You know nothing of my ordeal!" shouted Vinadan, pushing his father away from him and to the ground. A flame flickered in his eyes, and his muscles shook with adrenaline.

"You would dare lay a hand on your father? On your king?" Entallion replied in little more than a whisper. He stood, wiped his hands on his robes, and closed his eyes. He took a deep breath, and opened his eyes.

"Very well; we will do it your way." The king turned his back on Vinadan and paced around the glade, his feet crunching the frozen grass as he gathered his thoughts. At length he turned to face his son, every bit the king of Aclevion in bearing and in voice.

"Prince Vinadan Daelectus of Aclevion," he began, "I have ordered the King's Guard to launch an assault upon the city of Aillen, three weeks from this very night. Your brother, Prince Valahir will lead the force which will assail the city and destroy all that is left of Midhir's forces. As your king, I hereby appoint you to the battalion, and name you second in command behind Valahir."

Vinadan's face was a mask of barely concealed malice, "You think you're sending me back there, that I'm to lead the army, but I will not do it."

"You will do exactly as your king commands, or you will be hanged as a deserter."

With that, the king walked past his son, back the way they came, leaving Vinadan standing alone in the glade. Entallion did not look back as he made his way toward the citadel, and the cold winter wind stung his eyes and froze his tears upon his cheeks.

*

The rain fell hard and fast; its constant pitter-patter against the window of Vinadan's bedroom drummed out a rhythm to which his right leg bounced with nervous energy. He sat at the desk in his quarters, absentmindedly chewing his fingernails. He had made straight for his room upon returning home from the glade in his father's wake, and he had not ventured out once in the intervening hours.

He had lit candles only sparingly, and he gazed headlong into space in the half-light as he arranged his thoughts and processed his father's words. His bag was packed, and it stood ominously by the door. He had already resolved to leave, that much was now a given; his only decision now was whether or not he would return.

He stood up from his desk abruptly, and a tingle in his legs and an ache in his lower back told him just how long he had sat there, mulling over his plan. He gathered Midhir's journal and secured it beneath his cloak, and he picked up his sword. He held the blade out in front of himself, marvelling at how his appearance warped and shifted in the reflection of the weapon. He placed the sword within its scabbard and took a deep breath. Taking a length of cord from his dresser, he tied his long hair back behind his head, and strapped his bag over his shoulders and onto his back.

He turned before leaving, and cast an eye over his room, his bed, his possessions, but he did not feel grief or sadness at the thought he may never again see this place.

This is my father's home, he thought, *not mine. Well, not yet.*

He closed his eyes for a moment, and centred himself, drawing upon his newfound abilities. He opened his eyes and looked at each of the lit candles in turn. With a wink, they all went out, casting the room into darkness. He opened the bedroom door as carefully and quietly as he could, lest he wake anyone at this hour of the night.

"My prince," said the knight stationed outside of his room.

"All is well, Sir Ballister," replied Vinadan, casually waving away the other's confused look, "I have a sworn duty to perform for the king. I ask of you the utmost discretion; am I understood?" The knight hesitated, only for a moment, then relaxed his stance.

"Yes, my prince, of course," he said, bowing his head in deference, "do you require protection? With your leave, I would gladly accompany-"

"That will not be necessary, Sir Ballister," said Vinadan, "but I thank you for the offer, and will make sure my father hears of your service this night."

Vinadan nodded his goodbye to the knight, and made his way out of the castle as silently as he could. The rain was coming down even heavier now, and the wind whipped his cloak about him, chilling him to the bone as it screeched past at pace. Still, the young prince could not keep from smiling as he made his way through the darkened, empty streets of Aclevion. He knew he could slip past the outer guard with ease; there were ways to pass beyond the gate that he and Valahir had known since they were children, so his leaving would go unnoticed. Once he had cleared the gate, it would be simple enough to sneak a horse out of the outer stables, and then he would put miles between himself and Aclevin before anybody even realised he was gone. And even if he *was* spotted… *Well,* he thought, *it won't be the face of Prince Vinadan they encounter.*

Onward then, he decided with a smile, *onward to Aillen.*

*

Motes of dust floated lazily in the air, fleetingly illuminated in the rays of early morning sunshine which crept in through a break in the curtains. Valahir threw the doors open without knocking.

"What time do you call this?" he asked the empty room as he swept into Vinadan's chambers. He looked around the room, taking in the neatly made bed, and the folded garments which had been placed upon it - garments in the Daelectus family colours. A germ of dread began to coalesce within Valahir, and he looked again, harder this time, trying to place what it was that felt so badly wrong - so badly *off* - about his brother's room. And then it struck him.

It's practically empty, he realised.

"Ser Ballister!" Valahir called over his shoulder as he strode to the window and cast open the heavy curtains. The knight stepped into the room.

"Yes, Commander?"

"Where are my brother's possessions?" Valahir demanded. "Where are his books? His boots? His compass? Where are his pack and his sword? *Where is my brother,* Ballister?" The knight furrowed his brow in confusion.

"His mission, my prince; of course."

"His what?"

"For the king, my prince; I assumed you would know." Valahir's face began to turn red, and he breathed hard, burying the anger which threatened to spill forth.

"I would ask you to speak plainly, Sir Ballister. What happened? What did my brother say to you?"

"My prince," began Ballister, beginning to share a modicum of Valahir's dread, "Prince Vinadan left in the small hours, Commander. He was armed and bore a heavy pack. He told me that the king had entrusted him with an important mission; a secret mission, my lord. He asked for my discretion in the matter."

Valahir nodded, more to himself than to Ballister, and sat himself upon the edge of his brother's bed.

"Commander?" said the confused knight. Valahir gave no indication that he had heard him, and continued to nod to himself as if he had decided upon something unspoken. At length he stood, and walked to Ballister, placing a reassuring hand upon the knight's armoured shoulder.

"At ease, my friend. Worry not about my brother; that burden has ever been mine to bear. But I must ask you to seek out the stablemaster at once."

"The stablemaster, my prince?"

"Indeed," replied Valahir, graveley, "he will no doubt find that he is missing a horse."

Chapter Forty-Seven

Between the incessant sound of the dwarven smiths banging, hammering, shouting, and building outside, and the relentless prattle of the council members present in the small but opulent chamber, the king's head was beginning to throb. The sound of the dwarves, he mused, was something of a necessary evil as the grand opening of the new wing grew ever-closer, but the squabbling and lobbying of his advisors seated around the table was grating on Entallion today. He was a warrior king; his place was at the head of the army with sword in hand and banners flying high in his wake. Matters of the state, however - borders, taxation, budgets, treaties - these were matters better left to others. He sat at the head of the table, the queen to his left, trying desperately to remain interested, not to mention awake.

"Which is precisely why we must grant the Torundeli the funds they have requested," said Biltone, one of the king's oldest and most trusted advisors, "the border between Etain and Korrigand will only be strengthened if we agree to their request."

"While that may be true, my friend," said Edhal, the only Asarlai in attendance, "the crown simply cannot afford to grant handouts to every petty lord on the continent. The Torundeli do not lack wealth."

"I did not suggest we provide them with coin free of commitment, my lord; but perhaps a loan might-"

All heads turned to the wooden double-doors as they were thrown open with a creak.

"Forgive my intrusion, my lords," said Valahir as he entered, "but I must speak with the king and queen in private."

To their credit, the eight councilmen did not protest nor question the prince, but stood, bowed their heads in deference, and muttered their partings to the king and queen. The king, though more than a little concerned at his son's sudden intrusion, was secretly delighted to see the session brought to an abrupt close.

"Not that I lament the interruption," Entallion began as the last of the councilmen closed the doors behind him, "but what is so important that you felt the need to dismiss the council, Valahir?"

"He is gone, Father. Mother."

"Gone?" asked the king. "Who is gone?"

"Where is your brother, Valahir?" said Queen Arianrhod, rising from her seat and marching toward her firstborn, recognising in her son's countenance what her husband did not.

"I do not know, Mother. He played Sir Ballister false and departed the fortress in the small hours. He has taken a horse, and the hounds can find no trace of him."

"Who commanded the trackers to deploy the hounds?" asked Entallion.

"I did, Father, of course," replied Valahir, more than a little nonplussed by the question, "but that is not the issue here. Vinadan is gone, and his quarters are emptied - I fear he is not coming back."

"That's absurd," said the king, rising from his seat at last, "when I spoke to him yesterday, he-"

"You spoke to him?" asked the queen.

"Well, yes. In the old glade."

"What did you say to him?"

"Nothing specific; we spoke of many matters."

Queen Arianrhod took a deep breath and lowered her eyes for the briefest moment, before fixing her husband, with a look, the context of which she did not need to vocalise.

"I just wanted him to talk to me, Arian, like he used to when he was a boy," the king protested, arms wide, his voice gaining volume in the small room.

"What did you *say* to him, Entallion?"

The king's face flushed red, and he set his jaw defiantly.

"I just wanted to talk to my son the way we used to; he has been distant of late, and full of anger, and I thought that if I could just get through to him - especially there, where we have such fond memories, the four of us - that maybe I could help him."

"Go on," said Valahir, growing more and more concerned as his father spoke.

"And he threw it right back in my face," stated the king, with tears beginning to form, more in anger than sorrow.

"Then what happend, Entallion?"

"He is just so angry, Arian; he was arrogant, dismissive, downright disrespectful! So I said 'fine, if that's the way you want to play it, your King hereby commands you to-"

"*Your King commands you*?" the queen repeated, taking a quick step toward Entallion, "Gibrion's grace, Entallion; he's just a boy! He has endured a great trauma; can't you see he's hurting? He needs his father, not his liege-lord!"

"I tried, Arian, I really tried to get through to him, but he would not have it."

"And now he is gone, Aether knows where!" said Valahir. He stepped close to his mother and placed his arm around her.

"Come, mother; let us leave the king to his affairs." He cast a long glance at his father, shaking his head as he beheld the king. Queen Arianrhod did not protest, and allowed her eldest son to escort her from the council chamber, lest her husband see the tears he had caused to fall freely upon her face. She did not want to give him the satisfaction.

"That's right!" the king shouted to their backs, "leave me. You are dismissed by order of your king!"

As the double doors closed behind his wife and son, Entallion sat back down in his chair and held his head, eyes closed. His headache was now worse than ever, but it was still more bearable to the king than the ache in his heart.

*

"What are we going to do, Valahir" asked Arianrhod as she sat upon Vinadan's bed in his empty and silent room. Valahir paced to and fro, the image of his father with his jaw set and brow furrowed.

"I don't know, Mother," he said as he stopped pacing and turned to the queen, "my heart says we should saddle up this very moment and go find him, but my head…." he trailed off, shaking his head.

"Speak plainly, Valahir," said the queen.

"My head tells me I should remain here and attend to my duties. There is every chance Vinadan is just looking for attention, acting out in a bid to be seen or heard… I just don't know."

"You think he has merely run away in anger, and will return?"

"Who can say but he?" Valahir answered, exasperation creeping unbidden into his tone, "If I know my brother at all, then I would not put it past him. We know he has gone of his own volition and was not taken forcibly, so my heart is eased by this. I just do not know where he is, mother, nor could I even begin to guess." He ran his hands through his hair in frustration, and went to sit by his mother on the edge of Vinadan's bed.

"This is not your doing, Valahir," said the queen, as if reading her son's unspoken fears. "You are my son; you are Vinadan's brother, but you are also the commander of the King's Guard. You have your own life to live, and your own duties to perform." She sighed deeply and met her son's gaze with a fierce, stoic look in her eyes. "My heart also tells me we should stay in the capital. Your brother is troubled, and I fear he is stifled and stymied within these walls. He is my child, and I will always see him as my baby boy, but in truth he is nearly a man grown, and he must work through his trauma in his own way. I know he will return to us when he is ready. We will see him again, Valahir; of this I am certain."

*

Vinadan could hear the distant crash of waves to the north, and as he stood upon the outskirts of the coastal city of Aillen, he could see the outlines of yellow sandstone buildings on the horizon. The city had no real defences to speak of, as it had always been a domain of fisherman, academics, and scholars of the Asarlai. More recently, however, Midhir's orrec forces had taken up residence in the city, though they were not hostile to the locals. A strange peace held sway between the Aillenians and the orrecs, with neither group particularly fond of the other, but no blood had been shed upon the sandy, cobbled streets.

No blood, that is, until Vinadan had carried Midhir's head out of the city, unchallenged and unmolested. Power had swung, pendulum-like, in the city that day, and it had swung firmly toward the young prince. He had told Valahir that Midhir had not hurt nor tormented him, and this was true. He had told his parents that he was able to make good his escape and return to Aclevion uninjured, which was also true.

But there was much that Vinadan had omitted from his account. Chief among these missing facts was the procession of orrecs who had lined the streets as Vinadan departed, Midhir's severed head in his hands. Vinadan's eyes burned with the fires of the Asarlai; his own fledgling powers augmented by the teachings Midhir had openly volunteered to the young prince, and fuelled to an inferno by the knowledge which Vinadan had extracted from the old mage by terrible force. The orrecs had come out in their masses as Vinadan departed; their heads were bowed; they knelt in deference along the roadside; they swore fealty and barked oaths as they declared the young prince their new master.

Recalling this, Vinadan smiled. He checked and tightened the straps of his pack, patted the hilt of his sword reassuringly, raised his hood, and walked calmly into Aillen to take command of his forces.

Chapter Forty-Eight

The weeks passed slowly, and the day of Valahir's march to Aillen had arrived at long last. The prince had focused all of his attention upon the planning of the operation and the training of his men. Though he and his mother had sent scouts and other operatives into the wider lands of Etain and beyond the borders of their country, alert for any rumour or mere whisper of Vinadan, there had been no word of the younger prince to date. Valahir's heart was heavy, his eyes dark, and his jaw a mess of lazy stubble. He and the queen had grown closer these last weeks, and Valahir often visited his mother once his duties were complete, and they would simply sit and talk. While the talk was, more often than not, about Vinadan, lately they had begun to tentatively look ahead; to the grand opening of the new wing of the citadel - which itself was mere days away - and further still, with talk of Valahir's inevitable ascension to the throne under discussion. There was no malice in this talk, no plotting, nor undertones of any sinister sort, merely a mother and son looking forward to a bright day which was still some way off in the future.

Of King Entallion, little had been seen of late. He shunned court and performed his unavoidable duties with little more than a perfunctory vigour. He and Valahir had barely spoken since Valahir's interruption of the council session weeks earlier, and what conversation they did engage in was uncomfortably formal.

Of Queen Arianrhod, though she took no pleasure in it - in fact a deep sorrow was upon her, heart and soul - she could not help but view her husband the king through a prism; when she looked upon him now she saw him as a distorted, shifted version of himself; his very being tarnished by the fact that the queen deemed him culpable for driving their youngest son away.

Love still echoed within the walls of the citadel, but it was a cold, distant love.

The sun was low in the sky, but rising, casting the green plains ahead in a honey-golden light. Valahir led the procession on the back of the powerful albino Swiftstrike, though today he took no joy in the riding. A hundred men were behind him, similarly mounted and equally grave.

He should be here, by my side, thought Valahir as the green and yellow grasses, sharp, fallen rocks, and moss-covered boulders passed him by.

When this is over, he continued, losing himself in his own mind, *I will find him. I will retire my post, I will leave the capital behind me, and I will set out upon Shadowstrike to find my brother. Damn my father; damn the king.*

The journey was long but uneventful, and an unusual quiet lay upon the King's Guard. At length, the sweet, earthy smells of grass and trees faded, and was replaced with the sharp tang of salty sea-air. The vegetation took on a paler, browner hue, and the formerly muddy ground turned by degrees to sand under the hooves of the horses. Valahir had visited the coastal city as a child, and shook his head to banish a fleeting memory of himself and Vinadan building sand castles upon the beach, while the pale blue waters glistened and sparkled as if the goddesses themselves had cast diamonds into the fair northern seas. As he and his men passed the marker which signified that they had passed into Aillen, Valahir felt the hairs on the back of his neck stand on end. The main road into Aillen sits high upon a bank and, looking straight down the cobbled road, one can see all the way down into the city. Houses, stores, and stables line the road on either side as it slopes downward, and the sea and beach can be seen upon the horizon, peeking out from behind the pink and yellow stone buildings which seem to multiply and replicate, filling out the scene in all directions. Aillen has always been a vibrant place of fishermen, travellers, adventurers, and revellers.

But now it stood still, silent, and empty.

"Be on your guard," said Valahir to Captain Yulian, mounted directly to the prince's right. The captain gave a signal, and a ripple of readiness ran through the column at Valahir's back. With a tug of the reins, Shadowstrike stepped forward, and the rest of the force followed closely behind as the King's Guard slowly descended into the deserted streets of Aillen. No inquisitive gazes met them as they entered further into the city; no children played in the streets, and no trace of the aromas Valahir remembered from his childhood - the smell of sweet pastries and sugary treats which seemed to permeate the oxygen he breathed - could be found.

They moved further deeper, until they found themselves in an open promenade, more or less in the middle of Aillen, and still they saw no one. Valahir motioned for his men to halt, and they did so with a practised immediacy. The prince looked around, taking in all and alert for any movement. A large clock tower stood tall and proud in the centre of the square, its round face imposing and grand. To the left and right were shops, stores, and smiths', which usually sold cakes, toys, trinkets, and souvenirs to denizens and visitors alike. All were closed for business and devoid of activity. In front of Valahir, and the source of a new wave of dread which had begun to surge in his chest, was Daedan Asarlai's tower. As significant to Gibrion's history as it was, it was now little more than a tourist attraction and long since dispossessed of anything remotely arcane or dangerous. Nevertheless, seeing the old tower inside which, centuries ago, the ancient runes had first been deciphered and the Asarlai as Valahir knew them were born, sent a shiver down his spine and set his left leg bouncing nervously. He had seen the tower before, of course; and as he sat upon Swiftstrike, looking up at the old building, he remembered, though fleetingly, a keepsake his mother had purchased for him at the conclusion of the guided tour. A wooden replica of a gemstone, into which was carved a rune of power, though which one it was he could not now recall. He cast the thought from his mind, reimposing his concentration.

"Come, men. We cannot linger," he said as he tugged at the reins and set Swiftstrike into motion once more, his men following suit behind him.

"Leaving so soon, brother?"

The sound of Vinadan's voice could have burst Valahir's heart, rending it asunder as opposing waves of unbridled joy and a deep, cloying dread fought for control. Valahir had not moved ten feet, and he brought Swiftstrike to an abrupt halt and turned to face Asarlai's tower. He was forced to blink away tears as he beheld, about halfway up the tower on an overhanging balcony, his brother.

"Vindi?" he called, unsure why he was posing it as a question.

"Yes, Valahir. It's me."

"What…? How…? Are you okay?" asked Valahir, unable to organise his tumbling thoughts. "Come down from there, it's not safe here."

Vinadan smiled, and placed his hands on the rail of the balcony. He shook his head slowly, allowing his hair to sway to and fro in front of his dark eyes. "You are correct, as always, brother. It is not safe here; it is not safe here *at all*. Your men are about to find that out."

He took his hands from the balcony railing and drew himself up to his full height. He took a quick, deep breath, and thrust his right arm high into the air. A collective gasp rang out among the King's Guard as they watched Vinadan - their prince, their former guardsman - loose a column of orange and red fire high into the morning air. Born of his mind and body, Vinadan's fireball burned for only a few seconds, but seemed to last an eternity to Valahir. He shook his head slowly, his mouth open, as he watched his younger brother employ powers he simply should not possess. More than the fiery display, however, it was the look etched upon Vinadan's face which shook Valahir to his core.

Triumph, Valahir realised with a deep sinking feeling. *He looks triumphant.*

"Vindi," Valahir called once the fire had rescinded, "come down; let's talk, brother to brother." But the sound of orrec horns and war drums which suddenly rang out from every direction, echoing all around the central promenade - deafening in their din - told Valahir that his plea had come too late.

Far, far too late.

*

Calls went out and orders were barked as the King's Guard turned their horses about and drew into a tight formation as the orrecs closed in on all sides. All the while, Vinadan stood upon the balcony, his arms folded, wearing a tight grin. An orrec emerged from within the tower to stand at Vinadan's side.

"My lord?" it said.

Vinadan drew his sword theatrically, and pointed it at the crowd in the rapidly-filling promenade. "That one," he said, aiming the tip of his blade in Valahir's direction, "the leader; he is not to be harmed. He is mine. Kill the rest."

"Very good, my lord," said the orrec, bowing its head in deference. It took a single step forward and placed its left hand upon the balcony rail, and raised its right into the air. It made a series of gestures with the upraised hand, and barked instructions in a tongue not even Vinadan could fully understand. Once it had finished giving the order, a ripple of anticipation ran through the assembled orrecs; some three thousand in number by Vinadan's reckoning. They had their orders, and Vinadan could not see how the result would be anything other than an unequivocal slaughter.

On the ground, trying not to let panic overwhelm his rational brain, Valahir's heart thumped hard and fast inside his chest, and he could hear his pulse reverberating against his eardrums even over the din of the orrecs. His courage almost failed him as he watched countless orrecs break into cruel and ugly grins. They stepped forward as one, and arrows began to fly.

*

It was over in minutes. Vinadan watched from on high as his orrecs - those who had resided in Aillen under Midhir's control, and those with which he had reinforced the city in readiness of his brother's arrival - gave no quarter. Though the King's Guard fought gallantly and many orrecs now lay dead upon the cobbled streets, all but Prince Valahir were slain. Of Valahir, his eyes were wide in panic as he saw the last of his men succumb to the overwhelming numbers of the orrec host. His brother's host. He still sat upon Swiftstrike, trying to maintain his position as the horse reared and whinnied in the face of the surrounding orrecs. The smell of death was thick, and Valahir almost laughed as his panicked mind flashed childhood memories of visits to Aillen across his mind, but with the smell of sugar and sweet cakes replaced by the smell of decay.

"Lay down your sword, brother," called Vinadan. Valahir spun and looked at his brother, his wild and panicked face at odds with Vinadan's mask of calm assuredness.

"Vindi, brother," Valahir called back at length, "it is not too late. Come with me. We can fix this. Everything is going to be okay."

Vinadan grinned, but the look in his eyes betrayed the thin smile he wore. He waited, and simply stood staring at his brother, registering the army of orrecs which surrounded Valahir and Swiftstrike in his periphery, but he made no move of his own.

"Hold him," he said at length, and two orrecs immediately stepped toward Valahir with their swords raised. The motion seemed to snap Valahir back to his senses, and he tugged hard on Swiftstrike's reins and kicked at the horse's sides.

"Away!" he shouted, and Swiftstrike charged headfirst into the line of orrecs, scattering a group and creating a precious opening.

"Volley!" shouted Vinadan, eliciting a hail of arrows from his archers. Valahir was crouched low, his face all-but buried in his horse's powerful neck, and somehow managed to avoid taking an arrow. Swiftstrike, however, was not so fortunate, and Valahir was thrown from the saddle as his horse went down hard, skidding to a dead-stop. Valahir was dazed, but his instincts would not allow him to linger. He stood, applying his weight to his legs to test for breaks, and was relieved to find that he was still more or less in one piece. He cast one final look at Swiftstrike, and did not even attempt to hold back the tear which fell at the sight of the horse pierced by countless arrows, its lifeblood staining the yellow and pink cobbles a dark, portentous crimson.

With a heavy heart, Valahir turned his back on his fallen friend and set off at a run into the streets and alleyways of Aillen. As he passed down small streets and narrow lanes, he tried not to look at the terrified faces which stared out at him through windows, nor at the locks and chains which currently held the residents captive within their homes.

*

"You cannot hide, brother," came Vinadan's voice from somewhere behind Valahir as he hid, crouching low behind a small stone wall which stood between two houses.

"The city is overrun, Valahir, and more of my orrecs arrive every hour." Valahir did not respond, he merely closed his eyes and tried to steady his breathing. He must not panic; he needed to think. The sight of the sun high in the sky, its light glistening upon the waves below, would usually be enough to fill any heart with warmth and joy, but to Valahir it appeared only as a ticking clock; an hourglass slowly counting down to his inevitable demise. If he tried to run, the orrecs would surely see him. If he tried to fight, he would be overwhelmed in moments.

"Or you could try to hide, of course," Vinadan continued, turning here and there as he spoke. "Perhaps you mean to wait us out and make your escape under the cover of night." He grinned, though Valahir did not see it.

"I'm almost tempted to let you," the younger prince continued, "the haemori will be here as soon as the sun sets, and then we will see how you fare in the darkness. In fact, if you are fortunate enough, you may even get to meet Baron Diaemus himself."

Diaemus? Thought Valahir, opening his eyes wide in horror, *no… Vinadan would never…*

"He does not venture abroad much these days, truth be told, and rarely leaves his castle upon Skellt," Vinadan continued, "but it seems the opportunity to dine on such noble stock as *'Prince Valahir Daelectus; Captain of the Guard; Heir to the throne of Aclevion',* was just too tempting an offer to pass up."

"Why, Vindi?" shouted Valahir, finding his voice but not giving up his position, "why are you doing this?"

"Why?" snarled Vinadan. "You betrayed and abandoned me, brother; all three of you."

"What are you talking about? We have not-"

"Do not lie to me, *brother*. Did father tell you that he threatened to have me hanged as a traitor?"

"I don't believe you, Vindi," said Valahir, plainly, "he would never-"

"Oh, but he did, Valahir. What's more, I think that, deep down, you do believe me."

Valahir took a deep breath, held it, blew it out, and stood. He spotted his brother and stepped out from behind the waist-high wall. He was around twenty feet from Vinadan, and behind him.

Vinadan had not yet realised his brother had shown himself, and continued to cast his gaze here and there; high and low. Valahir stared at his brother's back, and slowly reached for the dagger upon his belt. He felt a single tear tickle his cheek as he drew the blade halfway out of its sheath. Time seemed to stretch out in front of Valahir like a road, a river, or the stars which could not yet be seen overhead. He felt his heart plummet in his chest, and knew that this would likely be his last day in this world. He slid the blade back into its sheath and folded his hands behind his back.

"Here, brother," he said quietly. Vinadan turned around, and assessed the situation in a heartbeat.

"You fool," the young prince said, taking a step toward his older brother, "you could have ended this." The younger man's countenance startled and terrified Valahir at once. Vinadan moved like an animal, every nerve taut and vein bulging, and his eyes were like that of a predator in the wild, stalking its prey.

"There is nothing to end, Vinadan. Come home, brother." Valahir held his ground, and did not raise his voice as his brother approached.

"I have no home. You all saw to that."

"You do have a home, Vinadan, and a family. Come home, brother, please."

"Do not call me *brother*, Valahir." Vinadan was now mere feet from his older brother, but still Valahir did not concede ground.

"Vinadan, this is not you; I can't imagine what Midhir put you through, but we can make it better - I swear I will make it better."

"Midhir?" said Vinadan with a grin, "you think this is about Midhir? I destroyed that old fool. But not before I bled him of every secret he had ever learned, every rune he had ever deciphered, and every power he had ever gained. I am stronger than you know, and I will be avenged."

Valahir became aware that orrecs had started to swarm the buildings and alleyways all around him and Vinadan. He was cut off, and alone. There would be no escape for him. No escape for Valahir, not without Vinadan at his side as brothers once more.

"There is still time, brother," said the older prince as Vinadan drew closer, "stop this, and come home."

Vinadan did not reply, but covered the distance to Valahir at a sudden sprint, surprising his older sibling. He drew his sword as he ran, and swung a vicious overhand strike which would have cleaved Valahir in two.

The clash of steel upon steel rang out loud and clear, echoing and reverberating in the morning air. The orrecs cheered as Vinadan and Valahir exchanged blows and parries, thrusts and counters. Vinadan pressed his attack, pushing ever forward. Valahir conceded ground as he fended off his brother's assault. Valahir was by far the more accomplished swordsman, but Vinadan fought with a ferocity his brother had never seen, fuelled by a hatred Valahir did not understand but lamented with every breath.

His brother was gone; this he now knew in his heart.

He knew it as surely as he knew he would not be leaving Aillen alive.

*

Kaal, Endeen Vinadan! Kaal, Endeen Vinadan!

The rhythmic chanting of the orrecs seemed to punctuate each cut and parry; the metallic din of the brothers' swords acting as percussion to the orrecs' foul cries.

Kaal, Endeen, Vinadan; Hail, Lord Vinadan.

Valahir had retreated deep into the city, warding off blow after blow of his brother's sword.

"You cannot win, Vinadan," he called through gritted teeth as his brother paused momentarily to catch his breath. The sun was high in the sky now, and some of its warmth still penetrated the winter cold. "I don't want to hurt you," Valahir continued, "but if you persist, my hand will be forced." Vinadan bared his teeth, and his brow furrowed.

"Do you really think you will simply walk out of here alive?" he spat.

Valahir reasserted his grip on the hilt of his sword and met his brother's gaze. "No," he said simply, barely raising his voice, "I do not. The only way I'm leaving here in one piece is with you at my side, Vindi, but I believe we will both die here today." He took a deep breath and set his feet, adopting a defensive stance with his blade held out in front of him. Vinadan charged.

The encircling mass of orrecs moved in concert with the duelling brothers, but did not interfere. They maintained a perimeter, and watched eagerly as Vinadan pressed his assault upon Valahir, but even though it had long since become clear that the young prince was no match for his older brother, not one of them gave in to the temptation to join the fray.

Kaal, Endeen, Vinadan!

Kaal, Endeen, Vinadan!

Valahir cast a quick glance over his shoulder, checking his way was clear. He registered that he was backing his way into a dense residential area, where the streets grew narrower and the concentration of homes increased, though all doors and windows were tightly locked shut. Any fleeting hope of aid, refuge, or rebellion were dashed at the sight of the locks and chains, and something inside Valahir changed; shifted; snapped. The sorrow he felt seeing his brother this way; the remorse, guilt, and the deep, heart-rending anguish began to fade, and fade quickly. He parried another strike, and sent Vinadan's blade wide. Valahir narrowed his eyes, and stared at his opponent. He felt the burgeoning swell of anger deep within his stomach, which fluttered to his chest, bile rising in his throat as his breathing intensified. He no longer saw his brother standing before him, but an obstacle; an opponent; an enemy. He suddenly wanted, more than anything else in the world, to be home. He wanted to embrace his mother, and could almost smell the jasmine scent of her hair. He wanted to feel his father's strong hand on his shoulder, and to share a drink with the man he had always idolised and been desperate to please.

He wanted to go home, and he would cut his way through every Aether-accursed orrec from Aillen to Aclevion to get there. But first he had to kill his brother.

Vinadan recovered, and made to launch a fresh assault upon Valahir, but the older prince sidestepped to his left, spun on his heel, and aimed a vicious backhand swing at Vinadan. The young man was not expecting this, and brought his own blade up to block at the last possible moment. Valahir had caught his brother off guard, and he was a blur of motion as he pressed his advantage. He took a few quick steps, and worked his blade in a masterful display of swordsmanship, and within seconds he had disarmed his brother, Vinadan's own blade having been spun out of his grip to land some ten feet away. Valahir did not stand on ceremony, but aimed a strong kick at his brother's midsection. Vinadan hit the ground hard, and struggled to catch his breath. With a single stride, Valahir was standing over Vinadan, his sword raised high in the air, the blade pointing downwards.

"This is your last chance, Vinadan," Valahir said, no longer trying to keep the anger from his voice, "surrender now, or I swear to you I will k-"

Valahir's eyes went wide with horror and surprise. He dropped his sword and slowly looked down. He could not reconcile the weapon which had penetrated straight through his stomach, its blade protruding from his back to point toward the blue midday sky.

A blade of pure red flame, summoned into existence from nothing. Vinadan's eyes were supernovae, and his skin burned with a thousand runes. He twisted the blade and stood, meeting his brother's rapidly darkening eyes with his own monstrous countenance. Vinadan barely heard the chanting and cheering of the orrecs; he was transformed, a being of flame and vengeance. The arcane arts of Daedan Asarlai, and the dark, corrupted teachings of the mad wizard Midhir were Vinadan's to command.

"W-what have y-you become..?" managed Valahir through free-falling tears.

Vinadan extinguished the flaming sword, and the fire in his eyes receded. He caught Valahir by the shoulder as his older brother began to fall, and he pulled him close, close enough to feel the other's failing, raspy breath upon his own face.

"I am a god, Valahir," he said simply.

He released his grip and Valahir's body fell unceremoniously to the ground. Vinadan turned and faced the army of orrecs which lined the streets, and he held his arms wide. The cheering intensified and, one by one, the orrecs fell to their knees in deference.

Kaal, Endeen, Vinadan!

Kaal, Endeen, Vinadan!

He gestured to gain the attention of the closest orrecs, and motioned over his shoulder. Three of them immediately moved to obey their new master, and hurried to Valahir's body.

"Bring him to the tower," said Vinadan, already walking away from his brother.

He did not look back.

He would never look back.

Chapter Forty-Nine

The citadel was on high alert, and a deep, dark foreboding hung thick in the air. It had been nine days since Valahir's guard set out to Aillen, and they should have been back by now. More than this, the scouts had reported no sign nor rumour of their imminent return, nor even of their departure from Aillen. The king and queen had not been seen for two days, and their duties had been divided and handed over to the council and the Asarlai. Against this backdrop of city-wide concern and uncertainty, a horse trotted lazily through the main city gates. Upon it sat an old man; he had a look of Adeniron about him, perhaps even further south, though he was no elf. His dark skin was withered from years of exposure to the bright southern sun, and his back stooped as he sat. Attached to the saddle was a dark hessian sack, its contents hidden from sight. The old man smiled and nodded to the guards as he entered the city.

"What is your business, traveller?" asked one of the guards, stepping out in front of the horse and raising his hand.

"Me? Oh, I'm here for the grand unveiling; wouldn't miss it for the world."

The guard nodded and waved the old man through the gates. He was not the first to arrive for the unveiling of the new wing, nor would he be the last.

"Thank you, Sir," said the old, stooping man as he continued on his way, "I simply can't wait."

The guard never saw the menacing smile the old man flashed as he went on his way, nor did he see the sparks which flickered to life in his eyes.

The horse trotted happily along the main road into the city, oblivious to the drama unfolding all around it. In the hessian sack attached to the saddle, prince Valahir's head slowly swung back and forth with the motion of Vinadan's horse.

*

Vinadan maintained the shape he wore for the rest of the day, though he struggled at times to hold his newfound form, and found himself deathly tired from the exertion. Still, that he had been able to control the shapeshift, hold it for this long, and to be so convincing as not to arouse a flicker of suspicion nor recognition among the masses pleased him greatly and fuelled his confidence and conviction.

The sun fell at length behind the tallest spire of the citadel, pulling down a curtain of deep blues and inky black in its wake. One by one, the stars twinkled into existence, as if they meant to bear witness to the coming events; events which would not only shape Vinadan's future, but would likely alter the course of history and set Aclevion - perhaps all the lands of Gibrion - on a new path.

His path.

Under the cloak of night, Vinadan finally released his grip on the shapeshift, and it was once again his own face against which the cold night air began to whip and beat. The beginnings of a fresh snowfall were upon the wind, but had not yet fully materialised. Vinadan fancied, for a fleeting moment, that the impending flurries, too, were watching, waiting for his command before they fell forth, blanketing the northern lands only at his behest.

He raised his hood, and moved forward toward the citadel.

*

'Rubble rats'; the thought came unbidden, and Vinadan smiled in spite of himself at the memory. His mother had called them that when she discovered them, only children at that time, sneaking and climbing through the myriad cracks and crevices which were to be found within the outer walls of the citadel. Boys, especially brothers, she had told them, seemed to have an affinity - a genetic predisposition - for getting into places they ought not to be.

Like rats among rubble, she had said of Vinadan and Valahir, so long ago. Before…

Vinadan shook his head and balled his fists, dispelling the thought. Though many of the offending cracks and breaks had long since been mended, there were still one or two which had been overlooked or missed entirely. It was into one such gap that Vinadan now squeezed his way, so that his entry back into the citadel would go unnoticed.

It would not do to be seen, especially given the reason for his return.

*

King Entallion was nothing if not habitual. Like his father, Ondellion, after whom the citadel was currently named and whose tomb he now stood before, the king was a man of tradition. Every morning since King Ondellion had died, decades earlier, Entallion had awoken early, gathered his furs about him, and descended into the Daelectus family crypt below the citadel to visit his father's final resting place. He would enter the crypt, lighting the torches in their sconces as he moved forward. He would then stop to kneel before the great statue of the three goddesses, close his eyes, and touch his chest, feeling his heart beat beneath his palm. He would then stand, and place a hand upon the cold stone sarcophagus in which his father's remains were housed.

"Good morning, father," he would say into the silence, "I trust you slept well."

The king had done this every morning, without fail, for longer than he could remember, and this morning was no different. Not only did Vinadan know that his father would never deviate from his routine, he was counting on it.

A loud click snapped Vinadan out of his thoughts; his father had turned the large iron key in the old lock, and a tall shaft of light broke into the darkness, lengthening as the crypt door opened at the other end of the long, narrow chamber. Vinadan hunkered down out of pure instinct, despite being all-but invisible in the darkness. He heard footsteps thumping down the stone stairs, and one by one the torches were lit. Closer and closer the firelight came to him, revealing the chamber by degrees, as if some sort of macabre procession had been arranged for precisely this moment.

Vinadan watched as his father lit the last torch, and knelt in front of the statue of the three goddesses. The king placed his hand upon his chest, and closed his eyes.

"Good morning father," said Vinadan, suddenly, appearing like a wraith from the darkness to materialise behind his kneeling father, "I trust you slept well."

*

Vinadan smiled as he left his father behind; the sound of the heavy door locking firmly back into place as he made his exit echoed around the cold, dark crypt, though no soul now lived within to hear it.

*

For years after that fateful morning, a myth would persist among the more superstitious folk of the capital that it was the very tears of Aether herself which had covered and the faces of the statue at the foot of which Entallion's decapitated and decomposing body was eventually discovered.

Dark tears, they said; *portentous, crimson tears;* tears which heralded a groundswell; a storm; a tidal shift in the fate and fortunes of the world.

The wave began inside a dark, cold crypt in the capital city of Aclevion, but it would soon reverberate far beyond the borders of Etain, the country of kings.

*

The meagre daylight which cautiously crept in through the window at this particular hour of the morning always seemed to illuminate every mote of dust and dander which the servants had missed. Not that Queen Arianrhod blamed them, not harboured the slightest bit of annoyance; in a citadel such as this - all rock and heavy oak - cleaning was nigh on impossible. The queen smirked as she watched the light creep across the cold stone floor, until it reached the heavy rug upon which she stood barefoot. Her and Entallion's private quarters were modestly decorated, and lacked the pomp and grandeur one might expect from a king and queen. The stone floor remained, and a number of thick rugs stood upon it at intervals. A tapestry displaying the Daelectus coat of arms hung on the wall above the bed, and there were plants of all sizes and colours here and there around the room. While the quarters were not flamboyant, they were large, consisting of a bedroom, a living room, a bathroom, and even a small kitchen area. It was in the latter that Arianrhod now stood, chopping vegetables before tossing them into a large pot. Though they had a veritable army of servants - three chefs chief among them - Arianrhod had always loved to cook, and could usually be found preparing rich smelling, often heavily spiced food whilst Entallion took his daily pilgrimage to the crypt. The servants would prepare the food for the day, but it was the queen who fed her family at night.

She heard the door creak open behind her, then click shut a moment later.

"You were a while today," she said without turning, "everything okay?"

"Everything is fine, Mother," said Vinadan. The queen spun, wide-eyed, and the knife fell from her hand to clatter to the floor.

"Vinadan?" she asked, barely daring to believe her own eyes.

"Yes, Mother."

She covered the distance in a single stride and pulled him close into a tight embrace.

"Where have you been?" she asked, releasing him from the hug but holding him by the shoulders, "why did you leave us? Are you okay?"

"Come, Mother; sit down." Vinadan strode confidently to the living room area and sat in his father's armchair. His mother followed him and sat opposite her son. The queen wore a look of puzzlement upon her face; she still could not quite believe the evidence before her, and that her missing son should simply walk into her room had left her utterly confused.

"How are you; are you okay?" asked Vinadan.

"Me? Am I okay? Vinadan: where have you *been*?"

"Aillen. I returned to Aillen."

"To Aillen? Why? Why would you go back there after what happened?"

"I went back there *because* of what happened. I had unfinished business there; I had more to do. And to learn."

The queen's sense was beginning to return, and she found her composure.

"Did you see your brother and the King's Guard?"

"I did," Vinadan admitted happily, "but I will come to that momentarily. There is much I want to tell you, Mother, and I would ask that you hear me out. Can you do that?" He stared at her, unblinking; stoic and composed.

"I can," she said at last.

"Good. There is much you need to hear, and some of it will not be pleasant."

"It's okay, Son, you know you can tell me anything."

Vinadan nodded, and took a deep breath. He stretched his arms out in front of him and felt a satisfying click in his left shoulder. He placed his hands upon his thighs and began.

"I am different, Mother; I have always been different. Valahir was always the soldier, not me. Valahir was always the one the people looked to to lead them in father's stead. Valahir always had his men, his friends, his share of admirers. I had none of that."

"Vinadan, I-"

"Please do not interrupt," Vinadan said curtly.

"What I did have, however, " he continued, "were my wits. Yes, Valahir could swing a sword with men ten years his senior, and he could ride a horse faster and harder than any man among the Guard, but he was sorely lacking in intelligence, wisdom, and a vision for the kingdom - for the world at large."

The queen sat silently and did not interrupt, nor did she give away any indication of the panic which was growing inside her. Her face remained impassive and her body still, but her mind was racing.

'He was'; she thought, *'he could'; 'he had'… He is speaking about Valahir in the past tense.*

"I, however, do not lack for ambition. Nor do I lack the wit or strength to achieve my goals."

"Vinadan?" the queen said, quietly, as if she were a student daring to ask a question of a professor, "where is Valahir? Where is your brother?"

"I said I would get to that," Vinadan snapped. "Father always mocked me for spending time in the library instead of the training yard; he belittled me for choosing a book over a sword, but it is I, Vinadan Daeletcus, who will have the final laugh. I have learned the very arts of Daedan Asarlai himself; I learned much at the hands of Midhir, and I have pushed my skills to the limit and found there is still a world of power out there for the taking." He grinned at his mother, but there was nothing etched upon his countenance but malice and arrogance. The queen felt a knot of anger creeping up her throat, mingling with the panic until it became an unbearable burden.

"Vindan," she began sternly, remembering that she was not only his mother, but queen of Aclevion, "you are wrong. Your father does not mock you, nor does he belittle you. He is proud that you take your studies so seriously - we both are. He thinks that if you put even half as much effort into your other duties, you will become a great man; strong as well as wise; cunning as well as learned. He will be back from the crypt at any moment; you can ask him when he… what's so funny?"

Vinadan sat back in his father's chair, and laughed openly at his mother's words.

"Of course you would say that," he said, "*Good Queen Arianrhod;* staunch leader and faithful wife."

"Watch your tone," Arianrhod snapped, pointing a finger in Vinadan's direction.

"Or what? Hmm? What are you going to do?" Vinadan stood up, but made no further move. "I'm giving you a chance, here, yet you do not have the sense to see it!"

"A chance for what, Vinadan? I don't understand!"

"A chance to *live!*"

The beginnings of tears began to coalesce in Arianrhod's eyes, and she found herself backing away from Vinadan, almost involuntarily, pushing herself as far back into the couch as she could.

"Vinadan," she said in a whisper, her voice cracking with emotion, "where is Valahir?"

Vinadan clenched his jaw tightly shut for a moment, as if to bite down on some unspoken confession, or to dispel an errant thought. He relaxed and met his mother's terrified gaze.

"He is in Aillen with the rest of the King's Guard," he said at length. "Well," he added as an afterthought, "his body is, at least; his head is in a bag under my bed." Vinadan flashed his mother a wide, satisfied grin.

The queen stood and strode to her son so quickly that he did not have time to react. She slapped him hard across the cheek, knocking him backwards into the armchair.

"You vile boy!" she screamed, "I cannot believe you would say something so despicable, so hurtful!" She leaned in and grabbed him by the lapels, hauling him to his feet. "I will only ask you one more time: where is your brother?"

Vinadan had regained his composure and met his mother's gaze with a deathly stare.

"I have already told you where he is. Both parts."

The queen let go of him and fell backwards onto the couch, her tears coming hard as waves of grief washed over her.

She believed him.

Vinadan took a deep breath, and blew it out. He straightened his clothing, and stroked his hair back from his face.

"Oh, Mother," he began with far more theatricality than the situation demanded, "you really mustn't feel too bad about it. He was a traitor to the crown; all three of you were, in fact. Well, at least that's what I'm going to tell them."

"Tell them? Tell who? What are you talking about?"

"Why, the people, of course," said Vinadan, as if the answer were the most obvious thing in the world, "my people." He turned and strode away from his distraught mother, and began pacing around the room.

"You will hang for this!" his mother shouted through tears, "when your father returns, he-"

"Funny," Vinadan interrupted, "both of my parents have now threatened to have me hanged."

"What? What do you-"

"Please," Vinadan spat, "please do not pretend you are innocent in this. Or did you truly not know that father was to have me hanged as a traitor if I did not accompany Valahir to war in Aillen? Aether's grace," Vinadan added, noting the look upon his mother's face, "you really didn't know, did you?"

His mother shook her head, but could not find words; not that there were any which would change the fact that her youngest son had just confessed to murdering his own brother. Through her grief, however, one shadow remained; one distant, hazy black gulf into which she dared not to look, but knew she must, despite the cost; despite the consequences; despite the increasingly inevitable answer.

"Y-your father, Vinadan; wh-where is your father?"

This time Vinadan openly laughed a cruel, mocking laugh.

"You'll love this one; a perfect blend of comedy and irony, I think." He turned to face his mother, stood tall, and placed his hands behind the small of his back.

"Father," he said, "is in the Daelectus family crypt; I thought it would just save time, in the end." The smile upon Vinadan's face and the glint of triumph in his eyes told Arianrhod that every word Vinadan was telling her was the truth; the black, abyssal truth of his actions. She did not realise she had been holding her breath until her vision began to cloud and panic set in. She breathed hard, irregular breaths, and felt tides of despair crush her, heart and soul. She fell to the floor, no longer seeing Vinadan, and no longer seeking to maintain a grip of her wits. The noise she made was neither a cry nor a wail; it was more the convergence of a groan and a whimper, but whatever it was was barely identifiable as human.

Vinadan sighed deeply and shook his head, disappointed.

"Oh, Mother," he said, "I came here hoping you, at least, would see what I was trying to accomplish; what I am on the brink of achieving. But, alas, your mind seems to have somewhat surrendered its grip on sanity. A shame, really…"

His hands still clasped behind the small of his back, Vinadan turned on his heel, casually strode back into the kitchen, and picked up the knife his mother had dropped.

Chapter Fifty

The morning air was crisp, and the wind blew gently. The Daelectus banners flapped in the breeze, and the sun was rising in the sky. The worst of the winter, it seemed, was now behind them, and as the morning stretched toward midday, the crowd of thousands each felt the fledgling warmth of the spring upon their faces.

The seasons were changing.

The day had been so long in coming that the men, elves, and dwarves in attendance could hardly believe it had finally arrived. The setting could not have been more perfect; the new wing of the citadel was impressive; its main feature a tall spire, stunning in its design and gleaming white in the mid-morning sunshine. A blood-red ribbon was draped before the main entrance of the new wing, tied between two free-standing gold posts.

The king and queen had not been seen in public for the last three days - nor Prince Valahir, for that matter - but the young prince Vinadan, returned from his latest sojourn, had assured the council, the Asarlai, and all concerned that there was nothing amiss. *A surprise,* he had told them; *all part of the plan.*

The crowd were in good spirits as they stood in the main square before the steps which led to the citadel. The smell of baked goods and sweet treats permeated the air, and more than a few of the attending onlookers were already a little drunk from the free wine which the citadel servants passed around. The red wine had been brewed specifically for this event; and King Entallion had allocated a sizable budget. Barrels and barrels of the thick, fragrant wine were stored in the cellar, and many had already been drained before the event had even begun.

Vinadan stood behind the main doors of the citadel, flanked by two of the king's council, and one of the Asarlai. He took a deep breath to centre himself, to calm his nerves and still the fluttering he now felt in the pit of his stomach.

It was time.

"You wait here," he said to the three men at his side.

"My prince?" said Alma of the Asarlai.

"I have given you a command, gentlemen; wait here."

"As you wish, my prince."

Vinadan bent his knees and picked up the ornate storage chest which stood at his feet. He exhaled sharply as he stood bearing the weight. A nod to Syan, one of the two councilmen, signalled that the older man should throw open the doors.

Vinadan walked out onto the landing area between the main doors and the first of the steps, and took his place at the temporary podium. All along the perimeter of the citadel behind him stood the city guard, resplendent in their ceremonial silver armour. He placed the chest on the ground in front of the podium, and stepped back around behind it. The Daelectus family crest shone and sparkled in the morning sun; the gold trim and inlaid jewels reflecting the light and dazzling the crowd.

The young prince took a moment to bask in the warmth and the cheers of the crowd, then raised his palm for silence. He looked to his left and nodded to one of the servants who happened past holding a silver tray. With a bow, the young girl hurried to Vinadan and handed him a goblet of the commemorative wine. He thanked her, and placed the goblet upon the podium without taking a sip. This was it; this was his moment.

"My friends," he began, projecting his young voice as far as he could. The crowd cheered, goblets were raised, and flags were waved among the masses.

Vinadan held his hand up to once again silence the crowd.

"My friends," he began again, "I cannot thank you enough for coming out to share in this celebration. My heart is moved to see so many of you here. Looking around, I can see that some of you have journeyed far to be here, and I am truly thankful that you will share in what will prove to be a most historic day." He took a breath; looked left, then right, scanning the cheering crowd.

"Today, we will declare the new wing of the citadel officially open. With this expansion will come greater opportunities for not just the crown, but for all. With such a grand expansion, and all that is inside, new jobs will be created, and new wealth generated. With that newfound wealth, we will expand further, invest, and not only Aclevion but all of Etain will benefit."

Vinadan allowed the crowd to cheer and raise their glasses once more, before he motioned for silence.

"Alas, where there is good, evil will surely follow in its wake, for there can be no day without night; no light without an opposing darkness."

What little muttering there had been among the crowd now ceased of its own accord, and the town square fell deathly silent.

"My friends," Vinadan continued, "I know many of you must be wondering why it is myself here, at this podium, addressing you all, and not my father." He paused for effect, and cast his eyes downwards, shaking his head slowly in an imitation of regret and sorrow.

"I am here to tell you - all of you who have come so far and given up your own time - I am here to tell you that we are betrayed."

A murmur ran among the assembled crowd, and heads turned here and there in confusion.

"Many of you will know of my imprisonment at the hands of the mad wizard Midhir; indeed, I have made no secret of it. What you do not know, however, and this goes for every being among you - even those among the citadel council - is that it was my father who was behind my kidnapping."

He let his words sink in for a long moment, revelling in the gasps of horror and disbelief among the crowd.

"You see, whilst I was at the mercy of Midhir, he told me things which I did not - could not - believe. Things about my father, my mother, even my brother. As many of you know, I managed, somehow, to free myself from Midhir's web, and I brought his head back to the capital."

Vinadan's eyes narrowed, and a darkness fell over his face.

"Once I returned, my father was desperate to learn what had transpired between Midhir and myself. At first, I believed this to be nothing more than the concern of a loving father for his youngest son. But, as time went on, I began to suspect a fouler motive. You see, my friends, my father was concerned not for me, but for himself. He wanted to know what Midhir had told me. He wanted to know how much of his own plans and schemes had been revealed."

The crowd were silent, enraptured by young Vinadan's passionate words. He had them, and he knew it.

"I am here, friends, to tell you - though it breaks my heart to put voice to these dark tidings - that my father, my mother, and my brother, were in league with Midhir all along."

Gasps went up among the crowd, and more than a few heads were shook in disbelief. A stirring of discontent began among the assembled onlookers, and the flags were waved no more.

"Ruling, you see," Vinadan went on, meaning to capitalise on his advantage, "was not enough for King Entallion; he planned to *enslave*, and your good Queen Arianrhod and courageous Prince Valahir were right there with him, in the thick of his treason." He went on, growing louder and more animated as he laid out his story.

"For this reason, they had me kidnapped, taken off the board, out of the picture, while they secretly plotted with Midhir to seize control of production, trade, gold, food, livestock… they wanted everything for themselves, and they were happy enough to watch you - the people - starve and suffer to feed their own greed." He was angry, now, fully committed to his lie.

"I had my suspicions, of course, and my return was not expected by my father; he certainly did not expect that I would be strong enough, wise enough, brave enough to take Midhir's head. So I left the capital, and Etain itself, to seek answers. With nothing more than a few essential possessions and my horse, I sought my answers. My journey led me, somewhat ironically, to Aillen; back to the very place I had been sequestered at my father's instruction. There, among Midhir's journals, I learned all. I saw letters from my father promising the old mage a fortune for his allegiance, and a fortune again if he betrayed his orrecs and installed a garrison of Aclevion knights upon the golden shores of Aillen. You see, I do not believe my father meant to kill me, at least not at first, but when word reached his ear that I had returned to Midhir's stronghold, he saw his opportunity. He sent Valahir and the King's Guard to Aillen with a single purpose: to kill me."

He wiped a non-existent tear from his eye with the back of his hand, and shook his head ruefully.

"I managed to escape with my life, thanks in no small part to Midhir's orrecs. When they, too, learned of Midhir's betrayal; when they learned that the old wizard meant to annihilate them, they rallied to my aid and slew the King's Guard. Valahir managed to escape the slaughter, but rather than return home, he instead sought me out among the carnage; rather than cut his losses, he determined that I still needed to be silenced. What he did not count on, however, was this…"

Vinadan held out his hands, palms raised to the skies, and drew upon his powers. His hands burst into piercing red flames, and his eyes burned with a power not witnessed in centuries. His feet left the ground, and he hovered an inch or two above the stone. The crowd gasped, and many threw their hands over their mouths in disbelief. Vinadan returned to the ground and the arcane flames receded.

"You see, my friends, I have grown stronger than my father ever dreamed was possible. With the blood of the Daelectus line coursing through my veins, and the power of Daedan Asarlai himself reborn within me, I will rule with strength from this citadel, which I now declare officially open."

He drew the sword at his hip, and took three long strides toward the red ceremonial ribbon. One swift slice, and the ribbon was cleaved in two. With a grin, he marched back to the podium and picked up the goblet of wine. He took a long gulp from the goblet and stepped toward the ornate chest at his feet, and kicked it unceremoniously down the steps. Gasps of horror and shrieks of terror went up among the crowd as the heads of King Entallion, Queen Arianrhod, and Prince Valahir spilled out.

"This is an outrage!" came a strong, deep voice from among the crowd. Vinadan spun to face the source, and saw with amusement the dwarven lord Thyrus pushing his way up the steps to confront the young prince.

"You lie, boy! Your father was a good, noble man! He would never-"

"Get him!" came an answering cry from the crowd. "Traitor!" came another. "Treason! Kill that fucking dwarf!" Within moments, an angry mob had surrounded Thyrus and the three dwarves who had encircled him, protecting their lord from the baying mob. Four members of the city guard drew their swords and ran toward the ruckus, but Vinadan held up his hand.

"No," he said, calmly. "Let them go. I do not believe Lord Thyrus had any part in my father's treason." The crowd around the dwarves receded, and Thyrus' guard breathed a little easier.

"You have not heard the last of this, boy," said a furious Thyrus, thrusting his finger toward Vinadan.

"I do not doubt it, Lord Thyrus," said Vinadan with a dark grin, "I get the feeling you and I will meet again before too long."

The dwarves turned and marched away through the crowd. Though they were jostled, shouldered, and were pelted with more than a few goblets of wine, they were allowed to leave. Once the dwarves had left the square, all heads turned once more to Vinadan. He held his goblet up, high above his head in victory. A cheer went up from the crowd, and the flags were waved once more. One of the city guard, though Vinadan did not know his name, marched toward the young prince and knelt, holding his word out in offering to Vinadan.

"All hail King Vinadan!" the guard cried aloud.

"Hail!" came the accompanying cheer from the crowd. "Hail King Vinadan!"

"No," Vinadan said, motioning for silence, "I will not take my filthy traitor father's title. The line of kings has ended. Whilst I will indeed answer my calling and serve you all from the throne, and while I will try to redeem the name of Daelectus, freeing it from the taint of my brother and parents, I will not name myself King."

A moment of silence ensued while the crowd digested the young prince's words.

"All hail Prince Vinadan, Lord of Aclevion!"

"Hail! All hail! All hail Prince Vinadan!"

Men, women, and children cheered and chanted his name. Flags were waved high above the heads of the masses. Wine flowed, and music played.

Vinadan smiled, and drained his wine. He turned to reenter the citadel, and tossed the empty goblet casually over his shoulder as he left. It clattered down the steps, though the noise was lost among the clamour of the crowd. Down it tumbled and bounced, until it rolled to a stop beside the head of Valahir.

673

Epilogue

Three days had passed since the unveiling of the new wing and the ascension of Prince Vinadan to the throne of Aclevion. Though his rule had officially begun, he had so far left matters of the state to his council. He sat now in the library, hungrily reading and making notes by candlelight. The hour was late, but Vinadan was wide awake. He made three heavy lines under a note he had just made, then placed his quill down upon the table. He cupped his chin and furrowed his brow. The candlelight flickered and wavered, reflecting in his pupils and sending shadows dancing upon the walls. Vinadan reached over and picked up his goblet, savouring the taste of the ceremonial wine. It really was *very* good. He placed the now empty goblet back down onto the table, and sighed heavily, pondering his notes.

Tennatir entered, a heavy tome clutched under his arm. He bowed as he entered, but Vinadan, lost in his thoughts, did not see the old man.

"A-hem," coughed Tennatir, announcing his presence. Vinadan blinked and shook his head, returning to the moment.

"Master Tennatir," he said simply.

"My lord Vinadan; the book you requested."

"Thank you, Loremaster," said Vinadan, taking the book from the old man and placing it upon the desk before him. It was old, very old, and a layer of dust covered the leather-bound volume.

"If I may, my lord?" asked Tennatir.

"Of course," said Vinadan, "what's troubling you?"

"With respect, my prince, it is what's troubling *you* that I am more concerned with."

"I don't follow, Tennatir," said Vinadan, turning to face the old man in the dim, flickering light. The prince's eyes were bagged and heavy, a deep purple which set his piercing pupils in stark contrast. His hair was tied back away from his face, and he looked tired.

"My lord," Tennatir began, "when did you last sleep?"

"Why do you ask?"

"You look tired, my prince. You need to rest."

"I will rest when I see fit, Loremaster. Please do not presume to lecture me."

"No, my lord, of course," said Tennatir, bowing in deference, "I only mean to say that I am old, and I have seen my share. I know what troubles you, young Vinadan."

"You do, do you? And what exactly do you think troubles me?" said Vinadan, somewhat irritated by the old man's words.

"Grief," Tennatir said simply. "I know why you lock yourself away in here, surrounded by books and scrolls. But no rune nor incantation can bring back the dead."

"You think that I-"

"It is okay, my prince, you need not speak of it. But I must tell you plainly: our loved ones cannot be returned from the veiled realm." Tennatir took a seat next to Vinadan, and gently moved his hand over the cover of the dusty, leather bound tome. "In all of our books and all of our scrolls, saying nothing of the records of the Asarlai, not a single mention is made of any who have yet defied death, nor of a single being who has been able to avoid its inevitable call - the accursed haemori aside, of course."

He placed a hand on Vinadan's shoulder, and offered a sympathetic smile.

"Not even Daedan Asarlai himself could escape the bitter cold grip of death. I am truly sorry to hear about your parents and your brother, my prince, but a dead man is doomed to his fate."

He gently patted Vinadan on the back, stood with some difficulty, groaning as he straightened his spine, and bowed to the prince. Taking one of the candles from the desk, he turned to leave the library to seek out his own chambers, so late was the hour. He reached the open doorway, and stopped mid-stride. He turned and looked at Vinadan over his shoulder with a studious look etched upon his face.

"That is, of course," he said, scratching his beard and tilting his head in thought, "unless they have somehow mastered the rune of *Necromancy*."

The End

To be continued in *Fall of the Unworthy King*

Concerning Evnissyen

An eternity of darkness, then a pinprick of light.

Larger it loomed, though it illuminated little, lost in the void. As it grew in stature, it revealed its secret: the single point of distant light was actually three; a trio of glowing lights, each orbiting the others in perfect synchronisation.

As the lights grew in radiance, they each revealed their true forms: goddesses; each as beautiful as the next, each with an orb of burning light shining brightly from somewhere deep within themselves.

Hemera: Goddess of Daylight.
Aether: Goddess of Darkness.
Gibrion: Goddess of Nature.

Together they were as one; balanced; each was a world unto themselves, yet was entirely dependent on the next; each of their individual strengths both a complement and a foil to those of her sisters.

As one, they beheld the all-encompassing darkness inside which they were still mere embers, as fireflies against the night sky; sparks, struggling against hope to catch fire in the void. Finding no foothold in this strange, dark plane, they deigned to forge a new world.

They held hands, closed their eyes, and united their souls.

Never had such a light shone in the universe, and never since has any new light come close.

Daylight, darkness, and nature became as one, and the unending emptiness from which the three goddesses were born was replaced with trees, rivers, fields, and mountains;
birds, beasts, and insects;
men, elves, and dwarves.

The world was born, and named Evnissyen by its people.

Upon this world, the continent of Gibrion – named in honour of its mother goddess – was most prominent, though other lands also flourished across the seas to the east and to the west.

But in the creation of Evnissyen, the goddesses were lost; their energies spent; their lives seemingly sacrificed for their world and its children.

The only traces of the three goddesses which remained were rumour, whisper, and folklore.

Stories; mere campfire tales, until one day when the world changed with the discovery of the first of three mysterious artefacts: huge, burning orbs; insubstantial; arcane spheres of pure undulating energy, scattered to the far reaches of Gibrion, held in stasis by colossal pillars etched with intricate carvings of mysterious runes.

The Soul of Hemera: orb of daylight.
The Soul of Aether: orb of darkness.
The Soul of Gibrion: orb of nature.

Were one to unite the orbs and harness their divine, arcane power, the ability to make or unmake the world as they saw fit would be theirs.

And so the cycles began, to renew every 330 years.

The first cycle of Hemera brought light, warmth, and joy into the new world of Evnissyen.

The first cycle of Aether brought grief, pain, plague, and long years of cold and darkness;

The first cycle of Gibrion returned life to the world following the darkness of the preceding cycle; trees grew tall, flowers bloomed, and birds returned to the skies.

Of the artefacts; at the time of the departure of Horith and Montagor from Ehronia in the year 307, in the ninety-ninth cycle of Aether, the Soul of Hemera resides with the elves in the forests of Eonis, and the Soul of Aether lies deep within the mountains of the capital city Aclevion under the control of Prince Vinadan.

The Soul of Gibrion, the orb in which resides the power of nature, is lost; long since forgotten to the passing ages of the world...

A Word on The Asarlai

Named for their founder, Daedan Asarlai, they are an ancient order of men and women who have devoted their lives to the study of mysterious runes. The first examples of the runes with which mortal beings came into contact were etched into the colossal pillars which hold the Souls of the Goddesses in stasis.

Since this monumental discovery, however, further examples of the ancient symbols have been found all across Gibrion, and beyond the borders of the continent in wider Evnissyen.

They have been found in carvings upon the walls of deep, formerly undiscovered caves; they have been witnessed in the sky, glimpsed for but a moment as celestial bodies align; they have been seen upon the battlefield, in shapes created by the running blood of the fallen; and once - only once in all of the recorded history of Evnissyen which remains intact - a child was born bearing a birthmark as obvious in shape as it was alarming in nature.

Whilst the runes themselves are known to most by sight, there are few - even to date - who can read them, let alone internalise and manifest their power.

Daedan Asarlai was the first; he devoted years of his life to their study, and his breakthrough changed the course of history.

When he finally translated the first rune - 'Influence', according to the histories - he did not make his profound discovery public, at least not at first. He had but a fraction of the key to decoding the mystery of these ageless runes, but one successful translation could be dismissed as fraud or fluke, to his mind.

He continued to work in secret, deciphering a second, then a third, then a fourth...

Eventually, almost two years after his initial breakthrough, Asarlai believed his knowledge - whilst scant in the grand scheme - was sufficient to dare to actually use the runes.

Knowledge is one thing, but its practical application is quite another.

He spent days going over and over his notes and sketches; reading, rereading, revising, updating, practising, practising, and practising again, until at long last he deemed himself ready.

He waited until the early hours of a cold winter's morning, when all was darkness and silence. He locked his door and pulled shutters over his windows. He unrolled one of his handwritten scrolls and closed his eyes.

He flooded his mind with thoughts of one rune, visualising its every line and curve, and from his heart he poured emotion, purpose, meaning.

His skin burned as the rune was reborn in his flesh, repeated over and over in irregular patterns.

Nature.

The ground rumbled, and the walls shook; the floor split open with an ear-splitting crack, and from the ground crept a thick green vine, only two feet or so tall, but summoned to life through the power of the rune.

A good start, he thought, but why stop there?

He closed his eyes, took a deep breath, and tried again.

Destruction.

He felt the heat on his face even before he had opened his eyes. As he did so, he could not help but cry out in triumph as he beheld the vine, now all but reduced to smouldering ashes.

Now that Asarlai had gained some small understanding of the runes and their deployment, he turned his attention to the lingering question he could not quite shake from his mind: how?

The answer, he was somewhat embarrassed to discover some weeks later, was disappointingly simple: the three Souls.

Daedan Asarlai had not only been the first to decipher the runes and utilise them in a literal, practical sense, but he had also made the connection between the runes and the Souls; after all, how can such power manifest itself without an energy source?

The Souls were the well from which the runes drew their power. If the Souls were indeed remnants of the Goddesses, then the runes were just as surely their divine language.

Asarlai did eventually share his discoveries with trusted fellow scholars and academics, and before long they inaugurated the Council of Asarlai in order to devote more time and manpower to the study of the runes.

Three years later, the council presented their findings to King Roran Rayneer II, who immediately took the council under his auspices and ordered his chancellor to devote a significant fund to Asarlai and his research. So captivated was the king with the runes and Asarlai's work, that he gave orders that the mountain pass in *which the Soul of Aether had been found thousands of years earlier - and was currently guarded day and night by soldiers of the crown - be expanded and made liveable so that Asarlai and his team may move their research from their current base in Aillen to the mountains above the capital.*

Seven years passed, and the small council of scholars had grown exponentially, and had become recognised as an order in its own right: the Order of Asarlai.

Of Asarlai himself, his achievements had brought to him great wealth and fame, and he had the ear of the King. The Asarlai order had taken on an advisory role at King Roran's request, as he held great stock in their wisdom.

Where once was glory, however, tragedy soon struck.

In the spring of the year 201, in the sixty-fifth cycle of Aether, Daedan Asarlai was found dead in his bed by a servant sent to wake him early at the request of the king.

His room had been locked from the inside, and Asarlai was found in his night clothes with a dagger in his heart; his eyes had been removed. There were no signs of a struggle in the immaculately-kept room, nor had any reports been made of unusual or suspicious activity in the hours leading up to the fateful discovery.

The bedroom window, however, was open, and the light curtain blew in the morning wind.

Centuries later, the order of the Asarlai still works to translate and truly understand the runes, the Souls, and the mystery of the Goddesses. They number in their hundreds, and as their knowledge has grown, so too have their powers. Many are now capable of summoning fire into existence, and shaping it as they see fit - tools, weapons, even animals can be manifested in the flames.

They continue to advise the Crown, and their monastery in the mountains above Aclevion is home to rooms upon rooms of books, scrolls, and tapestries containing the cumulative works of their order through the centuries, to say nothing of the rare and priceless artefacts housed within.

In the year 307, in the ninety-ninth Cycle of Aether, Prince Vinadan sits upon the throne of Aclevion, and the Asarlai are led by elder Alma Sindalli, whose second in command and closest ally is a gruff, irritable man named Xebus Anatalis.